podthology

THE POD COMPLEX

EDITED BY TIMOTHY REYNOLDS

WWW.DRAGONMOONPRESS.COM

podthology:
THE POD COMPLEX

ISBN 13 978-1-897492-09-3

DRAGON MOON PRESS
WWW.DRAGONMOONPRESS.COM

Printed and bound in the United States

podthology:
THE POD COMPLEX

Introduction

BY TIMOTHY REYNOLDS, EDITOR

On October 30, 1938, the CBS radio network aired *War of the Worlds*, a radio drama by Orson Welles, based on H.G. Wells' novel of the same title, and presented in a news bulletin format. There was much confusion and no small amount of panic amongst those who heard it—and even amongst those who didn't hear it but who heard about it from others. Now that's what I call good storytelling.

There's something viscerally thrilling about sitting alone in the dark, listening to a tale of suspense or horror, from the charge in the air raising the hair on your arms to the feeling that someone's looking over your shoulder even though you know you're alone in the room. That's why telling ghost stories around the campfire has been a tradition since the first time-traveler dropped his Zippo lighter in the camp of a Paleolithic hunter and the campfire was born.

I didn't really appreciate all of this until I fell asleep late one night listening to the podcast of Mike Bennett's *"Salvation"*. The story didn't bore me to sleep, it was just two in the a.m. after a long day when I slipped the headphones on and first heard that haunting theme music. Up to that point, I was sure that the worst thing I could experience as an adult sleeper was cheese pizza messing up my sleep with psychedelic 'bad-acid-trip' dreams. I was sooo wrong. I didn't sleep well for three days and when I did sleep, the dreams I had were filled with demons and hell-spawn and torture. As an older brother to two sisters, I used to *give* nightmares—I was hardly accustomed to being the one with cold sweats, jumping at every little sound.

Then I listened to Dan Sawyer's *"Angels Unawares"* and I could sleep again. There's something about a beautiful Celtic lass that banishes the demons. Of course, glutton for punishment that I am,

I then listened to Phil Rossi's *"Stranded"* and Scott Sigler's *"The Bag Man"* and all hope of sleep was banished.

I really shouldn't have been surprised that there were so many stories of horror and suspense and lost souls being podcast—for some twisted reason, we (humankind) like a good safe scare and always have. From the campfire to the radio to the podosphere, the oral tradition is very much alive, and that's what I wanted to bring to you here. I have tried to assemble a selection of stories which will in turn have you laughing, crying, sleeping with the lights on, and even wondering what the world in general (and podcasting specifically) is coming to.

The first sixteen tales come directly from the podosphere, that place where podcasts live and breathe. The only common element is that they have indeed been podcast. The final four tales are *about* podcasting. By the time this collection rests in your hands a couple of them may have been podcast, but their commonality is simply that they are about podcasting itself, from E.A. Zefram's present-day *"Soapbox 1.1"* to Jennifer Rahn's dark, distant futuristic *"ElectroFunkSeppuku"* and points in between. Then there's the final piece, *"From Anna to Yousef"*... think of it what you will, but I hope it raises more questions than it answers.

With each 'previously podcast' tale I have included where to find the original podcast and, to be completely honest, they really should be enjoyed in their original form, with all of the what-the-hell-was-that?! sound effects, original music, and voices born to scare the living crap out of you. Just remember to close the windows, lock the outside door, barricade the bedroom door... and don't hang your feet over the edge of the bed because darkness waits, just outside the light, whispering your name in the wind.

Foreword

By Tee Morris

H umble Beginnings
You might have recognized a name on the cover, or maybe you just thought the cover was cool. Perhaps you are just looking for something new. It was a simple thing that made you pick up this book. From humble beginnings, amazing things can happen.

Believe me, I know.

When people ask me how I got into podcasting, I point back to the publisher of this anthology, Gwen Gades of Dragon Moon Press. It was in the winter of 2004 when I still basking in the afterglow of my second novel (*The Case of The Singing Sword: A Billibub Baddings Mystery*) and in the middle of edits for Legacy of Morevi. Gwen and I started talking about promotional ideas for Legacy's book launch in the summer of 2005. (Yes, we were planning that far ahead.) I still remember what she told me: "Whatever you do, it's got to be as cool as your book launch for *MOREVI*."

If you're wondering what I did for *MOREVI*, I had commissioned the Sterling Swordplayers to play pirates that crashed my book launch. This meant witty repartee, fisticuffs, and (what else?) swordplay. So I kicked off my first novel with a stage combat show. Gwen wanted me to top that.

No pressure.

While brainstorming on what I could do to top what the Barnes & Noble of Manassas still talks about, I was listening to podcasts. As this was the winter of 2004, I was listening to a whopping five podcasts, and it was while listening to The Dragon Page's Cover-to-Cover that I realized the "topper" was right in front me. (Okay, actually, it was in my ears.) I plunked down $400 for a basic set-up, had Farpoint Media's Michael R. Mennenga walk me through the technical set-up, fired up the mic and started recording.

On January 21, 2005, the first chapter went live. What I thought I was launching was a neat promotion. Five years later, I realize I was changing the world with a new distribution for fiction.

That may sound as if I am suffering from delusions of grandeur, but no one else was doing what I was doing then. From my office, I started a movement that would introduce the world to stories from people like Scott Sigler, Mur Lafferty, Jack Mangan, Philippa Ballantine, J.R. Blackwell, Jared Axelrod, Phil Rossi, J.C. Hutchins, Mike Bennett, P.G. Holyfield, Chris Lester, J. Daniel Sawyer, James Durham, Mark Jeffrey, Matt Wallace, Matthew Wayne Selznick, and so on. That first podcast novel would also bring established authors like Tracy and Laura Hickman, James Patrick Kelly, Cory Doctorow, Paul Levinson, and Ian Banks into this audio arena, all anxious to offer their voices and their stories to the world. What was conceived as a publicity stunt became one of the hottest websites online, Podiobooks.com, where Evo Terra, Chris Miller, and a crew of passionate podcasters continue to produce podcast literature free to the public and open to all.

All this started with me, an MXL990, a $50 mixer, a Mac, and a wacky idea to podcast a really big book.

I could easily fill this page with the names of authors who have bravely stepped up to learn this "craft-within-a-craft" and share their characters, their worlds, and their stories on a global stage; but instead I will let this volume and the writers within speak for themselves. Maybe you have heard some of these stories before. Maybe this is the first time you have read them. What you are about to read are stories from the founders of this new art of storytelling. When you're done, I'd recommend looking up their bios and following the links they provide to their sites. There's a good chance you might find a few more stories from them, also available as podcasts. You might also follow their favorite links to other authors, and they may also have podcasts. And knowing as I do the podcasting community, those podcasts will lead to other podcasts.

You're getting all this here just because you recognized a name, really liked the cover, or craved something new. Humble beginnings. They can lead you to amazing places.

Trust me. I know. Boy howdy, do I know.

TEE MORRIS
CREATOR OF THE PODIOBOOK
WINNER OF THE 2007 PARSEC AWARD FOR *THE CASE OF THE SINGING SWORD: A BILLIBUB BADDINGS MYSTERY*

Stranded

By Phil Rossi

(Originally podcast: 10/31/08 at www.
podiobooks.com/title/notes-from-the-vault)

Randy didn't have to pee. Randy didn't need to take a leak. He straight up had to piss. That was the only way to define the inevitable outcome of "holding it" for too long. Piss, glorious, steaming, relieving piss. Snow had kept Randy from doing his business on the side of the road. He was no pussy, but the shit was really coming down and the wind was down right violent. He eyed his favorite thermos—partially to blame for his current predicament—but knew he'd never be able to drink out of it again, no matter how many times he washed it. The breaking point came an instant later. It was either in the snow or in the pants. Traffic showed no sign of moving. He reached across the cab for his parka and shifted his large frame into its down-filled confines. He pulled the hood up over his head and opened the driver-side door. The wind promptly slammed it shut in his face.

"I'm gonna need a bigger coat," Randy said and laughed, sans amusement.

He pushed the door open again and slid out of the cab. The truck's surfaces were thick with ice and snow. Randy was cognizant of every step he took. He hopped down and into the snow with a crunch. The white came up to his knees. His jeans would be wet when he got back into the truck, but melted snow was better than hot piss soaking his britches.

He unzipped his fly and pulled out his dick. The cold air made the urge to piss disappear entirely. *I was only kidding,* his pecker seemed to say, *So let's cut the shenanigans. Put me back in your pants and get back into that warm truck.*

Randy waited patiently, cock in hand, and watched the wind dance with the trees that lined the highway. Gray white curtains of menace throttled the naked branches as dusk fell toward night. Randy was ready to give up and put himself away. The flow of piss came with surprising suddenness. A pillar of steam rose from the snow. He let out a long sigh of relief, even as the cold bit at his exposed skin.

Something moved between the trees.

It was nothing more than a dark shape to his eyes in the fading light. A deer? The first shadow was followed by another and that followed by a third — this third paused, turned, and seemed to look directly at Randy.

It stood up on its hind legs.

The wind gusted and snow attacked Randy's eyes. By the time he could glimpse trees again, whatever he had seen was gone. *What the fuck is a deer doing up on its hind legs?* he thought and climbed back into the truck. *It's gotta be the weather.*

Snow exploded against the sixteen-wheeler's cab like a whip-lash and slammed the door shut, nearly flattening Randy's hand. If there had been a question before, there was no question now — it was a blizzard. Randy squinted past the windshield. Taillights faded into the white-out. He could make out two sets — just barely — and beyond that, nothing but snow and approaching night.

He bit off another piece of beef jerky and tossed the bag back on the dash. *Morrison Hotel* pumped from the rig's speaker system. The music was such a contradiction to the foul winter weather it almost seemed wrong to be playing it. *The Doors* were better suited to rolled-down windows and warm air. Balmier temperatures awaited Randy at the end of his route, but with the way things looked Savannah would be a long time coming. Traffic had not moved a single inch for quite some time.

Randy shifted in his seat and took his thermos in hand. He briefly considered the outcome of consuming yet more liquid, but the coffee within the thermos was still miraculously hot and he could not resist. He took a sip and then reached for the CB. Randy didn't keep the CB on most days. Some yo-yo was always trying his damndest to fire up a racial fight or prattle on about Satan and abortion. That nonsense got old fast. He took the handset from its cradle and thumbed the trigger.

"Eastbound," he said.

There were several seconds of hissing silence.

"Westbound. What's the word, Randy?" A familiar voice — Trey, a pal from way back — came from the speaker.

"Any news? Whaddya leave behind in the road that's holding me up, man?" Randy asked.

"Nothin' but snow," the voice replied.

Silence.

Static.

"Any word on the roads? There an accident I haven't heard about?" Randy asked.

"Dunno, brother. I'll look into it and get back to you. Over," Trey replied. He didn't come back on the radio for a long time.

Randy counted the minutes until the radio squawked.

"This is Trey out on Route 15 just south of Warrenton. Chicken coop is lights out. Just got word, folks, and that word is we are closed for business, both North and Southbound. Any other rigs on this stretch?"

Son of a bitch. Randy thought and thumbed the trigger on the handset. "Trey, this is Randy. Looks like we're the only two slouches on 15. Did you get any idea on when the road would be opening up?"

"When the snow lets up," Trey replied.

"Insightful," Randy said.

"You know it, baby," Trey said and laughed.

"Over and out." Randy ended the conversation.

Night came on slow, as if the dark was afraid to challenge the whiteout in progress.

Randy looked out the driver-side window. Snow, darkness, maybe the vague outline of trees—he couldn't make out much else.

Pam folded her hands in her lap and looked at the fogged window. The silence between her and Jay was a tense one. The rapid changing of AM stations—one brand of static to another—wasn't helping matters.

"Jay, I'm just saying," she began.

"What the fuck does that mean anyway? 'I'm just saying?'" he snapped back.

She struggled for an intelligent answer but kept coming around to a very bland *I don't know.*

"I just don't know why we had to take this back road," she said.

"Route 15 is a major highway."

Major, she thought. *Two lanes does not constitute major, you fucking dipshit.* She restrained herself from saying the words. She had already indulged in opening her mouth about the road choice in the first place. She knew it wouldn't change the fact that they were stranded. She felt a little guilty for pressing his buttons—Jay was laid back about everything except when it came to their road trips. He was the pilot and the navigator. She was just a little Miss Daisy.

"How long were those people stuck on that road?" she asked.

"What people on what road?" He looked at her. There was a Cheez-it crumb in his heavy beard. She brushed it away. She pulled down the passenger-side mirror to see if she had crumbs on her cheeks, but there were only two rosy circles. She pushed the sandy hair out of her eyes, lifted the visor back into place, and faced him.

"You know what I'm talking about. Those commuters that got caught in the blizzard last year. They had to call in the National Guard? Ring a bell?"

"Oh yeah," he said. "Right." He began to fiddle with the radio again.

"Was it 48 hours or something ridiculous like that?" she asked.

"Look. We're not too far south of Leesburg. That's almost a major city out here. We're not going to be stranded here much longer. I'm sure the plows are digging out the road now."

She looked back at her fogged window. *It depends on visibility.* She thought, *that's the cruxt. As long as we can't see more than a few feet ahead of ourselves, they're not going to let us go anywhere.* She wiped a hand across the condensation-laden passenger window and peered into the night to see if she could make anything out.

Something slammed against the glass.

She shrieked and practically jumped into Jay's lap.

"What the fuck was that?" he said.

"Something hit the window," she said, the words a rapid staccato.

"I know that. What the fuck was it? Was it a deer?"

"I don't know. It happened too quickly and it just looked dark to me. Could a deer have run into the car like that?" she asked him.

"It happens all the time. Deer aren't the brightest of animals and they're probably just as blind in this as we are," he reasoned.

Snow-blind deer running into cars? That makes total sense. She kept the sarcasm to herself. Jay laid his head back and closed his eyes. Pam pressed her face to the window to see if the deer had knocked itself unconscious.

All she could see was white, gray, and black.

Benjamin wasn't sure how to handle the situation. At first, he told himself that it was a fluke. He'd hear a new traffic advisory in five minutes stating the road had been reopened. He'd let Kathy continue to sleep and when she woke up they'd be moving again and he'd tell her about the original traffic advisory and how it made him feel like he was going to shit in his pants.

But the truth was, Benjamin still felt like he was going to shit in his pants and the advisory still stated that Route 15 South of Leesburg was closed and that motorists were advised to use alternative routes — or if travel wasn't necessary, to stay off the roads until conditions improved. *So what about us idiots who are on the road now? Do you have advice for us?* He glanced in the rearview mirror. Daphne was sound asleep. She leaned to the left of her car seat. They had just turned the seat to face forward that week. That's was the prize for the one-year-old traveler. You got to face forward.

He tried to remember when they had last fed Daphne. Had it been an hour ago? Two? She would be hungry soon. Too soon, he knew. Inevitably, he would have to wake Kathy to feed their daughter and he'd also have to explain to her the situation.

The wipers were on high but still the snow was tenacious, obscuring his view. He leaned forward, wrapping his arms around the steering wheel. The result—his chest triggered the horn. Kathy opened her eyes instantly and Daphne began to stir.

"Is everything okay?" Kathy asked. The horn had given her a good start.

"Well," he said.

"Was there an accident?" She squinted at the windshield.

"I don't know." He did his best to avoid prolonged eye contact.

"I heard the horn," she said. Daphne started to whimper. Kathy turned around in her seat. "Are you hungry, honey?" She began to unbuckle the seat belt.

"The road is closed," he blurted. He had meant to deliver the news in a calm and reassuring voice, but the anxiety frothing beneath the surface had spewed forth the words.

"What road? This road?" she asked, concern tugging at her features. He nodded and took a deep breath.

"Yeah. Both north and southbound are closed."

She sensed his anxiety and put a hand on his thigh. Her face relaxed.

"Well, just get us off on the next exit. The snow looks bad. We'll just find a place to stay the night."

That was Kathy—eternally calm. He didn't have the heart to tell her nothing had moved in a couple of hours.

She finished unbuckling her seat belt. She was halfway between the front and back of the car—wedged between the driver and passenger seat—when the crash came. Something hit their hood like a load of bricks and then leapt off into the snow. Benjamin only caught a glimpse of the hind legs, slender and muscled, as the—well, it had to be a deer—sprang off into the blizzard. Kathy tried to turn and face forward, but her foot had become stuck between the center console and the passenger seat. Daphne was crying full tilt now. A thud sounded on the car roof. Another crash on the back of the car. The rear windshield was obscured completely in snow—there was no way to see what the hell was going on. And then a terrible clicking and scratching began. Like something was trying to claw it's way in. The traffic advisory began to repeat, but Benjamin couldn't hear it.

Randy was dozing. But not for long. The cab of his truck erupted with the sound of clicking and scraping. He thought for a beat that it was hailing. Then he saw the long fingers splayed out on his windshield; a face peering in at him. The flesh was a ghostly white, mottled with occasional gray blotches. Its head was inverted and vaguely triangular, resulting in a permanently-grinning mouth that was open wide. It's teeth were needle-thin icicles. The thing stared at him with eyes like black marbles.

There were more slender-fingered hands beating on the passenger-side window. He pressed himself against the driver-side window. A slap came on the glass and Randy screamed. There were more hands at the window with the inhumanly long fingers and savage, curved talons—the hooks explained all the clicking and scarping. The things were trying to open the cab like a can of tuna.

"They're everywhere!" Trey's voice came over the CB sounding thick with dread. "Dear sweet lord, what the fuck?!"

Then came the sound of breaking glass over the radio.

"...you son of a mother fucker...Get out!" Trey screamed. There was another crash. Followed by another.

Randy began reciting the Hail Mary at the top of his lungs.

"They're not deer! They're not deer!" Pam was screaming over and over. Jay reached over her lap, yanked open the glove box and spilled out the messy contents. Crumpled receipts—there were so many crumpled receipts. Two Big Mac wrappers—he couldn't remember having ever taken his car to McDonald's. There was a half smoked pack of American Spirit cigarettes that he'd spent an entire night looking for, a month or more past.

"Drive, Jay. Drive."

"I can't," he shouted into the dashboard. "I can't. There's no where to go."

The back windshield cracked after taking a massive blow. Pam screamed. But Jay had found what he'd been looking for. The letter opener almost sparkled beneath the dome light. It looked a lot smaller than he had envisioned. In his mind's eye, he recalled a mighty scimitar, but this thing would have a hard time buttering an English muffin in a single pass.

"What are you going to do? Open their fucking mail? Drive, god damn you." She slammed her foot onto the gas. The car was not in gear. The RPM needle slammed into the red.

Trey's screams rattled the CB speaker, but it wasn't terror that fueled the cry now. It was agony. Whatever these things were, they were killing him. Randy did the only thing that came to mind. He leaned his weight on the truck's horn. The big rig emitted a blast of sound, guttural, and huge. Like a dinosaur. Another blast, this time longer. The monsters disappeared.

The horn kept on roaring.

Jay refused to ease his grip on the letter opener—but the things were gone, that was clear. The sound of their nails and the pounding of their ghostly white fists had been replaced with the low, loud roar of a truck horn. Jay almost thought he could see the rig less than a hundred feet ahead of them. He dropped the letter opener and laid into his own horn. The cars around him were all doing the same, stealing the might of the blizzard's wild voice.

One by one, horns dropped out of the chorus until it was just the truck blowing. And then the truck stopped. The voice of the traffic advisory guy was the only sound in the car. *That didn't just happen,* was all Jay could manage to generate in his brain. No course of action, no logical train of thought on how to get them out of the situation, only his mind's stubborn refusal to accept the brief but vivid events of the past five minutes.

"Jay," Pam said from the passenger seat.

He turned and looked at her. He forced a weak smile. *Gotta be reassuring for Pam,* he thought.

He reached out to place a hand on her knee.

The passenger window exploded behind her. Two spindly thin, tightly muscled arms were in the car. They embraced her.

"Jay!" His name was drawn out—*Jaaaaaaaaasoooon.* He reached out and grabbed one of the assaulting limbs. The flesh was ice cold and rock hard. The strength of the grip was terrifying. Pam screamed his name again. He reached for the letter opener. It lay on the driver-side floor mat. He wrapped his fingers around it, lifted it above his head, and brought it down in a devastating arc.

And missed.

The letter opener buried itself in Pam's shoulder. Her eyes went wide. She opened her mouth to scream again. But instead, she fainted. Her limp body was pulled out of the car before he could move to grab her feet. He sat there dazed and then remembered the horn. The horn. How could he have been so stupid?

The driver-side window exploded.

He hit the horn.

There were arms on him. Hands. Nails digging into his flesh and releasing terror like it had been stored up in the destroyed skin cells.

Pam was screaming again.

Gone from Jay's head was intelligent thought. The primitive brain, nestled deep and reptilian within Jay's cerebrum, fired survival commands to his arms and hands. Jay grabbed at the steering wheel, at the dashboard, at the seat belt strap. He grabbed at anything and everything—but his hands couldn't find purchase.

He was outside the car. The snow and wind cut through him.

A face came in close to his. It wore an impossible grin. Its breath was cold. Cold teeth brought hot blood. Jay's hands reached up and grabbed the side of the thing's head. It was thick with hair. It felt like human hair. The rational, human part of Jay's brain sparked.

The hair is soft, came Jay's final thought as life pumped out of the hole in his throat. His blood soaked into the freshly fallen snow.

One two. One two. One two.

Randy was fixated on the wiper blades as they fought against the accumulation of snow on the windshield. Randy brushed his hand over the lever that controlled the horn with a detached sort of reverence. The horn seemed to scare the things away—at first. But then they had come back, and Randy had not sounded the horn again. Instead, he had watched the creatures overcome the car immediately ahead of his truck. The things had ripped the automobile apart. He knew he should've hit the horn again, but he had been paralyzed by fear. Now, as he watched his wipers go to and fro, he knew it had been more than simple fear. There had also been a grim, selfish brand of logic employed. What if the horn didn't work twice? Then he'd only alert the snow devils to his presence. So instead, Randy had cut the truck's engine and had killed the headlights. The heat ran off the battery now. He didn't have the heart to stop the wipers. He needed a portal to view the blizzard stricken highway, or else he would have felt like he was being buried alive.

Still, he couldn't afford to run the heat and the wipers off the battery for long. Not if he wanted to start the truck again.

What I need is the National Guard to get here and dig me out, he thought, and then imagined a snow-suit clad team of National Guardsmen prying open the truck's driver-side door only to find him frozen solid. This version of Randy would be wearing icicles dangling from a blue nose and a dusting of frost on stiff eyelashes. *Probably better than being ripped asunder by those devils,* Randy contemplated. Still, the thought of freezing to death would not do. Not when there were warm Georgia nights, rolled-down windows, and the *Doors* lying ahead. Randy occupied himself by determining how many hours traffic had been stopped for. He couldn't do it. The trauma of the last...how long had it been? Fifteen minutes. Thirty minutes? His brain was scrambled. By rights and by his wrist watch, only fifteen minutes had gone by. The dashboard clock insisted it. He compulsively shoved several pieces of beef jerky into his mouth and began to chew.

"Fifteen minutes," he said with his mouth full.

There was a rapid pounding on the driver-side window. Randy attempted to leap the distance from driver-side to the opposite end of the cab, almost choking on the jerky. Snow fell away and a women's face filled the driver-side window. She was holding a small child.

Holy shit. What the hell are they thinking?

Randy scrambled to get the door open.

"Hurry, get in!" he said.

The woman was silent, but, what was more disturbing was the child's silence. The pair slid into the cab. Neither of them were wearing jackets and melting snowflakes were trapped in mother and daughter's matching auburn hair. Randy slammed the door shut and locked it.

"My husband," the woman stammered. "He's still out there. He... distracted them so we could get up to your truck. He used the flares. He's still out there."

He's dead, Randy felt like a bastard for thinking it. But, in times of trouble, one had to be realistic.

"What's your name, ma'am?" Randy asked.

"Kathy," she said and peered out the window.

"Well, then, we'll keep an ear out for him."

"You have to go find him," she said, and there was a pleading in her voice that Randy found hard to dismiss. "It was Benjamin's idea to come up to the truck. He said you'd have a fire axe and that would give us a chance to fight these things off."

"Fire axe?" Randy said. "No such luck. I've got a fire extinguisher."

This seemed to deflate her entirely. Kathy began to tremble. She clutched at the light girl who had her face buried in her mother's neck.

"Then we left the car for nothing? And now Benjamin is out there alone?"

Oh hell, Randy thought.

Acura. Randy said the word to himself as he trudged through snow that had drifted up along side his truck. He was surprised at how deep it had gotten. It rose to his thighs. *Acura.* It was a funny little mantra. The trailer seemed to be blocking most of the wind and for that, Randy was thankful. He could almost see. *Acura. Is that Japanese?* Randy didn't even think he knew what an Acura looked like. *Acura.* He held the fire extinguisher out in front of him. *From fire axe to fire extinguisher to what the fuck am I doing out in this snow,* he thought.

Acura.

He saw the car—the snow on the hood formed a sort of outcropping and beneath the white ledge, the fancy letter *A* had weathered the storm, suffering only a thin layer of flakes. The car's parking lights glowed yellow through a snow drift. The Acura looked empty and Randy contemplated not going the full distance. He turned and looked back toward his truck. All was quiet. Maybe the creatures wouldn't return. He looked back to the Acura. *I told her I'd really look for him. I should at least go all the way to the damn car.*

So he did, and when he got there, he knocked on the windshield. Nothing.

He turned from the Acura. Before he could step away, Randy was grabbed savagely by the ankles. He tried to run, but instead dove straight into the snow. He managed to roll onto his back. The fire extinguisher, his only weapon, lay just beyond his reach.

A man with foggy glasses and wet hair emerged from beneath the car.

"You almost killed me," Randy said. He got to his feet and struggled to convince his heart to slow down.

"Did my wife make it?" The man, presumably Benjamin, ignored Randy's comment.

"Yeah. They're safe in my truck." Randy said and retrieved the fire extinguisher. Benjamin looked at the red metal cylinder.

"You left the axe with them?" he asked.

"This *is* the axe, buddy. I bet you'd think something called an "extinguisher" would make me feel safe, but it doesn't. So let's hurry the fuck up and get back to my truck before those things come back."

It was just before dawn when Randy stirred to the sound of car horns. The honking sounded far ahead of the 16-wheeler. How far off was hard to discern. The wind still dominated all other sounds, although occasionally, between horn blasts, the blizzard carried a scream. Benjamin, Kathy, and baby Daphne slept huddled together on the opposite side of the cab. Randy grabbed Benjamin around the ankle and gave him a good shake.

The horns blasts were getting louder and that meant the god damn snow devils were getting close.

In the pale dawn light, Randy could discern the shapes of the cars ahead of him. And he could see the creatures on top of the cars—ghostly figures, with long, freakish limbs that flailed, that pummeled, that dragged victims off into the dark trees bordering the road.

"Wake up, Benjamin," Randy said. Benjamin's eyes shot open.

"They're back," Benjamin said and Randy was amazed that two simple words could convey such a sense of defeat and terror.

Only a handful of cars remained between the creatures and the truck. The blizzard was letting up and Randy could see the beasts clearly now. *Sweet Christ*, Randy thought, *there's a lot of them.* He started counting—he didn't know why. He should have been moving, he knew. And there were more devils than he could count. The sinewy animals ate up the highway like a white-gray wave. They moved with a bizarre grace that was almost mesmerizing. *It's not safe in here*, Randy thought. *But maybe…*

"In the trailer," Randy said. "We'll be safe in the trailer. I think. But we gotta move now."

"Okay," Benjamin said. He attempted to wake his family with gentle nudges and softly spoken words. Randy wanted to punch him in the head.

"I mean now!" Randy yelled. The shout was enough to wake Kathy. Daphne stirred and rubbed the sleep from her eyes. She looked scared and confused. Randy had the driver-side door open. He jumped down into the snow. He helped Benjamin out and then helped Benjamin get his wife and daughter out.

The snow grabbed at Randy's legs with each awkward step he took. His mind screamed, *Run, you son of a bitch!*

I can't run, Randy thought. *I can't.*

Take your time, the snow cooed.

It filled his boots and soaked through his socks. Randy looked over his shoulder and saw that the creatures had no problem staying atop the drifts. They skittered to and fro, dancing across car tops as they moved. The beasts were forever graceful, even as they yanked stranded drivers from their cars through broken windows.

Randy and the family of three made it behind the trailer without being noticed. Around them, the snow fell lightly. He fumbled a key ring from his pocket. His fingers were numb, but he still managed get the key into the lock. He turned it and the lock popped open. Together, Randy and Benjamin lifted the heavy door. They hoisted it just high enough so that Benjamin and his family were able to crawl in. Randy hazarded a peek around the side of the trailer. The snow devils were on the cab now. Snow fell off in big clumps as the creatures moved about. In and out of the cab they went — through the open driver-side door, out a newly broken passenger window. The creatures swiveled their heads. Long snouts sniffed at the frosty air. The devils flowed up and onto the trailer's roof. They moved with the slow, stalking pace of efficient predators. Randy slipped back behind the trailer. He'd seen enough. He climbed into the darkness and pulled the door shut. He flipped a switch and a single, naked bulb flickered to life.

"Now we wait," he said.

There were tears in the following hours. Benjamin cried. Kathy cried. Daphne wailed until she passed out.

The blizzard picked up again to join the lament.

All the while, the creatures prowled on the trailer's roof. Their claws clicked and scraped. Their bodies thumped and rumbled. The things were always busy and Randy thought the sounds were surely going to drive him to insanity. Somehow, he fell asleep.

The trailer door began to trundle up, jarring him back to full waking. Pale, cruel hands appeared in the small space, followed by an elongated face. Randy was on his feet and at the door in seconds flat.

"Jesus. Help me, Benjamin!" Randy shouted as he struggled to pull the door back down.

The two men used their full weight to keep the creatures shut out. But the monsters were strong. Several times the door rose inches before they slammed it back down again. Despite the cold, Randy and Benjamin were sweating. Randy knew they couldn't keep up the fight for long — surely, not as long as the abominations who were so very eager to get inside. No, the door needed to be braced.

"Toward the back, in those blankets," Randy yelled to Kathy.

"There are two crowbars. Go. Fast. I can't hold this door down."
Kathy obliged.

Daughter in one arm, crowbars beneath the other, she half-ran, half-stumbled to the back of the truck.

"Wedge them in the tracks," Randy commanded.

Kathy set the toddler down and jammed the crowbars into place. The door rattled but did not rise again. Outside, creatures screamed now—screamed as if they could sense they had been thwarted.

They beat on the trailer door for what felt like an eternity. Baby Daphne cried herself hoarse. Randy didn't think he'd seen anything sadder than the little girl's mouth and throat working soundlessly. At long last the devils relented, but Randy could still hear them out there. The sound of their movement was quiet—nearly silent—but every once in a while there was a click, a scrape, or a thump. They were waiting.

Randy never thought he'd be able to get back to sleep with the noises, but he was wrong. When he woke next, it was mercifully silent. Even the blizzard had stilled. Benjamin, Kathy, and Daphne were hidden beneath the pile of blankets. Morning squeezed itself through the thin spaces in the trailer's door. Randy did not move to wake the family. Instead, he crept to the door and placed his ear against it. A heavy pounding came from the other side, as if in response to his presence.

Randy's startled yell woke the baby. Her crying, in turn, woke her parents.

"National Guard!" the voice on the other side of the door shouted.

Randy didn't believe his ears.

"National Guard. We're here to get you out of here."

Hesitant, Randy removed the crow bars and stood back. The door flew open on its tracks. The National Guardsmen, there were four of them, looked in on the refuges, making no effort to mask their surprise.

Mounds of white stretched out for miles behind the truck. A graveyard of buried cars and SUVs.

Not a thing stirred.

Thousands of tracks disturbed the undulating white. The prints led off into thick woods surrounding Route 15.

Randy did not look to the trees. Instead, he cast his eyes skyward and thanked God for the daylight.

A Pint to Prophecy

By Marie Bilodeau

(ORIGINALLY PODCAST: 10/4/09 AT
WWW.STORIESRETOLD.CA)

In the dark corner of a pub sits an old man, bent over his golden ale, wearing heavy clothing to cover his bulky frame, his hair still defiantly red despite the wrinkles on his face, his left eye covered by a patch of leather.

He sits alone, yet his surroundings throb in his veins and the smell of humanity coats his senses. Odin, creator of this world, takes a deep swig and watches his children at play around him.

He smiles at the sight of two lovers reuniting, but in their laughter he hears the familiar and distant voices of the Norns, the three fates who predict what is to be. He sighs and takes another deep gulp before placing the glass carefully before him. Every sound seems to conspire to form the syllables of their prophecy, from the clinking of glasses to the roaring of cars outside.

> *An axe-age, a sword-age,*
> *shields will be cloven,*
> *a storm-age, a wolf-age,*
> *before the world's ruin.*

Odin lowers his head. No one but him had heard it, of course.

He feels the vision of the Norns teasing and goading him. He lets it slowly wash over him as he takes hold of his glass. It's cold. Too cold. The frost crawls into his blood, seizing muscle and joint until his breath crystallizes before him.

A storm age. Three consecutive winters, the worst ever felt, will cover this world. Crops will fail. Animals will die. Children and the elderly will perish. Humanity's dark passions will erupt in the failing world. Husband will betray wife. Brother will take sister. Mother will kill child.

Odin feels the warm hush of the pub wash over him, and he sees beyond his thick breath again. A diamond wedding ring, small but big enough to reflect the light, catches his attention. In it, he sees the moon.

A wolf-age. A great wolf will rise up from the depths of Hel and swallow the moon, and her brother wolf will also rise up, swallowing the sun; and the stars, frightened, will vanish from the sky, casting the world into total darkness and chaos.

He has to look away. He closes his one good eye and takes a deep, long drink. A transport truck rumbles on the street outside, and he feels the ground below him shake. The tremors grow until everything trembles and tumbles. He forces himself to sit still, the sounds of laughter around him vanishing as he hears the earth crack and shudder so violently that trees are uprooted, and far away the mountains fall.

His grip on the drink tightens as he feels every bond fetter and snap, freeing his forsaken brother, Loki, the God of Mischief, as well as his ferocious son Fenrir, a wolf so terrible with a mouth so wide it scrapes across the floor as he walks. Flames dance from Fenrir's eyes and leap from his nostrils.

It is only a vision, Odin repeats over and over again, fighting the battle call boiling his blood.

The world calms, and his vision of Fenrir vanishes as he stares at the fireplace at the other end of the pub. A few gathered around it glance back at him warily. They sense unsettling in him, but dare not approach. Odin cannot blame them, for he fears the vision makes him reek of death.

It's karaoke night, apparently. Odin sighs and takes another swig, wishing he had gifted all of his children with the gift of song. A man staggers to the mic, goaded on by his friends, and screeches some destroyed rock and roll song.

Then his voice is replaced by the crowing of a cock, for which Odin is momentarily grateful. He sees the watcher of the dead strum his harp, smiling grimly as a cock crows and raises the dead in Hel.

The vision refuses to let him be, now. He sees the great Midgard serpent lashing and breathing poison, staining the earth and the sky. Loki's monstrous creatures rise from the oceans and the earth, causing the sea to rear up and lash against the land, a great tsunami that wipes out most of what remains of humanity. The world is screaming around him and on fire. From every corner of the Earth the darkness rises.

And the gods stand against it.

He sees it, as the earth quakes and booms. He sees himself leading his gods against the dark forces, leading his brethren as well as the over 450,000 brave souls gathered in Valhalla since the dawn of days.

And then he sees the great wolf Fenrir, feels his foul poisoned breath and the warm blood trickling onto his sword arm as muscles rip and ligaments sever. His heart stops pounding in his chest. He knows he is dead.

He watches with pride as his son avenges him.

In his passing, the last of humanity quakes, children, men and women gather and clutch the old bark of the Yggdrasil, the world tree on which Odin built this world for them. He tastes their fear and despair and wishes he could wash it away from them, but he knows he is dead and gone, and his creation must survive on its own.

If it can.

Fumes reek and flames burst, scorching the sky with fire. The earth sinks into the sea.

The Norns' craggy hold on his mind weakens. He looks down and notices with some chagrin that his ale is gone.

"Here you go," the waitress offers him another, placing the condensation-riddled glass before him, the ale cold and dark and inviting. "You look like you could use another," she winks at him and walks away, her bleached blonde hair reflecting the low lights, and in it he sees the sun rising again, beyond his creation, her dark roots like the horizon.

He sees barley ripening where it had never before grown, fresh water and lush grass. The field of the gods sprouts again, some of his surviving brethren enjoying it in peace. Then he hears laughter and he sees them, strolling alongside the gods. Humans, laughing and well, the gods sharing stories with them as he had always done.

He takes a soothing, long taste, and cringes as another terrible singer takes the mic. He shakes his head and smiles.

Downing the rest of his drink, he leaves ample tip on the table and dons his jacket against the cold, early summer night. He steps outside, his breath thick and heavy before his sight.

It seems that winter was returning early, this year.

Cold Duty

Selected Readings from the Diary of a Gelusian Repairman

By J. Daniel Sawyer

(Originally simultaneously podcast: December 24, 2008 on www.clonepod.org/2008/12/24/ep-25-cold-duty-by-dan-sawyer/ and steampod.org/2008/12/steampod-episode-9-cold-duty/)

PREFACE

What follows are edited transcripts from the audio diary and excerpts from the written journal of James Broadman, technician and stockholder, Broadman Royal Materials Corporation. These transcripts were created from the original handwritten journals and the recordings on prototype Seanaic wax cylinders with a grant from the Broadman Estate and was committed to the Museum Historical Collection's Reading Room, July 1, 1940.

15 NOVEMBER, 1860
SOURCE MEDIUM: WAX CYLINDER #109

It ain't every day a man gets his first real job. I probably wouldn't ha' gotten it had me father had his way. He pegged me as shorter on brains than me brother when I was a young'n, and sure'n if he weren't proper in that. I don' mind. I liked me work in the stables, keepin' the horses clean and fed and healthy when I was a lad. The rest of the track ran around me, with a Watts engine runnin' the Davy arcs and the well pump and the starter gates and old Jimmy keeping the Watts in good nick. I kept the animals happy. First just the family's, then all the boarded ones. I wasn't supposed to have nothin' else to do. But time came when the old Jimmy couldn't keep on his feet anymore for the drink, and I didna wanna see the old goat get shipped, so I gave him a fresh bottle of whisky and stole his tool belt from him.

Turned out to be no great thing to replace the gaskets, or clean the valves, or service the giant puffer. Nobody told me how, it was just came kinda natural to me, fixin' things—no different than findin' a little rock in an animal's hoof.

I've always reckoned I'd run the stable for the rest of me life, and you know, that woulda suited me just fine. Me days filled with the horses and the smithee and the sounds of the engine, me nights taken down at the pub with Simon or trying to coax Charlotte out onto the green.

But it was me brother Sean that finally caught me at it, last night. The turbine on the Watts engine had gone, and the two Davy's arcs were dim. They were supposed to stay lit, and with everyone else gone home, it was down to me to get it up again, and without settin' the shop on fire with the candles or the gaslights.

When I got the pressure vented and the turbine cowlin' open I found a few copper brushes set to stroke against some brightly colored disks that the turbine spun. I'd seen inside before, when I were nine and Jimmy replaced one of the disks. I remembered then that the brushes were actually supposed to drag along the discs, but tonight several of 'em brushes weren't makin' contact anymore, and two of 'em were worn all down to the nub. Old Jimmy wasn't anywhere about, and I'd never needed to do up any of the generator parts from scratch before.

Looking around, I found a couple of the brushes at the left end of the turbine were new and had a lot of slack on 'em. I could tell Jimmy in the morning that he needed to make new ones—for now, I'd just snip the slack and use it to replace the ones that had gone off, which was all well and good until I heard Sean's voice behind me when I was closin' the cowlin'.

"How long have you been doin' that, now?"

I jumped. Me brother never came down to the track except for the races. Turning round to face him, I saw his arms crossed and his eyebrows raised. "Who taught you to fix the Watts?"

I told him nobody taught me, it just had to be done.

"Good with machines then, are ya?" Sean had his full dress on, military from toes to crown. I felt shabby standin' in front of the family genius, but then I always had done. I took me 'cerchief out of my pocket and mopped the oil off my hands.

"I reckon so."

"Clean it up. Guv wants you down at the house."

He spun around on his heels and strode out of the stable. When his back was turned I didn't feel like a kid so much anymore.

I thought cleanin' up would be enough, but when I walked into the Guv's study I felt like a grease monkey all over again. Sean was there, sitting with a brandy in his hand in one of the Guv's matched wingbacks. Opposite him the Guv had his pipe going, and right after I come in he moved his horse and said, "Check."

"'Scuse me, Guv?"

"Jamie, good." He didn't really even turn to look at me. I didn't really expect him to. "We're taking Brass Farthing down to run her in the Royal Ascot. Have her ready to board the eight-fifteen tomorrow."

"Yes sir. I'll have 'er up for ya." I made to go, but after Sean made his move they both stood an' Lord above if the old Guv didn't walk straight up to me and clap me on the shoulder.

"Jamie, your brother here tells me you've got a way with machines."

Now I don't know how this'll change, now that this all gone down, but Sean and I never were the best of friends. He's six years older than me and smarter than an owl—got himself learnin' at university and all—and he always made sure I knew I was dim as candle drippings. But he looked pleased, in that kinda friendly way, and not mean at all, so I decided not to lie to the Guv.

"Yes sir, I s'pose I do. They just makes sense to me, and I ain't never met one I couldn't get along with. They got spirit, like a good horse, but they ain't as hard to talk to."

The Guv nodded his head in some earnest, like he just found the final piece to a puzzle. "Well then, you'd better pack your bag then, too. We could use a man like you at the plant in London. Someone in the family, someone we can trust. Yes, pack it well, my boy. If you work out, you'll be vital to our operation." He gave me a final nod, then looked back to Sean and said. "Well, that's done. Who's move is it?"

The two of 'em went back to their game like I wasn't even there. I s'pose I shoulda been put out, but I was set and fit to bust. I took the carriage back out to the track and brushed Brass Farthing down, packed in her tack, and then sidled up to my quick room above the stables. I got me bed and room all proper down at the estate, but I stay here most nights. I got me kit all packed now, everythin' I might need for weeks. I wanted to go tell Simon and Charlotte the news, but I ain't gonna get the chance before we're off in the morning, so I'll have to post them from the train.

It ain't every day a man gets offered a job on merits. Not every day at all. But Jesus come home, it sure is a fine thing.

25 DECEMBER, 1860
SOURCE MEDIUM: WAX CYLINDER #145

The thing they don't tell you about London when you're livin' up in the 'interlands is how bad it stinks. Or how crowded it gets in the markets and the streets and everywhere. I never seen so many people crammed into a spot before, like sheep runnin' through chutes for the shearin'.

It's hard not bein' back home for Christmas. Last year I got to take Charlotte to the Boxing Day market, where we danced most of the afternoon and helped keep the lines in order. Then we had hot wassail back at the pub 'afore I walked her 'ome. I won't be doin' that this year. Not in London. Best I can hope for is a warm letter back from her before the new year come and go. Sure'n but this club do get lonely at Christmas.

But there's plenty of work to keep me crankin' spanners till my dyin' day, I reckon. Turns out the Guv and Sean got themselves a laboratory set up where they make magic colors out o' the coal tar what gets thrown out by the gasworks. You ain't never seen colors like these. They got the whole city done up in 'em now. Streamers, banners, posters, and scarves everywhere for Christmastide.

Well, any road, they needed someone they could trust to run the Watts engines they use to do fancy compression experiments and God knows what else. It's a curious thing, though—they done modified all their engines so they freeze air on the...oh, what was it they called it...the compression stroke. Don't know what they use it for yet, but I found out if you set your beer on the cowling around the piston, it chills it down right pretty.

There's lots of places they won't let me go yet. One of the doors off the floor has the Mason symbol on it, and that one's always locked. It don't matter much, I just get curious around the locked doors.

Funny thing though, this working for money. Back north I ran the stables because that's what you do. The Guv owned the track, and 'e needed one of his sons to keep the nags in good nick, so I did it. If I needed something, I asked John the butler, and he saw to it that the Guv gave me an allowance. Here, end of every week I get paid. They train me serious—I ain't never heard so many new words in one place before—and then they give me money that's mine to do with what I like. Sean shown me how to use the bank scrip and make my deposits, and got me a membership to the club where I live. Seems that they don't like workers in there, but because I'm family I get some owners dispensation. It's a strange world down here in this awful damn city, but I gets me own money an' me own room and... well, me own.

It's me own life, not like I had back home. And there's enough money that I can afford a wife proper and all. I got a letter off to

Charlotte back home, askin' her if she'd come down this summer when she's of age and help me get on about the business of a family. I didn't know how much I'd miss her when I left, but any time I get to missin' home, I hear her voice singin' like she always did when she'd wipe down the bar before close. I hope she'll help me make a family. That's what a man what's got his own life has to do, if he's not in the army or fixin' as a fop.

Simon sent a post tellin' me he's gonna ship off with the R.N. next summer. Wants to see the world—I'm 'opin' he takes off after the weddin'. Can't have a proper one without your best mate standin' by you.

City life is treatin' me good. I like makin' me own way. Sure'n I miss the green, though. I ain't seen green since I got here. I hear tell from Sean that the parks turn green in May. I hope he's right.

Right proper fellow, Sean turned out to be. Not the tosser I figured him for at all. Right proper bloke, treats a man well what plays fair with him.

The city sure is pretty at Christmas. There's always music every-where, like it were magic somehow.

25 August, 1861
Source Medium: Wax Cylinder #280

I don't got no more money for the pub this week, nor for the bar downstairs here at the club. Sure and I wish I did. I spent it all, wanting to be a man and pay for me own weddin', even though the Guv offered anythin' I wanted.

Now I don't got nothin' left to raise for the wake, what after I got the telegram from Clayton. Charlotte was comin' down with her family, and they met up with Simon in Brighton—he'd got leave to come to the weddin'. The cretin signalman waived their train through a tunnel what was already occupied.

Now they're both gone. Burned to death when the steam vented.

God grant me some brandy and a bridge to fall off. Now they want me back at the factory for some emergency order. Gotta keep the engines runnin'! Gotta keep the pipes cold! I hope they freeze hell over for the soddin' signalman.

19 FEBRUARY, 1877
SOURCE MEDIUM: LEATHER-BOUND JOURNAL #4

I never did intend to write in this book or touch a wax cylinder ever again. I didn't intend to keep a diary again, ever. Didn't want to think about the last time I recorded my thoughts. Still don't. Not now. Not ever. But I need to get as much of this down while I still remember it. I didn't think it would be so important.

Three years gone now Sean shipped off for an army posting in India. Three days before leaving, he had lunch with me at the club, said there were things I needed to know before he left.

When the fish came, he pulled a hip flask out of his coat pocket and put it on the table.

"You know what that is, Jamie boy?"

"It's just an ordinary flask."

"Is it now? Watch this." Sean slid the lamp from the middle of the table and held the flask over it.

"Careful, Sean, you'll burn your hand."

"Shh. Watch." He held it there for about two minutes, then took it off the flame. "Give me your glass."

I passed my empty tumbler to him, and he opened the top of the flask and poured a couple fingers, then pushed it back across the tabletop to me.

"There now, take a nip on that."

Now, I know Sean is a scotch man, and I don't rightly fancy scotch in the first place, let alone scotch what is boiling hot. But Sean smiled at me with this mischief look, so I decided to play along.

"Jesus, it's like ice. How the hell you done that?"

"What do you know about the vacuum?"

"That's what gets made on the backstroke that chills the cylinder, right?"

"Right. Well, when I was fifteen, I saw how to trap a vacuum between two bottles. It keeps heat or cold in no matter what goes on outside."

"Blimey. May I..." I reached out for the flask and felt it—not even warm, except right there on the bottom where the fire'd been licking' at it. Inside the mouth, I could see how much smaller the inside was than the outside, but whatever join there was were invisible. "How did you get metal..."

"There's a lot you don't know, little brother, but now's the time to learn. But think, with this you could freeze things and keep 'em frozen. The better the vacuum, the more perfect the container."

"Why would you want to keep things frozen, aside of ice?"

"You remember how we used to hang the beef in the winter?"

"Sure'n it never went bad, neither..."

"Exactly. Cold keeps things fresh. Specimens from India, meat in the winter. Keeps it all from spoiling."

"So then that back room, behind the Mason doors, next to the three big Watts engines with the cold pumps, them's..."

"It's a Gelus room. That's Latin for 'ice.'" Sean leaned across the table and pulled me so he were nearly whispering to me. "Think of it like a tiny slice of the North Pole in that little room. Now this is important. I need you to follow me here, Jamie boy. What's in that freezer has to stay cold, no matter what happens. Coal shortage, you keep those Watts spinning and pumping. War comes to London, you keep 'em working. Rest of the factory's burnin' down, you make sure that nothin' that keeps things cold behind that door ever gets touched. No matter what. Ain't nothin' more important in the world."

"What's in there?"

"There's things in there the Queen herself wanted looking after."

The Queen herself. Well them's some words you don't hear everyday. Or didn't, up till then.

Last two days he gave me the whole rundown how the system works, the whole "Gelusian Infrastructure." As many times as I'd seen it over the years before, as much as I knew it had to work, I couldn't believe it. Turning fire into ice, they were.

But it was what Sean told me before he left that stuck closest all these years.

"I'm going off to India to do my duty, little brother. Duty what makes us Broadmans different from the other slouches from the north. Our good name is all we got. I gots to go and do my duty, Jamie. Be sure that you see to yours. Don't let me down."

I told him I wouldn't, no matter if the Queen herself told me not to. Truth was I didn't have much else to do. I'd made a good life with me work. Never had the stomach to do much in the way of finding a woman again. I had me job, I had me time playing snooker at the club, or going to the shows now and again. It were a good life. Maybe not enough...but I reckon I got over wanting it to be 'enough' a long time back.

If I hadn't, I did by the time we heard back from India, where Sean went septic after falling off his horse. Once that happened, I was more or less on me own. The Guv's health had been failing for years, and he'd retired back up to the home counties, so all I had from him were his letters telling me when something out of the ordinary had to be done.

The chem lab went on running itself for another year and a bit without a hitch. Sean and the Guv had a good team of men working things there, a lot of them what we poached from old man Mackintosh's shop. Of course, it didn't hurt that Mr. Hancock, what Mackintosh beat out with his jacket, were an old friend of the Guv and easy to poach off, too. Ain't much we didn't steal when we could, I daresay, but in the years we been down here, I learned that's business. Figure out what the other guy's doing, find out what's wrong with it, then do it better and cheaper and use the profits to pay for your own lab. Some days I wish I had a better head for the particulars, but I'm no Sean, and I'm no Guv, and the best I'm ever gonna do is managing the shop. I inherited some of Sean's stock when he packed it in, but I don't go to the board meetings. I signed my voting rights over to the Guv—he knows his plans, and I don't, and it'd be dashed embarrassing to show up and have to ask what all them fancy business law terms mean, anyhow.

Or, at least that's what I thought, and was content to go on thinking as long as I drew a breath. And I might have done, till Christmas last come with its snow. That's when it changed, and now my head's too full to think straight without getting it out on paper again.

I came home from my nightly walk Christmas night to find the old Guv's solicitor at the door of the club. I just about felt my heart drop out of my chest. I weren't ready for the Guv to be gone yet. Not after Sean and Charlotte and Simon.

But when I got to him, running in front of my hound between the horses and nearly spooking a mess of them, he just handed me an envelope and walked off. I chased him to ask after the Guv, but he weren't a friendly sort, and told me to read what he gave me, before he jumped into a hansom.

What was in that envelope set the world on its head just as surely as if the Guv had passed over. It was a letter from the Guv.

He told me I'd done good since he let me out of the stables, and now I had to step up and take things over as he got on.

Sean invented something when he was still a boy, he said. Something brilliant, more brilliant than the wax cylinders I sometimes record on. Something terrible. He didn't say what, just that it was the reason the company was made for: to keep the secret safe. And to change the world forever.

He said that since I were running things now I needed to take responsibility for more of the operation. There was a room, round the back of the chiller, what contained some secret equipment. The equipment needed keeping, oiling. He said all the directions would be right there. He told me where the room was, and where the key were, and how to find the door, which was hidden behind a false wall.

I found everything just where he said it was, but I don't know as the Guv ain't still guessing me low. I know what it was the minute I laid eyes on it. I've studied every drawing I could get my hands on for the last ten years. I just didn't know they'd ever gone and made one.

It had a nameplate: Babbage, Mark 3. The Analytical Engine.

I've had months now oiling it, changing its parts, rewinding its Jacquard spools, and I ain't any nearer to understanding any of this than I was on Christmas night. What in the hell are we using it for? Why couldn't Sean be here? Why's the Guv hiding up north and leaving me to stumble round blindly down here?

Maybe Sean was right, and every man does have his duty. But sometimes, duty can be damn cold.

28 MARCH, 1884
SOURCE MEDIUM: LEATHER BOUND JOURNAL #13

The Guv's solicitor brought us orders from the old goat to take a day off, shut the lab and the Gelusian cabinets. Well, he can say what he likes about when and where and who should work, but I got my stock in this place and I got my promise to Sean to think about, so I stuck around and stayed out of sight most of the day. Playing spy ain't quite dignified for a man my age, but I've done more ridiculous things in my time.

So what am I to see when at three in the bleeding afternoon the front door opens and two carriages come in, horses and all. First a full blown trolley cart with a four-horse team, and then a hansom cab.

And I'll be blighted and laid in the grave if the first person what stepped out of that hansom weren't the Queen herself. She directed a team of royal guards to move two giant things what looked like metal beer kegs as long as a man from the trolley cart and through that bloody locked door, the one behind the Watts engines what I still don't have keys to. The one with the Mason's compass on the door. Soon as they was stowed, she up and left. The guards stayed in there for an hour more, before they walked out and took a hansom.

What was it Sean said all those years ago? "The Queen herself."

15 APRIL, 1890
SOURCE MEDIUM: LEATHER BOUND JOURNAL #20

Talked to Henry Babbage last week. Our partnership with his new company is already turning over something amazing in his new line of electric cooled servos running on special materials we make over in the lab. Gonna bring some fine changes to the next version of the engine, it is. Or so he tells me, and I always known him to be a trustworthy bloke. Got to know him after I told him we had one of his old Dad's engines in the back. Between the two of us, we'll salvage old man Babbage's reputation right proud. No one will remember what a prick he was when everyone's using them engines.

I felt my first rainstorm coming on this afternoon. An hour beforehand, a deep ache down in my fingers. Wasn't much I could do but take a tincture of laudanum and wait for the clouds to bust. I have my forty-seventh birthday next month. Guess the years are finally starting to have their way with me. Henry said he's going to bring some of the blokes around for a snooker tourney. I was looking forward to it until today.

It were this morning when word finally reached me that the old Guv decided to go fox hunting in the wet. Old, damn fool. Never knew when to stop. Well, when a half ton of mare loses her legs in the mud and takes you down under her, you stop pretty much whether you're fixing to or not.

Now I gots to find me a wake for the old cuss, and then find out what I gotta do with the lab and the Gelusian cabinets now he's gone.

16 APRIL, 1890
SOURCE MEDIUM: LEATHER BOUND JOURNAL #20

The order came in at ten o'clock last evening to shut the company down. I got the wire at my club. That was three hours ago. Two hours ago I made it across Piccadilly to the lab and slipped into the warehouse by the back door.

I started getting cramped in my seat on the catwalk above the Watts engines by the time I heard the lock. That's a Hobbes lock, unpickable. After last time I made sure we had them on every door. Whoever it was had a key.

They came in just like last time, a hansom and a trolley. But this time it wasn't the Queen what got out of the hansom. It was my father's solicitor. He directed a crew of workmen who pulled what I thought was a trunk out of the trolley, and they all went behind the Mason's door.

I followed, peering through the crack in the door like a little child spying on an undertaker. They opened the trunk and worked on its cargo with hoses and pumps, draining out one thing then putting in another. It took almost an hour, all of them bustling about. By the time they was finishing up, I decided I needed to stay inside and find out what was what. When they covered the trunk and slid it into a drawer, their backs were all turned. I slipped in through the crack in the door, spry as I could, and ducked behind one of the tall standing tanks.

Once they'd put their cargo into the drawer, they closed its door, set a dial on the front, and filed out. The door closed behind them, and I heard the bolt slide in. Didn't worry me, there was a latch on the inside.

What I found inside that drawer though...

It was the Guv, floating under glass in some kind of green pickling solution. All cold, like a side of meat. Like they was being kept for the Freemasons. Like the stories about them being cannibals was true.

I gotta go and think on this some more.

16 April, 1890: Second Entry
Source Medium: Leather bound Journal #20

I found another solicitor's envelope on my desk when I come into work this evening. This time, there was a key in it. The key to the Guv's office.

On his desk was a letter to me.

Sean invented something that kept a body from freezing, if you replaced the blood. Something that made it possible to freeze fish and bring them back. He reckoned he could do the same with people.

They'd been on their rampage ever since. They got money from some banker and set it up, snapping up wealthy old clients, putting their cash in trust and living off the interest, using it to build the lab and maintain the Gelusian room.

They'd got the Queen herself to go in for it when Prince Albert died, and now I think about it that day I saw her here, that were the day her son Leopold died.

They got all them buried in there like cadavers, until someone can bring them back. He left a whole book on how to tell when to bring someone back.

The Guv closed his letter with "Broadman Chemical is all yours now. Keep that room functioning; it is the only reason this company exists. It's more important than you can ever know. I know you'll do right by the trust I've put in you."

All these years, he still couldn't call me "son." He still thought I was dim. Maybe I am. I can't see how it's nothing less than monstrous what they done, and I can't believe I helped them.

18 APRIL, 1890
SOURCE MEDIUM: LEATHER BOUND JOURNAL #20

A nasty joke. That's what it's got to be. Sean and the Guv working me over for the prank of a lifetime. I'm gonna wash my hands of them both and all their awful plans. I want no part of it. Not anymore. I'm gonna go to Calais and sell my shares off, then live the rest of my life never seeing a Watts engine or a goddamned Gelusian room. Never again.

19 APRIL, 1890
SOURCE MEDIUM: WAX CYLINDER #320

I got as far as Dover before I realized I don't have nowhere else to go. If I live to be a hundred and fifty I don't reckon I'll ever have nowhere else to go. I'm almost fifty years old and I ain't got no one but Henry Babbage to play snooker with. Even me old hound is gonna go soon. The streets are changing with people riding the new steam carriages and leaving their horses at home. All I got that I know anymore is me rooms at the club, and that damn lab and the machine shop.

I don't want to work in no mausoleum. I don't want to see no one coming back from the dead. But what if Sean's in there? God help me, I sure would love to see him again. Show him what folks are doing now with that flask he invented.

He was right. All men have their duty. Even when they don't like it.

I reckon I got mine figured out right enough.

3 May, 1905
Source Medium: Wax Cylinder #515

Supervised installation of the electro-mechanical Babbage Analytics Mark 6 to replace the old Mark 3 last week. It takes a load of work off my hands, continually checking temperatures in the Gelusian room. This one'll ring an alarm if anything goes wrong, then me or one of my shop boys can see to it. I fit all the cabinets with special locks last month, so that I didn't have to worry no more about people breaking in.

Then, after all that work, I find out that King Edward gone and granted monopoly rights to the Maxwell Power company to supply electrical to London—means we can't generate on site no more once their cables reach us. What's to happen if their generator fails, I'd like to know? Gonna have to figure out some way to keep the Watts engines running for backups, I guess.

20 August, 1909
Source Medium: Leather bound Journal #62

Maxwell Electrical hooked us up to their grid last week, and the last of the big Watts engines went off line. I managed to move one of the smaller engines to a secret room and run a drive shaft to the secret turbine that powers the hydraulic lifts and presses in the synthesis lab, in case the grid ever goes off. Good thing I did, too.

When Prince George brought Czar Nicholas and his boy Alexei to tour the facility this afternoon, just that thing happened. The boy got loose from his two minders and started prodding at the machines with a spanner he swiped from one of the repairmen. No one even knew he'd gone missing until the capacitors blew and all the lights went out. Nicholas found the boy frozen, stuck into the junction box with the spanner. He tried to pull the boy out before any of us could stop him, and he got stuck too. We was lucky one of the men had the good sense to cut the lead from the street before anyone else came in, but by the time he did both the boy and his father were burnt so's you couldn't see them no more.

6 NOVEMBER, 1915
SOURCE MEDIUM: LEATHER BOUND JOURNAL #73

If it were gonna happen anywhere it would've been here, and it would have been yesterday. The Bolshies gave us all a big Guy Fawkes present, bombing the factories for something they're calling "the revolution." They bombed up and down the whole street. I was in my office when they blew out the pressure pipes that pumped the vacuum through the Gelusian room. When I led me boys in to repair it, two of them got trapped when the flywheel jolted from the pressure going mad.

Now I ain't as spry as I used to be, but I got in there with a lever and pushed down so as they could crawl out. The other men pulled the boys out before my grip gave way. When the flywheel snapped loose it went right through the wall of the Gelusian room.

We had to fix the wall and the engine before the people thawed, and I had to do it without letting the boys know what was up. I set six of them to work on the wall—copper plates welded in to the other copper plates that made up the vacuum seal. While they made with the acetylene I took the rest of the boys and lit the fire on one of the two big Watts engines what we decommissioned under King Edward. I've kept 'em in good nick on my spare time, just in case.

With the fire lit, we filled the boiler. We kept the pressure valves wide open until it was at temp, then closed them off right quick. The engine started turning, and moved at a good clip. The boys got the room patched and I used the valve outside the room to pump the air out of the seal once again so the room would keep nice and cold.

It was when I opened the valve to let the cold in that the fitting burst. It went right through my left leg.

The boys were fast. They stopped the bleeding and gave me some laudanum and got me down to Charing Cross right quick. The doctors reckon they can save my leg, but I'll probably walk with a cane the rest of my days.

20 NOVEMBER, 1915
SOURCE MEDIUM: LEATHER BOUND JOURNAL #82

I got in to inspect the damage today in a wheelchair. All the Gelusian cabinets seem fine but one, where the flywheel landed.

It's probably just as well, he'd never have borne the women and the Indians getting the vote. But the old Guv ain't never gonna see the world what's come out of his company, and the Empire.

25 DECEMBER, 1915
SOURCE MEDIUM: LEATHER BOUND JOURNAL #82

Went out to the factory in my wheelchair again, late at night when no one was around. I managed to get the Guv's body out onto a cart and then into the firebox of the Watts engine what powers the Gelusian room, and said my prayers over him.

25 DECEMBER, 1917
SOURCE MEDIUM: LEATHER BOUND JOURNAL #84

When I came back by the factory for the evening check in, I saw they finally put the sign on the old derelict across the way what they been knocking down with steam shovels. Looks like our new neighbors are going to be Germans, manufacturing more of the six-stroke carriages with help from William Morris. I never thought I'd see me a Morris-Mercedes factory, not in a thousand years.

In the fifty-seven London Christmases I seen, I reckon I've seen just about every kind there was. Plague years, snow years, wet years, years when everything changed and the world opened up, like this one. Never thought I'd see German industry in London, but there it is across from my company. A strange sight, but maybe not the strangest. Not as strange as the year after the Ripper when everyone were afraid to stay out after dark, until the carolers came and filled the streets with music. Christmas is special. The demons don't come out to play when the candles and holly is out.

I heard carolers today on my walk at Hyde Park. They stood in the middle of where the Crystal Palace used to stand, for the Great Exhibition. I only ever got to see photos of it, they tore it down before I arrived in the city. Sometimes, it's hard to remember being anywhere else.

The snow was fresh. The sounds of the city—the six-stroke steamolines, the hoof clops of horses on the sidewalk, the voices of lost people, sifted through the trees and the powder, carried on the wind, rushing through the trees like it were a cold steam. Their voices, singing "O Come Emmanuel," sounded like God took the world's heartbreak and made it into a diamond, then wrapped it around a symphony. I don't know if I've ever heard anything so beautiful.

31 OCTOBER, 1920
SOURCE MEDIUM: WAX CYLINDER #535

The day of the dead is here again. I'm getting close to my last one, I reckon. The old Guv died at eighty, I'm only three years off from there.

It don't matter anyhow. The life I know began because I understood machines and could fix them without asking questions. In the time I been doing this, I came to run the company for thirty-five years now. I helped Morris adapt the Mercedes gasoline engine to work with steam, give it more power and get rid of those god-awful cooling systems so they can run forever. He went and built an airfoil with that engine, and they're building them across the street from my office. I worked for years with Henry Babbage, my best friend, and our chemicals helped him build computers what run on bioelectric power, or plugged into the Maxwell grid, before he passed things on to his son and went off to Berlin to retire. Our scientists found metals that can lift other metals when you cool them down, and minerals that can pick up long-wave lights what people can talk over. I seen everything change so much I don't recognize it anymore. I can't look at a machine anymore and see how it works. I don't even know if we truly run our machines anymore. I'm obsolete. That what I know how to do won't need doing much longer, and I know it.

Been thinking on Charlotte lately. Of what might have been. I don't got nobody to pass the factory on to. Ain't got nobody to entrust the secrets to. It's all going to die with me.

I tried. I really did. Henry Babbage kept trying to fix me up, first with whores and then with widows. Every time I looked at one all I could see was Charlotte, what she must have looked like with her face all burnt. I never could, God help me, and now I've failed because my duty will die with me. Sean wouldn't approve. All his inventions—his bloody-minded genius—it's all gonna go for nothing.

They're never gonna find a way to bring them all back anyhow. And what if they did? What would they know of this world without horses on the street, where Germany is part of Britain now, where you can drive a prop-powered dirigible anywhere in the world? They wouldn't know what to do anyhow.

Just like me.

Maybe it really was all for nothing. Maybe I should have stayed in the stables, never let them see what I could do with machines. I could have had that life with Charlotte—children, grandchildren, horses, the country and billiards with dear old Simon down at the pub. It would have been fine. Someone else could've done things here. Sean and the Guv would have found someone else to run it.

It would have been better. Maybe I wouldn't have lived so long. Maybe I would. But I wouldn't be rotting alone in my club night after night.

I don't want to be tired no more. Only reason I don't off myself is I know Charlotte is up in heaven waiting for me, and Saint Peter won't let in no suicides. And I ain't got nobody to feed my hound McTavish. I can't die until he done served his time too in this prison. It wouldn't be right, nohow.

6 JUNE, 1932
SOURCE MEDIUM: WAX CYLINDER #615

I thought if I lived to be a hundred I'd never see anything so strange as the Queen showing up in my lab. I'm eleven years shy of that now, and I've seen more strange things than I care to count, but nothing takes the cake like it got taken today.

The curried pheasant was quite fine, and tender enough that it didn't get caught in my false teeth. What got me was when I sent the empty back I got a course of royal guards instead of fish.

"Sir James Broadman," they says, "His Royal Majesty has requested your presence."

Well, I wasn't going to refuse, was I?

They wheeled me out the front door and into a limousine. When we stopped and they unloaded me, I was shocked to find myself back in front of the factory. I don't come every day anymore. My body is too frail for it. Babbage's boys helped me set up a new system for the Gelusian room a few years ago, fully automated with backup generators. If anything goes wrong, it automatically rings me club with a recorded message.

But there I was, with the royal guards pushing me into my own company's foyer, and there in the waiting room on one of the deco chairs was the King himself, with a tall gentleman in a gentleman's proper hat.

He asked for a tour. I didn't even know half of what we did anymore, so I called my Vice President down, and he toured for all of us. I don't even remember half of the new words I heard today, and I've never heard so much about plastics in my whole life.

When I started out the lab was a bunch of wood and marble workrooms with Bunsen burners. Now it was white-painted, every surface clean and shining like it just came from a factory itself, and between every room there was an airlock. Every employee wore protective suits, safety goggles, and nose plugs. I'd last been in there fifteen years ago, and I didn't recognize the place at all.

I spent the whole afternoon with them pushing me around, with the King nodding at every new fact or process that was explained to him. When the tour was done, he dismissed my employee and then looked down at me.

"Sir James, I wonder if you could show us the family room?"

I shook my head, not understanding for a minute.

"I believe my grandmother called it 'Gelusian.'"

"Oh." What could I say? You don't refuse the King, and he knew about it already. He'd just said Victoria had told him about it. "Certainly."

I had the guard push me back through the little access door into the second lab. I still kept the key to the Mason's door on me—I wouldn't ever let it out of my sight for any money—and turned the lock myself.

It was cold in there. Colder than I remembered. These old bones don't hold their own heat anymore, and every breath made the marrow itch like a nettle rash.

I explained to them the workings of the room, and as much as I understand of the theory of how the freezing process works. The lanky man in the gentleman's bowler, who had hung back all afternoon, interviewed me on points I'd never learned about. It was like he knew more about the process than I did.

When he was done and we wheeled out of that hellish cold, the gentleman, who still hadn't introduced himself, took the King aside and talked to him excitedly for a while. I don't know how long. I dozed off like I do sometimes now. Charlotte is in my dreams. It's the only time I'm really happy anymore.

I woke to the man's gentle shaking.

"Who the hell are you?" I'm ashamed to admit I snapped at him, but goddammit he was a stranger shaking me awake.

"Arthur Unwin, m'lord. I'm the King's personal advisor on these matters."

"These matters...?"

"Occult sciences."

"Occult?" I hated to repeat everything like a pedant, but this man wasn't playing fair with the language we'd both agreed on. I'm no scientist, but the one thing science isn't is 'occult.' It's only because it's in the open that it moves so fast.

"Hidden things—areas of research that are so far out on the edge we're not sure they're science yet. Or, at least, we don't know what to do with them. There's a lot of that going on now. It's my job to understand all of it within the borders of our fair island."

Well, at least he'd started making sense. "What you have here is incredible. That your brother cracked the problem of suspended animation almost eighty years ago..."

"Now hold on there a minute, young man. My brother figured out how to freeze people. Ain't nothing but a goldfish ever been brought back. For all we know all these people are as dead as Jacob Marley."

"I think we may have a way to find out. I've been talking to some of the experimental physicians at Charing Cross, and they've found ways to fix things that would have killed people ten years ago. I think...it's too incredible to say, but I think that, if we found someone who died from the right cause, we might be able to fix them and revive them..."

"I won't give consent, and I've got rights here even against the King. These people are in my care, and if we wake them up we could kill them."

"Maybe there's a way."

And he laid it out to me. The whole plan. He wanted to start with a dog—euthanize it in a way that they were sure they could fix, then freeze it for a month, then bring it back. They were sure they could fix a problem with the heart or the lungs by giving the patient new organs. I don't want to know where they'll be getting them. Mr. Unwin said he thought they could even make the brain work right again with therapy, like they do for stroke victims.

McTavish is getting pretty long in the tooth. Sleeps most days, his old bones paining him all the time. I've put off putting him down because I can't bear to see him go. But if there's a chance I can live to see Sean's dream come true...

Well, I gave them McTavish. I hope to God he survives.

13 AUGUST, 1932
SOURCE MEDIUM: LEATHER BOUND JOURNAL #100

It's not Friday.

That's what I kept telling myself when they thawed out McTavish today. It's not Friday. It's Saturday. Saturday the 13th isn't bad luck. I didn't think it was. Maybe I was wrong.

For me, today, thirteen is a lucky number. McTavish thawed out fine, and they replaced his lungs, which they'd scorched after they sedated him. I saw him after the surgery, his belly fur all shaved and him strapped down like a naughty child. They had him immobilized, but he could see me, and he whined. He knows who I am.

It worked.

Now I have to go through every file for every patient, and look at every cause of death. Find someone who we can revive. Maybe... maybe...it will be worth everything after all.

20 OCTOBER, 1932
SOURCE MEDIUM: LEATHER BOUND JOURNAL #100

Unwin told me that the best case would be someone what died of shock, or someone what suffocated, or at worst, a heart attack. Those things, they think they can fix.

I spent the last two months sending numbered files to the blokes at Charing Cross. They knew what they were looking for, and I didn't. Besides, I understand medical jargon about as well as Egyptian hieroglyphics.

First word back was one they made me break to the King's man. None of the Royals would suit—they died of hemophilia and cancer and other things they can't fix. When I broke it to them I found I wished the old Guv hadn't spoilt in that accident, I'd have loved to see the look on his face.

Eventually, we came down to a stack of ten. All of them died young. All of them died of injuries or of infections. When I got the list of file numbers, I started at the top. I looked the number up in the card file where the name and lock combination were kept. When I saw the name, my old heart about stopped right there.

It was Sean, at the top of the list. I should have expected it. The old Guv would've saved him if at all he could. Still, he died in India. Or I'd thought in India.

There was one thing left from the packet the Guv's solicitor left behind. It said "open before thawing."

I took it from its place in the locked drawer and opened it with the bone knife I kept on my desk—elephant's bone, sent to me from India by Sean so many years ago. There was a book inside, an instruction manual for successfully removing a body from the deep freeze.

And inside the front cover there was a letter, old and yellowed, nearly falling apart. It was written in the Guv's hand.

Jamie,
If you're reading this, it means that you're ready to undertake the thawing process. We've been very careful with who we freeze, my son. Only the best and brightest found their way in here, scientists, intellectuals, members of the royal family. The flower of our generation preserved to offer wisdom again to a future, darker age. Keep them safe until they are needed.

You'll also find in here names that you recognize, even some people you've known. We've been careful to keep low priority patients, and it was Sean that prevailed upon me in the choice of who they were.

If I was lucky enough to receive Gelusian preservation, I may see you again, and tell you then. But life is risk, and my conscience cannot bear any longer the risk that I may not come clean. You have excelled at every task put before you. You've *forged alliances I could never hope to, and built our company into a lion of British industry. The world will remember you, and all you did with it.*

I treated you poorly, my son. I underestimated you, and it is one of the many regrets I count in my long life. I hope what follows might, in some small way, make amends.

In the Gelusian room, you will find your brother Sean. When it was clear he would not recover from his illness, we shipped him back home. He died in port, close enough to make it to our facility in time.

You will also find two people Sean insisted we take in, over my objections. Your childhood friend Simon, and your fiancée Charlotte. By the time you read this, I daresay their injuries will be considered minor.

They weren't burned like the Guv told me—they both died of smoke inhalation in the fire.

If you have made it this far, you've done your duty well.
Proceed carefully.
Bring life again to those who once knew it.

I read it over two or three times. Then I took my cigar lighter out of my pocket and burned the paper in the ash tray on the desk, too numb to understand anything it said. I thought I could forget it, but it looks like I can't. I remember every word.

The list I left alone for the afternoon. The book, I posted to Charing Cross.

I wheeled my chair out onto the balcony overlooking the city. As autumn fell below me over London, I wept.

2 NOVEMBER, 1932
SOURCE MEDIUM: LEATHER BOUND JOURNAL #100
I had only three choices for our first subject. How can a man

chose between the friend of his boyhood, the love of his youth, and the brother he worshiped from birth? Which of them to bring back? Which of them to risk on the table? To face again the possibility that they will die, when his whole life a man has failed to let the dead rest in his heart?

I have not slept for two days. But there is only one choice. The file says that her injuries, as near as Sean could tell when he supervised her suspension, are the least severe. The easiest to repair.

If she dies again, I don't know what I shall do. And if she lives, I don't know that I can bear to see her again.

10 November, 1932
Source Medium: Leather bound Journal #100

Charlotte has revived today. They tell me she doesn't remember who she is, but that she keeps calling my name in her sleep. I called my solicitor and changed my will. Even if she never fully recovers, at least she'll be taken care of when I die.

I've decided not to go see her. I'm too tired. Too old. I'm stuck in this damn chair all the time. Can't even hold up my own weight up anymore. She should get to keep her memories—the evenings walking on the green, kissing in the stable, flirting across the bar. I won't take that from her by letting her see me like this.

She wouldn't even believe it was me anyway.

Post Script

On December 25th, 1932 Sir James Broadman entered Charing Cross Hospital to converse with Miss Charlotte Hunt, a patient in the recovery ward. The meeting lasted thirty minutes, during which time Sir Broadman demanded that no medical staff attend. Hospital records indicate that the interview terminated abruptly when a nurse was summoned to attend Sir Broadman, who had stopped breathing. Attempts to revive him succeeded in restarting his heart, whereupon it became clear that he had suffered a stroke.

Sir Broadman suffered a second stroke at 11:00 P.M. Following the stroke his respiratory system collapsed. Attempts to revive the patient were unsuccessful. Time of death is recorded at 11:23 P.M. in the Charing Cross intensive care log.

Per the instructions left in his will, the patient was cremated on Boxing Day, and his ashes scattered on the green in Hyde Park by Charlotte Hunt.

Fractura

By Jack Mangan

(Originally podcast: 08/27/08 at www.
jackmangan.com/2008/08/27/fractura)

My love.
I only regret that I did not survive you.
As your feral mind claws its way back through savagery, madness, genius, and divinity, you will continue to rediscover these words, embedded in the code of the universe.

Eons may dull your memories of me, but the salvation of our love will touch your every regeneration. No matter the place, no matter how cruel its God, my love for you will be there, your armor against fortune's slings and arrows.

I recall the night we met.

The skyscraper had impaled that world, protruding two hundred stories out at one coordinate, jutting out another three hundred at its exact opposite point. The party had been on the 2001st floor, six levels down from the building's southern roof, in celebration of this dimension's La Muerte de Dios. Reality had reached its limit of expansion, and begun the long journey back inward upon itself.

I'd been driven out onto the ledge by desperation, agoraphobia, claustrophobia, and boredom at the party. Seeing no easy way through the crowd to the door, and seeking only a moment of fresh air, I'd slipped out the bathroom window, dangling my feet, then dropping onto the narrow ledge.

Apparently, it was your self-loathing that had put you out on that concrete precipice. There you were, sitting on the edge, leaning precariously out over the distant streets below, your hair falling forward like a straight black curtain to obscure your face.

"Hi," I said, approaching with cautious steps. You ceased your rocking and sat upright. You swept back your hair to reveal red-rimmed, wet eyes, and a sweet, embarrassed smile. "May I sit?"

You nodded. I sat down at an uncertain distance and you started talking. About pleasant nothings. My anxiety diluted with marvel, with charm, with wonder, until at last I was only enamored. I slid myself marginally closer to you as we talked. Your pathos increased with each inch of distance closed.

You began to speak of your pain, to tell me of the hurt that had riven your soul. By the time our lips met, you had told me of your wish for death.

"My love," I'd said, pausing the kiss, my words drenched in youthful awkwardness and melodrama. "A soul such as yours must endure."

Your lips pressed again against mine; you spoke softly: "My soul will endure."

It took a moment for me to fully understand what happened next. I felt a sudden intense pressure in my neck, felt your hands closed tightly around my throat. I gasped at your strength, wondered what had triggered this wilfull, unexpected malice. My hands clutched at yours to free them from my windpipe, but could not break your grip.

After long, agonizng moments, you finally shoved me roughly away, where I lay crumpled on the ledge against the wall of the building, reclaiming my ragged breaths.

On hands and knees, I looked up into your eyes, which were as sorrowful and as dead as this plane's Dios Muerte.

"Te quiero," you said, then leaned back. As I struck my hand out, you let yourself drop from the 2001st floor. I dove forward to the edge, but you were already gone, plummeting through the clouds below.

I clutched the ledge's rim and looked over, my tears falling after you to the city streets far below.

I'd remained upon that world for millennia, through hundreds of lives full of stagnance and existential boredom. I occupied every form and sentience level that world had to offer, loved and reproduced and quarreled and died repeatedly, my true mission with each rebirth to find you again in that universe.

I almost never did.

The time had come for all beings to abandon our tangible lives and enter the Conveyance, forsaking this imploding dimension for the next. The universe had very nearly completed its compression, begun so long ago on that fateful night when we'd met. Fractura del Universo. I joined the queue for the next reality with the heaviness of failure upon my soul.

And there, without form, in that channel of light and void between existences, I found you again. We'd just been random strangers, waiting on nearby lines. We existed in a state beyond the sensory; we both simultaneously became aware of the other's nearby presence...A chance reunion at the edge of cataclysm.

The bodiless embrace was as sweet as it had been in our physical forms upon that skyscraper ledge. Our beings mingled in the nothingness between dimensions, tasted each other again, and intertwined at the most minute subatomic level.

There we'd danced ethereal for that universe's last remaining years, basking in each other, our souls enmeshed. As time drew on, as our atoms grew into each other, I felt the sting of your life's pain grow more pronounced throughout my being. I soon realized that this was not incidental or merely empathic, that you were purposefully inflicting your misery upon me. I wanted to confront you, but instead chose to remain silent, to forgive and overlook this. For a love this pure, this deep, I could compromise and endure shared pain from one who'd suffered so much on her own.

I recall that in the final seconds before reconstituting in the new, infant plane of existence, we'd drifted far from the crowds at the lightbeam's vacuum center, had flickered out into the fringe zones. I'd tried to pull us back, but you were bent upon continuing the unbridled dance of the void.

Here, against the walls of the dimensional tunnel, we felt a swelling of intense, encompassing heat, as if we'd been dipped into the roiling broth of the Sun.

A terror gripped me unlike any I'd ever known, a fear for my mortality in the truest sense, of a death without regeneration. I pulled frantically at you, tugged with all of my strength to draw us both back to the void center, back toward the transitional vehicles to the next dimension, but you resisted my every effort. I could taste your rapture within the scalding heat, your utter joy at the horror in which we'd become submerged. I felt the sourceless fire burning through my entire form, my mind, my self, scarring me, altering me, implanting changes that would never be undone.

I cried out, pulling frantically, until finally at the last moment, you'd angrily relented, allowing your resistance to deflate, to be pulled back into the transitional channel with the rest of the relocating souls.

Once we'd rejoined our fellow travelers, I became acutely aware of the terrible pain that still coursed through me. The agony was near-unbearable. I'd tried to pull your being into mine, to interweave the threads of your self with mine, to find comfort in you, but you'd rejected me each time...your coldness rivalling the intensity of that terrible heat from which we'd just escaped.

Finally, as we drew nearer the switching station, you slipped your hand free of mine. In an instant, you'd disappeared into the crowd. I fought down my agony and called out for you, but could find no response at all. I jostled and shouldered my way through the otherwise orderly lines, repeatedly shouting your name, but to no avail. I finally allowed the flow of the passengers to carrry me across the platform, and onboard the awaiting Conveyance, alone once again without you.

There'd been no sign of you anywhere, once we offloaded at our new destination. This new universe had already begun an ambitious expansion cycle, and there was an infinity of miles to cover to find you.

I searched oceans of time, fathoms of space, but never uncovered the vaguest trace of your presence. I began to wonder if you'd succeeded in terminating your being.

Sibling aches nested in my bosom, one from the heartbreak of losing you, the other from the injuries I'd suffered at the fringes of the transition tunnel. I knew that both had changed me, scarred me deeply. I sensed that both would one day claim me altogether. None of this mattered. I only sought to find you again.

I don't recall how many millennia had passed, but our lives would not touch again until years after I'd given up hope.

I'd been centuries into a peaceful, tranquil, happy, satisfying union with another, with whom I'd found a lesser, though not insignificant, degree of love. We lived simply together as oxygen-farmers in a primitive undersea village. It was in this particular life cycle, my dear, that you had come in search of me.

I'd swum out alone to a floating, artificial traders' island to peddle some of my useless items. You were there. Cries of happiness turned to an embrace turned to a kiss turned to passionate love turned to abandonment of all else. I wouldn't learn until much later that you'd tracked me to that world and that trading flotilla, seeking again the comfort of our partnership, the depth of our love.

We fled the sea and found a quiet pre-industrial paradigm. There, you and I took up residence together in a remote mountain cabin, living simply off of the generosity of this God's grace. Our days there were not without strife, but it was still the most beautiful time I'd ever known. We grew close in this place, talked at length about our experiences. You described to me the roots of your pain. Your father. Your mother. Those who'd wanted you too forcefully. Those who'd wanted you too little.

When you grew restless beneath the mountain's quiet shadow, we set out to make a new life in some other location across the light-years. A few worlds were investigated, then abandonded, until we finally came to rest at the Great Organism.

Once there, we embedded ourselves into its subcutaneous metropolis, a place teeming with as much activity and bustle as our previous home had held stillness and calm. We dove into this new life—you moreso than I—flowing gleefully through the veins of the Organism's magnificent cities of flesh and bone. We spun through many adventurous generations here, exalting in daring leaps from mindless low creatures to cycles as sophisticated, privileged demigods.

Though our environment had drastically changed, our tumultuous love persisted through all of these generations. City life had merely framed the continuation of our happiness and horror together...our shared and mutually inflicted pain and joy...our fighting and co-existence...the insanity and the peace...betrayals and reaffirmations...reveling each day in the rapture of our souls' union.

My pain over losing you before had matured and moved on. Its sibling physical ache also grew over time, however, remaining embedded in me through each life cycle, just as we inhabited the Great Organism.

I remained haunted by the wounds inflicted at the end of the former universe. Although we'd both touched the light tunnel's perimeter, its disease had apparently only infected me, not you. As profoundly sad and angry as you perpetually were, you had remained as healthy as a god. There were days when I felt lost within the feverish heat of my sickness, which threatened to consume my body altogether, leaving only a pile of ash in its wake. During some of these occasions, you comforted me and soothed me, but mostly, you just acted irritated by my incapacitation. You avoided me and hailed scorn and derision upon my pain. During these years, I was often forsaken for the sake of others' attentions. I never cried or cursed you for the salt of your cold indifference...I forced myself to accept it. It was only during my spells of terminal illness that I wept over you.

And it was during one of these that I left.

It broke my heart to go, and if you'd been at home, I'd never have found the will. But as it was, I dragged my weakened body out of the bed, left my every material item behind and drifted away, to surrender to whatever fate this universe would give me.

I drifted for ages in a fog of heartbreak, fear, and sorrow... conscious of very little around me. It was not an animal life cycle, for I was still extremely self-aware of my thoughts. It was a plague of the mind, which would either take hold of me and never let go or eventually release me. I was powerless to influence its decision.

I awoke to coherency at a healing station.

They'd rehabilitated me, even as they'd confessed complete bafflement at the cause of my injuries. I never told them what I knew about the transition tunnel's oven-like edge.

Upon my full recovery, I stayed on as a volunteer to pay for my medical bills, working amongst the sick and the impure, giving solace and sympathy when I could offer nothing else. My mind was constantly occupied then, but still found time to yearn for you. I confess though, that the longing was dulled somewhat by time and distance and my practical responsibilities. The hospital eventually thanked me and said that my karmic debt was in balance. I left that place feeling physically better than I had in eons.

Invigorated with a health I hadn't felt in lifetimes, yet still stained by a gaping emptiness, I drifted from place to place, world to world, soul to soul, star to star, job to job, house to house, galaxy to galaxy, form to form, lover to lover, life to life, until one day, I'd finally noticed myself settling again.

I was living a bachelor's existence on a Theater World, basking alone amongst millions in the sound and the glow of the films that played across the sky. I eschewed social tendencies there in favor of quiet solitude, only to discover my strong ambition. In lieu of friends, I craved the authority to determine which movies were played across the skyscreen. I would still have found yearning for you, if I'd searched my heart and mind, but my strongest desire now was for power on this world.

And so I started from the bottom and worked my way up. I delved in with a solitary, determined purpose, working as a humble cleaner but steadily promoting my way upward.

This universe's La Muerte de Dios had passed unnoticed for me, but now, as I ascended the theater's employment ladder, my peers had begun to talk of its impending implosion. Even as my career goal drew within reach, people had begun to let go of their lives. Every day, thousands more joined the Exodus to this dimension's way station. This was, in fact, how I'd finally achieved my dream position.

The End of Days were upon us when my immediate superior finally abandoned her post, departing with her loved ones for the Conveyance. The pressure of the steadily shrinking cosmos could already be felt in every atom, but I was determined to realize my career purpose, for however long I had left.

I searched through the theater's archive cellar of film reels, well aware that I probably only had time to run one movie before the universe's death. Titles leapt out at me vertically from the shelves, but still, I could settle on nothing...until I finally saw one that reminded me of our first night together, eternities ago on the ledge of that high-rise.

I fed the first reel of "2001" into the projector, watched with awe as its first images played out upon the sparsely clouded night sky. Just as a few stars remained visible in the dissipating heavens, so did I see that a few stragglers remained in their seats, apparently indifferent to the oncoming apocalypse.

And as the film's monolith appeared on the cloudbank, I spotted you, seated in one of the theater's back pews. You were turned around, looking directly at me, through the projection booth's window.

Lightning played across the backdrop behind you, jagged lines streaking across HAL's glowing computer eye. Savage winds ravaged the landscape as the dumb theater planet rebelled in protest to the demise of its home universe. Its tectonic plates quaked in fear. Some theater-goers fled their seats, some remained. The movie continued playing; you and I remained fixed with our eyes upon each other.

The planet's natural fury shattered the wall of the projectionist's booth behind me.

It was only then that I became aware of the most penetrating cold I'd ever known. With surging terror, I realized that this bitter chill was the mirror image of the deadly, roiling heat in which we'd bathed so long ago, at the edges of the transition channel during the last Fractura del Universo. The cold I felt was the end of the universe.

The violence swelling in our midst could no longer be ignored; the terrible power forced me to my knees, and then into a fetal position on the trembling floor. Even as the panic welled up in me like bile, I felt your touch upon my flesh, your lips upon my skin, your soul upon mine. You had left your seat, come up to the projectionist's booth. I allowed myself to absorb into you as you merged into me; we made love as "The Blue Danube" played, and the electric, burning, violent chill of the dying universe vanished from my perception.

We lay in naked afterglow beneath the projector's beam, even as the fabric of reality tore itself apart around us. We were an island of pure bliss in a tempestuous sea of chaos.

The theater had shaken itself to ruins when I finally rose from our embrace. "Come, my love. You've restored my desire to live on. We should make our way to the transdimensional channel. I will never let you go again, in the next plane. My love will be there for you always." I stood, reached out my hand for you to take.

Your smile was utterly devoid of joy. I'd thought I'd seen love on your face earlier, but now there was only the stark blankness of the abyss.

Your attack was too swift; I had no hope for defense. All of these millennia later, I found myself gasping once again for breath in your clutches, while your hands squeezed around my throat.

As the Theater World fragmented into rubble around us, your fingers remained locked beneath my chin. Gravity had become a forgotten theory. Our forms began to dissipate, even in this murderous embrace. I'd begun to black out, but felt my mind fighting back to retain whatever shape this dying universe would still allow.

I was not liberated from your clutch until our bodies finally disintegrated altogether. Although I had no further need for oxygen, it still took a few metaphysical moments to feel my soul breathe again. The rhythmic binary of inhalation-exhalation gently relaxed my taut dread. Your distorted voice echoed fiercely in my mind.

"My soul will endure."

Though I'd believed myself no longer tied to a physical manifestation, I felt what could only be described as a swift kick to my chest. With no laws of physics or gravity, I felt myself drift off into the bitter burn of this disassembling universe. I flailed a bit, but soon relented and fought instead for stillness, accepting my utter helplessness.

The pain was unlike anything I could ever explain to you, my love. As terribly as you claim to have suffered in your lives, I can now assure you that I've endured far worse.

Yet even as the unbearable chill consumed me, I found my mind recompiling itself into something new. As I was torn apart in the death throes of this reality, I found my soul continuing to adapt.

I realized that I was viewing the very blueprints of the new everything in the atrophying organism of this passing universe. I did not delve too deeply into the code, lest I risk a corruption that would annihilate the very foundation of this ceaseless, cosmic regeneration cycle...even tempted as I was to attempt to find a way to live on in the new paradigm. Instead, I chose to embed this message that you read now, which should recirculate indefinitely through all future universe regenerations, programmed to be discovered by you during each of your sentient life cycles.

Even as the cold tore through me, I was aware of others. There were many who'd forsaken the Conveyance, who'd remained behind to die along with this universe and with me. Whether they'd been trapped, as I had, or whether they sought to witness the bare code structure of it all, I cannot say. I saw no faces, managed no interactions, was only aware of their fading presences.

In those final, final moments, even as the incessant torture had become reduced to familiar routine, as the dead universe's withered corpse had turned to dust and ash, I became aware of something else.

A new portal, strikingly unlike that one which had transported us so many times from one old universe to a newborn one. It was a circle of tangible blackness in the void of non-existence. Its pull was slight, but undeniable. Whatever I could define as my self passed slowly through this spinning hole. There was no feeling, no sensation, no memory, no mind. Nothing.

What followed was an age of darkness.

I woke one last time in the body of this man. He'd lived his entire life in a quiet patch of suburbs. I watched from infancy into approaching middle-age as the city's sprawl encroached and overtook his hometown, eradicating the natural tranquility, replacing it with metropolitan bustle and concrete vitality. The city, meanwhile, had become a terrain unto itself, with roads winding up the skyscrapers' exteriors like mountain highways.

He'd married the girl who lived next door on his suburban street, who'd loved him back ever since their earliest shared childhood, who'd many times fled the horrors of her own house to seek the solace and refuge of his family's home.

I recognized you in her, just as you recognized the final generation of my soul in him. We were both just subconsciously influential passengers in these two lifetimes.

She toyed with his affections, reveling in the attention that her beauty attracted, using her suitors as pawns in games to taunt him. They'd both left the small town to pursue further study in their late teens. He traveled the world, learning other languages and cultures. She went to the city's wilderness and lived as a socialite. When he'd finally completed his global education and come back to visit her, he found that she'd been unable to hold the reins of her lifestyle. In the openness of the city's freedom and limitless possibility, she'd courted chaos and disorder. She was living out of control, mired in trouble, and falling fast into the misery that had preyed upon her entire life.

He took her home to the small town where they'd both grown up. There, they married and bought a house on the same street where they'd fallen in love as children.

But even with your knowledge of my final lifetime in this man, she'd continued to levy her pain upon him, punishing him for his love and for his concerns for her. Their love continued to co-mingle with betrayal, their joy with misery, their peace with chaos. But even as you and she hurt him, he remained steadfast by your side, faithful and devoted to this truest love, sparked uncountable eons before his birth.

Your animosity was not restricted merely to her city disappearances; it was administered to him often at their suburban home, rarely sparing full brutality and force. The cityscape was certainly her favorite destination, though, when you felt the need to exercise your sharpest malevolence. You and she disappeared countless times back into that range of skyscrapers, requiring him on a few occasions to go in and pull her back out.

Including this last time.

Even impending middle-age had not tamed her desire for trouble, although the kinds of trouble available had evolved over the decades.

He found her at a party near the top of an apartment skyscraper. When he'd quietly entered the room, she'd berated him with her most refined deluge of scathing vitriol and hatred. He'd stood quietly until she'd finished, then wordlessly taken her hand and led her outside to the car, which was parked on the snaking skyscraper road just outside.

He'd opened the passenger door for her, but she'd seized the keys from his hands, insisting that she drive. With a sigh, he climbed in through the door he'd opened. He and I watched her swerve in her inebriated state down the winding, narrow road, headed for the street far below.

She screamed furiously at him when he suggested that she was driving dangerously...and when he asked that she pull over so that he could take over, she barraged him with a volley of insults, letting go of the wheel to strike at him.

He fought back to restrain her, but she shoved him roughly into the passenger door. Momentarily free, she aimed the car at the skyscraper highway's fortieth floor guardrail and accelerated. They bounced up off of the metal barrier; the vehicle's undercarriage slid across the railing, sparks flying. The car's spinning rear wheels finally found purchase on a another stretch of elevated pavement. With one final screech of tires, they went over.

The car erupted in flames when it hit, scorching a black stain into the street surface. My tears were useless against the fire.

Her body died. You moved on to another form. I watched you leap into the refuge of a simple creature-life, where no surface memories or introspection could reach your mind.

The man somehow survived the impact, but his shattered body lies here now in this hospital bed. The medical staff's forced pleasantries tell him all he needs to know about his chances. They offer sedatives for the intense ache, but he refuses them. He spends most of his waking time just remaining still, an island of quiet amidst the hospital's bustle of noise and activity.

And he waits.

And while the dying man lies in the bed, this broken, tired old soul waits patiently to vacate his broken, tired body.

La Muerte de Dios.

The Bag Man

By Scott Sigler

(Originally podcast: 07/30/08 at
www.scottsigler.com)

Thursday, 9:17 p.m.

The phone rang. I pulled myself away from a Seinfeld re-run, picked myself out of my Lay-Z-Boy and shuffled towards the cordless. I always put the cordless back in its little holder, so when it rings I have to go get it anyway. Kind of defeats the purpose of having one, but hey, it was a gift.

"Hello?"

"Hello, sir," said a little boy's voice. "May I please speak to Mister Frank McMillian?"

"You're talkin' at him," I said. I didn't recognize the voice, at least not right off, and I wondered how the kid got the number. I also wondered if I'd have to change it—again. I'd changed it four times in the past three months. The price of stardom, I suppose ... and the price of writing newspaper articles that piss people off.

"This is Frank McMillian?" the voice asked.

"Yes, kid, this is Frank McMillian. Who is this?"

The pause was only slight.

"Good evening Mister McMillian," the kid's voice said. "This is the Bag Man."

My knees went instantly weak and I felt like I'd been kicked dead square in the nuts. My head swam. I needed a deep breath, but couldn't draw one. I shuffled for the Lay-Z-Boy, grateful it was only five feet away. Cordless gadgets come in handy after all.

"This some kind of sick fucking joke?" I fell back into the chair, breathless and weak.

"No sir," the tiny voice said. "No sir, this is no joke. You've heard enough of the police tapes, Mr. McMillian. I think you recognize my voice by now."

"No, I don't recognize it," I lied. Somewhere in my head it seemed that if I admitted recognition then I was accepting this call as real—accepting my own doom. A part of me refused to recognize the voice's identity; but I knew damn well who it was. "I don't know who the fuck this is, but you're not funny."

"That may be the case, Mister McMillian, but I assure you I am the Bag Man. You're in denial, now. It will pass. I'll be paying you a visit tomorrow at 3 p.m."

I'd heard such conversations before, but those were tapes. Tapes of other people. He was talking to me now, and that was a whole different story. I wondered how he could be so fucking polite. He sounded like he was drumming up candy sales for the local little league team, not announcing my death warrant.

"You've made a mistake," I said.

Claudette...

I still couldn't breathe, and my words were more puffs of frightened air rather than an actual voice. "Really, I think you've made a mistake."

"That's not the case, Mister McMillian. We both know that. I'll see you tomorrow. Tell the police the code is Tweety, Sylvester, Daffy. Can you remember that, sir?"

Tweety, Sylvester, Daffy. My mortality spelled out in Looney Tunes characters. I had no doubt the cops would have the same code.

"Good-bye, Mister McMillian. Have a pleasant evening."

I heard a click, then a dial tone. The phone dropped from my hands to fall noiselessly on the shag carpeting. On the TV, Kramer burst through the door. The crowd roared in delight. I didn't think it was funny.

THURSDAY, 10:02 P.M.

I was on the phone again, this time with Shawna Perreault, police commissioner. I remembered when she earned that honor—note the word *earned*; it wasn't handed to her because she was a woman in a man's world, like most bitches who get high-ranking jobs. Shawna was the real deal, not some affirmative-action entitlement piece of shit getting a job over some hard-working stiff who made the poor career choice of being born a white male.

"Did he give you a code?" Shawna asked.

"Yes," I said. I didn't say anymore. I didn't want to. I'd recognized the Bag Man's voice. I was almost one-hundred percent sure my ass was fried.

"Well?" Shawna said. "What was it?"

I swallowed. I didn't want this to happen. I knew the game. Bag Man always called the cops and gave them a code. He gave that same code to the victim. Even after two years of killings, the fucking cranks were still calling 9-1-1, claiming the Bag Man had called them and that they needed protection. His codes solved that problem. He was a damn courteous kid.

Thing was the codes became more of a warning to the cops than a way to separate out the sick, attention-starved loonies. The cops wanted to confirm Bag Man's targets—not so they could stop him, but so they could stay the hell out of his way.

My mouth was dry. I wanted a drink. I wanted seventeen drinks, all stiff ones, but I hadn't decided if I wanted to spend my last seventeen hours on Earth three sheets to the wind. I closed my eyes; it was time to find out if this was for real.

"Tweety, Sylvester, Daffy," I said. I waited. Then opened my eyes. Shawna didn't say anything. I knew, once and for all, that I was a dead man.

"I'm sorry, Frank," she said. I could hear despair in her voice. I couldn't blame her. Two years of watching this circus freak kill people at will would be enough to exhaust any cop.

"Yeah," I said. "Me too."

"What did you do?" she asked. "Why is he coming after you?"

"I don't know," I said.

... *Claudette Peters.*

"I know I've been a shit, you don't win two Pulitzers by being nice, but I haven't done anything to deserve this." In the back of my head I wondered if there *was* something, some forgotten sin, some repressed memory, but I couldn't dredge anything up from my swampy mind.

"Frank, you know the deal," Shawna said. "If you want police protection, I can't deny it, but I urge you to think that over strongly. You could be causing the death of good men."

That was how bad it had become in the past eighteen months. The cops wouldn't go near the Bag Man unless they were ordered. Even then, most of them just quit instead. Nobody blames them now; it's one thing to lay your life on the line in the name of duty, it's quite another to risk death knowing there's absolutely nothing you can do. Nobody wants to die—especially the way the Bag Man kills you.

Death by massive brain hemorrhaging. No external wounds, no broken bones, no internal bleeding other than the head. Coroners said the victims' brains looked like they'd been cooked in a microwave. A real mess. I saw one of those brains. Microwave wasn't my choice of descriptive kitchen appliances; I preferred a blender set on *puree.* I saw a coroner open up a victim's skull with one of those spooky bone saws. Fucker's brains spilled out like a damn milkshake. I wasn't surprised to see most everyone lose their lunch, but the coroner puked, too. The *coroner.* You know it's some sick-ass shit when the fucking *coroner* pukes.

The first four or five victims had everyone stumped. City authorities had no idea what caused such bizarre deaths. The CDC sent a team down and everything. Then the calls for help started coming in. Word gets around on the street, and seeing as the Bag Man gave everyone twelve hours to live people talked. It didn't take long for the story to spread—by the twentieth victim, even die-hard gangstas were calling the cops for help.

Sure the strange killings made the news, but no one knew what we had on our hands. Not till Rocco "Pizza Face" Salvatore called the cops for protection. Told the DA he'd give up everything he had on the Caprizi family. Everything. The DA almost shit himself. All the cops had to do was keep him alive. The cops guarded Rocco like he was the President that night. Even squirreled him away to a safe house. The protection, the move—it didn't matter. The Bag Man showed up at the appointed hour and turned Salvatore's brain to oatmeal. Two cops died that night. The Bag Man ignored their bullets, ignored them until they tried to tackle him. Then he touched those cops, and they died.

"Frank," Shawna said. "Did you hear me? Do you want police protection or not?" Her voice sounded shaky. If I asked, she had to send the cops. None of them would volunteer. Not anymore. Twelve cops with pureed brains assured that.

"No," I said. "Forget it, Shawna. No cops." She breathed a sigh of relief. Insensitive as hell, but I didn't hold it against her.

"I'm authorized to give you a gun, Frank. Anything you want."

"I've seen you guys shoot a fucking bazooka at him," I said. "It won't make a difference."

"The gun's not for the Bag Man," she said. "It's for you."

Now there was a little detail I'd missed in two years of covering this story. The cops were willing to give people guns—suicide instead of facing the Bag Man. How's that for civil rights? My die-hard reporter nature should have jumped on that story like a bum on a baloney sandwich, but that part of me was dead already. It died the minute the Bag Man said he was coming for me. Hard to care about the news when you won't be alive to see tomorrow's evening edition.

"No," I said. "No gun." I hung up. Shawna didn't call back.

FRIDAY, 9:32 A.M.

It's funny how much time I spent on the phone my last few hours. Ironic, really. People say the pen is mightier than the sword.

Naw, that's bullshit. Words aren't a reporter's weapon—the phone is. Hours and hours and hours on the phone, calling contact after contact. Call one guy to follow up a lead, get a name, call another guy, get a name, call another guy, set up a meeting. At that meeting what do you get? More names and numbers. Words ain't shit. Too many of my colleagues think their dainty little fingers type out brilliant prose that wows the reading audience. Bullshit. All people want is the story. Any schmuck can string together a few sentences around some nice tasty facts. It's not like we're T.S. Elliot, although some of these conceited, arrogant bastards seem to think they are. There's only one talent in the reporting field—that's getting the story.

After a lifetime on the phone, I guess I couldn't quit. I called my ex-wife Sheila at work the next morning. Hadn't talked to her in four months. She was pissed because she divorced me back when I was making reporter wages, peanuts. Now I had two Pulitzers under my belt and a bona fide New York Times number-one bestseller about the Bag Man's childhood. I had money falling out of my ass. The greatest joy that money gave me? That Sheila didn't get any of it.

"Pratchert Enterprises, Sheila McMillian speaking." She'd kept her married name. Never could figure that one out.

"Hi Toots." She'd loved being called Toots when we were married, at least until she found out that's what I called all the women I was fucking at the time. She kind of hated it after that.

"Hello, Frank" Her voice held that odd mix of ice and familiar warmth only an ex-wife can master. "I haven't talked to you in months. How's life in the fast lane?"

"Great." I wanted to get this over with fast. It wasn't like I had much time. "Listen, Sheila, there's something I want to tell you."

"Ohhh, sounds serious, Frank," she said. "You never were too good at serious."

"I know. Listen, Sheila, I wanted to say that when we were together I really loved you. I've never loved anyone but you. I screwed up things for us both, and I wanted to tell you that I was wrong. And I'm sorry."

She was silent for a moment, then her voice came shaky and weak. "Frank, I...I don't know what to say." The coldness in her voice was gone. Now there was only shock. I knew why. We'd known each other for twenty years, spent six of them married, and I don't think she ever once heard me say 'I'm sorry' to anyone about anything.

She started to say something else, but I hung up. I sat back in the Lay-Z-Boy and clicked on the TV. Re-run of Grey's Anatomy. The phone rang. I knew it was Sheila. I didn't answer.

FRIDAY, 11:34 A.M.

Seven-year-old Tommy Archer. From the South side. Died in a drive-by. The kid never did anything to anyone. Just in the wrong place at the wrong time, and that could be anywhere anytime of the day in this fucked-up city. Stray twelve-gauge blew his head clean off. I saw the pictures. Hell, I was the one who broke the story.

That was Pulitzer number one. In the first months of the Bag Man's reign he was the biggest story on the planet. Everyone was trying to figure out why bullets didn't stop him, why he didn't burn when they turned a flame-thrower on him, how he could get into any building, any prison, any fortress at the appointed time, things like that. He was so inhuman with these weird powers that no one stopped to see him as a little boy.

No one except me.

He always looked blurry on film or on TV. Never clear. But if you saw him in person, and I had thirty-seven times in the past year alone, you could recognize his face. I've seen him more than anyone outside of the police department. What can I say? I'm a old-guard senior reporter who used to go out drinking Manhattans with the Chief of Police. Membership has it's privileges.

Took me four weeks of looking through archived articles of every story concerning young white boys. Four weeks; twelve hours a day staring at newspaper clippings. Didn't write a single story in that time. Almost got fired. It was worth it. 'Worth it' is spelled P-U-L-I-

T-Z-E-R, by the way. I broke that story. Tommy Archer, seven-year-old victim of urban violence, back from the dead to kill sinners.

FRIDAY, 12:02 P.M.

No one complained anymore, not even the liberals. Police did everything possible, tried every weapon, even brought in psychics and parapsychologists, if you can believe that. Those schmucks couldn't do anything, either.

Sick fucking world we live in. Full of sick people. The Bag Man became my only beat, I covered him day-in and day-out. I wasn't the only one. Every major metro has a reporter in this city, including a dozen European papers and rags as far away as Japan and South Africa. Everyone loves watching American scumbags bite the bullet. I have to admit, I kind of liked it too. At least I did until Tommy called *me*.

So there's around fifty print and broadcast reporters who do nothing but cover the Bag Man. His day-to-day killings don't make much of a media splash anymore. Don't do much but cause grief and humiliation for the victim's family as reporters scramble to find out what the poor bastard did wrong. You never know when he's going to off a celebrity, and that's news. Guess I'm a celebrity now—I'll be good for a few headlines myself. Yeah, about fifty people covering the Bag Man, but I've got an advantage, I lived here before little Tommy got rolling.

That's how I won my second Pulitzer. Got a tip from Shawna Perreault that Hasbro, the toy company, was filing all these Freedom of Information Act requests with the police department, trying to get a clear picture of Tommy's face. Took me three weeks to get the story, but I got it. They wanted to make dolls. *Dolls.* Can you believe that? This supernatural freaky dead boy is turning people's brains into porridge and Hasbro wants to turn him into a Cabbage Patch Kid or something. I cracked the story wide open. It drew gobs of national attention. Hasbro quickly forgot about the plan. Didn't matter. Sweatshops made the dolls anyway, and they sold like hotcakes. Bag Man shirts, hats, greeting cards with the clever slogan "Don't answer the phone!" People were making a killing off Tommy. Pardon the pun.

Like I said, a sick fucking world.

FRIDAY, 12:37 P.M.

I tried to reach my daughter at her college. Hadn't talked to her in weeks. We're not very close. She's living with this black guy. Not that I care, mind you, but it's still unsettling even if you're not a racist. She's in college, you know? You worry about rapists,

...Claudette Peters Claudette Peters

you wonder if this black guy is a good man or if he's ghetto trash getting a free ride to college because of the color of his skin. You wonder if he's going to take her whether she wants it or not.

Got her answering machine. I left a regular message, told her I loved her. She'd find out the rest soon enough.

FRIDAY, 2:54 P.M.

The doorbell rang. Can you believe that? He rang the doorbell. Little fucker could get into any building, anytime, anywhere, and at my house he rang the doorbell. I wasn't getting up to let him in, though. Fuck him. He was there to kill me, after all.

There was no point in playing games. No point in running or hiding. When your time was up the Bag Man found you. No one knew how. He just did. Some ran. Some hid. Some fought. They all died. Me? I preferred not to waste my last few minutes in some useless dash for freedom, for survival. I'd covered this story for two years. I'd seen the shit people had pulled to stay away from the Bag Man. None of it ever worked.

I remember the best one of all, the incident that *really* let us know there was no way to stop Tommy Archer. Vincent Emil was a rich bastard, a Croatian immigrant who made a killing in real estate deals, owned the QuickieBurger restaurant chain, even owned a minor-league baseball team in Kansas, of all places. Pompous bastard, I can tell you that for free. Wore a lot of jewelry, Italian silk suits, that kind of thing. He got the call just over a year ago. Did he panic? Not Emil, no way. He called his private jet, had the pilot fuel it up, then he called me. Said he was going to be the first to outrun the Bag Man, that he'd be at 10,000 feet at the appointed hour.

He invited me along, wanted the world to know that Vincent Emil wasn't going to be "bagged" by anyone. Craziest shit I ever saw. We were at 9,500 feet. Emil was laughing his head off, drunk on life, elated that he'd escaped certain death. Then the bathroom door opened. Tommy came out. Didn't say a word. Walked right up to Emil and touched his head. Emil dropped dead on the spot. Tommy walked back to the bathroom and shut the door. It was only then I realized I'd shit myself. No one went near that bathroom. We landed twenty-five minutes later. A cop finally opened the bathroom door. Tommy was gone, of course. He'd somehow boarded a plane while it flew at 9,500 feet, did his thing, then disembarked. Crazy shit. Crazy kid. No way to outrun him, no way at all.

So I sat there in my Lay-Z-Boy, waiting in as much comfort as I could muster. My house. My things. No running for this old reporter. I had, however, decided to have those drinks. All seventeen of them. The Bag Man was here for me, and I was good and smashed.

"It's open, Tommy old boy."

The handle turned, the door opened and there he was, smiling politely with his perpetually-missing left incisor. I wondered if he'd cashed in with the Tooth Fairy before his head absorbed that rogue slug.

He shut the door behind himself, rubbed his feet on the throw rug in front of the door, and came in. There was a rosy glow on his cheeks. His straight blond hair was caught somewhere between combed and wild. It's a look only little boys can carry well, because they don't try, it just happens. I wondered if that's what his hair had looked like before the slug ripped through his head like a Ginsu through a tomato. No trace of the wound, by the way, just a normal little-boy head. I'd drank a bottle of Southern Comfort to blur things. It hadn't worked. Somehow I was suddenly sober, despite the liquor. I'm sure that was his doing.

I'd meant to ask him why he called himself the Bag Man. Some last act, eh? No one knew. We assumed it was because he "bagged" people, as in "body bag." Like I said, I meant to ask him, but when he walked through my door it just didn't seem to matter.

"Hello, Mister McMillian," the Bag Man said.

"Hiya Tommy." I wanted to run, but that wouldn't do any good. It was three minutes to 3:00. I'd watched this scene many times as an impartial observer. No one got away from Tommy Archer the Bag Man. I offered the bottle to him. "Care for a swig?"

"No thanks, Mister McMillian," Tommy said. He just stared at me. He had the face, hair, body and gap-toothed smile of an innocent seven-year-old, but his eyes were something else. They seemed very old. Older than me.

"Tommy, are you sure there hasn't been some mistake?" There was a whine in my voice I hadn't heard since Sheila walked out on me. I'd promised myself I wasn't going to beg, that I would die like a man. So much for promises; I was never that good at them anyway.

"You're a liar, Mister McMillian," Tommy said. "You've hurt a lot of people in your job. Printed stories you knew weren't true just because they were sensational. You've made quite a name covering me, but before you won that first Pulitzer you were not a very nice reporter, sir."

"There's no such thing as a nice reporter! The only nice people write that useless social-page shit, those feature puff pieces. I'm a hard-news man, Tommy!" I whipped the bottle at him. It went right through and smashed into the wall on the far side. Shards of glass sparkled in the flickering light of the television. Uzis don't work on him, but I could hurt him with a half-empty fifth of liquor. Right.

"Come on, Tommy," I said. I felt tears coming down my cheeks. If my ass hadn't been socked into the Lay-Z-Boy, I'm sure I would have been on my knees. "I was a scumbag reporter for years, sure, but that's not any reason to kill a man."

"No, it's not," Tommy said. "That's not why I'm here. You remember Claudette Peters, don't you, Mister McMillian?"

My blood temperature dropped to zero in a fraction of a second. From the moment I'd heard his voice the night before, I'd known why he was coming for me. I'd known, I just hadn't allowed myself to remember. I blocked the memory, just as I'd blocked it for the last thirty-two years. But as soon as he spoke her name, I couldn't stop the flood of memory.

"Tommy... Tommy that was thirty-two years ago. I was a drunk kid, for God's sake!"

"I don't care if you were drunk or sober, sir," Tommy said. "You raped her."

I broke. The tears came, uncontrollable. I'd raped her. She'd wanted it, *flaunted* it, then played games with me. I hit her. Only once, but it was enough. Took the fight right out of her. In a drunken stupor I'd taken her virginity by force. I almost told Tommy it was just a date rape, but I didn't bother. The mere fact that he was here, in my living room, meant I was dead. There was no bargaining with the Bag Man.

"She killed herself last week, Mister McMillian," Tommy said. "She never married. Never had kids. From the night you raped her, she could never trust anyone. Counseling didn't help, nothing did. It's unusual for such an event to cause such a high degree of trauma, Mister McMillian, but it destroyed her life and you're to blame."

"I was nineteen years old," I said, crying like a little girl. "It was a frat party, I was drunk."

"This is true, Mister McMillian, but it's still a sin. And you've got to pay for it."

"There's no one else out there to kill? No one worse than me?"

"They're all gone, Mister McMillian," Tommy said. "You were one of the people who cheered me on while I cleansed the city of that scum. I read your editorials in the beginning, about how someone had to get rid of these criminals anyway. 'Good' people like yourself loved me until all the really bad people were gone and I moved on to the 'only a little-bit bad' people. No one liked that. You knew some of those people. They weren't gang-bangers or assassins, they were neighbors, friends, co-workers. But they were also pedophiles, child-abusers, spouse abusers, con men. They were also rapists. Like you. And now it's your turn. It's 3 p.m., Mister McMillian."

He stepped towards me. I shut my eyes, I didn't want to see it coming. I heard his hands vibrating, thickly, like a dozen bumble bees trapped in chocolate pudding. I felt a tingle on my forehead.

His hands came for my head, but I didn't think about myself. All I could focus on was Claudette Peters and those tears of fear and pain and betrayal that streaked her face thirty-two years before.

I remembered her now. Every last detail.

What the Damned Owe

By Jared Axelrod

(ORIGINALLY PODCAST: 04/15/08 HTTP://PLANETX.
LIBSYN.COM/INDEX.PHP?POST_ID=329286)

Barry Sturgeon calmly put down the file his accountant had given him, carefully cut the ring finger on his left hand and drew a summoning circle on the floor in his own blood. As the hardwood inside the circle crumbled and fell away to reveal the pit of flames beneath, Sturgeon sighed inwardly. His demon would know what to do about this tax mess.

Nysrogh rose slowly out of the flames, his suit immaculate, his manner refined. He smoothed out his waxed mustache with an index finger, his lacquered nails glinting in the firelight. "I'm not usually summoned after a transaction has taken place," Nysrogh said, his voice a languid purr. "And certainly not so soon."

"I'm sorry, I'm…look, you said I could, whenever I—" Nysrogh cut Sturgeon off with an upraised palm.

"And I meant it, my dear boy, I meant it. Customer service is very important to us. Now, what seems to be the trouble?"

Sturgeon swallowed hard. "Well, it's tax season, and when I sold my soul to you for wealth, fame, and Cecilia—"

"How's she working out then?"

"Oh, she's fine, fine."

"Wonderous." Nysrogh polished his fingernails on his lapel, admiring their sharp edges. "I'm particularly proud of her. Carry on then. When you sold your soul—"

"Right, well. When I sold my soul, that naturally put me in a new tax bracket, so I hired an accountant to take care of it. Now, he's pretty much taken care of the wealth part and all that. But, um…

what about the rest of it?"

Nysrogh slowly moved his attention away from his nails. "I'm not sure I follow."

"Well, the fame, and, you know, Cecilia. Those didn't just happen. I bought those, there was a transaction. So, the question is, do I owe taxes on that?"

The demon seemed confused. For a moment, his immaculate manner cracked. He eyed the pit of flames from which he came nervously. "Well, I don't think...I don't think you do. After all, who can put a price on such things?"

"Well, you did. My soul. So, what do I owe on that?"

"Look, I'm not really sure."

"You're not sure? You're not sure," Sturgeon pinched the bridge of his nose. "Maybe I should talk to your supervisor."

"I beg your pardon?" The entire room burst into flames with Nysrogh's indignation. His nails turned into claws and his eyes glowed with an unholy light. He grew so large the office walls seemed to strain to contain him. "I am chief of the houses of the princes of Hell, a second order demon! And you will treat me with the respect I am owed!"

Sturgeon stood his ground. "But you're not sure what I owe on these taxes."

Nysrogh's voice and body shrank. "No."

"I think I better talk to a first order demon then."

Nysrogh's coughed into his fist and removed a thin, shiny device from his inside jacket pocket. He slid his finger along its black face and it lit up.

"Hey," said Sturgeon. "Is that an iPhone?"

"We all have them." Nysrogh said, dialing. "Part of the deal with Jobs."

"Can I..?"

"There's one in your right desk drawer." Nysrogh said "Ipos. Yes, I'm sure...Hello Ipe, this is Nys and I've got a— Look, I understand you're busy...No, that's not like that. Of course I can handle a...

You're not listening to me. Will you listen? It's about the IRS, okay? Yes. Them. Thank you." Nysrogh returned the phone to his jacket and stepped out of the circle of flames. He sat cross-legged on Sturgeon's leather chair. He folded his hands over his knees and refused to look in Sturgeon's direction.

"So, um, is he coming?" Sturgeon asked. Nysrogh gave Sturgeon a quick nod with an overly enthusiastic grin and then resumed glowering at the wall.

Suddenly, two large meaty hands blackened with soot and blood burst from the hole in the floor. The head of a lion followed set upon powerful human shoulders. The creature clawed and forced his armored body through the hole, flames pouring out of his mane and cascading down his torso.

"Who summons Ipos, Demon Count of Hell, Commander of Thirty-Six Legions? Who dares summon me?"

Nysrogh pointed to Sturgeon who shifted from one foot to another. "Yes, well, it's about my contract, you see, and...and taxes."

"Speak no further," said Ipos. A pile of papers appeared in his outstretched hand out of a puff of flame. A delicate pair of bifocals also appeared on top of his lion's muzzle. "I have your contract here. It appears fairly standard: wealth, fame, beautiful wife. Many of the laws that govern inheritance taxes also apply to this, so it should be easy to sort out. Fame is immaterial, so no need to pay any on that. And the wife, hmmm. This, ah, Cecilia, who was she before the contract was instated? There doesn't seem to be any documentation here."

"She wasn't anyone." Nysrogh said "I created her. Barry here was extremely explicit about the kind of woman he wanted. Tall, but not too tall. Smart, but not too smart. Large breasts, but not too large. Funny, but not too funny. Rather than search the world for that sort of woman, I just made her from scratch. Seemed like a good idea at the time."

Ipos removed his bifocals. "You couldn't have just wanted your high school sweetheart like everyone else. If she was created for the contract, that makes her a thing. But I imagine she has some degree of sentience, knowing Nys's attention to detail, so that makes her a person, too. Which means that you might owe on her, you might not."

Sturgeon was feeling increasingly uneasy. "You don't know?"

"I do not. This is a grey area, past my experience. I will have to call the boss."

The way Ipos said "boss" made Sturgeon's blood run cold. "You don't mean…?"

"Me," said a man dressed all in black, suddenly standing in front of Sturgeon.

Nysrogh and Ipos were gone, as was the hole in the floor. There was only Sturgeon and the man in black in the room, as if it had always been that way.

"Lucifer?" Sturgeon whispered.

"Mr. Morningstar, if you don't mind. Let's keep this professional, Mr. Sturgeon, shall we? I don't really have the time for this, but quite frankly, neither does my staff. If you are going to waste time, I'd rather you waste my time, okay? Now, taxes. You're worried about taxes."

Sturgeon could feel the man in black's voice deep within his bowels. Behind each word seemed to be an ocean of screams and wails. "Yes."

"I see. Sold your mortal soul for earthly joy and you're worried about taxes." The man in black turned his eyes to the ceiling. "You created them, not me."

"I just don't want to get audited," Sturgeon said, in a strained voice. The man in black sighed and picked up the folder Sturgeon's accountant had given him.

"I really shouldn't have to explain this to you. Number one, if they audit you, they audit you. Bend over, spread your cheeks and take it like a man. Because I can assure you, Mr. Sturgeon, no matter what they do to you, it will not hold a candle to the everlasting torment I've got in store for you once you pass on. Do. You. Under. Stand. Me?"

Sturgeon was intensely aware of the smell of urine and the dampness of his pants. He managed to croak out a small, "Yes."

"Good. Now. Number two." The man in black tore the folder and the papers it contained in half, and then half again. "This is ridiculous. Everyone knows that the rich don't pay taxes."

Salvation

By Mike Bennett

(Originally podcast: 04/13/08 at
www.mikebennettpodcast.com/?q=hall_of_mirrors)

G eoffrey Leech burned in the fires of Hell. He had no knowledge of time; he could have been in perdition for thirty seconds or thirty thousand years. All he knew was the agony of his soul's unending torment. Like flesh, it was vulnerable to damage and pain; it tore and bled and burned. But unlike flesh, it regenerated as quickly as it was destroyed. Sometimes the fires relented, giving Geoffrey and the other damned a darkness to lie and smoulder in, to weep and howl and regret; to repent and beg the forgiveness of a God that could no longer hear them.

Demons prowled these smoking catacombs, passing through fire and brimstone unharmed; their souls, or whatever it was that formed their substance, seemingly impervious to heat and pain. They came and took their pleasure in the torture and abuse of their charges. They were the masters of Hell and the damned were theirs to play with. Geoffrey's master was known still by the name he had borne in life. It lacked the classic demonic cadences of the names of some of his peers, but the mention of it brought as much horror and dread to those he preyed upon as might any other name in the ancient registers of Hell: it was Clive. Clive liked to hear his name twisted in screams and whimpered in pleas for mercy. He would occasionally take a moment's rest from his labours specifically to hear the music of the misery he created; and to his ears, the most enjoyable music of all issued from Geoffrey Leech.

Geoffrey, when he wasn't making said music, would wonder in dread and awe how Clive and his kind had come about. Evidently

Clive had once been mortal, so how had he attained his demonic form and position? Why didn't he suffer? Why didn't he burn? After all, wasn't this Hell? Weren't they all supposed to be suffering?

And now, on the occasion of our story's beginning, Geoffrey had finally found the courage to ask. Clive had been torturing Geoffrey for some time and was taking a break from his exertions when the object of his pleasure reached out a trembling hand to him. "Please, please, Clive, my master. I beg of you, stop."

Clive laughed. He sank his burning talons into the soft, sizzling flesh of Geoffrey's face and twisted it up to face him. "What is it, wretch? Do you tire of my attention?"

"No, master, I beg of you, if I may…a question. One question."

"A question?" Clive smiled, baring rows of pointed teeth. "How interesting. What makes you think I'd answer it?"

"I," Geoffrey stammered, struggling to speak in spite of the burning talons in his face. "I have no hope that you will, master, I only beg that you might consider."

Clive did consider for a moment. Then he said, "Very well, little shit man. But be warned, there is nothing you can ask of me that will bring you anything other than unspeakable pain."

Geoffrey tried to nod. "I know, my master, and I humbly accept it."

"Very well then," Clive withdrew his talons from Geoffrey's face and licked the hot blood from his fingers. "Ask."

Geoffrey knew that unspeakable pain was going to be administered anyway, so he raised his eyes as far as he dared and asked his question. "How do you get to be a demon?"

Clive laughed. "A demon?"

Geoffrey looked up into the face of his master. "Yes, master. I, I want to be like you."

Clive punched Geoffrey in the face. "Don't look at me, you stinking arsehole. Did I say you could look at me?"

As if summoned by Clive's anger, fire swept through the cavern and consumed them both, though only Geoffrey burned. He screamed and Clive came around behind him and climbed onto his back. The firestorm passed and Clive, his flesh smoking but unharmed, leaned in close to Geoffrey's ear. "You want to be like me, do you?"

"Yes." Geoffrey's tears steamed over his freshly burned flesh. "Yes, master."

"Why?"

"Because, because you don't burn. You don't suffer. None of the demons do. I've seen how you—how all of you demons—you inflict pain, but you never seem to feel any and I, I've been thinking: if I am to be damned for all time, then I'd like to be like you, a demon, a master, a bringer of pain rather than a, a receiver of it."

"You think we don't suffer, my pretty fool?" Clive gave a low, humourless cackle. "Oh, we suffer. Not quite in the same way as you do, granted, but we suffer nonetheless. And when we have endured our suffering, we come out looking for wankers like you so we might take our pain and anger out on your wretched carcasses. Your suffering makes us feel better again. Your pain is our soothing balm. As they say in the mortal world, shit rolls downhill. It's a popular ethos of those of come to Hell. And as I recall, you yourself were a great advocate of that practice in life. Rolling your shit downhill; a bully, using your position to make the lives of your juniors, shall we say, less comfortable?"

"I'm sorry."

"For what, for being a bully? What about all the other things? Your sexual appetite for young girls, the younger the better, hmmm? Oh, that was, of course, your final undoing. A heart attack while fucking a poor child prostitute," Clive chuckled. "Oh, you despicable hound."

"Forgive me, master."

"Forgive?" Clive laughed. "It is not my place to forgive, shitty man, it is only my place to punish. I personally applaud such behaviour, it seasons the soul and adds a certain delicious…" he sniffed at Geoffrey's face and head. "Piquancy." Geoffrey cringed away from him, but Clive seized him by the ears and pulled his head forwards.

"Come now, Geoffrey Leech, don't be coy. You should be proud of your life: your physical and psychological abuse of others was genuinely entertaining." Clive stroked the burned and blistered skin of Geoffrey's scalp and he gave a low chuckle. "I personally enjoyed the way you treated the fair sex. Especially that poor cow who married you." He tutted. "You really made her life Hell, didn't you Geoffrey? You didn't even cry when she killed herself, you heartless bastard. Some might say that a man driving his wife to suicide would be worthy of demonic status in itself. But unfortunately, it doesn't work like that." He leaned forward and licked the blood that ran from the ruptures on Geoffrey's neck.

Geoffrey struggled to keep his voice steady. "Then, h-how does it work, master?"

Clive was beginning to lose himself in the taste of Geoffrey's blood; he slowly sank his teeth into Geoffrey's shoulder. The scream that followed did nothing to awaken him.

"Master, please! Please don't eat me again!" Geoffrey screamed. "You said you'd answer my question."

Clive lifted his mouth from the wound he had made and savoured for a moment the little piece of Geoffrey that steamed in his mouth, enjoying its delicate, lightly barbequed flavour. "Oh, yes, of course. How do you get to be a demon?" He watched as the wound began to heal, wet and sticky like hot treacle, ready to be enjoyed all over again should he feel the urge. "Well, that's a decision to be made by your master and mine."

Geoffrey felt a surge of hope, which he tried to keep from his voice as he replied, timidly, "You mean... ?"

"Yes. Him."

"But, but how does He get to know my wish? Do, do I tell Him, or do you?"

"Fortunately for you, He knows all. If it were up to me, the last thing I'd do is pass on your request; I like having you here too much." Clive's tongue slaked across the back of Geoffrey's neck.

"Then," Geoffrey blurted, closing his eyes and desperately trying to keep Clive's attention on his words rather than the taste of his flesh. "Then, what happens next?"

"Oh, I don't know," Clive mused. "He considers your request; if he deems you worthy, you get your chance to please him. If you please him, you become a demon."

"How will I know his decision?"

"I pass it on to you."

"When does he tell you?"

"He already has."

"He has? When?"

"He lives in my mind, as he does in yours; you just aren't as clearly tuned in as we demons are."

"S-so," Geoffrey stammered. "What is his decision?"

Clive sat up on Geoffrey's back and looked lovingly at the scorched flesh of his favourite charge. It saddened him to have to give Geoffrey Leech a chance at demonic status, but he had his orders, and Geoffrey now had his mission. He sighed and bent to kiss the bubbling wound he had made earlier. The smell was too much resist. "Oh, I'll tell you later. Right after what I sincerely hope isn't our final supper." Clive drew back his lips and sank down to the wound on Geoffrey's shoulder.

Geoffrey screamed; his desperate struggles to be free of the monster on his back only adding to its pleasure in devouring him. They writhed together, one lost in pleasure, the other in unspeakable torment. And presently, when a strangely focused fire howled around them like a whirlwind, Geoffrey welcomed it as a blessed relief; his screams dissolving into the roar and crackle of the flames, before dissolving into nothing at all.

Geoffrey's eyes fluttered open to a deep, incomprehensible whiteness. He stared into it for at least thirty seconds before he realised he was in no pain; in fact, he felt comfortable. Then he became aware of air moving in and out of his lungs; he was breathing air. He blinked, and moved his hands; he felt softness beneath his fingers, warm and dry, like fabric. He raised his hands before his face and a sound issued from him that made the nearby nurse look over in alarm.

"Mr. Leech?"

"I'm not burning," Geoffrey croaked. "I'm not dead."

The nurse smiled and came over to his bedside. "No, you're not, but it was a close call. We thought we'd lost you for a while there. Fortunately, the doctors were able to bring you back."

Geoffrey touched his face, running his fingers over his lips and cheeks. He touched his hair and ran his fingers through it, rubbing at his scalp and delighting in the sensation. "I'm not dead!" he laughed, but the rush of air snagged in the dryness of his throat and he fell to choking uncontrollably.

The nurse steadied him. "Easy now, Mr. Leech, you've undergone a very traumatic experience. Here," she handed him a glass of water. "Drink this, slowly."

He accepted the glass with both hands, marvelling at its smooth, clean touch. Then he drank, and the sensation of the water running over his tongue and into his throat was the greatest pleasure he felt he had ever known. He drank, savouring every drop, washing the water around his mouth like it was the most precious substance on Earth—which, he now knew, it was.

"Hey, not so fast," the nurse laid her hand on the glass to slow him. "Sip it."

Geoffrey let her ease the glass away from his lips and he turned to look at her. She was beautiful: a plump and plain young woman, unremarkable in every way. And yet all he could see was the selfless kindness in her deep brown eyes. And her smile; she was happy to see him. His heart ached as the vision of her face began to soften and swim in his tears.

He was alive.

"Now here's an unusual customer and no mistake," Doctor James Montague pointed out Geoffrey with a subtle inclination of his pen as he and Doctor Lucinda Scott walked along Geoffrey's ward later that day. "Came in last night—heart attack. Found in a hotel room when an anonymous caller contacted room service." James stopped Lucinda with a light touch on her arm. He arched an eyebrow. "A 'young' lady."

"How young?" The two doctors regarded Geoffrey at a distance as he dozed amidst a nest of wires and tubes.

"Let's just say when he checked in to the hotel, it was with his 'daughter'; when he checked out, she had mysteriously disappeared."

Lucinda grimaced slightly. "Any family come forward? Daughters or otherwise?"

James shook his head. "Not yet. He had another attack on the gurney as the ambulance crew were bringing him in. We lost him for a bit but managed to jump him back after a few jolts."

"How long did you lose him for?"

"Forty, fifty seconds; maybe more."

"Lucky man."

James nodded. 'You don't need to tell him that, the chap's almost deliriously happy to be alive."

"So what's so unusual about him? Surely a spot of delirious happiness isn't unusual, given the circumstances."

"No indeed. Nothing unusual about that, but it's the stuff he's been coming out with about Hell and damnation that's giving me cause for concern. I think we may have to get him over to Psychiatric."

Lucinda frowned. "What sort of stuff? What's he been saying?"

James gave a wry smile. "Ah, he's on a mission, Lucinda."

"A mission? What kind of a mission?"

"Ask him yourself." James put a hand gently to her back and guided her over to Geoffrey's bed. Geoffrey's eyes fluttered open at the sound of approaching footsteps. "Mr. Leech. Sorry to disturb you. How are we feeling?"

Geoffrey smiled. "Wonderful, thank you, Doctor."

James came around to Geoffrey's bedside and raised a hand to indicate Lucinda. "I've just been telling Dr. Scott here about your brush with the Devil."

"Not the Devil, I didn't actually have any contact with him," Geoffrey turned to Lucinda. "But I was in Hell, yes."

Lucinda smiled as she came around to the opposite side of the bed. "Now then, Mr. Leech. I'm sure you've just suffered a particularly vivid nightmare. That, coupled with the joy of surviving a near-fatal heart attack—"

"No, Doctor," Geoffrey interrupted. "Please, forgive me—I don't mean to be rude, but you're mistaken. I died. I went to Hell. I was in Hell for an eternity."

James glanced up from taking Geoffrey's pulse. "You were only dead for a minute at most, Mr. Leech, not exactly an eternity."

"There are no clocks in Hell, Doctor," said Geoffrey. "A minute or a thousand years: it's all the same. Time is *our* construction, our way of ordering our world. Hell has its own order."

Lucinda exchanged a discreet look with James. "Go on, Mr. Leech."

Geoffrey addressed himself to each of the doctors in turn. "Well, I was the—I don't know—the regular victim of...a demon. A demon called Clive. I was his to torment forever. At least, at least that's how it seemed."

"Clive?" Lucinda sounded surprised.

"Yes, Clive. He was human once but he died and went to Hell. He became a demon. His body—or rather, his soul—was transformed somehow. He left the tormented to become one of the tormentors. You see, demons—they don't burn and suffer like the ordinary damned."

"I see," said Lucinda.

"And so, I asked him," Geoffrey continued, "if it could be possible for me to be like him, and that's when he gave me my mission."

"Oh? And what mission is that?" asked Lucinda.

"I-I have to kill a man," Geoffrey's voice quavered slightly. "It's the will and command of Satan himself. He communicated the information to Clive, and Clive communicated it to me."

"How do you mean, communicated it?"

"Well, he just put the knowledge in my head," said Geoffrey. "It grew there, just as my flesh re-grew whenever it burned or he—Clive—ate it."

"He *ate* you?" Lucinda couldn't suppress a look of revulsion.

"Yes, often. He did whatever he wanted to me. As I say: I was his."

James patted Geoffrey gently on the shoulder. "Well, thankfully the nightmare's over now, Mr. Leech. You're back in the real world. No Clive, nor any other demons to worry about." Then he pointed a cautionary finger at Geoffrey's nose. "Except maybe cigarettes: I understand you get through a packet of twenty a day, is that right?"

"Oh, that's all over now, Doctor. I'm a changed man. I'll never do anything to endanger my health again. Nor will I do any harm to others, or cause anyone to suffer, not even so much as say an unkind word. I'm changed, you see, Doctors; I'm born again."

"Quite literally," Lucinda smiled. "So I guess this means you won't be fulfilling your mission then?"

Geoffrey's knuckles tightened on his blankets and he shook his head. "No, Doctor. I couldn't. I can't do it!"

"That's the spirit, Mr. Leech," said James. "The last thing we need in B-Ward is the Devil's hitman."

Geoffrey managed a smile. "No, Doctor. No fear of that."

It was just then that the elderly man in the next bed pitched in with a laugh. "He won't like that, will he? You think Old Nick will let you off just like that do you?"

Geoffrey's face tightened into a grimace of terror. "No!" he screamed. "No! No! I can be saved! I can be saved!" The man in the next bed stopped laughing as James quickly drew the dividing curtains between the beds and cut him off from view.

"It's alright Mr. Leech," Lucinda tried to calm Geoffrey, but he was raving and screaming uncontrollably. Nurses were running over now, they moved in quickly and eased Geoffrey back against his pillows. James tugged up Geoffrey's pyjama sleeve and injected him with a sedative. A few moments later Geoffrey's struggles began to abate; a few moments more and he was asleep.

James and Lucinda stepped away from his bed. "So," said James, "you see what I mean now about him being an unusual case?"

"Rather!'

"So, what do you think?"

"Well, we'll see how he is after surgery, I suppose. He's obviously terrified of death, so once we've operated and he understands that he isn't likely to drop dead at any minute, he may become more rational. In the meantime," she nodded in the direction of the man in the next bed. "A private room away from Mr. Rich-Tea-and-Sympathy there will probably work wonders."

"Yes, but still, quite an elaborate delusion, eh?"

"Oh yes, the maddest thing I've ever heard." She chuckled. "Clive. Whatever next?"

That night, Geoffrey dreamt of the image Clive had planted in his mind whilst simultaneously feasting on it. He saw again the face of his designated victim; the man's mouth was moving but the voice that issued from it was Clive's. "This is the face of your mission on Earth, Leech. This is the face of the man you must kill. And, provided you have spunk enough to rise to the task, before you dispatch him you must say these words: 'Hallelujah, I am your salvation!' When you do this, you will die again, but this time you will return to Hell in triumph."

Then the voice changed to that of another, it grew deeper and more commanding. Geoffrey whimpered as he heard again the voice of Satan in his mind. "You have asked a blessing of me Mr. Leech, and I do consent to charge thee with mine task. Fail me not, for Hell is only the beginning for those who displease me. Fail me not, Geoffrey Leech. Fail me not." The final command resounded through his whole being as if it was echoing straight from the halls of Hell.

Geoffrey awoke to the sound of his own screaming. "I won't fail thee, master! I won't!"

"Mr. Leech?" The night nurse ran into Geoffrey's room, turning on the lights and coming to his bedside. "Mr. Leech, shhh. It's okay. It was just another nightmare." She put an arm around his shoulder as Geoffrey fell to crying, his sobs heaving his chest.

"I can't do it, Nurse. I can't! But I have to. He commands it."

"Is this the Devil you're talking about again?"

Geoffrey nodded.

"It's all right, Mr. Leech. You don't have to do anything you don't want to, and no-one's going to command anything of you." She smiled. "Other than you lie down and relax."

Geoffrey turned to her. "I'm so afraid, Nurse."

The nurse squeezed his hand. "I know, Mr. Leech, but you don't have to be. Have you said a prayer?"

Geoffrey shook his head.

"Why ever not?"

Geoffrey's voice trembled. "I, I never believed in God. I—" His sentence broke apart, shaken by sobs.

"Well if you've been to Hell as you say you have, perhaps you ought to start believing."

"But, why would God listen to me? I'm evil. I must be! Judgement has already been passed on me—I belong in Hell."

"God listens to all, Mr. Leech, especially those who turn from Satan."

The nurse looked around; outside, the corridor was silent. She took Geoffrey's hand in both of hers. "Pray with me, Mr. Leech. Our Father, who art in Heaven."

Geoffrey repeated her words. As he did so, the prayer came back to him. He hadn't spoken them since his schooldays—then, it had been meaningless to him. But now the words soothed him; his sobbing abated and his voice lost its tremble. Afterwards, when the nurse had given him a sedative and gone back to her station,

Geoffrey repeated the prayer quietly, over and over, until he fell into a deep, dreamless sleep.

"I've never seen anything like it," said James, handing Geoffrey's pre-operation test results to Lucinda. "It's like he's just had a successful heart transplant."

She looked at the charts. "Are you sure these are his?"

James nodded. "The X-rays were taken this morning."

"He's made a complete recovery overnight? That's impossible."

"And yet, there it is. Its seems our Mr. Leech is a living, breathing miracle."

Lucinda held the pictures up to the light. "What on Earth do you think is responsible?"

"Well, it's not omega 3 fish oils, that's for sure. When he died, the arteries feeding his heart looked like someone had melted a kilo of cheese into them. Now they look like those of a fit and healthy adolescent."

"So there's no need to operate?"

"Well, there's nothing to operate on. Nothing malignant or even vaguely worrying."

Lucinda leafed further into Geoffrey Leech's chart. "Evidently damnation is good for your heart."

"Yes, but it plays havoc with your sanity. Poor chap's become obsessed with religion. Says he wants to join the priesthood and spend the rest of his life doing the Lord's work."

"That's hardly insanity, James. I believe they call it a calling."

"Well he's been called, all right. He wants to leave immediately and go off to become a missionary in Africa or some such place."

Lucinda indicated the chart. "Well according to this, there's no medical reason why he can't just do that."

"Well, perhaps, but according to this," James tapped his head, "he shouldn't go anywhere. I want to do further tests."

"Understandably. But what does he say to that?"

"He says he's already wasted one life and he's not prepared to waste a moment of his new one being a guinea pig for us."

"So he wants to leave?"

James nodded.

"Well, you can't hold him here against his will. If he's fit enough to leave, we can't keep him prisoner."

"I know, I know. But it's, it's bizarre, isn't it? I mean, it really is like some kind of," he shrugged. "Some kind of miracle."

Lucinda smiled. "Don't tell me you think Jesus is responsible for this."

"Oh, I don't, and nor does Leech."

"So what does he think, not—?"

James nodded. "Exactly. According to Leech, this is the Devil's work. He can't fulfil his mission with a diseased heart, so Satan's fixed it for him."

"I see. And so he's turned to religion for…salvation?"

"Presumably."

Lucinda shook her head and handed James back the charts. "So, what are you going to do? You could try and have him temporarily committed, insist he be handed over to Psychiatric for tests?"

James smiled. "Only if sudden religious piety qualifies as dangerous madness—and correct me if I'm wrong, Lucinda—but I don't believe it does."

"It doesn't."

"In which case," James looked at the X-rays on Geoffrey's chart then looked up to Lucinda with a shrug. "Who are we to stand in the way of the Lord's work?"

The first thing Geoffrey did upon his release from hospital was to go to his local Catholic church. The night nurse, Nurse Baines, was a Catholic, and she told him that if he really wanted to serve God he should become a Catholic. However, upon speaking to Father

Matheson at St. Peter's Church, Geoffrey discovered that his new life as a missionary wasn't going to be starting any time soon.

"But Father, you don't understand," said Geoffrey. "I need to begin serving the Lord immediately. My soul depends upon it." They sat in the front aisle of the church. Behind and above the altar, Christ looked down on them from the cross, his eyes filled with sorrow. Father Matheson laid a hand on Geoffrey's shoulder. "Patience, my son. The first thing you need to do, if you're really serious, is to begin your formal conversion to Catholicism."

"Well, how long does that take?"

Father Matheson made a gesture of uncertainty. "It varies, depending on the individual. Is anyone in your family already a Catholic?"

"No."

"Well then, have you ever been to mass?"

"No."

"So, may I ask, what it is that attracts you to the Catholic faith, Mr. Leech?"

Geoffrey wrung his hands. He wanted to tell the priest everything, but after the reaction of certain hospital patients and staff to his revelations, he had learned to exercise restraint. "I, I've had a religious experience."

Father Matheson smiled. "I see. May I ask the nature of this experience?"

Geoffrey looked into the older man's eyes. The lines around them were etched with compassion and understanding. If this man couldn't understand what had happened to him who could? "I died, Father. I died and went to Hell. And now, I've been given a mission from the Devil."

Father Matheson seemed to stiffen slightly. He straightened his back and took his hand from Geoffrey's shoulder. "I see. And, er, what is this mission?"

A tear spilled down Geoffrey's cheek. "I have to kill a man."

Father Matheson regarded Geoffrey steadily for a few moments.

Then he took a deep breath. "What you are saying is very serious, Mr. Leech. It's no joking matter."

"I'm not joking, Father, I swear to you. I've burned in the fires of Hell. My flesh has been flayed and eaten by demons. I was eaten alive again and again by a demon called Clive who said he liked me and didn't want to give me up, but I begged and I begged and I got the chance to become a demon myself, and so I took it, and when Clive was eating my brain he put the—"

"That's enough, Mr. Leech!" Father Matheson got to his feet. "What you are saying is insane!"

Geoffrey's face contorted with disbelief. "But, you believe me, don't you? You have to—you're a priest!"

"And you are suffering from some kind of severe mental or emotional stress, Mr. Leech. Have you seen yourself lately? Have you looked in a mirror? Whatever work you are doing, you need to take a break from it, sir." Father Matheson watched as Geoffrey sank his face into his hands and began to weep. He turned away and instantly became aware of the figure looking down on him from the cross. He raised his eyes to Christ's and immediately regretted his words. He turned back to Geoffrey, then slowly returned to his side and laid a hand upon his shoulder. "Please. Take a holiday, my son. Take the Bible with you, read it, study it; and pray. Seek the Lord's help and you shall find it. And when you get back, come and see me again. If you still want to become a Catholic, we'll see about getting you enrolled in some classes."

Geoffrey took the priest's hand in both of his. "You believe me though, don't you, Father?"

Father Matheson closed his other hand around Geoffrey's. "Yes, my son. I believe you. But you need rest, and you need to learn something of our faith. I have some literature I can give you and I presume you own a Bible?"

Geoffrey hung his head and shook it once in the negative.

"Well, I'm sure I have one of those too, somewhere."

"Thank you, Father."

Father Matheson smiled. "If you want to thank me, my son, take a holiday."

Geoffrey brought Father Matheson's hands to his lips. "I will, Father. I will."

The next day, after reading all the sections of the Bible Father Matheson had marked for him plus a good deal more, Geoffrey returned to work. He felt happy; his fear of the Devil had been calmed by the scriptures and he felt that he was well on the way to becoming a devout servant of the Lord. When he walked into the offices of Dobson and Shaft that morning, it was as a changed man.

His colleagues in middle-management were sympathetic, and keen to make his work burden as light as possible, but Geoffrey didn't want any charity. He had work to catch up on, and work was good for the soul. He spent the morning working at his desk with an assiduousness that no-one had ever seen from him before.

"Bloody Hell, Geoff," said Tim Whitely. "Ease up or you'll make the rest of us look like a bunch of layabouts."

"No offence, Tim," said Geoffrey over his computer monitor, "but you are a bunch of layabouts. I used to be nothing more than a layabout myself before I saw the error of my ways. We're being paid, Tim, and an honest day's pay should reward an honest day's work. We're not here to email jokes and silly videos to each other all day."

"Jesus, mate. I thought you had a heart attack, not a bang on the head," Tim held up his cigarettes. "Coming out for a fag?"

Geoffrey gave Tim a patient look. "I just had a heart attack, Tim. What do you think?"

"I think you should chill out a bit, mate. Maybe a lungful of nicotine is just what you need."

"Thank you Tim. I know you mean well, but I have no desire to commit suicide. Suicide is a sin."

"It's a *what*?"

"A sin, against God."

Tim laughed. "Since when do you care about what God thinks?"

Geoffrey's eyes narrowed slightly. As much as he'd love to tell this slovenly fathead about what had happened to him after death, what would be the point? People like Tim wouldn't listen, they didn't care about their souls, just as he hadn't. But Geoffrey was a changed man. He was born again and he had a duty to God. He smiled and answered the question. "Since I was saved, Tim. Just as you can be, if you see the error of your ways and put your trust in the Lord."

Tim laughed. "Now I know you're taking the piss, mate." He shook his head. "You crack me up, Geoff, you know that? I'm going out for a smoke. Catch you later."

Geoffrey scowled. Oh, Tim, you and all the billions of fools like you. You are *so* damned.

At eleven-thirty, Geoffrey looked at his watch and decided he had time to quickly pop down to the canteen and grab a coffee from the machine. When he got there, he grimaced; the canteen seemed always to be full of temps eating rabbit food: yoghurts and oranges and wholemeal sandwiches from silly little Tupperware lunchboxes. Geoffrey loathed them, but tried to keep a pleasant expression on his face as he joined the end of the queue at the coffee machine.

The line was going nowhere and he looked impatiently to the front to see a temp, who obviously had no idea how the bloody machine worked, fumbling with the reject button. Geoffrey rolled his eyes and muttered under his breath, "Oh, for fuck's sake."

The girl in front of him turned around. "Oh, hi, Geoff." It was Sarah White. Geoffrey had fucked her at last year's office Christmas party, an act which he had later regretted.

"Oh, hi," he said, looking back to the front of the line.

"I hear you had a heart attack?"

"That's right, yes."

"And they brought you back?"

He looked at her. "Obviously."

She smiled. "Pity."

He looked at her. "Oh, do leave it out, Sarah. I'm trying to be a better person and right now you're making that very difficult."

She laughed. "You? A better person?" The eyes of numerous temps turned discreetly in their direction. "How do you plan on doing that?"

Geoffrey spoke through gritted teeth. "By minding my own chuffing business, for one."

Sarah came close to him and spoke in a confidential tone. "You didn't use to want to mind your business, Geoff. You used to like to mind mine."

"Perhaps once," Geoffrey was taller than Sarah and he looked over her head to the coffee machine where the temp had now been joined by another clueless dolt who was giving the machine an ineffectual beating. "But not anymore."

"Oh come on, Geoff. It's not like your wife's still around, why not take me out for a drink sometime?"

"Thank you Sarah, but I'd rather not."

"Oh?" Sarah deftly cupped his genitals and gave them a friendly squeeze. "Don't tell me you don't miss me."

"Get away from me, you whore!" Geoffrey struck out, shoving her back with both hands. Sarah fell stumbling into the backs of the people ahead of her in the line, causing them to fall in all directions. One man fell onto a table and a yoghurt carton ruptured all over his shirt.

"Jesus Christ, Geoffrey!" Sarah shouted from where she now sat on the floor. "You fucking lunatic!"

"Yeah," said another man who had stumbled in the queue. His shirt was tight, accentuating a muscular physique. "What the fuck do you think you're playing at, mate?"

"I'm sorry," said Geoffrey, raising his hands before him. "I'm just trying to be a good person."

"Well you're going a funny way about it, you fucking idiot!"

"He's fucking crazy," said Sarah.

"No." Geoffrey offered her his hand. "No, I'm not crazy. I'm sorry,

Sarah, I—" As Sarah's hand closed about his, the room seemed to suddenly slow down and stop. All around, the angry scene stood frozen, as if some higher power had pushed a reality pause button that only Geoffrey seemed unaffected by. Then he felt Sarah's grip tightening on his hand—a fierce, burning grip. He looked down and saw the hand that held his was no longer Sarah's. He screamed as his hand burst into flame. He looked up to see Sarah's face beginning to liquefy like a waxwork under a blowtorch. Her smile widened impossibly, revealing row upon row of small, pointed teeth. It widened still, splitting her cheeks. Blood and fatty tissue crackled and spat as the shell of her face fell apart to reveal another face growing within. It was Clive.

"Hello Leech," said Clive. Sarah's hippy chic clothes fell away in burning rags as Clive grew to his full size. "What's all this nonsense about being a better person, then?"

Geoffrey fell to his knees before the demon, watching in horror as the flesh of his arm began to burn. "No, master, please, I never meant—"

"Never meant what, wretch? To seek the counsel of a priest? To shit on the trust of the Lord Satan?" A scorching heat radiated from Clive and all around him office workers began to blister and smoke. "Did you honestly think you could ever get away from your bond to the Prince of Darkness?"

Geoffrey screamed as the fire began to spread to his body.

"You have no life of your own, Leech. Lest you forget, your very existence is a gift from Satan; a gift given solely on condition that you fulfil his mission."

In his mind, Geoffrey saw again the face of the man he had to kill. He knew his name and his address, saw his house and the faces of his family, and then, like a death knell, heard the words he must speak when he took the man's life, "Hallelujah, I am your salvation." They echoed through his mind, over and over, discordant and drowning out all other thought. Geoffrey screamed in a hopeless effort to smother them. "Yes, master! I'll do it! I'll do it!" Fire consumed all his flesh now, and yet, despite the fact that his eyes were sizzling in his head, he could still see perfectly well. He watched as Clive's horned head loomed in close while all around, office workers blazed and melted in the inferno.

"Good," Clive grasped Geoffrey's head in both hands. "Because if you continue to fuck around with silly notions of being saved by God, you're going to be really fucking sorry. Do you understand? You're dead, and your worthless fucking stinkhole belongs forever in Hell."

Geoffrey screamed as perdition's flames rose around him. He couldn't escape. He could never escape. He nodded and felt the skin of his face come away in Clive's hands.

"Good," Clive opened his mouth and dropped the burning skin inside. "Mmmmmm." He smiled. "Yummy." He chewed for a moment before looking distastefully at his hands. "Oh dear, do you have a napkin, Leech? I seem to have you all over my fingers."

Geoffrey collapsed, his hands over his face, screaming and rolling from side to side on the floor.

"See? He's fucking crazy," said Sarah. "It's like he thinks he's on fire or something."

"Maybe he's having a fit," said the muscle man. "Quick, get something to put between his teeth in case he tries to swallow his tongue."

"Chance'd be a fine thing," said Sarah. She took advantage of the general hubbub now surrounding Geoffrey to go to the front of the now-disordered coffee machine queue. She gave the top of the machine a hefty shove and the little light came on indicating the machine's readiness. She dropped her coin in and selected a hot chocolate. "Bloke's a fucking mental case."

That night, Geoffrey sat in his car outside the house of the man he had been sent to kill. He stared at the windows and the front door, tensing occasionally whenever a shadow passed behind the curtains or an upstairs light clicked on or off. He opened his packet of cigarettes and lit one from the one he'd been smoking. What did he have to lose? Lung cancer was the least of his worries. He was dead already. Judgement had been passed upon him and his fate was sealed. The best he could hope for was that his eternity in Hell might be more comfortable as a demon.

He drew on the cigarette and thought about the things Clive did to him: the torture, the abuse, the tearing and eating of his flesh; Jesus Christ, would he be able to do those things to others? To be that way took a special kind of evil, and he—all he'd ever been was a bully. A bit of a pervert perhaps, but he'd never tortured anyone for pleasure. Or had he? It depended on how you defined torture. He remembered his wife's suicide note and his fingers trembled as he drew hard on the cigarette, causing the long ash to tumble onto his jacket. He looked back to the house.

Maybe he'd be able to get out of Hell sooner as a demon. Maybe he hadn't even been in Hell—maybe he'd been in Purgatory? A wave of hope flowed through him and he flicked on the car's reading light. He put the cigarette in the ashtray and pulled the sports bag he'd brought with him across the passenger seat. He rummaged among its contents; the sound of metal on metal as the knives, hammer and large adjustable wrench shifted around inside. Where was the fucking Bible Father Matheson had given him? The stupid thing was black and Geoffrey couldn't make it out in the poor light. Then his fingertips brushed against its soft cover, it was buried under the tools. He pulled it out and held it under the light.

Purgatory, Purgatory, where the fuck was Purgatory? He flicked to the back to try and find it in the index. Shit! There was no fucking index! How was anybody supposed to find anything in this stupid book? He threw it aside and felt fresh tears coming to his eyes. He flicked out the light, threw his arms across the steering wheel and buried his face in his sleeves. He bit down on the fabric, stifling his sobs, muffling them, hating them, knowing that somewhere, Clive was watching him and laughing.

"Motherfucker!" He sat back and punched the wheel. "You motherfucker, Clive! I don't want to do this! I don't want to kill! For God's sake, I don't want to die! I want to live!" His thoughts raced. What should he do? If he refused his mission, he'd go to Hell and face the wrath of Satan. If he went through with it, he'd still go to Hell and become a demon; a monster and a tormenter of others for all eternity. Truly, he was damned if he did and damned if he didn't. He struggled to weigh the lesser of two evils and found them both of equal, unbearable weight.

A light went out in the front room of the house and Geoffrey's seething anxieties were silenced as his whole attention shifted to the front door. It had a pane of rippled glass set in the centre and through it he could see the silhouetted shadows of the occupants as they passed; first one, then another on their way upstairs. The children had been put to bed hours ago, so this had to be the man and his wife going to bed. This was it.

A bedroom light went on upstairs. Geoffrey opened the bag and considered its contents. He knew it would be impossible to bludgeon the man without waking his wife, so perhaps he should use a large knife? He could place a hand over the man's mouth and slit his throat, quickly and quietly. No, he'd fight; the woman would wake up. Then he remembered: it didn't matter. When the man died so would he. He'd die and go straight to Hell: though this time, as a Clive had said, in triumph. He reached into the bag and took out the hammer, feeling its weight and heft. Yes, it would be very quick. He turned back to the window and watched the light go out. How long should he wait? Half an hour? An hour?

He put the hammer back in the bag and lit another cigarette. He opened the glove compartment and took out the bottle of whisky he'd brought along to steady his nerves. He unscrewed the cap and took a slug. What did it matter if he got drunk? He wasn't going to be driving anywhere afterwards. He looked at the glowing clock on the dashboard. It was eleven forty-five. He'd give them three quarters of an hour. Then he'd do it.

Geoffrey woke up. Grey daylight revealed an empty whisky bottle and an overflowing ashtray. He looked at the clock: it was eight fifteen. The clamour of young children came to his ears and he realised that they were what had awoken him. Geoffrey looked out of the window. His quarry, a heavy-set man in his forties, was helping his wife usher the children out of the house and off on their way to school. Geoffrey's face looked like it had aged ten years overnight, but the sight of the family, alive, happy and going about the ordinary business of another day, brought a smile to his face that almost wiped those years away again. Sometime last night, between the parents going to bed and his finishing off the whisky, he had evidently changed his mind and made his final decision.

He looked into the rear view mirror, expecting to see Clive sitting in the back seat, but he was alone. He ran a hand over his stubbly chin and looked around at the passers-by, watching for a ripple of heat or a tendril of smoke from an unseen source. Surely Clive had to be here somewhere? But he wasn't. He must be waiting ahead, around the next corner or the one after that. Perhaps a shop assistant or a policeman would turn around and there the demon would be, the world would slow down and burst into flame and Clive would be upon him again, playing with him, like a cat plays with a mouse, before leaving him, screaming and writhing alone, like a lunatic. Was this how his remaining time on Earth would be? Was this the new shape of his damnation—Hell on Earth?

Then he knew the one place where Clive couldn't go: the church. He whimpered as a sudden hope shook his heart. He had to speak to the priest again and this time, he'd tell him everything. He turned the key in the ignition and stepped on the clutch. Then he hesitated. What if the priest wouldn't listen to him—to what would almost certainly sound like the ravings of a madman? His hand tightened on the gear stick and he shifted it slowly but firmly into first. He'd have to listen to him. Geoffrey glanced at the sports bag by his side. He'd make him listen, whether he wanted to or not.

On entering St Peter's church, a feeling of blessed safety so overwhelmed Geoffrey that he stumbled back a step. He stopped and wondered if he had mistaken the feeling; if in fact, Hell-spawned thing that he was, he was being forcibly repelled by the Holy Spirit. He steadied himself against the door-frame and cautiously reached out into the church. He held his breath, waiting for pain or an inexplicable force that might compel him to withdraw, but he felt nothing other than a divine stillness. He straightened up, composed himself, and walked inside. The sense of sanctuary deepened with every step he took away from the door and the outside world, the world where Clive and others of his kind were able to prey upon his soul and sanity.

At the entrance to the centre aisle he genuflected before the crucified Christ as he had read he should do in the literature the priest had given him. He looked around. Two or three other people knelt or sat at prayer, but there was no sign of Father Matheson. Geoffrey moved to a pew near the front, set down his bag of tools, and knelt to pray. He soon became lost in his prayers, a whispered stream that poured unceasingly from his lips as he rocked back and forth on his knees.

"Mr. Leech?"

Geoffrey looked up and saw Father Matheson standing close by. He smiled. "Yes. Hello, Father."

"I'm delighted to see you here. How are your studies coming along?"

"Fine, I—" Geoffrey couldn't think where to begin. "No, actually, they're not. Father." His voice began to lose its steadiness as he spoke. "I, I have a terrible problem."

Father Matheson sat down on the front pew bench immediately before Geoffrey. "Please, tell me."

"It's that thing I spoke to you about before. I know you said I, I needed a holiday, and believe me, you were so right. But a holiday isn't going to make my problems go away. You see, I, I'm damned. I died and went to Hell and the Devil sent me back to kill a man."

Father Matheson nodded. "Yes, I remember. You told me this."

"But there's more, Father. After I left you, I was determined to do as you said: to lead a good life, to study the Bible."

"Good, my son."

"But he wouldn't let me." Geoffrey tried to hold back his tears. "He came to me and told me I had to fulfil my contract."

"Who came to you?"

"Clive, my demon. He possessed a woman where I work," Geoffrey's words began to tumble. "He brought Hell into the canteen and everybody was burning. I was burning. He told me there was no escape and that I had to kill him, to kill the man, because Satan commanded it and I-I was so afraid, I, I said I would." He paused a moment, looking uncertainly at the priest, who then nodded for him to continue. "But, but then," Geoffrey went on, clinging white-knuckled to the back of the pew before him, "when I went to do it, I couldn't. I was going to do it, but he was there with his children and his wife. Oh God, God help me, Father, I couldn't do it. I just couldn't do it, and now I'm completely fucked! I've blown the deal and the Devil's going to be fucking furious with me now—he's going to drag me screaming and kicking all the way back to Hell." He lowered his head onto his hands and shook with silent sobs.

Father Matheson laid a hand on Geoffrey's shoulder. "Mr. Leech, you're clearly going through a dreadful trauma. Have you spoken to anyone at the hospital? The surgeons who saved you?"

Geoffrey shook his head. "No. What can they do? This is beyond them. Only God can help me."

"Well, it's possible that this kind of thing has happened to people besides yourself; other people who have come back from," Father Matheson hesitated a moment. "From death."

Geoffrey looked up at him. "Do you think that's possible?"

"Anything is possible."

"Really? Then you, you must at least accept the possibility that what I'm saying is true? That I've been resurrected from Hell to kill a man, and now that I haven't done it, Satan's going to be after me?"

Father Matheson frowned. "I believe that *you* believe it, my son, and that if this condition has afflicted you, it may have afflicted others."

Geoffrey pressed his hand onto the priest's. "Father, please, this isn't a medical situation. It's, it's an exorcism situation. I need help, and not from a doctor, but from you, from a priest."

"You think you're actually possessed by demons?"

"No, not possessed by them, but, enslaved or something. I've entered a contract with the Devil and I haven't kept up my half of the bargain. And now he's going to get me."

"You believe the Devil will take your life?"

"Yes, exactly."

"And how do you think he'll do this? The Devil cannot harm you in life, my son. All he could do to our Lord was to try to tempt him from the path of righteousness, and that's all he can do to any of us."

"Really?"

"Yes," said Father Matheson, encouraged, sensing he was getting through. "Our lives are filled with choices, and the choices we make in this life decide our fate in the next. We know the Devil can walk upon the Earth if he chooses, and he may well do so. But if he does, it is as tempter, not assassin. Temptation is the weapon that the Devil wields against us. Turn from temptation and the ways of sin and you shall be saved."

Geoffrey's eyes filled with tears. "Do you think so?"

"Yes, Mr. Leech. I think so."

"Then he can't get me?"

Father Matheson shook his head. "Not in this world, my son."

"But what about Clive, the demon?"

"I don't know what to say about that. I've never heard anything like it before. I'm not a psychiatrist, but it's possible that he was a creation of your own mind in your hours of uncertainty. Perhaps now that you've decided not to go through with this murder, he may simply go away. The battle to lead you into sin is lost. As long as you stay on the path of righteousness then, with God's help, hopefully you'll have seen the last of him."

Geoffrey's face broke into a smile. "Oh, thank you, thank God. It might be, mightn't it? What you say makes sense, Father."

Father Matheson nodded and stood up.

Geoffrey also got to his feet. He felt a need to hug the priest, whether it was appropriate or not; he had never wanted to embrace anyone so much as he now wanted to embrace Father Matheson. He hurried to the end of the pew and came around to stand before him. "I don't know what to say, Father, I feel like a terrible weight has been lifted." He took the priest in his arms and hugged him. "Thank you. Thank you so much."

Father Matheson gently eased him away. "There now, Mr. Leech. Please, no thanks are necessary. I'm just—"

"A man of God, doing the Lord's work?" A hoarse voice came from out of the shadows further back in the church. A figure stood up in the darkness there and slowly began to walk towards the front of the church, down the aisle to the right.

Father Matheson frowned. "Do I know you, sir?"

"Perhaps," said the man. He had white hair and he was dressed completely in black. He stopped and turned to face them. Then, as he entered the far end of the pew that Geoffrey had just vacated, his white dog collar became clearly visible. He smiled.

Father Matheson frowned. "Father McBride? But you're—"

"Under investigation?" Father McBride continued along the aisle towards them. "Following allegations about myself and certain... young boys?"

Father Matheson nodded slowly. Yes."

"I was, Father. But the investigation has now been more or less decided."

"Oh? How so, Father?"

"I was guilty. A case of what you were just telling our friend Mr. Leech here about: temptation. I allowed myself to be tempted. I followed my basest animal passions and did unto others as had been done unto me."

"But Father—"

"I forgot, you see, the truth of everything we believe in." Father McBride laughed bitterly and shook his head. "I felt as long as the authorities remained unaware then I'd be fine. I forgot, or rather, ignored the higher authorities." He stopped a moment where Geoffrey had been sitting and bent to pick up the bag. "Tools, Mr. Leech? Why do you need tools in a church?"

"I-I just had them with me when I came by," said Geoffrey.

"Surely you could have left them in your car?" Father McBride carried the bag around to the front of the church and joined them.

"I didn't want to leave it unattended."

A smile spread over Father McBride's face. "Of course you didn't." He looked up at the effigy of Christ on the cross.

Both Geoffrey and Father Matheson saw the red mark around his neck. "You seem to have hurt yourself, Father." Father Matheson touched his own throat to indicate.

"Oh it's worse than that, Father, much worse. When I woke up this morning I was hanging by the neck from a light fitting."

Geoffrey's face darkened with realisation. "Oh Jesus Christ, no."

Father Matheson frowned at Geoffrey. "Mr. Leech?"

Father McBride gave a low laugh and reached into the sports bag. "Oh, don't talk to me about Jesus Christ, Mr. Leech." He drew out the hammer. "He doesn't want me for a sunbeam any more."

"No," Geoffrey screamed. "Please, it's not too late."

"Oh yes it is, Mr. Leech, for both of us. But at least I won't be burning anymore." Father McBride swung the hammer in an arc. "Hallelujah! I am your salvation!"

Chuckles Mulrooney, Attorney for the Damned

By Scott Sigler

(Originally podcast: 07/30/08 at
www.scottsigler.com)

*D*evon Collingsworth swayed slightly from side to side, a testament to his lack of sobriety considering that he sat at the kitchen table, leaning heavily on both elbows.

In front of him stood a half-empty bottle of Five-Star Vodka, its clear warmth and the promise of forgetfulness beckoning to Devon like a mermaid calling to a wayward galleon. His right hand clutched a cellular phone—the call heralding the "good news" he'd passionately visualized for over a decade could only be moments away.

His other hand gripped the handle of a beat-up .44 Magnum, a present from his dead father. An inheritance, actually, seeing as father's last act was using the .44 to splatter his brains all over the rumpus room.

Devon had kept the gun as a morbid memento—he was the next big horror writer, after all, and such a grisly talisman seemed to fit his pre-fabricated image of a twisted literary superstar. He'd never planned to use the gun for anything other than interviews with People Magazine reporters, a publicity stunt to show just how "messed up" he was. People got off on that shit if you were a horror writer; they wanted to know you were damaged in some way, as if your deviance and lack of normalcy justified creation of dreadful yarns.

How ironic that he now planned on using the .44 in the same

fashion as his dear old dad—like father, like son. The hollow-point rounds would do more than just take a chip off the old block.

Devon's head hung down until his precisely shaggy hair brushed the tabletop. He'd just written his masterpiece, clearly the best work he'd ever done. After ten years of mediocre manuscripts, ten years of striving to be the new master of horror, Generation X's answer to Stephen King, ten years of wading through the ego-laden short story market, ten years of supplementing his "full-time writer" income by doing freelance high school football and basketball stories for the local paper—after ten years of pure *bullshit*, he'd written something that simply could not miss.

He'd just e-mailed that something, that can't-miss something, to Morty, his agent, who by now had surely read over the brief manuscript. Devon knew Morty would rave over the piece. The way things were going, Morty would probably just happen to be having lunch with some major publisher, Morty would share the story, the publisher would flip over it, then instantly offer at least a cool million.

Devon knew these things because, after all, when you sell your soul to the Devil, fame and fortune are a done deal.

The phone beeped softly. Despite his dulled reactions, Devon clicked the talk button without a moment's thought. He slowly pulled the cellular to his ear as if it was a thirty-pound dumbbell and he was on his last, excruciatingly slow rep.

"Hullow?"

"Devon!" Morty's enthusiasm ripped through Devon's Vodka-addled brain. "This is Morty. I just got your manuscript, kiddo! I have to say I never thought I'd see you write something like this, but it's incredible."

"Thanks," Devon said.

Morty screamed each sentence as if he were an orgasmic guest of a Playboy Mansion orgy. "I mean this is a show-stopper! You're going to be a household name, my boy. I knew there was a reason I stuck by you—where have you been hiding this stuff the last ten years?"

"Beats me," Devon said, his words thick and slurred. "You might say the muse struck me."

"Well I'll buy that muse a drink!"

"Beat you to it, Mort."

"Sounds like it, kiddo," Mort said. "Listen, you're not going to believe this, but I just happened to be having lunch with Robert Reffleman, the publisher of Penguin Books."

"You don't say." Devon took a quick pull from the bottle. His taste buds were long dead from the cheap liquor, and at room temperature the vodka went down like lukewarm water.

"Yeah! And he read the manuscript just now. I mean, of course it's only ten pages long, but he loved it! He offered us $1.6 million for US rights, and we haven't even talked about international!"

"Imagine the luck," Devon said.

"I have to admit, when I saw the title 'Fanny the Fluffy Little Kitten' I thought you were nuts, but it's the best damn children's book I've ever seen! Robert loved it, wants to get the art and have it on the presses by this Christmas."

"Whoopee," Devon said. "Just cut the deal, Morty. Do whatever you think is best." Devon hit the talk button again, disconnecting the call. He set the phone down and lifted the gun.

After a decade of ceaseless writing struggle, Satan had come to him in—of all places—the soup isle at Meijer's grocery store. There was no fire and brimstone, no tail, no horns, not even that cool hipster pointy goatee the devil always sported in the movies. He was actually kind of fat. Wore a three-piece suit with Gucci shoes. He didn't look at all like Satan. He looked more like Dom Delouise posing as a lawyer.

"Got a deal for you, Devon," Satan had said. With one syllable from his mouth, Devon knew instantly who it was. Devon hadn't wasted time with all that "how did you know my name?" and "how do I know you're really the Devil?" bullshit, because something inside him identified *Satan* as sure as a redneck knows a new Garth

Brooks tune from the first twangy white-trash lyric.

"You want to be a writer, Devon?" Satan had asked. "Fine, you'll be famous as all get out. Make over a hundred million, be a household name, do the Oprah thing, book tours, have movies made of every book you put out. The American Dream. Exactly what you always wanted, Devon—to be *famous*. To be a *writer*."

Devon surprised himself by not even thinking twice. He made the deal. They slunk out to Satan's black Cadillac Escalade to sign the contract, as if Satan were a cheap $20 hooker and they were knocking out a quick blowjob. Satan, of course, had parked his obnoxiously huge vehicle in a handicap spot. Devon abstractly wondered how the Escalade handled on hot brimstone.

He had to prick his finger and sign in his own blood. His signature was damn near illegible, more a smear of thick red streaks than a name, like the writing of a five-year-old tripping on a double-hit of acid, but somehow Devon knew penmanship didn't really matter.

Satan handed him a copy of the 150-page contract, grumbled something about beating rush-hour traffic, hopped in the Escalade and drove away, ignoring a "no left turn" sign as he did. Devon looked at the contract. No human skin, no parchment, just standard office paper. It was even notarized.

Devon ignored the chill that swept over his brain and scrambled to get home and attacked his computer. He'd just fucked his immortal soul, but his mortal frame still had work to do. Would he write the next horror masterpiece? The new Frankenstein? Dracula? Dr. Jekyll and Mr. Hyde? And none of that cheap rip-off vampire bullshit that paraded as talented writing—he wanted something *original*. How long would it take him? A month? Two months?

It took him all of twenty-five minutes.

When he started typing, he couldn't stop. For only the second time in his life, he felt true terror. The first time he'd felt that coppery emotion, he was an 11-year-old on a new Huffy Trailmaster dirt bike freshly assembled from K-Mart. Riding along happily on the shiny new bike, he nearly went under the axle of a Fritos semi captained by a man who collected both empty Jack Daniel's bottles and DUI citations.

As Devon wrote, the terror mounted. Try as he might, the only thing he could think of was the quirky story of a little lost kitten named Fanny. He wrote Fanny's first misadventure—how she got lost in a mall and couldn't find Clara, her seven-year-old human owner.

Sweating, shaking, horrified, he finished the story, knowing that he'd been duped. He started a new document, trying to think of death and terror and malice. He'd just met Old Scratch himself: how much more inspiration did a budding horror writer need? Despite the visions of death, dismemberment and despair that raged through his head, all he could find was an uncontrollable urge to write about a wacky camping trip in which Fanny made friends with Gweneth the Greedy Grasshopper and Sally the Soft-Spoken Squirrel.

Tears streaming down his face, Devon e-mailed the first story to his editor, pulled the bottle of Five Star from the top shelf, fished the gun out of his closet, then sat down at the kitchen table to wait. He'd known, somehow, that Fanny the Fluffy Kitten was a guaranteed smash hit. According to Morty, that guess had been dead-on. Now Devon was on the precipice of fame and fortune from his writing—and he wanted none of it. He'd sold his soul (which was a truly admirable act for the next King of Horror) and wound up writing cheesy children's books.

Devon lifted the gun to his temple. He was heading to hell—what good was another thirty or forty years compared against eternity? It was the briefest tick of the clock, so he might as well end it. After all, he didn't really *want* to live another forty years reviled as the person who invented the next annoying and probably pedophiliac purple dinosaur.

With his thumb, Devon pulled back the hammer and felt the spring-catch vibrate lightly through his skull. He lifted the bottle for the last time, a one-for-the-road drink, so to speak, took a big swallow, and set it down. His finger slowly squeezed the trigger...

His doorbell rang.

He blinked, finger still on the trigger. The doorbell rang again. Devon set the gun down, grabbed the Vodka bottle and stumbled towards the door to his apartment. Maybe it was a pair Jehovah's Witnesses. Wouldn't they get a kick out of this situation? He'd head to hell clutching a copy of "The Watchtower."

Devon opened the door, and looked out at a clown.

A clown with a briefcase.

The clown wore a baggy pink suit with lime-green ruffles at the sleeves and collar. His giant, patent-leather red shoes stuck out at least a foot in front of him. A nose, which was almost as red as the shoes, stood in sharp contrast to his white greasepaint face. A severe black-greasepaint frown covered his mouth and most of his cheeks and chin. A ratty red and black Dr. Seuss hat stood up on his head—which added to his six-foot frame, making him seem almost seven feet tall. To complete the ensemble, a plastic blue flower protruded from his lapel. Devon could make out a tiny squirtgun-like opening in the blossom's center.

Devon was speechless. That didn't seem to phase the clown.

"Devon Collingsworth?" the clown asked.

Devon nodded.

"I'm glad I caught you before you did anything stupid." The clown produced a business card. "Allow me to introduce myself. I'm Chuckles Mulrooney, attorney for the damned. May I come in?"

Chuckles Mulrooney, attorney for the damned, sat on Devon's living room couch, concentrating on Devon's contract with the devil. A copy of Fanny the Fluffy Kitten, still warm from the laser printer, sat on Chuckles' briefcase. A once-white sheet covered the couch, obscuring patches of duct-tape and disintegrating red-and-yellow plaid fabric. Bits of ancient stuffing still escaped despite the blanket, and found their way onto the worn lime-green shag carpet like furniture dandruff.

"Nice decor," Chuckles said. "Kind of post-apocalyptic Brady Bunch."

Devon sat in a splintery rocking chair, his only other piece of furniture except for the kitchen table and chair, his dresser and a mattress that lay on the bedroom floor. He clutched the Five Star bottle, now three-quarters empty, and stared at the clown on his couch.

"You could have done better for yourself," Chuckles said. "One-point-six million for your eternal soul? Not much of a deal, Devon."

"You don't say," Devon said.

"Yep. You could have netted at least two million *and* written a real book. Not that I didn't like Fanny the Fluffy Kitten, of course. If I had kids, I'm sure they'd love it. But a mere one-point-six mil? You didn't even try and sweeten the deal?"

"I wasn't aware one could haggle with the Devil," Devon said.

"That's the problem with kids today, you all don't think twice about paying retail."

Devon said nothing, but took another long, burning swig.

"Listen," Chuckles said. "Here's my offer. You got tricked, and there's nothing you can do about that, but you should realize how much money you can make in the course of your life. What I'm offering you is this: I get half of everything you make. In return, I'll get you back your immortal soul."

Devon stared and said nothing. There was a clown on his couch, reviewing the pros and cons of a bona-fide contract with Satan. The sureness of it all stunned him into silence.

"What do you say, kid?" Chuckles asked.

After a brief silence, Devon finally spoke. "Who, exactly, the fuck are you? I'm supposed to believe you're some kind of...clown lawyer? How did you find out about my deal?"

"I'm not a *clown lawyer*, as you put it, I'm an attorney for the damned. It's my business to find people like you. I find loopholes in contracts with the devil and get my clients' souls back. For this service, I get half of everything they make from said contract."

"And you dress like a clown...why?" Devon followed up the question with another long hit of vodka. He was so bombed he couldn't even smell the pungent alcohol.

"Because I was once like you, Devon," Chuckles said. "I used to be a struggling lawyer. I worked hard, *very* hard, but I just didn't have it. I wanted to be the greatest lawyer of all time, better than Cochran, better than Darrow, better than *all* of them. The devil came to me while I was buying condoms in a 7-11 and we hashed out a deal—he gets my soul, and I get to be the greatest lawyer that ever lived."

"So what happened?"

"He came through on his end," Chuckles said. "I mean, I'm the greatest, a legal Mohammed Ali. I can give a deposition that will make your head spin. Most cases would be over by the time I finished my opening statement. I've become a master of the spoken word, a manipulator of emotions, an artist of legalese and I have a photographic memory of every case and precedent in the history of man. Not just America, mind you, but every case that's ever come to trial anywhere under any system. You should hear some stories about Cro-Magnon law. Fascinating stuff. And that Cherokee legal system, where they slice open your scrotum, insert a burning coal, then sew it back up again. Now *that's* capital punishment.

"At any rate, I'm the best lawyer of all time. The devil came through on his deal. He added one little clause, though. Every day I wake up with the uncontrollable urge to dress like a circus clown. I can't help it."

"If dressing like a clown is wrong, you don't want to be right?"

"Don't be a smart-ass, Devon. The first thing I do in the morning is shower, the second thing I do is put on the greasepaint. You should see my wardrobe. It looks like a trailer from Barnum & Bailey. As you can imagine, it's difficult to practice law when you show up with size twenty-seven feet, honk your nose every five minutes and squirt the judge with a lapel flower."

"I can see where that would get in the way." Devon said, then polished off the bottle.

"Satan scammed my ass," Chuckles said. "He is, if you'll pardon the expression, one crafty old devil. They don't call him The Trickster for nothing. I have all this legal prowess, and I can't use it in a real court of law. But you know what? He fucked with the wrong guy. About a week after realizing the best suit I'd ever wear would have the Bozo label on it, I decided to kill myself. Why bother living for another thirty or forth years. It's only a tick of the clock, anyway, you know?"

"Yeah," Devon said, glancing at the still-cocked Magnum on his cheap kitchen table. "I know what you mean."

"Then I realized: that's exactly what he wants. That's why he tricks us, so he can get our souls faster. I found out later he's got a monthly quota to fill, but who would have thought of that?"

"A quota," Devon said.

"Yeah, like a state cop with speeding tickets," Chuckles said. "Anyway, that tricking stuff got me thinking. If he can trick us, play with the wording, come up with new meanings, then it means the contract is just a starting-off point. It's open to interpretation, if you follow the logic. Then I decided to get even with the forked-tailed bastard."

"Get even," Devon said. "With the Devil."

Chuckles nodded, his big hat flopping in time. "I decided to represent people who've made deals with the devil and get them out of the contract. I do this for three reasons: one, because I'm getting amazingly rich off it; two, because I'll keep doing it until he tears up my contract and gives me my soul back; three, just to piss him off."

"You want to *piss off* Satan?"

"This is America, kid," Chuckles said, his smile bizarrely magnified by the black greasepaint. "Don't fuck with a lawyer."

"You've done this before, right?"

"Sure kid," Chuckles said. "The Devil hands out deals for fame and fortune all the time. You don't need talent to be famous, just a good contract. Bob Saget was my first client, and I just found a loophole in Britney Spears' contract."

"I always wondered how she made it."

Chuckles busily ran a highlighter over the contract and made notes in a yellow legal pad.

Devon watched, or tried to, but he was a bit too drunk to see straight. "And you think this is going to work?"

"I think it will work, but it's up to you, kid," Chuckles said. "As your legal counsel, I have to warn you that Satan won't be happy to hear from me. If we don't succeed, you'll be in for a pretty rough eternity."

"There's varying degrees of hell?"

"Sure, sure," Chuckles said. "As you may have guessed, Satan isn't a nice guy. If you think burning in eternal flame is the worst he can do, you've got another thing coming."

"So if I hire you, and we don't win, then I'm fucked."

"Let's face it kid, you're already fucked. It's just a question of degree. Personally I think we're going to kick his forked-tailed ass all over the place—in a metaphorically legal sense, of course—but it's up to you. As your legal counsel, I'm obligated to give you all the facts."

Devon sat back on the Very Dysfunctional Brady couch and mulled the possibilities. An eternity spent writhing in burning agony, skin perpetually blackening under the caustic kiss of sulfurous flames, internal organs cooking forever and ever—and that was the *best* he could look forward to.

"Fuck him." Devon said. "I was misled in this contract and I want out. I am, as you say, a victim of the system."

"That's the spirit, kid." Chuckles pulled a piece of paper from his briefcase.

"What's that?" Devon asked.

"This is a writ of formal protest." Chuckles started filling out the form. "The party in the first part—Satan—has entered unto a binding agreement with the party of the second part—you—and the party of the second part finds the contract inconclusive with his original intention of verbal agreement, than the party of the first part, when formally served with this writ of notice, becomes—"

"Whatever," Devon said, cutting off Chuckle's windy explanation.

"What's it means in layman's terms?"

"It means as soon as you sign this, Satan or an official representative has to come down here and do battle."

"Battle?"

"A legal debate, if you prefer," Chuckles said. "It all comes down to a battle for your soul. Just sign here." Chuckles offered Devon the paper and pen.

"After I sign, how long till we get our day in court?"

"Right now," Chuckles said. "No judge, just me and the legal representative of Satan. You remember how you *knew* the fat guy in the three-piece was Satan, the real McCoy and not some crackpot? Works the same way in debate—we just *know* who wins each point. We know when it's over, and we know who won."

Devon started to sign, then paused. Varying degrees of hell. That left a lot to the imagination of a horror writer.

"Just sign it, Devon," Chuckles said. "You got something better to do first? Like maybe wait for Fanny the Fluffy Little Kitten's Saturday morning cartoon to be all the rage?"

Devon signed the paper.

A stench-laden cloud of sulfurous smoke billowed in the midst of the living room. Devon, for one, was glad to see at least *something* a bit more along the lines of demons and what-not. Considering the stakes, a little dramatic entrance couldn't hurt.

Satan himself, resplendent in an immaculate three-piece, stepped forth from the rapidly dissipating cloud. He stared hard at Chuckles.

"I am pissed off," Satan said. "I want you to know I was in the power tools aisle of the Home Depot in Des Moines, closing in on this aspiring actor."

"Gee, that's too bad," Chuckles said.

Satan glowered at the lawyer-clown. "So you and I finally we meet on the field of battle."

Chuckles smiled his greasepaint smile. "It's a long cry from the condom isle at 7-11, eh pal?"

"*Finally*?" Devon said. "Chuckles, what does he mean *finally*? I thought you'd done this before."

"Sure, but not with the Big Dog himself," Chuckles said. "I usually deal with one of his minions. Think of them as a combination demon/legal aide."

"Did he tell you he's lost two in a row?" Satan asked with a smile. "Did he tell you about those poor, tortured souls?"

Devon looked at Satan, then back to his clown lawyer. "Is that true? You've lost your last two cases?"

"Don't sweat it, kid," Chuckles said. "I've still got a *winning record*."

Satan laughed. "I'd hardly parade five wins and four losses as a winning record, Chuckles. He didn't tell you much, did he, Devon? You really should ask more questions. I bet you *always* buy retail."

Devon sat on the couch, head in his hands, moaning with the noises of the doomed and the damned.

"My client's shopping habits are irrelevant," Chuckles said. "You misled my client into a fraudulent contractual obligation. Since Mr. Collingsworth did not fully understand the agreement into which he entered, he is free of any obligation to you."

"Your client had the opportunity to review the contract," Satan said. "Your client waived that right. Ignorance of the contract's content is not a defense."

"My client wanted to be a horror writer," Chuckles said.

"He is," Satan said. "I happen to be quite terrified of fuzzy kittens. Horror is in the eye of the beholder, wouldn't you agree?"

Chuckles looked down. He picked a piece of furniture dandruff off his big red right shoe. "That's a good point," he said, "but the eye of the beholder in this case happens to be the marketplace. In the case of Greenwell vs. Mephistopheles, I proved that contractual disagreements of standards must be based on the accepted standards of mortal society, not the opinions of pawns of Hell, agents of Heaven or the voice of the damned."

"Yes, but you forget Simpson vs. the State of California," Satan said. "In that case it was established that societal standards of behavior are irrelevant in the face of physical evidence, and I believe you'd accept the contract as physical evidence."

Devon's stare bounced from Satan to Chuckles, from Satan to Chuckles. He didn't follow the argument, but suspected Chuckles was down 30-love.

"True," Chuckles said. "But in the case of Grog vs. He-Who-Walks-Like-Death-Amongst-Men, 16,301 B.C., you yourself ruled that the verbal agreement is more important than the written contract."

Satan's arrogant smile faded. "You're citing Grog as a precedent? They didn't even have writing then. They signed deals by leaving teeth-marks on sticks, for crying out loud!"

Chuckles shrugged, as if he were a helpless victim to the pure force of fact. "What you say is true, but a precedent is still a precedent."

"Grog," Satan said again. "But you haven't used that precedent in all nine of your cases against Hell."

Chuckles' white teeth flashed from beneath his black greasepainted lips. "Been saving old Grog just for you. Does it piss you off? Back to the subject at hand. Since we've established that the verbal is the primary form of agreement, and nowhere in your contract does is specifically state that all verbal agreements are secondary to the written form, than we must gather that your verbal agreement with my client takes precedence over the written contract, correct?"

"That's a fucking loophole and you know it," Satan said.

"There are no loopholes," Chuckles said. "Only interpretations. You said you would make him a horror writer, and there are no societal standards anywhere on Earth that would construe 'Fanny the Fluffy Kitten' as horror, which puts you in breach of contract."

Satan stood quiet for a moment. Devon had a feeling that something big had just taken place, a major swing in momentum. Judging from the conceited smile on Chuckles' face and the look of fused hatred on Satan's, Devon dared hope that he'd won.

"Soon," Satan said. "Very soon, I'll have you where I want you. I'm going to take a century's vacation when you die. I'll invent tortures that will make you beg ceaselessly."

"Hey," Chuckles said, "how's that quota coming, anyway?"

Satan growled.

Chuckles started putting his notes in his briefcase. "You know, I've got two more cases coming up. All you have to do is rip up my contract and I'll let them slide."

"You'll run out of loopholes sooner or later," Satan said. "I'll keep making the contracts tighter and tighter, you fucking clown."

"I'm not a clown," Chuckles said. "I'm an attorney for the damned. Don't forget, *you* made me the best. I'll keep finding ways to beat you."

"We'll see," Satan said. "We'll see." With that, the billowing cloud returned and Satan stepped inside, disappearing from Devon's living room.

"What happened?" Devon asked.

"You're off the hook, kid," Chuckles said. "Your soul is your own again."

"What about Fanny the Fluffy Kitten?"

"The invalidation of the contract frees up any and all intellectual properties generated from said contract, and all rights revert to the creator free and clear of contractual obligations."

"What?"

"You can publish the 'Fluffy Kitty' book and your soul still belongs to you. Don't forget I get half. Remember, I found a loophole *for* you, I can just as easily find a loophole *against* you should you try and renege."

"What if I don't want to write that book?" Devon said. "What if I don't write about Fanny at all?"

Chuckles smiled a *do-you-really-want-to-fuck-with-me* smile. Devon felt as if an icicle tickled down the back of his neck. He didn't like the look on that painted face, not one bit, and suddenly found himself wondering if he was any better off indebted to Chuckles Mulrooney than he was to Satan.

The cellular chimed lightly. Devon answered, never taking his eyes of the smiling Attorney for the Damned.

"Hello?"

"Devon, this is Morty. Listen, they're insisting that Fanny be a series. I've got Robert right here, and he's offering $2.3 million for the next book and wants to option two more at $3 million apiece. Now how soon can we get another book?"

The numbers danced in his head. Over $8 million for just over an hour's effort. A far cry from a few thousand dollars for ten years' work. As yet, he hadn't signed any contract to publish Fanny the Fluffy Kitten—but if he didn't, he knew Chuckles would find some interesting clause and hand his soul over to the devil once again.

Cellular still pressed to his ear, Devon walked over to the kitchen table and picked up the .44.

"Devon," Morty said. "When can we get the next story?"

Devon stared at the gun, stared at the still-cocked hammer. There was only one way to keep his soul *and* his integrity. And he had to do it *now*. His eyes traced the length of the rust-speckled barrel.

"Devon?" Morty said. "You there, kiddo?"

"For the moment," Devon said.

"Well? When can we get the next story?"

Devon made as if to point the .44 at his head, then sighed and let the weapon hang heavily near his hip. "I just happened to have one done. Fanny's taking a little camping trip."

"Sounds good, kiddo," Morty said. "I'll be waiting for it. You're *rich*, kiddo. Rich to the tune of $8 million." Morty disconnected. Devon pocketed the phone.

"Sounded positive," Chuckles said. "So, just how much are you making for me?"

In that moment, Devon knew he'd spend the rest of his life writing cheesy children's books. The money made it just too hard to pull the trigger. His spirit hung low. He'd escaped the deal with the Devil, but his soul remained sold.

Somewhere in his imagination, Devon heard the squeal of tires on hot brimstone, and the jovial laughter of a fat man dressed in a three-piece suit.

But...there was a way out.

For the first time in his life, a truly inspirational idea jumped into Devon's head. He'd just beat a deal with the Devil. He'd be damned if he'd let anybody share his sellout money.

"How much?" Devon said. "We'll make $8 million. Or should I say, *I'll* make $8 million."

Devon raised the .44. Chuckles' face probably went white, but who could tell under all that greasepaint?

"A vacation?" Mephistopheles asked. "You're taking a vacation? For how long?"

"A century," Satan answered with a wide smile. "I haven't taken a vacation since humans beat the Black Plague."

"But a whole century?" Mephistopheles asked. "What the hell are you going to do for that much time?"

Satan's grin was a mixture of joy and creative evil. "I've got a few things in mind. Did I ever tell you I hate lawyers?"

Creature of God

BY JACK MANGAN

(ORIGINALLY PODCAST: 01/24/09 AT
WWW.VARIANTFREQUENCIES.COM/2009/01/24/
CREATURE-OF-GOD/)

She touched the head to her tongue, felt its slight electrical charge.

"This battery is good," she whispered, tossing it to me. I nodded and clicked it into the compartment, then shone the laser sight's red dot on the ground. Her jaw clenched; it was time. We stepped out from behind the Ryder truck and walked purposefully toward the hangar. Margot kept her .45 holstered, but displayed openly on her left hip; I carried the sniper rifle in my hands.

"Like I said, the deal should go nice and smooth," she said. "The guns are just a formality. Without 'em he don't take us serious."

Just as I did during most of our disputes at home, I nodded agreement rather than express my true feelings. It rarely did any good anyway, and this was hardly the time for an argument.

A figure stepped out into the open hangar doorway. He'd cultivated a number of thug stereotypes; shock of white-blond hair, mirrored sunglasses, dull tie, black suit that seemed to grow directly out of the darkness of the hangar.

The unpaved yard was a vast, open expanse, dimly lit and sparsely decorated with rusted forklift carcasses. Loose gravel crunched under our feet as we approached. My eyes darted everywhere, sensing other presences but seeing no one.

Margot stopped us at a distance of twenty yards. "You alone?" she called.

"Alone as a corpse," the man replied. Relaxed smile, slight southern accent. "Wait there, Margot; the gentleman will come to me."

My anger hissed upward, like steam above a kettle. "That wasn't the arrangement."

He said, "Either we do things the way I dictate, or I drive away with your feet tied to my bumper."

I gripped my rifle's handle, but Margot shook her head.

"I don't like changes in the deal and I don't like being threatened," I muttered, for her ears alone.

"Go ahead," she said. "It will be all right."

I sighed but said nothing. Letting him see my gunbarrel's silent O, I began the lone approach. He watched me cross the sixty feet, his smile slightly more visible, his outline melding into the cola-dark gloom of the hangar. The red laser dot danced and bobbed on his torso as I drew nearer. I stopped abruptly with the forward sight nearly touching his tie, letting my feet kick forward a dust storm of gravel.

He ignored the gesture, and apparently, so did his clothes. The dirt seemed to refuse to cling to him; his pants and expensive shoes looked as clean and impeccable as they would at his wake.

"That's impeding our business here," he said, inclining his head at my rifle. A number of hard-ass, sub-witty replies came to mind, but I could hear Margot's voice in my head, telling me to just cooperate, goddammit.

Three seconds of stalemate followed, the air as charged as a playground slide.

With a sigh, I let the rifle relax.

The moment my gun was lowered, he drew a heavy pistol from within his jacket and fired two fast shots over my shoulder. The flurry of sudden movements and noise dazzled me, caught me completely off-guard; my tinnitus screamed at the high-decibel cracks. I staggered slightly, chanced a quick look behind me to see Margot on her back in the dirt—not moving. I raised my gun again, but blondie caught its barrel in his strong left grip. With his right hand, he smashed his pistol hard into my knuckles; the rifle went skidding across the gravel.

I managed to swing my fist out and up into his chin, could hear the sickening, satisfying click of teeth snapping together. As he staggered back, I grunted and hit his chest with my shoulder, tackling him hard to the ground. I quickly had his torso pinned beneath my legs, punching wildly at his face with feral rage. He struggled to break free, but my hold was too secure. His hands came up for counterstrikes, but could muster no leverage, and his weak cuffs were easily parried.

But no matter how many blows I struck, not a drop of blood appeared. I landed hits that would have re-broken a boxer's nose, shattered any other man's front teeth, but he seemed to absorb them with indifference. I broke the right lens of his sunglasses, exposing a cold, mud-brown iris beneath, but the only apparent injury was to my lacerated knuckles. Hell, his pretty blond hair wasn't even getting dirty.

I don't know how long this went on; it ended abruptly with a pinpoint pain in my lower back. The sharp sting was so unexpected, so out-of-place, that it took a moment for me to acknowledge. I reached around and felt something solid-yet-feathery protruding from my backside, like a dart. I tried to pull it out, but my fingers were suddenly unable to grip anything. I was distantly aware of the blond man tossing me, of lying on my back in the dirt. He was hunched over me now, his face uncomfortably close to mine, his exhalations not warm, but icy cold on my skin.

"A tranquilizer dart, Johnny boy," he said, his one eye boring into me through the rim of his ruined sunglasses. "You were correct when you sensed that we were not alone."

I could muster no response. That dark, dark eye grew and morphed into a great yawning mouth, stretching wide to devour me.

I awoke to white gospel music and engine hum, strapped into the powder-blue front seat of an early '60s Cadillac. It was raining, and still dark outside. Other than the safety belt, I had no restraints.

"Welcome back to consciousness. Here." A manila folder was tossed into my lap. I opened it and saw a small stack of pictures, Polaroids and big black-and-whites. All of Margot in various stages of negotiations and other activities in a motel room with the man I'd just fought at the hangar, the same man who sat in the driver's seat right now. Blondie. The dashboard glow reflected in his flawless mirrorshades, identical to the ones I'd ruined. I spun quickly to look into the cavernous back seat, certain that someone else was in the car, but there was no one. It was just me and him.

"She set you up," he said. "The original deal was for me to shoot you and leave you in a box inside that old building. She and I were to keep the cash and fence the goods elsewhere."

I looked at the pictures, one in particular, feeling all of the negative reactions boiling inside. I punched him hard again, squarely across the jaw. The car swerved a bit on the highway, but otherwise the man betrayed no reaction; he remained seated face-forward, hands at 10 and 2 on the wheel. I wanted to hit him again, but felt too groggy and tired.

"So why did you shoot her instead? Why welch on the deal you guys had?"

"I received a different set of orders from above—or below, depending on your point of view. My employer has taken an interest in you, Johnny."

"How fucking special I feel. Who is your employer? And what does he want with me?"

"We're on our way to see him now. With luck, you'll soon find out why he's chosen you." His grin was downright...creepy. "And you can call me Belial."

"I'm not gonna call you anything," I muttered, closing my eyes. "Asshole."

The woman on the radio crooned that my salvation lay in Jesus Christ.

I'd never before seen a bar with stained glass windows. A small, battered sign proclaimed it EVIL EDDIE'S BAR. Every parking space was taken, so Belial pulled the Caddy onto a patch of grass at the lot's edge and we ran through the rain to get inside.

Lightning punctuated a thunderclap as we crossed the threshold. I was utterly soaked, but wasn't surprised to see Belial looking dry and neatly groomed.

The place was empty, and nearly as dimly lit as the hangar had been. It seemed that they had the same radio station on in here that Belial had been playing in the car. The unmanned bar occupied the entire left wall of the first room, half-full bottles and mugs on its surface in front of unoccupied stools. At the far end, a row of caramel-colored shots were lined up, waiting to be drunk.

Belial nodded to the bar as he walked past it, entering into the alcove for the men's and ladies' rooms. He looked up to indicate that I should follow.

The bathroom had a bank of filthy urinals to the left and two stalls to the right. Underneath the second stall, a woman's legs were visible, knees on the floor before a pair of men's jeans and black boots. I frowned, looking at the woman's khaki pants and tan sneakers; they were exactly the same as the ones Margot had worn to her shooting.

Belial and I stood for a few moments, the room utterly silent; I felt as if my anger was being teased toward climax. The moment I'd decided *enough already* and resolved to walk up and kick the stall open, to demand some answers, Belial hit me. Unprovoked, unexpected, just a sudden impact of knuckles upon chin. I stumbled into a sink, rubbing my jaw, staring back at the big Aryan.

"I owed you that one," he said, grinning under his sunglasses. I took my weight off of the cracked porcelain, balled my fists—

The stall door swung open with a screech, and a tall, repugnantly handsome man stepped out. His neat, casual dress clearly marked him as Belial's boss. Red-black flannel tucked into blue blue jeans, brown leather belt lining the border. All dynamics, all psyches, all atmospheres, all certainties, all confidences, all faiths, all intentions withered and vanished in his presence. Belial and I had been about to indulge in a fête of violence and extracted blood; I now felt like an embarrassed schoolchild caught misbehaving by the principal.

"Hello Johnny," he said, his voice as deep as the cosmos. "Welcome."

He stuck out his hand for me to shake. I paused, taken aback. A hideously detailed tattoo of a vein-stricken, leather-brown eye canvassed his right palm, but that was not the horror. A smear of blood, like stigmata tears, trickled down to his wrist. My glance darted back to the gap beneath the stall's wall where he'd just been, but the woman's legs were no longer visible there. The slightest trace of impatience touched his face; cold liquid fear poured into me like wet cement. I steeled myself and returned the handshake.

The momentary tension abandoned his features, and he smiled a warm avuncular smile. "Come, let's go have a drink." I sneaked a quick glance at my hand as we exited the dingy bathroom. No trace of red.

The barroom was still as deserted as a bomb scare. He led us to a dimly lit booth in the corner; each of us sat down before tall glasses filled with some black fluid. "To Johnny," the man said, raising his glass and draining it. Belial followed suit and I reluctantly did the same, taking the tiniest sip from my glass. It was Pepsi.

"You're going to like being one of mine, Johnny boy," he said.

I was barely aware of my own helplessness, succumbing to the awe that his presence inspired. But some final reserve of defiance screamed out from my core.

"Your thug here killed my girlfriend. Why the fuck would I ever work for you?"

The Man looked at me blankly for a few seconds, then burst into laughter. Belial chuckled appeasingly, but I just sipped my flat cola, waiting.

"OK," the Man soon said. "You're going to accompany Brother Belial here to a meeting in End Town. Couple of gentlemen there call themselves the 'Bad Feelings', apparently desperate to contact me. It should just be a simple conversation, a transaction of words and facts, nothing more."

I knew that I'd do exactly as he'd said, but he still must have interpreted some trace of hesitation in my face.

"Johnny, you're mine now, surely you can feel that. You're a part of my grand machine, a cell in my bloodstream." There seemed almost a fatherly tenderness to his rumbling voice. "But don't worry, don't worry! I treat my boys real good. You need money? A new car? A new woman, one who won't betray you? I'll get you whatever you need."

Something in his gentle tone touched me, steadied me. I'd long ago shattered the mirror that reflected upon my psyche, hung draperies of denial in its place, no longer willing to look inward and see my forsaken soul. But through his soothing, fatherly words and acceptance, he'd made accessible a new lens, one which offered a fresh view of myself. And for the first time in years, decades, it felt safe to look inside.

My inner landscape of surrendered virtue, of drought-starved, corrupted morality had been unchanged by time, had likely even degenerated further from the years of neglect. But somehow, through this scope of his presence, it looked righteous. My compromised soul appeared wholesome and correct, honest and good.

A tear escaped down my cheek.

The Man reached across and gripped my fingers in his tattooed right hand. "Go with Brother Belial to End Town. And forgive him his trespass against you, son. His actions were to your benefit, after all. The bitch had set you up to die." A ghastly orange twilight flickered in, tainted the color of my soul's landscape, like the sudden tint failure of an old television. The Man reiterated, "She'd conspired to kill you for a few hundred dollars. Direct away your anger at your brother, rather aim it at her memory."

I nodded in agreement, in spite of my true feelings.

An hour later, I was back in the Caddy's passenger seat, listening to twangy gospel music while Belial drove us south. I'd been unconscious and groggy for most of the ride to Evil Eddie's, but this time I made sure to memorize the twisted directions to the Interstate.

He only tried once to spark up conversation; I ignored him and closed my eyes.

I woke to the rumbling transition of tires from pavement to the netted steel surface of a bridge. Dawn had recently begun to establish its presence in the east. We passed over some kind of marshy wetland, driving into the heart of some factory zone. Belial pressed us on past the mills and the stacks, leading us inevitably to the dingiest and most decrepit of the abandoned factories. A few drops of rain hit the dry windshield as soon as we stopped.

I felt a presence again behind me in the Cadillac, but a quick look back showed the seat still empty. I saw that the front flank of the storm had followed us south, and was about to lay siege to the land where we'd stopped.

The downpour began in earnest as we ran across the lot into the building's open truck bay. Again, I was soaked, Belial was perfection.

"We're a few minutes early," he said. "The Bad Feelings boys should be here shortly."

"I'm unarmed," I said, looking around the loading area. "I'm gonna need a gun."

He smirked. "Not going to be that kind of meeting, brother. The Man told you; it's just a friendly conversation."

"Seen lots of friendly conversations turn bloody real quick. I ain't standing here without something to protect myself if these guys turn hostile."

I stared right into his sunglasses; he seemed to be considering my words. Then he sighed and pulled a .45 from his shoulder holster; the same he'd used to shoot down Margot.

He handed it to me. "Trust me, there should be no reason to use th—"

I interrupted him by placing the gun against his forehead.

Tight trigger on a .45.

The report of the shot echoed loudly throughout the loading bay. Belial's head whipped back from the blow; he staggered a step, then stood looking at me, powder burns, broken sunglasses, and a look of surprise on his face.

It was an awkward moment.

I shot him again in his cheek. And again between the eyes; he staggered again but still remained standing. The bullets ripped holes, but I was alarmed and terrified at the utter lack of blood. It took one more shot to the temple to finally fell him. I exhaled a relieved sigh as he slumped to the ground and didn't move. I stood over him, watching closely for motion, preparing to pump more shots into him, when I noticed them.

There were six, they'd entered stealthily and circled us; I had no idea how long they'd been there or how much they'd seen. Each of them wore bad ties and white shirts, like waiters at a diner. Each aimed a weapon directly at me.

"Greetings," said one of them.

"We are the Bad Feelings," said another.

"You and Belial had a disagreement?" asked a third.

"He killed someone precious to me," I replied.

"Is he dead?" asked the one behind me.

I bent down and touched his cold neck, felt no pulse. I wondered if he'd have felt like that before I shot him. As I began to stand, I noticed that he had another pistol tucked into a second shoulder holster.

"He's dead," I said, standing fully upright.

"Doornail," said one of the Bad Feelings.

"I see the dangerous idea spinning in your mind," said another one.

"But you fired four shots."

"That gun in your hand only holds six."

"Not enough bullets for all of us."

"Kill two, the other four will kill you."

"So drop your gun."

"Deliver our message to your master."

"Just as Belial was sent here to do."

I kept the gun pointed downward, held up my left hand. "OK, you guys are getting on my nerves. Please; have one guy do the talking, the rest of you shut up."

The one standing at 2 o'clock from me spoke: "Here is the message we wish you to convey to your master."

"Father Vitor of Saint Joseph's Church is the anointed," said the one next to him. "The man prophesied to blind the eye."

"The priest cannot be allowed to live. Understand?"

"You must memorize this message word for word," said another.

"Repeat it exactly as we dictate it to you."

I shook my head in disgust. "OK, I asked nicely."

I shot the one at 9 o'clock from me, then fired across at midnight. The other four returned fire, but their bullets whizzed overhead as I dropped to the floor. Two o'clock and eight o'clock managed to shoot each other in the crossfire. I scooped out Belial's backup pistol and shot down the remaining two. One of them managed to squeeze off a second shot at me, but his bullet dug into Belial's body, missing me by a matter of inches.

I stood up in a hurry and emptied the second pistol into the Bad Feelings who were still moving.

Trembling with fear and adrenaline, I left them all in the stillness of the abandoned mill and drove the Cadillac back to the Interstate. The windshield wipers were barely effective against the torrential rains. I made only two stops: the liquor store and the motel.

It was in the dingy solitude of my room that I noticed the neat, clean hole in my chest, ringed in black scorches. One of the Bad Feelings' bullets had indeed found me during the shootout, though I'd felt nothing.

After a difficult, yet alarmingly painless self-surgery, the stubbed lead was extracted from its crater.

No blood spilled from the wound.

THREE A.M.

It had been two days since the slaughter of the Bad Feelings. Two nights of his face in my nightmares...that tattooed hand caressing my face, staining my skin, causing me to wake in terror and sweat. I sat up in the darkness, imagining that I'd just heard his rumbling voice, and felt gaping emptiness in its absence. He hadn't sounded angry at my betrayal or desertion... No words were discernible at all, only his fatherly, reassuring tone. But then I woke and he was gone.

I sat on the bed and wept, feeling utterly alone in the motel room, listening for his voice but hearing only the sounds of the rain and the distant thunder.

Finally, I rubbed my eyes and switched on the television, curious to see if late-night CNN could tell me when the rain would abate, or even to see if the Bad Feelings had been found and if their slaying had made it to national news.

All thirteen channels were static. I was about to turn the set back off when I noticed a shape beginning to emerge within the dead image. I realized that what I'd thought to be white noise from the TV's speaker was actually the sound of running water. Listening more closely, I also detected the mingled click-clack of a train passing nearby.

The shape lurched forward suddenly, distorting the static,

seeming to stretch it as if breaking through a web. The fabric of the static suddenly seemed to give and something dark broke through.

It was him.

He blinked and leered, seemingly scanning the room. His gaze hadn't yet landed on me; I switched the TV off and scooped up my clothes from the floor.

The TV turned itself on again, back to the undulating static wall.

I grabbed as many of the remaining Bud cans as I could carry out to the car and sped away from the motel, flowing north on the Interstate.

I got ammo for my guns and a burrito at Walmart, then found a secluded place to park the Caddy and sleep. The sun was getting ready to punch out for the day when I awoke. It was fully dark, forty-five minutes later as I was pulling into Evil Eddie's parking lot. Again, every painted space was taken. Light from within illuminated the building's stained glass windows.

This time, the inside was just as crowded as the lot. Every barstool, every seat at the tables and booths was occupied, every collar blue or scented with cheap perfume. Liver spots and yellowed teeth. A thick, hairless bartender worked to maintain the flow of booze, grinning as he pulled the taps and filled the shot glasses.

The jukebox's low current of organ-heavy, crackling, aged vinyl Delta blues defined the atmosphere.

A ceiling fan spun lazily, bathing me in its warm, humid breeze. The air smelled stale, stagnant, impure. No one looked directly at me, but I could feel the sidelong glances from all sides. I caught many gazes flickering away as I scanned the place.

No familiar faces; I headed back to the men's room.

A toothless old-timer had quite a scare when I kicked open his toilet door, but there was no sign of the Man anywhere.

Cursing to myself, I went back out into the bar proper. The thick bartender stared at me as I approached. I pointed to a bottle and crossed myself as he poured its contents into a glass for me.

As soon as the bourbon touched the rim, I shot two holes in his chest. The whiskey scorched down my throat; I turned around to an audience of staring faces.

My guns began firing.

What followed was a sort-of blackout; I came to walking along a semi-paved side road, vaguely aware that I was following the sound of a church bell. All that noise at whatever late hour this was? I held a half-empty Bud can in my left hand.

The tolling eventually led me to a humble, one floor structure, with a brass bell swinging in its lone central tower. There was no stained glass, only dull neon images of crucified Jesus in the windows. White paint flaked on its beveled wood siding. A weathered sign staked into the grass read: "St. Jos p 's Chur h of Jesus C rist the Savior".

I climbed the steps and was about to enter when I noticed the stain on my right hand. There were only the slightest traces of red on my clothes, and my left hand was spotless; it was mainly on the right. Rivulets of blood trickled down to the wrist, exactly mimicking The Man's tattoo. Through the thin coating of blood on my palm, I thought I could see the outline of an eye.

"Jesus fucking Christ."

I kicked open the church door, immediately spotted the holy water bowls to my left and right. I stumbled to the right, immersed my red-smeared hand into the basin. The water darkened and—to my alarm—began to steam.

Then the burning sensation set in, ravaging my skin up to where the wrist emerged from the murky red fluid. The intense pain forced tears from my eyes, but I gritted my teeth and swished my hand around, until finally all of the tainted holy water had evaporated.

I held my throbbing right hand over the empty basin; it was wet, but seemingly clean. My palm was a blank slate of wrinkles again, no blood or tattoos. There was a sudden rustling noise from somewhere; I looked up just in time to see the skirts of a priest's robe entering the church's confessional.

I gulped down the rest of my beer and entered the booth through the other door.

"Bless me father for I have sinned."

"Sounds tragic," came the reply through the screen. "Go say some fucking Hail Maries."

I sat in startled silence, forming questions, but not speaking them. The priest said nothing more, though his outline was still visible through the patterned screen. I heard the flick of a lighter, smelled faint cigarette smoke. With a defeated sigh, I left the booth and headed for the front doors. I stopped at the other basin and began to scoop up holy water into my emptied beer can.

"Hey, don't taint that!" came the priest's voice from behind me. He'd emerged again from the confessional cocoon, the cigarette clinging precariously to his lip. I looked over at the red-stained basin, then back at him.

"Look. This may sound a little strange, but I seem to have gotten myself mixed up in something bad. Something evil. I'm going off now to fight this man... devil, demon, witch; hell, I don't know what he is. But I think I'm going to need this. Sorry." I gestured with the beer can.

"You'll need much more than that to face Him, my son."

"Father Vitor."

He nodded and walked toward me. "Your coming here was no accident, Johnny."

"The Bad Feelings said that you're the prophesied—"

"—yeah, yeah; I know. I've never felt confident that I could do it alone. Just been waiting for them to send you here."

"So you'll come with me to Evil Eddie's?"

Vitor shook his head and stubbed out his cigarette in the Holy Water basin. "He lives under the viaduct at the edge of town, that's where we'll find Him. We can walk to it from here, but do as I fucking say—at all times—or we'll both end up far worse than dead."

"Aren't you a little foul-mouthed for a priest?"

We walked for awhile through midnight's teeming mist, traversing unpaved roads and sometimes directly through damp thickets of trees. Finally, we emerged from someone's wooded backyard into a large clearing. By now, the mist had graduated into an aggressive downpour, the rain spurring on the fast-flowing river that bordered the field to the west. A railroad track lined the hilltop at the far southern edge, eventually reaching an architecturally gothic viaduct across the water.

The place appeared deserted, but I knew he was here.

Father Vitor and I continued to walk through the tall grass, pressing on toward the bridge. The structure seemed to loom larger and larger overhead as we approached. Eventually the tall growth gave way to patches of wet clay and brush adjacent the riverbank. The cold rain soaked me relentlessly, plastering my hair to my head and sinking my feet into the muddy earth. I looked up just in time to see him step out of a shadow from beneath the railroad bridge.

He smiled at the Father and me. We closed to a distance of about twenty feet and everyone stopped. I tried unsuccessfully to keep the holy beer can from trembling in my grip. Conceding all initiative, I said fuck it and drew the gun in my other hand. I'd walked away from Evil Eddie's Bar with two bullets left. Enough for us both.

The Man seemed even taller here tonight than he had at the bar. He looked down into the .45's barrel and grinned broadly.

Father Vitor spoke, "I've brought him to you as you requested, Master."

"What?!" I turned and shot him a look of outrage, but he only gazed lovingly at his true patriarch. "You goddamn—"

Suddenly the Man was right in front of me, his strong hands upon my shoulders, rubbing affectionately. He smelled of burnt copper. I looked up into his smiling face, but he pulled me to his chest in a firm, fatherly embrace. He felt warm and dry and safe.

"You've done all that I asked of you, Johnny. Made me very

proud. Everything you've done was according to my design."

I was too immersed in dread fear to say anything in response. He continued to hold me close to him, but I could sense that we were moving. My feet were walking on their own to stay near him as we approached the river's edge.

"You're going to succeed Belial, Johnny. You'll be my favorite son now." As he said it, I knew I'd never desired anything so strongly in my life.

I was dimly aware of a single gunshot, somewhere very far away.

Immediately following the harsh crack, the Man let go of me and took a few steps back. He held up his right hand, looking at it with mild curiosity. There was a black hole, a second iris in the eye, directly in the center of the palm where the bullet had passed through. I looked down to see the literal smoking gun in my hand. The spell was momentarily broken.

"Master!" shouted Father Vitor.

I screwed up my courage, raised the beer can high and swung it low in an arc, dashing holy water out at the Man. There was fierce hissing in the places on his palm where the water made contact.

His face twisted into deep crimson rage, filled with hatred of a purity unattainable by mortal man. He emitted a roar of pain and fury that shook the very storm clouds from the sky. It took every fiber of resolve I could muster to remain where I stood and keep swinging the can at him.

The blessed elixir splashed out in agonizingly small doses. Each new spray burned on the skin of his hands and face, but it didn't seem effective enough. The Man was writhing and bellowing in smoking anger and pain, but I could feel the can getting lighter and he showed no sign of dropping.

I caught a peripheral glimpse of Father Vitor rushing in to attack and easily sidestepped his blow, tripping him up as he charged. Acting on instinct, I fell upon the priest and shoved the can's aluminum nozzle into his mouth, forcing him to drink what was left. He began to cough and retch as the last drops of holy water coursed down his throat.

Then I felt a strong hand grip the front of my shirt and pull me off of him, lifting me high up in the air. The Man punched the can into the field and then lowered me so our faces were level, though my legs dangled freely two feet above the ground. It seemed that his already impressive height had increased since I'd broken from his arms. I raised the gun, but he snatched it and tossed it into the river. His tattooed hand twisted my shirt in its strong grip and he pulled my face to within an inch of his. His breath smelled of sulphur.

"Some boys just need a little more discipline," he growled. He tossed me with a casual gesture; I flew back twenty feet, landing painfully on my neck on the wet riverbank. I looked up to see the massive Man walking toward me, his calm masculine anger invoking deeply-repressed fears from childhood. A streak of lightning highlighted his outline.

Behind the Man I saw Father Vitor stand up; he looked at his Master in awed fear, then shot me a look of sympathy. The Man unbuckled his belt and slid it free as he approached. I stood up, my knees trembling almost comically.

"Father," I called. "There must be something of your faith left, otherwise you wouldn't have been able to bless the water. Help me now."

The Man snapped two lengths of his belt together; the sonic boom it created knocked me backward into the river. I struggled to stand quickly and waded out further, seeking an escape that I knew to be impossible. The Man stepped directly off of the riverbank into the swift current. I risked a look over my shoulder and saw him closing the space between us with each stride. There were fresh burns from the holy water on his face and his outstretched right hand.

"Father!" I shouted to Vitor, who stood now watching from the muddy bank. "Father help me! Bless the river water!"

He adopted a bewildered expression. "Bless the river? A priest can't conduct sacrament on so much water at once... and besides it's in motion..."

I felt the sting of the belt leather on my Adam's apple, then the moment of painful asphyxiation as it dragged me backward. I fell to the riverbed, swallowing huge gulps of water. My hand closed on something hard and metal among the submerged rocks. The Man hauled me up gasping and struggling for breath.

Even through the commotion in the river and the noise of the rain, I heard Father Vitor's clear voice carrying from the bank. "O water, creature of God, I exorcise you in the name of God the Father Almighty, and in the name of Jesus Christ His Son, our Lord, and in the power of the Holy Spirit."

The Man turned from me and shot him a look of disappointment. "You'd turn from me so quickly, boy? I'll have to deal with you next."

Father Vitor's incantation faltered.

"Don't stop, Father! Please!" I screamed and pulled up Belial's gun. With a roar I pressed the muzzle to the Man's throat and squeezed the trigger.

Nothing happened.

"Tsk tsk, wet gun jammed. You're going to need some severe punishment, boy." The eye on his hand slapped me hard, sent me splashing back ten feet. I struggled to remain upright; the water was significantly deeper where I landed.

I heard Father Vitor's tremulous voice speak out again. "I exorcise you so that you may put to flight all the power of the Enemy..."

The Man laughed a terrible, inhuman laugh. Even as he spoke to his wayward priest, his eyes remained fixed upon mine. "Your holy water may have stung me, padre, but you have no real power to do me any harm."

"You're wrong, asshole," I called. "Heard it directly from the Bad Feelings themselves. Father Vitor is the one prophesied to blind the eye."

All amusement drained from his face. "...and be able to root out and supplant that Enemy with his apostate angels: through the power of our Lord Jesus Christ, Who will come to judge the living and the dead and the world by lire. Amen," Vitor finished and waved the sign of the cross.

A streak of lightning seemed to have struck the running river directly in front of me. There was a brilliant flash, followed by a great explosion of water. My eyelids fluttered; I felt my body growing numb, and suddenly the river's fast current seemed too strong a thing to resist. I knew I had to swim to the safety of the shore, knew I'd never make it. I was aware of a strong hissing noise, and great deal of steam.

And then the bellowing began. Oh God. It was the last thing I heard before the dark current of unconsciousness swept me away.

I came to, tangled in the gnarled branches of a tree growing out of the riverbank. The viaduct and the field were nowhere in sight. I was slow to realize that I'd been shaken back to wakefulness by a strong hand on my shoulder; Father Vitor stood leaning out to me from the muddy shoreline. I felt relieved to see his smile, which now showed the benevolence that you expect in holy men. It was then that I noticed the denim blue sky of early morning overhead. The storm clouds had finally dispersed.

"Come on, Johnny, let's get the fuck out of here." With Vitor's help, I climbed back up onto solid land. As I tried to shake some of the damp out of my clothes, my body remembered just how sore and beat up it felt.

Father Vitor and I found our way out to a dirt road, and he led us from there. We walked in silence, taking what appeared to be a roundabout way through the town toward his church. The dirt eventually turned to cracked pavement beneath our feet. I was about to question the indirect route, when I noticed a dilapidated shack nestled amidst the tall weeds and grass to my left.

A faded sign next to a broken stained glass window on the building read, "EMIL & EDDIE'S BAR", but two parts of the letter "M" had broken away, causing it to resemble a capital "V". The ampersand had also long ago dropped from the board and never been replaced. The rusted hulk of a powder-blue Cadillac rested in decay not far from the ruined shack.

I hurried to catch up with Father Vitor.

The priest finally spoke as we drew near to his church.

"Every priest in seminary secretly dreams of banishing demons, though few would admit it," He lit a cigarette, shielding the disposable bic with his hand. "I... have been a lost man. Thank you."

I shook my head. "You saved my ass twice, Padre. I should be the one saying thanks."

We crossed the remaining distance and entered the churchyard where last night I'd been drawn by the tolling bells. "So I guess I'll just—" I began, but saw that he'd frozen in the walkway, his face as white as the paint flakes. I followed his gaze, after a moment saw what had drained his color.

An eye had been drawn in blood on the front door.

Rivulets of glistening red had trickled down from the image, spreading into the pattern I'd seen in the Man's tattoo, and later on my own wrist.

Fighting back the icy dread, I bounded up the steps and touched the mark.

Dry.

Comprehension dawned and I exhaled deeply in relief. "Don't scare me like that, Padre. This is from me. This is the mark I made on the door when I got here last night."

The gray horror held fast on Vitor's face a moment longer, then scattered like thunderheads before the sun. He grinned and shook his head, chuckling out cigarette smoke. "Sorry. Still a little jumpy."

"Understandable." I opened the church door and walked in.

It smelled faintly of cheap perfume and beer inside.

Was there a flitter of movement by the confessional?

I looked another moment, but no one was there. Vitor seemed oblivious.

Someone seemed to have refilled the Holy Water basins since we'd left last night. But... was the water supposed to be yellow? It hadn't been last night. Both containers looked to have been filled with piss—or flat beer. I ran over to one and sniffed it; nothing. I dipped my fingertips and smelled them. Still nothing. Maybe it was just the bronze of the basin, or—

"Christ's hands," Vitor gasped. "His stigmata bleed in the shapes of eyes." I followed his gaze to the cheaply-sculpted, crucified Jesus above the altar. I walked slowly up the aisle, saw the painted blood on His chipped ceramic palms, but the trickle looked normal to me, like any other crucifix I'd ever seen. A moment later, Vitor shook his head and pinched the bridge of his nose. "Sorry. Never mind."

"Dammit, Padre—" A rumbling engine dopplered closer outside, loud 1950s gospel music blaring from a car stereo as it passed by. I bolted for the church doors, flung them open, but too late. The car was gone, its music and engine fading into the distance.

I closed the door quickly again, stood leaning against it. We looked at each other now, ready to join in mutual, self-conscious, self-deprecating laughter at our paranoia.

But in his mud-brown eyes I only saw fear... his fear and my own, spreading dangerous ideas like viral preachers, threatening to stage a coup and overthrow rational thought.

We both began to speak aloud.

"There's nothing going on here."

"Nothing."

"We're both just tired."

"Exhausted."

"Drained."

"Minds playing tricks on us."

"Jumping at shadows."

"Obviously."

"We blinded the eye."

"The evil is dead."

"Doornail."

"The Man is gone."

"Exorcised."

"Shut up."

"Water blessed."

"Prophecy fulfilled."

"Shut up. Shut up!"

I knew this last bit was my own voice; it echoed a few moments longer around the small church's ceiling. I sat down heavily in the nearest pew.

Vitor dropped his smoke on the tiled floor, stamped it out with a trembling foot. "What the fuck do we do now, Johnny?"

Before I could respond, the wooden bench creaked next to me. I sensed a presence there, felt it, heard it, smelled it, tasted it; as clearly as I had when riding in Belial's blue Caddy. As clearly as I had when drinking Pepsis in the booth at Evil Eddie's. With a start, I jumped out into the aisle, breathing in short, ragged gasps.

The pew was empty.

Panic had now assumed almost total control; I had to fight to keep from hyperventilating. Vitor and I looked at each other yet again, neither of us wanting say it aloud.

This will never be over.

This will never be over.

"What do we do now?"

Angels Unawares

By J. Daniel Sawyer

(Originally Podcast: 09/28/07 at sculptgod.
jdsawyer.net/?p=1)

This is how it happened. I swear. What you are about to hear is the absolute, unvarnished truth—I don'a give bugger all about whatch'a found in the histories. It wasn'a a suicide, and it wasn'a murder. I was there, and I saw, and no one else did. Their "forensics" don'a mean a bloody thing, because I *know*. And what I saw is more amazing than what they think happened. But I kept it to myself, just to be sure that no one would ruin it—because I promised her, you see. And I had to keep the promise—no one could have broken it after seeing the look in her eyes.

But first, I suppose you'll want to know about how it started—what it was like in this town back then. The commotion started back when her body was found beaten against the rocks like so much driftwood. That wasn'a the unusual part—a lot of people fell from that trail on the bluff. That's why the laird put the fences up when I was a lad. It never stopped anyone from going down there, you understand, just made him feel better when there was a fuss. Great spot for the spring frolic, it was, and of course we were all up there as normal. When they find bodies down in the surf there it's usually a suicide or an accident—someone gone off their melon on too much whisky. But they're always *normal* people. She was unusual, and the lengths they went to trying to explain it made the whole town start locking their doors at night.

They said that she was mutilated—or deformed; that her body wasn'a like a woman's body, but they weren'a sure if the fall did it or if it was something else. They said that the policemen fought with each other to avoid having to be near her. It was hideous and beaten, and they'd never seen anything so brutally done. In the end it was only her cloak that identified her.

It was always her cloak that announced her.

Dark, it was, and seemed to fall about her like water. She always wore it up there at the frolics. Even when one of the youths would bring a guitar or a penny whistle and she danced for us with those dances that would pull us away from the material world for a moment or three—even then the cloak was her companion. She liked it because it kept her safe in the shadows, blended right in when it was dark, no matter where she was. Glorious, shimmering dull blue, deep but faded, fastened round her neck with a dull golden braid—thinking of it now I realize that she and the cloak seemed to be two expressions of a third, hidden thing. Like she was a tired faerie from an older, forgotten world. But that's maybe the mists of fond memory speaking.

So they became convinced, eventually, that she had killed herself, though they couldn'a imagine why, and eventually the memory of her faded into the ghost story the young ones all hear from the older ones upon their first visit to the frolics. Everyone was sure that it was suicide, or that she'd been killed by a lover—an older, married man they fancied she'd been seeing. And partly the reason was that no one they questioned had seen her that night after the moon rose.

But I saw her. And I know what happened.

We always called her Aadi. One of the other young men who came to the frolics heard it from his father serving in India—he said it meant "beginning." She was the first one to clear the grove on the bluff, and as far as anyone could remember she had begun the spring frolics. I suppose the old druids would have called her the May Queen or thought she was a dryad, but we had no use for superstition. The dawning future had enough magic of its own. The twentieth century was coming, nature was being conquered, and, in our little lowland village far away from the noise and dirt of the factories at least, there was nowhere to look but forward and up. Of course, all of us knew her real name—though none of us knew her age—but Aadi suited her better than the name she called herself, and that is always how I'll remember her. The sound of it was always soothing, and she seemed to me as ageless as the hills she lived in. My father told me, before he passed on, that someone had always been up there—when he was a lad, he too had gone to the bluff and met the woman in the trees who lived up in the hills, but that one had been a minstrel. Aadi was no minstrel—when pressed she might have been able to squawk.

It was early May—late enough that the rain had stopped the pretense of snow and had contented itself merely with being wet. Ten or fifteen of us went up to the grove on the bluff as often as we could to catch the scent of the changing seasons, to dance and play, to wrestle with the lassies among the tall grasses, and to watch the moon set on the sea. Someone had brought a book of poetry that night, and we handed it around with the Glenlivet, reading to each other while the wind came up. On that cold night the drink was like hot butter, coating inside with warmth, smooth as a woman's neck. When mixed with the pine fire and the smell of drizzle, the glow of faces in the firelight, the sound of Shelly being read in the halting voice of a seventeen year old Scots lad, it seemed to thin the veil between the worlds. It was a night that felt more real than any other, perhaps because it was as unreal as any I have yet lived. An evening when, for a moment, time stepped outside of itself and flirted with eternity.

When I'd first happened upon the grove, as a twelve-year-old explorer, it seemed the perfect place for a hideaway. The tall grasses and thistles that grew around it made it all the more private for being a nearly impenetrable grove of pines. It was already clear in the middle, and there were endless tunnels and paths wending their way through the trees and under the bushes. One of them led to the bluff above the ocean, with a view so long that you could almost see the continent peaking over the horizon. I started bringing my friends up there. At first it was just other lads from the mill—after all, what group of boys doesn'a need a place to retreat to, to learn to smoke and drink Dad's pilfered scotch, to brag about imaginary conquests, to dream about finally growing up, and to share the old spook tales that we'd all heard in the nursery. We made plans about hiking the highlands, joining the RN, getting away to the cities where life was wild and free. It was the place we stole away to when we ducked church to read the subversive books that the Priest never preached from. Eventually we started bringing girls along, using the beauty and secrecy of the place to find out exactly *why* their breasts were like two fauns running in a field, to learn about the peculiar lilt of a lass's voice that could make you fall asleep contented, and to learn exactly how many scratches thistles can give you while you're concentrating on other things. No one really knew when Aadi started showing up. Looking back, it feels like she had always been there, hiding just outside the firelight. When she finally showed herself, no one thought to ask where she came from. I don'a think anyone really cared—she knew the stories that kept us all coming back. Not just the old stories about sleepwalkers and faeries, but the real stories behind them. The stories of armies getting lost in the fog, of great battles won and lost to keep Scotland free, of times long forgotten in arid lands far away. She told us how the sleepwalkers were invented to explain why the wildcats only came out at night, about how the old bones of the world frightened the ancient Pict. She taught us about life, brought us news of the outside world. She didn'a look much older than we did, but she understood the *whys*. She taught us to love the world we were in, even though we all wanted to grow up and move out and away into the world. Under her, we learned patience, to savor life as it went by, to not be pushed under by cares. We learned to love life because it was real, and to love stories because they were not. She taught us gratitude, even for sorrow. She taught us what it meant to be alive.

And that night, Aadi sat behind the circle, watching with her eyes glowing in the firelight, looking for all the world like a raven eying an egg. Her eyes were bright with mystery, smiling at the clumsy joy and comradeship around the fire. She took the drink when it was passed to her, and then the book. But when she opened it to read she stood and stepped into the circle. And she read. She could not sing a single note, but she read—in a voice that was full of sorrow, like a willow branch weighed down with snow to the breaking point. Her voice was music, but that night it did not draw us to sing. Although I don'a remember the words she spoke I do remember the sound. It was the sound of deepest regret, the loss of a mother whose children were grown. It was the last frolic—we had all finally reached maturity. We were moving on, having a last evening together before the first of the lads shipped out with the RN. In the cold of the night, in the glow of the fire, her voice was the strength of weakness and loss.

When she was done, we sat around for a long time, looking at each other, knowing truly for the first time that something magical was ending. She passed the book, and the readings continued, but what had been a frolic had become a meditation. I was actually surprised when couples started fading into the shadows as was customary. I wasn'a ready for the night to end, and although the closeness of the lass on my arm was comforting, I wanted to be alone. Before the book came around to me again, I stood and faded into the shadows myself. I quietly stepped back from the fire and took the path leading down to the edge of the bluff. The pale sliver of the waning moon overhead threw just enough light to pick out the path amid the low brambles.

A chill wind blew up from the sea below, carrying the usually distant sound of the waves straight up to me. I couldn'a see many stars through the scattered clouds, but the moon glimmered faintly on the waters below. It felt as if the world were changing around me, as if I wasn'a walking completely in the realm of flesh and blood. And despite the wind, the air felt still and portentous—I couldn'a hear any owls or other sounds of the night. It felt like there should have been mist in the air, but there wasn'a. Rather it was clear all the way to the dark horizon. I pulled my lamb-lined oilskin tighter around me to keep out the cold, but I didn'a want to return to the warmth of the fire and my friends.

I don'a know how long I stood there on the cliff, looking out at the seam, but when I turned away I caught a glimpse of her a few yards down the bluff. She stood, little more than a black shadow against the pale dark sky, gazing out at the water as I had been doing, and I was surprised to discover that I wanted to know more about her. Oh, she had told us about herself, about her parents, about being raised in the hills outside of the town and traveling to visit family in London for holidays, and I certainly knew her well enough. We had shared many moments around the fire and in the heather, enjoying the camaraderie of the group and more private moments of discovery. I had talked long with her over the years—she was, after all, my friend. But I was suddenly seized with the notion that I didn'a know her at all. As if our time together—all that time—had been merely a dream, and I was truly seeing her tonight for the first time.

As I walked over to her, across the brambles and grasses, she turned to me, cloak clasped shut with one hand, and cocked her head to one side, pulling the wind-blown hair out of her eyes. Her bare feet and legs held her up against the wind, and she seemed small. For the first time since I knew her, she seemed small.

"Aadi?" I called out to let her know it was me.

"Yes?" She looked at me as if I had interrupted something very private, and I stopped for a second while she studied me. Standing there, against the grey of the sea and the blue-black horizon, she seemed pensive and vulnerable, more so than I had ever known her to be. And yet it seemed improper to approach, so I began to turn away.

"Nothing."

I walked a couple of steps and she called out to me, "Wait! Please?" I turned back and walked towards her.

"Are you sure I'm not intruding?" I arrived at her side, and she dropped her hand and turned back towards the ocean.

"No. I thought I wanted to be alone, but I'd rather have you here. I just wanted to look at it one more time before I go."

"You're leaving too? You hadn'a said..." I stumbled, and stopped.

Even though I was going away to the army in a few weeks I had trouble imagining that place without her presence. "Where are you moving to?"

"I'm going home."

"Home?" Her home was in the hills, I had walked her there many times, I had seen her room. I knew her siblings. "I thought this was your home."

"No," she said, "I haven'a been home in a long time."

I let the comment pass, not knowing what to say to it, and we shared a long moment standing by each other, looking out over the vast expanse of dark water.

"I've wanted to go home for so long, I never thought the day would come," she said. She seemed far off, even as she unconsciously took my hand. "I never thought I'd miss this place. But now I almost can'a bring myself to leave."

"I thought you had always been here."

"No. I was sent to accomplish a task." I turned and looked at her, baffled, but her gaze didn'a drift from the sea. "And now it's done. I was to return when it was done, but..." Her voice trailed off, as if there was nothing more to say.

"You can always come back to visit. I'll be back on break from university to visit my family, the others will come back for holidays."

She looked at me, amusement and tenderness fighting over her gaze, and I saw for the first time that she had been crying. I reached up and brushed a tear away from her face. "No," she said, "you don'a understand. I'm not like you, I can'a come back. You—all of you—have grown up, so my time is done. I've helped you all I can."

"I don't understand..." But she put her finger to my lips to silence me, and then gently kissed me.

"Thank you." She smiled, "I'll miss you, and this place. But I have to go. Promise me you won't tell anyone?"

"Tell them what?"

She let go my hand and stepped back from me, toward the cliff, and turned once again to look at the sea. "Don'a forget me."

She dropped her arms and let her cloak fly free behind her in the wind, baring her body beneath to the night air. For a moment I thought she was going to jump so I stepped towards her, but when the wind caught her hair she began to glow. All around her, the grass, her cloak, her body, her hair seemed to be on fire with a warm, dim, phosphorescent orange glow. It started like a halo, but quickly the wind whipped up and it seemed to pull the light farther away from her, a pale, shining copy of her form, blurring behind her like a trail of yellow fire. The wind built and built, until her cloak was thrown out almost straight behind her and she seemed to be flying even while her feet were still on the ground. She swelled up, breathing deeply the cold wind. Her eyes, which had been clenched shut, relaxed as if she was sleeping yet still held aloft by the wind.

And then the fire seemed to leave her, not dying out, but separating from her by inches, clinging to her cape and hair like tendrils. The tendrils, one by one, whipped free, and when the last one let go the entire glow caught the wind and flew away towards the mountains. I watched it fade, too dumbstruck to say anything, but when I looked back her body had collapsed half over the cliff.

There was nothing I could do. Before I could get to her she slid over on the loose gravel at the edge. I looked down after her but the night was too dark to see anything. I wanted to jump down after her and save her, wanted to run back to the fire and get help, but even as the thoughts crossed my mind I knew that it was no use. She was gone. And whatever was left at the base of the cliffs was only her vehicle.

I do not know how long it took me to walk home that night. The moon was still in the sky when I lay down in my bed and looked out my window, but the entire household was silent. I fell asleep wondering just what she was.

I wonder still.

But it wasn'a suicide. And it wasn'a murder. I know. I saw.

I was there.

The Curse of the Forward-Thinking Gentleman

By Jared Axelrod

(Originally podcast: Part 1: 01/17/06 at
http://planetx.libsyn.com/index.php?post_
id=49132 Part 2: 01/25/06 at http://planetx.
libsyn.com/index.php?post_id=51567)

I t has been both my luck and immense misfortune to be involved
with the singular institution known to the public as Basil
Fohrsight. While the inherently tumultuous events that seem to
surround the actions of this man are at once exhilarating and voltaic,
I must confess that, in the wake of the currently peaceful stretch
after the Stormby Smith affair, I had quite enjoyed the respite from
Basil's usually unusual circumstances. I oftentimes wondered if Basil
was leading an all together different life, leaving behind the bizarre
companions of former days. But I need only to look at my good
friend's trademark knowing grin to be aware that the next adventure
could very well be around the corner, and I would be caught up in
his opulent whirlwinds yet again.

It happened far sooner than any of us, perhaps even Basil
(though, in all honesty, I scarcely believe that to be true), had
supposed. It was an unseasonably warm January that night in 1906.
We were leaving yet another sumptuous dinner at the residentry
of Lord Canterbury. To my mind, I am still unclear as to why Basil
attends these functions, beyond the obligation to Lord Canterbury,
who is, even in Basil's austere estimations, a good man who does
much for the Philadelphia society at small and the world at large.

But the fellow seems perhaps a bit too taken with all that is new and unheard of, and as such are his salons and dinners littered with intellectuals and those who merely consider themselves so, each with a new idea about the proper way to live. Basil, naturally, launched into one attack after another, but, again, laying into my good friend's nature, would let the argument languish each and every time it became apparent that he wasn't really being listened to. I often wondered in those moments if Basil actually did doze off, or if he merely appeared to, in order for his sparring partner to get the point.

We were met outside of Lord Canterbury's edifice by Rupert Fohrsight, Basil's brother. Rupert was, as far I was aware, still clinging to the latest of his kaleidoscope of occupations, that of a private detective. When his eyes happed upon us, he gave an unquestionable look of surprise, and confessed later that he had been so intent on watching Lord Canterbury's house he had not seen us enter. "Detective work," he said, "is that engrossing."

"I am not at all surprised," said Basil, with a polite smile. "Lord Canterbury has excellent taste in molding and shutters. I myself have often taken a moment before entering to gaze upon them admiringly. Although it has never occurred to me to spend an entire evening doing so. Perhaps I should."

"It is not what the outside of his house that intrigues me," Rupert said. "It is what lies within."

"Chairs?" volunteered Basil. "Tables? That rather suspicious brandy he served with the venison? I admit the sofa by the bookcase in the parlor did require closer inspection, but you might have come in for that."

"I did not wish to come inside," intoned Rupert with palatable gravity. "For I did not wish to alert my quarry that I was on to him."

"Who?" I asked, slightly ashamed of my own excitement "On to who?"

"That man there!" Rupert said, pointing. The man in question carried himself with a slight hunch and wore an overcoat. The only other distinction he possessed was that I remember him being one of the few people at dinner who did not argue vehemently with Basil.

"Algernon Feldspar?" Basil veritably blinked with incredulity. "Rupert, you must be joking! The man has a tendency to be off his head quite a bit, but then, such is the way with all inventors, I should imagine. You were one once, and you're off your head quite a lot."

"Did not, while you were dining with such a man, notice his left arm?" Rupert was well into his traditional method of locomotion whilst detecting, his nose jutted forward in a hound-like stoop, his greatcoat flapping about his boots. Basil, no doubt in anticipation of Rupert's usual long-winded explanations of detected guilt, turned his gaze upwards toward the stars, his great white hair reflecting the moonlight wondrously.

I admitted to Rupert that I had not noticed Algernon Feldspar's left arm, nor for that matter, his right. I had been distracted, as I'm sure most of the patrons of Lord Canterbury's dinner were, by the suspicious brandy that was served with the venison.

"I noticed his left arm," Rupert said, with an unclear amount of pride. "It is swollen and stiff, and barely moves. I saw him try to lift a teacup with it, and it caused him to perform an impressive display of strain."

"Could be an injury," I mentioned. "A strained ligament, perhaps."

"Perhaps," Rupert said. "But then why does he glove his left hand, while the right is exposed to the elements? And then there are peculiar stains on his trousers . . ." Rupert Fohrsight's explanation continued along those lines, enclosing about Algernon Feldspar a fine net of possibilities. I will confess, I did not pay attention to most of it.

There are some parts of Philadelphia that look out of place, as if someone removed those buildings from other parts of the city, and then forgot where to put them back. Such a house Algernon Feldspar was now staggering toward, huffing and puffing, as if he were carrying a great load. Rupert Fohrsight took this as admission of guilt, saying that such a man would not be so exerted unburdened, and ventured a guess as to the thievery that was perpetrated at Lord Canterbury's abode.

"Seems a bit unusual for theft, then," I ventured. Algernon Feldspar seemed almost handicapped by that left arm, and should its lack of comfortable motion have something to do with actual injury, such suppositions of guilt and theft seemed a bit cruel and ungentlemanly. "Didn't you say he had a suspicious arm going in to the salon?"

"Indeed," said, Rupert, his eyes narrowing. "That is because he is a poor criminal."

"Finally, something we can agree on," Basil said, snapping out of one of his self-induced trances. "Algernon is a very poor criminal indeed. An absolute failure at it, you might say. No doubt through lack of trying."

Rupert rounded the corner of his quarry's incongruous domicile, extending farther than I thought humanly possible in order to have a scan though one of the inordinately high windows. He shrank back, frustrated. "Black as pitch in there. We'll have to go inside. Basil, could you lend a hand?"

"I'm afraid not. I need one of them to light this cigar and the other to shield it from the wind. I'm all out. But you two go ahead. This cigar seems to have utterly captured my attention, and I fear I shall simply be without use until I finish it."

So it was that I squatted and formed a stoop with my hands, hoisting Rupert up to the windowsill, his voluminous coat smothering my face. He was quite surprised to find it already opened, and Rupert muttered something along the lines of how only criminals have unlocked and open windows, for what do they have to fear of their own kind, or some other line of thinking along that nature. My ears being muffled by Rupert's raiment, I can only assume what he was speaking from the few words I could grasp and my knowledge of the speaker.

Rupert slipped into Algernon Feldspar's window, and held out a hand for me to follow. Housebreaking was never the hobby for me that it apparently was for Rupert Fohrsight, and I had a great deal more trouble breaking my particular entering than he did. But I managed in my own scrabbling way, and entered the darkened room. The floor was oddly cold to the touch (it shames me to say so, but I more tumbled into the house than anything else, and found myself immediately on my hands and knees), and smoother than the rough planks that covered the outside of the building would allow one to believe. It was only when Rupert, impatient at the lack of light, lit a match, that I saw my reflection in the floor and came to the conclusion that it was not made of wood at all, but rather polished copper.

"Rupert, did you notice the floor..." I began, but then trailed off when I noticed why he did not.

Propped up against the walls of this metal-lined room, in various states of posture, were what can only be described as the bodies of men, yet men as if they were birthed by radios and steam engines. Globular glass eyes glared and glinted by Rupert's match-light. Strange terminations collected at the end of each metal arm, some like claws, some like grapples, but most like elements I have never seen in either machine or man. They all seemed based upon a human form, but only as if their creator had heard of man by rough description, and decided to fill in the blanks with whatever he had lying around the house.

Rupert had lit another match in order to gain a closer inspection of the nearest body, but his appraisal was cut short by an ominous clanking noise from down the hall. As the clanks got progressively louder, so too did Rupert and myself get more and more rigid, as if rigor mortis set in by expectation alone. With a sound not entirely unlike a plumber's main tool releasing itself after a hard day's work, a door upon the far wall erupted. From the faint light in the hallway, we could only dimly make out another one of these misshapen mockeries of men, with its bulky limbs and oversized head. Further distracting us from the details of such a creature were the eyes, for they were lit, they seemed, from the very fires of Hell itself, or some other, similarly powerful inferno.

The creature made motions toward us with some sort of shiny claw-hand which was more than enough to launch Rupert and myself toward the window, out onto to the street and toward Basil, who, oblivious to the near-demise we had experienced was puffing away on his cigar, humming to himself. In excited tones and extensive vocabularies, Rupert and I described what we had witnessed, and Basil regarded us with one eye open, cigar smoke carelessly spilling out the corners of his mouth.

"I didn't think such a thing was possible," Basil said when we finished. "I scarcely believe it myself. But there's no denying it. You have completely robbed this cigar of my attention. I'm not sure if it shall ever get it back." Basil stubbed out the cigar, reverently. "And not even half-way down. Shall we go into the house, then?"

What little color Rupert contained in his complexion was suddenly and dramatically drained away. "You don't honestly mean that, do you, Basil? Weren't you listening?"

"I was indeed," Basil said, adjusting his white hat with his unique combination of fastidiousy and carelessness. "Which is why I must see these wonders for myself."

"Don't go, Basil!" Rupert pleaded, his pallor now matching the whites of his eyes, giving his entire face the look of an unfinished painting. "It's not safe!"

"Nothing is, my dear boy, with the possible exception of death." said Basil. Confident and composed, Basil strode up to the front door full of purpose and posture. He reached out to ring the bell with a determined finger, only to pause, and turn back toward us. "Maybe backgammon," he called back, over his shoulder.

"I'm afraid I don't understand," Rupert sputtered through chattering teeth.

"Backgammon. Could be safe. Granted, it's been several years since I played such a game with a truly masterful opponent, but I'm willing to venture a supposition. Though, I would consider it a kindness if you don't hold me to it. Hate for one of you to start playing the game recklessly and then keel over due to some confounded board-game mishap. I'd feel guilty for weeks." And with that, he rang the bell.

The massive door, no less heavy by the exposure to Philadelphia weather and the indignities of the city itself, creaked open, yet the hand that moved it so was not made of steel. Standing amidst the weathered doorframe was the round figure of Algernon Feldspar, clad in shirtsleeves, polishing his glasses with his now-apparently-functional left hand.

I fear that if young Rupert Fohrsight had not had the lamp-post to cling to, he certainly would have been facedown in the cobblestones.

Basil and Algernon Feldspar chatted jocularly for several minutes, as was Basil's way, and, as a revelation that was somewhat of a surprise considering his tight-lipped attitude at dinner, it seemed that it was Algernon's way as well. By the time they had finished their handshakes, the two had already become great friends.

Basil motioned to Rupert and I to follow him inside the house, but Rupert cared not a whit for such invitations. "I'll not go back in that house," he called to his brother. "Not again."

"I'm terribly sorry, Rupert," Basil called back. "But I cannot possibly be asked to understand what you are saying when you stand — or rather, lean — at such a distance. I'm afraid if you wish to talk with me you must come inside."

I looked at Rupert and shrugged. I will say this, however great my fear may have been when last inside that deceptively careworn abode, so much greater was my curiosity that I found myself chasing after Basil, not wanting him to get swallowed up by the house before I had my chance at such a tour as well. I imagine a similar feeling ran through Rupert, for the young Fohrsight brother was at my heels, not wanting to miss a moment.

Algernon Feldspar had one of the more peculiar parlors I have ever seen. I often heard the expression "littered" used synonymously with "cluttered" (much to my eternal chagrin), but let me tell you true that in every aspect the room was very much literally littered with one form of taxidermy or another. Beyond the various heads and outstretched birds of prey that lined the walls, several smaller mammals lay underfoot, and Algernon was in the process of removing a handful of nuthatches and a small fox from one of the chairs in order that Basil might have a place to sit down. A quick scan of the room proved that he would have to do similar acts three times over if Rupert, I, or even the host himself had any notion of sitting down ourselves.

"I apologize," our host said, scraping a small, perfectly preserved menagerie off a sofa. "I just don't use the parlor much. Not for entertaining, leastways. This was all," he gave a vague motion to the morass of paws and claws that surrounded us, "Inherited."

"And a fascinating collection it is, too," Basil said. "But I'm far more interested in these things here." Basil pointed to a deer's head, or, rather, not so much to the cranium of the young buck shot in it's prime, but to the unusual sheets of unquantifiable material that were festooned about it's antlers. "What exactly are they?"

At this, our host visibly brightened. "Those are in fact several layers of custom-sculpted latex resin meshed together in such a way that ..." And so he went in on in such a way that only inventors and certain parents do when referring to their own beastly progeny. I will allow that I was much more interested in Rupert, who, already shaken by our adventure in the copper room, was looking incredibly uncomfortable to be in an enclosed space with a myriad of glass eyes glaring at him. His elder brother, however, no doubt used to such stares from his many years in the classroom, seemed right at home.

"Why, that's astounding, my good man!" Basil exclaimed. "The application of such a device! In the field of marine biology alone!"

This was about all poor Rupert Fohrsight could take. "Marine biology! Basil, this man shares his house with literal monsters, and you want to talk with him about fish!"

"Indeed I do," said Basil affixing upon Rupert a gaze not unlike a steel vice in temperature and effect. He then turned back to Algernon

Feldspar with a much more relaxed countenance. "However, I must admit that my two friends here have had an experience that I envy a great deal. Might I persuade to you, dear sir, to allow us to visit your copper room?"

"Certainly," said our host, and sprang to the door way (as much as one could spring, what with all the little animals underfoot), only to stop and turn around and face Rupert and myself. "That wasn't you two a moment ago was it? Oh, I am so dreadfully sorry. It's extremely difficult to see through the glass at first … but then, you'll see." Our host allowed himself a slight chuckle.

Algernon Fledspar led us down a series of narrow hallways toward a door that looked like nothing so much as the porthole to the engine of a steamship. Our host placed his hands upon the great wheel-lock that sealed the door in place, but then, as before, stopped what he was doing and turned around.

"You do realize I'm not supposed to show anyone this. My employers were quite explicit on that matter," he seemed a bit worried, as if his employers themselves were on the other side of the door, laying in wait should he open it while others were present.

"And I respect the great burden this must have laid upon you. However, I would ask you to remember that these two fine gentlemen have already seen what lies beyond in the copper room. As for myself, seeing as how they have described the room to me, I already have an inkling of what lies within. Better to have me carry the reality of this situation about in my mind than some fantastical approximation. Better to have the fantastical firsthand, wouldn't you agree?"

"I suppose you do have a point," said Algernon, as he turned the wheel and wrenched open the door with no small amount of effort.

The inside of the immense copper room looked amazingly less sinister than when Rupert and I had come through the window. The room itself was unchanged, but illuminated by our host's gas lantern, the menacing inhabitants of the room now reflected a friendly glint off their copper skin. Most curious was the drain in the center of the floor, a detail that, in the darkness of our previous visit, Rupert and I had failed to see.

"Are you familiar, gentlemen," Algernon said, as the rest of us wandered about the room to take it all into account at greater detail. "With the recent innovations in sub-marine transportation?"

"No…" Rupert began, with a look on his face that betrayed a feeling of being lost and confused. No doubt a similar express was painted on my own.

"That's because there hasn't been any." The tumultuous echo of the room added to our host's authority. "However, my employer, a quite wealthy ship builder who unfortunately shall remain nameless, has several men working on the project as we speak. He's of the belief that submarine transportation will be the way of the future taking humanity from one continent to another without having to worry about storms, or indeed any sort of weather at all. And he reasons that once such vehicles are able to transport people safely, there will naturally be a need to walk about the ocean floor once we're down there. Hence," he said, motioning to the copperplate monstrosities.

"But you said the technology had no recent innovations," Basil said, adjusting his tie in the orange reflection of one of the mechanisms.

"There hasn't been. Most of them still sink."

"Isn't that what they're supposed to do?" countered Basil.

"Yes," said our host, with a slight tinge of melancholy. "But I do imagine they are supposed to come up eventually."

"Mayhap they are just waiting for the right time?" suggested Basil with a weak, if hopeful, grin.

"I don't…don't understand…" sputtered Rupert. "But…your…your arm…?"

"Oh, you mean at the party! Were you there? I don't remember seeing you…"

"No, Rupert prefers to attend parties unseen," said Basil.

Algernon gave them both a quizzical look, then continued. "Yes, well. I had wanted to test the out the new suit in a long-term trial. So I donned the suit at the wee hours of the morning and proceeded to keep it on for the rest of the day. With the exception of a delicate incident preparing lunch, I had gotten through most of the day with out any damage or strain. But then came the realization that Lord Canterbury's invitation to dinner, which there was no way I could miss. Not wanting to arouse suspicions, yet at the same time unwilling to cut short my test, I decided to wear only the left arm under an oversized suit. Due to that new insulation I was telling Mr. Fohrsight about in the parlor, the arm itself is not that bulky. I surmised that everyone else would be too distracted by the suspicious brandy that Lord Canterbury insists on serving with the venison to notice anything unusual about my arm.

"In fact, with the exception of a stuck wheel that made its presence known right before dinner, the arm worked out beautifully.

"You know gentlemen, it's good that you got out when you did. I was about to flood the room to do some underwater testing." Algernon pointed to the multitude of faucets dangling from the ceiling. He then moved his finger to a door similar to the one we had just entered from, only smaller. It was open now, but looked as if it fitted right over the sole window in the room, sealing it tight. "I was letting the chamber air out during dinner. But I would have had to seal it up again before releasing the water."

"So you build diving suits," I said, attempting to put my thoughts in order aloud. "For submarines that haven't been built yet?"

"Quite so," Basil said. "Quite so. My dear friend Algernon here is a futurist. The poor fellow is cursed to build machinery who's use is dependant wholly on the technology of others."

"It's not half as bad as he makes it sound," Algernon said. "Why, these latest suits are merely modifications of a design I did for a previous employer. I fancy I'll see an adequate submarine before I see what he had in mind."

"And what else could they be for?" I wondered. Looking at them, I could not think of a single purpose other than the sea, and said so.

"Space," the futurist said, in the flat tones of a skeptic. "Damn batty fool swore he was going to build a rocketship."

Pirates of the Crimson Sands

By Justin R. Macumber

(Originally aired on September 19th, 2009. www.deadrobotssociety.com/2009/09/19/ pirates-of-the-crimson-sand-an-audio-adventure)

*D*on't be so grit," Shana said as she planted her small brown hands on her hips and dug her feet into the rust-colored desert sand beneath her. "We go for the *Skulper*."

A man twice her height and three times her age glared down at her with his one fierce eye, and hard sunlight winked off the studs in his nose and upper lip as he frowned. "Ain't grit, Cap'n," he said. "It's wit, sharp as ever. The *Skulper* is a tag fools run, and we all knows it. We should go for the *Behemoth*. Loads of sparkle in that."

"True nuff," another man said. He wasn't much taller than Shana, but he could have held several of her in his hairy stomach as it poked out from beneath the shirt that was stretched taut over his chest and gut. "I'm just a bosun, Shana. You the Cap'n, so we follow you as ever, but Braka's true. We should go for the *Behemoth*."

Thrusting her lower lip out, Shana clomped over and shoved a finger in the fat man's belly. "You grit then too, Chim. What, you think the *Behemoth* got just one cannon on it? We gonna sail up and gut her pretty as we please? And how many swabs we lose last time we try that? Half? You talk tag fool run? Goin' after that *Behemoth* with what few we got now, that be a tag fool."

Braka sighed roughly and ran a calloused hand through the sun-bleached hair that sprang from his head like a desert fire. After a moment of grumpy silence he said, "True and wit, Cap'n. True and wit."

Shana saw Chim glance at Braka out of the corner of his eye, and she could tell that neither of them was entirely convinced, not that she could blame them. She wasn't being entirely honest with them, and they'd sniffed it out. She knew the only thing that held them back from calling her on it was their respect for her family and her rank.

At that moment she missed her dad in a way that was deep and painful. The crew had never given him backtalk. Then again, he would've been upfront with them and told them that the mission wasn't really for gems and engine juice, but for medicine to save a sick little boy. He would've told them his decision was based on emotion and nothing more, and they would have accepted it. But her dad was dead, and her hold over the crew wasn't strong enough yet to show them any weakness, even if they would've understood it.

"Fore we make a run at the big sparkles," she said, looking at each of them in turn, "we gotta get our names back, our reps. That last hit nearly did us in, and every scag around here knows it. If we make a solid hit or two, it'll all be blue skies again."

"I hope you're true," Chim said.

Shana glanced over at the bosun. "Ain't I ever?"

Chim's eyes twinkled like he wanted to laugh, but his lips clamped together and caught the sound before it could escape. "Enough so, yeah," he replied.

Since her dad's death Shana had stepped up and become as good a Cap'n as she was able, a right solid splinter off the old man. But, in doing so she'd lost some of the humor that had once been as much a part of her as her long black hair and grey eyes. Above all else she demanded respect, so she didn't deal well with laughter at her expense. Not even from Chim. More than one bar rat had come away with a blackened eye and broken nose after making a joke loud enough for her to hear.

Seeing that she'd won the day, the taut skin of her dark face softened and she smiled. When she did, she felt like an actual fifteen-year-old again, and not like the gruff old skipper she'd had to become. "Good nuff," she told them. "Da always said, 'Be right more than wrong.'"

"He was wit," Braka said.

Chim nodded in agreement.

"Mark you true," the little captain said. "Now that we has our course, get my ship made worthy and the crew chinned up. Aye?"

Chim and Braka snapped their heels together and saluted. "Aye aye, Cap'n!" they replied in unison before hustling off to the creaking hangar that stood at their backsides like a fossil from a bygone era.

Shana watched them go for a moment, and then walked toward a small shed that sat in the sand a short distance away. Scarred from decades of howling winds that blew sporadically through the desert without rhyme or reason, the hut's metal walls leaned dangerously inward, but they remained standing, and she knew that somehow they always would.

As she entered the hut she heard humming, and beneath that the sound of sand and wood rubbing together. A grin rose to her face, but then the overwhelming heat nearly burned it away. The hut was as hot as a wheatwork's oven, and instantly beads of sweat broke out across the coffee colored skin of her cheeks and arms.

"That you, Sissy?" a tiny voice asked.

Her grin widening, Shana stepped through the curtains that fell from the ceiling just inside the door. Once past it she had a clear view of the hut's interior, and it looked the same as it ever had. Layers of blankets were spread across half the room's sandy floor, and on them were piled pillows beyond number. The rest of the floor was uncovered, and that was where her little brother sat, wooden boats in each tiny hand. She could only imagine what epic battles he'd been playing out in the sand.

"Of course it's me, Sweets," she replied.

The young boy frowned. "I hates that name, and you knows it."

"I do," Shana replied as she settled onto the floor next to him. "But Sweets is much choicer than Swain."

Her brother thrust out his lower lip, his hands shook as he held onto his boats, and a small tear rolled past his nose. "Only Da calls me Sweets."

For a brief moment she wanted to reach out and clout the boy, both for his stubbornness and for his tears, but the thought left her as quickly as it had come, and instead she reached out and rubbed his bony little shoulder.

"You're true," she said. "Only Da can call you that. I'll know better nexty."

Like the sun rising out from a reaving cloud, Swain smiled. "You bring me any sparkles?"

"Not much glitter to be got," she replied as she leaned over to one side, "but, I did brings you this."

From a pocket in her billowy pants she pulled a toy. It was similar in size and shape to the wooden boats her brother held, but the new one was made of metal, and the paint on its hull was still shiny and fresh.

"Ow!" Swain said, bouncing up and down in the sand as his eyes caught sight of it. He tilted forward to grab it, but a coughing fit suddenly ripped through him, and he fell onto his side.

Shana scuttled over as quickly as she could and took hold of his shoulders. Powerful coughs shook his chest, and in them she could hear what sounded like wet paper tearing. Flecks of blood coated his lips.

"My breath," he said between coughs. "Get... me... my breath."

Even before the first word was out Shana was reaching into the pockets of his tattered linen pants. She felt metal against her fingers, and from his left pocket she pulled a small, brass object. Swain weakly grabbed for it and put it in his mouth. Small white wisps of vapor rose from the object, and after a few moments his coughing jag ended.

"Thanks, Sissy," he said, too drained to rise from the blankets. "I know... I know we don't have many breaths left. Sorry for having to use one now."

Shana shifted around and tucked pillows beneath his head. "No need for that. I'll get more, no worries. You my li'l bra, Swain. I may not be Da, but I'll do my true best to care for ya."

"Forever and all?" Swain asked, his tiny face slowly clearing up.

"Forever and all."

He smiled, but when he looked down at his empty hands his eyes went wide and he started struggling like an up-turned turtle. "My new boat, Sissy! I lost it!"

Shana shushed at him and picked the toy up from the ground. "It's right here."

Contentment spread across his face as his tiny fingers closed around the metal ship. As he brought it close to his chest, he closed his eyes and sighed.

"Now," Shana said as she got to her knees, "I has to sail. You be good?"

"Good and true, Sissy." Swain smiled, but the small blood droplets that freckled his face undid the expression's sweetness.

Shana pulled her shirt tail out, shifted forward, and used the material to wipe his face clean. Once that was done she held his head and watched him for a moment. His skin was cold against her own, and she knew that no matter how warm the hut got, it couldn't be warm enough.

Swain opened his eyes and looked up at her. She marveled at their light blue clarity, like an untroubled summer sky.

"I love you, Sissy," he said.

A sob nearly tore from her throat, but she held it in check and nodded. "And more love back to you, bra."

As he closed his eyes again, he said, "S'okay. I trig you call me Sweets. You're not Da, but you care for me like he did."

"I do as I can. If you needs for anything while I sail, ring the bell, and Momma May will come a'runnin'."

"All righty," Swain replied as he rolled over and curled up in a nest of blankets and pillows. He said something else, but his voice was little more than a whisper as he put his thumb in his mouth and began snoring.

Shana smiled, rose to her feet, and then turned toward the curtains and the door beyond. Minutes later she was inside the hangar and on her boat. When she looked down at the deck of her ship, the *Cloudstrike*, she flashed a wicked grin. The grin was echoed back at her by a dozen grizzled faces, faces she loved and had known since birth.

"Alright, ya flea-ridden sundogs," she said, propping a foot up on the railing that ran across the front of the bridge deck, "when last we sailed, twice our number crewed this boat, but that's the past. Today marks our future, so chin up and keep a salty eye for what's to come, aye? Yon distant *Skulper* might seem a light tussle, but she's got sparkles in her belly and it needs be ours, aye?!"

A chorus of "Aye!" rang up at her.

"Then step witty, ya mongrels! Bosun, lash the hindmost. I want us swimming in spoils come supper!"

Chim grinned, and several golden teeth glinted in the sunlight. "Aye aye, Cap'n!" He then turned to face the crew that stood behind him. "Taverd and Russa, stoke the plasma drive! Doog, you and Neven trig the wing stabilizers! Keiff, up to the crow with ya. As soon as the *Skulper* comes on screen, I better hear you bellow. The rest of ya, get to your stations and stand ready!"

Swarthy bodies moved across the deck of the *Cloudstrike*, and soon Shana could feel a surge of power thrum through the ship's hull. It was a sensation that was as familiar to her as her own breathing. The *Cloudstrike* was the only home she'd ever truly known.

Behind her Braka popped the wheelhouse hatch and said, "You tendin' the helm on this hit, Cap'n?"

She nodded firmly. "So long as I've two hands to me, Braka, they'll be on that wheel."

The older man nodded and cleared the hatchway. As Shana entered the wheelhouse, the chilled air sent a shiver through her. Moments later every panel and screen was activated, and a constellation of lights blinked across the helm control station.

"The drives are trim, Cap'n," Braka said as he read a display. "So say the stabilizers. Keiff's called a clear sky. We're answerin' all bells. *Cloudstrike* is fit and ready."

Nodding, she put her left hand on the large metal wheel that dominated the center of the room and reached forward with her right hand to press a red button. The ship's gravity lifts kicked into life with a powerful burst of sand and sound. When the horizontal stabilizers showed a clean lift, she grabbed the throttle and pushed it upward. Bells rang through the air, and the *Cloudstrike* sailed forward in a smooth rush.

Once the hangar was cleared, she had an unfettered view of the Saara Basin, but that wasn't saying much. All she could see were shifting dunes. Scarlet sand stretched out beneath blue-white skies, and there was little to break up the monotony of it. Even so, Shana felt a kinship with the desert that let her see it as few others could. Its sand pumped through her veins and surely as her father's blood.

Braka turned a knob next to the forward radar display. "Zepple had better been trim with us."

"He's been trim so far, yeah?"

"Aye, but there's ever a first time not, and I'd rather we not be it."

"For the shiny we flipped him, he'd better have steered us wit."

The older man sighed. "Mayhap so. . . Mayhap so."

The *Cloudstrike* sailed through the Basin for nearly an hour, its keel well above the dune line, before Shana's right hand pulled on the wheel and turned the ship to starboard. The sand began to thin as they left the Basin and entered Azazel Ridge, until eventually it was replaced by flat and seemingly endless hardscrabble dirt. Rocks and cacti littered the ground like a demon's garden.

"Cap'n, Keiff spies an active radar pinging to the north-northwest."

"Is it the *Skulper*?"

Braka shook his head. "Not sure less we ping 'em back, but won't much else be grit enough to sail these wastes."

"Alright then. Let's go."

Pushing up on the helm, the *Cloudstrike* shifted its course slightly to port. Shana then grabbed a lever and pulled it down several inches. In response the ship dropped altitude until it was only a meter above the rushing ground.

"Cap'n, we're getting a friend-foe signal now. It's definitely the

Skulper."

She grinned. "Get the crew set for boarding. I'll zoom her so fast she can't bring cannon to bear. Once we're locked to her I want everyone over the side and looking for sparkle. Her crew should be few, so no needs to rampage. Kill if we must, but otherwise truss 'em and lock 'em way."

"Aye aye, Cap'n." As he turned, alarm bells suddenly began to ring out. The older pirate glanced down with his one good eye, and a moment later he said, "Ah, no, this ain't well. Zepple either ain't trim, or someone else weren't trim with him, 'cause the *Skulper* got two gun skiffs flankin' her."

Cold water filled Shana's middle. "Have they spied us?"

Braka looked at Keiff's report and said, "Don't seem to. Not yet anyways. We gonna break off, Cap'n?"

Part of her wanted to nod and turn the ship around, but there was too much at stake to let a small thing like gunships quake her innards. "We still hit her, Braka. Too much juice been spent gettin' here, and we needs the sparkles too much. 'Sides, ain't never seen a skiff that could tend with *Cloudstrike*. Not even two. So, go man a cannon. I want those gunnies downed 'fore they even know we're hittin'."

Braka saluted and was out of the wheelhouse in record time.

Gritting her teeth, Shana dropped her ship's altitude even lower. Cactus tips whapped at her keel so quickly that it almost sounded like rain, and she could feel it in the soles of her bare feet. Behind her was a wash of flying cactus milk and needles. Flying so low went against her instinct as a captain, but in the broken expanse of Azazel's Ridge it was the only way to avoid radar detection.

To her left was a screen that showed the *Skulper* and her escorts. They were several kilometers out, but the distance was narrowing quickly. Her left hand held a white-knuckled grip on the helm as she steered the ship down into their wake.

"Cap'n!" Braka said over the ship's intercom. "The cannon are ready!"

"Unseal the starboard gunports on my mark," she replied.

"Aye aye!"

Shana kept one eye on her passive sensors and the other on her flight screen. She didn't want to sneak up on the gunships only to end up hitting a boulder and flipping through the ridge like a flaming cartwheel. After several minutes of dodging debris and slipping through engine wash, the *Cloudstrike* was behind and below the gun skiff on the *Skulper's* port side, as close as she could get without triggering their proximity alarms.

"Fire in five!" she yelled as she grabbed the throttle and shoved it upward. The ship leapt beneath her in a savage flood of power. "Four!" She turned the helm to port and exited the skiff's wake. "Three!" She moved the altitude lever up, and the *Cloudstrike* rose higher into the air. "Two!" The skiff shifted its heading suddenly, but Shana's boat was already beside it, boxing it in. "One!" Four gunports opened along the *Cloudstrike's* starboard hull. "Fire!" The ship shuddered as four Gauss cannons shot heavy rounds across the short distance that separated the two ships. The skiff never had a chance. Seconds later it hit the ground in a shower of broken steel and fire.

The element of surprise now gone, Shana knew that getting the second skiff would require skill and a steady hand. She tried putting herself in the place of the skiff's captain, thinking what he might think, making her plans on what he'd think they would do. After a few seconds she had an idea.

With a grin she hit the afterburner button on the throttle, and like a rocket the *Cloudstrike* blasted forward until it was ahead of the Skulper. She then spun the helm to starboard with a hard yank, which brought them directly in front of the second skiff.

"All hands!" she said in the intercom that hung near her mouth. "Brace for impact!"

Skiffs were small ships, Shana knew, built mainly for speed and agility. Guns could be stowed along each side of them to add a bit of bite without limiting their movement, but one thing they couldn't add was armor. A heavy, ironclad skiff was a useless skiff. Even knowing that, she had a lump in her throat when she reached for the throttle.

"Da, if you're out there," she whispered, "let this work."

Without allowing herself more time to think about it, she pulled her throttle down as hard as she could and then hit the switch that triggered the ship's breaking flaps. Immediately she was shoved forward as the *Cloudstrike* radically reduced its speed. Behind them, the skiff turned hard to starboard as its captain saw what was happening, but by then it was too late. The skiff slammed against the rear of the *Cloudstrike* and was broken nearly in half by the impact. A shudder ran down her ship as they collided, and alarms rang out, but Shana saw that her hull integrity held firm. There'd be a dent or two to repair later, but they'd come out of the impact better than she'd thought they would.

Ahead of them, the *Skulper* was racing as fast as its engines would carry them, but she shook her head as she pushed the throttle upward again. The *Skulper* could have had a half day's head start and it still wouldn't have gotten away. Cargo transports were built for hauling freight, not for racing.

"Braka, get ready to board!" she said into the intercom.

"Aye, Cap'n"

She turned her radio on and then said, "Skulper, heave to!"

"Chaff you!" the *Skulper's* captain replied. "We've got guns aplenty on this boat!"

"We got you, *Skulper*! Both your escorts have been planted! Heave to and you might get to live."

A laugh rang across the comm channel. "Promises from a pirate! What a lark! The day I thinks you scags are trim is the day they put me under!"

"Mayhap you true, *Skulper*," Shana said. "Don't cry I didn't warn you."

She shut the radio off and refocused her eyes on her target. Her throbbing engines brought her to them in less than two minutes. The *Skulper* tried throwing them off by tacking back and forth, but the lumbering transport didn't have the agility to match the *Cloudstrike*. As soon as they were broadside to broadside, she hit a button that fired a series of magnetic grappling hooks. Once they established a lock, powerful winches reeled the carbon nanofiber ropes in. The two ships' hulls clanged together seconds later.

"All hands, begin boarding!" she yelled before activating the powerful magnetic clamp that would keep both vessels secured to each other. Once the automated guidance systems were engaged, she was out of the wheelhouse and running down the ramp to the lower deck. Ahead of her she saw her crew as they scurried across the carbon ropes to the *Skulper*. Wind whipped past her furiously, but with a practiced jump she was on the ropes and running across them like a crazed acrobat. As her feet hit the foreign deck, she pulled the pistol that was holstered to her right hip.

She'd expected a bit of fighting to greet her crew, and she wasn't disappointed. Several well armed marines fended them off from a hatchway that led to the bridge. Her men tried to shake them loose, but their number just wasn't enough to pound them out.

Seeing no other choice, she took matters into her own petite hands and started running. The marines saw her coming, but her small size and youthful speed was too much for them, and moments later she let fly two sonic grenades through the hatch. She nearly went deaf when they detonated. The hull rang like church bells all around her. But, the marines also stopped firing, and her crew swarmed past her before she could rise to her feet.

Marines deeper in the ship tried to stand against them, but by then her crew had the momentum, and soon they'd secured the bridge. The *Skulper*'s captain, when Shana finally saw him, wasn't nearly as defiant as he'd been earlier. Tight ropes around his hands, arms, and legs saw to that. He had no other crew on the bridge with him.

"You so grit," she said with a grin.

The captain looked at her with a scowl. "You talk big for one so wee."

Braka lashed out and smacked him hard across the face. "Mind your tone, scag."

Shana approached the tied up captain and said, "Mayhap I'm wee, but I'm not the one trussed up like a winter goose. Now, be good and give us the keys to your hold. If I has to ask twice, Braka will hit you again, and not so gentle that time."

Looking up at the large man that towered over him, and then at the armed pirates that sneered through scarred faces, the captain shook his head and replied. "Sigma-Five-Epsilon."

"There now. Tweren't so hard, yeah? Braka, take the crew and secure all the sparkle we can carry. Dump the rest for the scavages."

"Aye aye, Cap'n" Braka said before gathering the men and exiting the bridge.

Once they were gone, she turned to the captain and said, "Now, my little goose, I know you also has a secret hidey hole up here, and all you need to open it is your voice. Open 'er up, and smartly, or I'll get really nasty."

"Don't be grit," he said. "That's meant for a hospital, it is! A children's hospital at that!"

Shana laughed and shook her head. "You think I'm grit? You got no med supplies writ on your manifest. I looked. The black market is where you've plotted these to go. You knows it, as do I, so don't cuff with me. You're no mercy saint. Now open it."

"You're a monster," the captain said.

In a rush Shana stood before him and had her pistol pressed again his right temple so hard that it dimpled his skin. His face was level with her own, and she could smell traces of soap on him, but beneath that was more than a little fear. "Mayhap so, scag, but I'm the one standin' here with the gun, so open the hold. Now."

The captain gritted his teeth hard, and his cheek muscles jumped, but when Shana pulled down the hammer on her pistol he said, "Red sky at night, sailor's delight."

Behind her she could hear the sound of rushing air as a vacuum seal broke. When she turned she saw that a small panel had opened on the port wall, and in it was a box. The container was cold to the touch, but she was able to grab it and pull it into the light of the bridge without any trouble. Red medical symbols were painted on its sides, and they made Shana smile. When she opened it and saw what seemed like a hundred brass mouth pieces, each one identical to the one she'd pulled from her brother's pocket hours before, her smile widened.

"Ow, ain't you pretty," she said.

"I hope you get not one copper bolt for the lot of them," the captain said behind her.

Shana turned and fixed him with a cold stare. "These ain't for sale, scag. I have a love who needs these, so to me they're worth more than all the sparkle in the world."

The captain's expression softened for a moment as understanding dawned on him, but then he sneered and rolled his eyes. "If lies help your head rest at night, so be it."

A reply rose to her lips, but she knew her words would be wasted breath, so she kept her mouth closed as she walked over to him. He looked at her with eyes filled with venom, but as she raised her pistol he began to plead for his life. He fell silent when she struck the butt of her pistol against the side of his head, and he was unconscious before his kneeling body hit the deck.

"Braka," she said into the comm wrapped around her left wrist. "Everything trig?"

"Blue skies all the way, Cap'n. Our hold is brimmin'. Want we should set charges as we leave?"

Shana thought about it, but she shook her head. "No. This old tug's no menace to us, and if they do drift to harbor any word they say about us will only get our reps up again. Leave her be."

"Aye aye, Cap'n. See you back on the *Cloudstrike* shortly."

Shana nodded as she lowered her wrist. After closing the medical supply box and tucking it under her left arm, she left the bridge of the *Skulper* and retraced her steps to her ship. With any luck, the winds back to their hangar would be fair, and she'd be home in time to read her brother a story before he fell asleep. Her dad had read to them both once upon a time, and she was only too happy to carry on doing it. Her brother meant more to her than anything else, and she knew that she would do anything for him, no apologies asked, and none given.

The Man in the Rain

Dedicated to the memory of Herbert T. Fuqua

BY J. DANIEL SAWYER

(ORIGINALLY PODCAST: 08/01/08 AT
SCULPTGOD.JDSAWYER.NET/?P=16)

"*D*une kaffe, tall, no crème."

"Si, senor." The small, leathery barista dressed like Juan Valdez nodded his head and pulled the coffee from the antique tapped carafe on the bar. The rain flowed down like a waterfall, thick enough to obscure the other side of the narrow dirt and gravel road. The tourist bureau said it always rained like this during January. "Kaffe."

"How much?"

"Dies."

"No, no. Quatro."

"Siete."

"Cinco."

"Si, senor. Cinco."

"Gracias." Mondu laid down a five-credit chit. The money was pretty much the only modern thing allowed in public here. He wrapped his fingers around the base of his coffee cup and flipped his oilskin up over his head, his boots squishing in the mud as he ran across the road to his shop.

The water against the palm frond thatch chattered like cloud of courting locusts. Per local regulations, the building was constructed of traditional reed materials, with only the barest of Fullerine and steel reinforcement to protect against earthquakes and looting. The nature preserve in the Brazilian basin didn't just preserve nature in a more or less arrested state, it preserved material and human culture too. The twenty-second century's answer to the Amish lived here—men and women and various intermittents who wished to experience life as it once was in the wilds of the Amazon, along with a handful who wanted to disappear for a little while.

Coffee on the counter, oilskin on the hook, Mondu hopped over the low gate and stepped up to the register. A customer—short, Asian, and heavily scarred—sat on the wicker chair in the small lobby. Seeing Mondu return from his coffee break, the man stood, meticulously folded his newspaper, and strode over to him like he'd forgotten to take his rejuvs for a few years. Knotty joints—a man with arthritis eating his bones like a...what did they call those fish? Prianahs, piranhas, something like that. Poor cunter. Somebody should've given him the facts of life while he could have taken advantage for cheap. Nanobot joint lubrication was painless—leg transplants weren't.

"Helgretes, amigo," Spanish never set well in his mouth, and he didn't dare try Portugese. English was bad enough—the mishmash creole he'd learned in the bowels of the Nigerian IT world was his first language, and he liked it that way. Efficient, short phrases stolen from English, Afrikaans, Mandarin, and half a dozen programming languages cobbled together to express thought elegantly, simply, and directly. Still, he had to make himself understood as best he could—as long as he worked the counter. "What service can we give for you, sir?"

The man set his Panama hat down on the glass-top display case—real glass, too, not the cheaper and stronger Fullerine composite—and tapped his finger over a gaudy native bracelet. The term "native" was used loosely—the Yanomami and Awa maintained show settlements as tourist attractions, but aside from their sentimental and commercial devotion to family history, they had long since melted into the South American Confederation's pot.

"Que é o preço?" A voice like cracked sheepskin. Mondu could understand the question perfectly well—programming AIs for hierarchical metabase bots required a dozen different languages. Speaking it...well, that was quite another matter.

"Sid sid, fifteen on'a ticket."

"You speak English?"

"Sid sid, I do."

"Good. I need this here."

"Having a ticket?" Mondu hadn't seen the man in before, but the boss might have dealt with him. The item he wanted wasn't one Mondu had logged in, so it was possible the customer was trying to reclaim a pawned item.

"What is a ticket?"

"Returning customer..."

"No. I have not been here before. How much?"

"Twenty-five, less gots you something to hock."

The customer rifled through his pockets and pulled out a ring, setting it on the table. "Here."

"Gold." Mondu placed the ring under the scannerscope, sampling its purity and checking to make sure it didn't have a tracking mark that he'd have to remove. "Good good. Straight swap plus ticket. Good for you?"

"That will suffice."

Mondu printed the claim number, carefully and by hand, on the ticket alongside its trade value. The man would have three days to reclaim the property before it went on general sale. He listed the price value of the swapped bracelet as the redemption value, and handed it to the customer.

The man took it without meeting his gaze, and shuffled out as if every step pained him. Aside from his gait, he didn't look that old—but then, neither did Mondu. Cheap rejuv kept looks from meaning much—had done since as long ago as Mondu could remember. People looked the age they wanted to, and that's all there was to it.

The rain still came. It felt safe. The thing he'd missed most about life back home after he left was the rain. His city, Calabar, grew up right out of the middle of the rainforest in southern Nigeria where, when the air wasn't thick enough to chew, it rained. The rain always felt right. Here, even though between the canopy and the clouds he rarely saw the sun, the rain felt close. It felt like all the parts of home that he actually missed—and there weren't many of those.

The thatch did leak a bit, here and there. The boss kept a bunch of cotton towels under the counter to keep the glass clean. Mondu wiped the glass down, and then settled on a stool at the end of the counter, leaning up against the reed wall. He couldn't really tell where his sweat ended and the humidity and rain began, but he didn't really care. His coffee, still warm enough to drink, stank of too much cinnamon and over roasting, but the bitter smoothness slid down his gullet like chicha.

From his perch he had a view, through the door and the rain, of the cafe patio. The array of umbrella-hooded small tables were usually abandoned—at least since the rains started—but not this week.

The man arrived in a Fedora hat and trench coat to keep off the rain—far too warm for this weather. For the third day in a row, he drank his coffee with his hat set on the table as if reverence required his head remain uncovered in the presence of the ramshackle canteen knocked up out of corrugated metal and banana leaves. Rain or shine—mostly rain—he showed up precisely at 1200 and left precisely at 1250, as if he were billing by a psychiatrist's watch. A tourist might have stayed two days waiting for his guide to arrive for his trek through the jungle. A professional's schedule would have varied depending on the needs of the day. This man was more precise, and three days was too many.

Mondu studied him for a while, wondering if he would stand and come into the shop. For days now the stranger's eyes had scanned the environs as if he were waiting for someone. All that time, the one place Mondu hadn't caught him looking was at the old hockshop. If he was here for one of the boss's special services and wanted the boss to do it personally, he'd be waiting a while till the boss got back from his jaunt to Sao Paulo to see his mistress.

The afternoon stretched on. No further foot traffic came in through the door. A couple of calls rang in on the antique phone—actually rang, like a bell—freelance guides checking in for loitering clients, tourists calling in advance asking if they had steel machetes, and the like.

He wished he had a computer. He hadn't been on the net in almost six months; for all he knew the universe had been and gone in that time. He wanted a new wetware cube and a terminal to hook up to it just as it was decanted. Use the delicate chemical signals to coax the fiber lines into place, stimulate it right to lay down the language strata, etch the programming onto the protoneurons, and come out the other end with a custom AI well suited for the ordered task. He missed the communion with the emerging mind, the challenge and precision of the work—the artistry.

Night came on with a slackening of the rain. Mondu closed up the shop and made his way through the file room where he took his dinner of tapir, Brazil nuts, banana chips, and mango before climbing into his hammock. It wasn't much, but it came free with the job. Besides, if he was going to live for a six month rotation in a nature preserve he might as well get all he could out of the experience.

It didn't hurt that it was a more comfortable way to sleep than any bed he'd ever used.

Morning found him snoring lightly with a cockroach on his head. Sometime during the night he'd shifted his arms, flopping them outside the deep valley created in the cloth by his body, and holding open what was otherwise effectively a cocoon for keeping out the bugs. When he cracked his eyes open against the light, he saw the sectioned abdomen of the creature squatting comfortably over his left pupil. Nothing in the world looked bigger than an Amazonian cockroach, but when you woke up enough mornings with them sitting on you, or crawling over your coffee maker, they lost their effect. They really weren't much more than small, creepy-looking six-legged birds. He flicked it off his forehead and rolled out of bed, landing squarely on his feet.

The rain wasn't falling, but the humidity hadn't taken much notice. It's suffocating moisture meant the night had offered no relief from the heat, so he stripped down to skin and soaped yesterday's grime off his body, then dusted himself head to toe with antifungal talc before slithering back into a pair of camo BDUs and a three-sizes-too-big white silk button-up. He grabbed a papaya out of the tree that grew out his back window and chewed it over while he opened the shop and planned his day.

Not that there was much to plan. No tour groups were due through for another four days, and the casino wouldn't be open until they were in town, which meant there probably wouldn't be anyone coming through the shop who needed to go into hock to cover their debts. It was even less likely that people would be through for souvenirs or deals selected out of the display cases of previously pawned items.

If business was slow again today, he might tempt fate and slide out early with a blowgun and a machete for a walk through the jungle. He still had a few hunting tags for the season—perhaps he'd bag a tapir and make a bonfire for a spit-roast. The village folk might like the odd excuse to gather during the long stretches of rain. He didn't know for sure—they weren't a sociable set. But, even if only a few showed up it would help. He was running low on books to read during the evenings.

Mondu found a mount plate in the boss's office, and used it to display the gold ring from the day before. Front and center in the display case, he should be able to move it when the next pack of tourists came through—it might make a good wedding ring, and there were always one or two couples looking to stage memorable nuptials in front of a banyan tree or down by the river.

As the day dragged on, Mondu perched himself up on his

195 | The Man in the Rain

stool against the wall and digested a trade paper he'd printed up in Rio—no PPDs allowed for residents in the preserve, so all his reading material was dead tree. There was no lack of trees to print them on, not in the Amazon. Nor, he thought as he nipped back to the old-fashioned outhouse privy, for toilet paper. No saddles and suction here, no built-in bidets, just a handful of paper to get enough of the crap off to keep his ass from staining his shorts. It wasn't really sanitary—but then, what in the 20th century had been?

As he was marking his place in the book and pulling up his drawers, he heard a loud rapping on the counter.

"Hola?"

"Si Senor. Une momento, por favor." Mondu grabbed his book and meandered out from between the hallway of inventory shelves and around the corner to the front of the store.

There, at the display case-cum-counter, stood the man in the rain. His white Fedora rested loosely in his hand on the counter, and his half-bald head glistening with water beads under the hot, old-style incandescents.

"You speak English?" An American. In the six months he'd been here he hadn't seen a lot of Americans.

"Sid sid. I speak English okay."

"Good. This ring here, how much?"

"Twenty."

The man nodded, then he chewed his bottom lip thoughtfully. "And this here?"

"The machete, or the stylus?"

"The machete. I have some hunting I may need to do."

"Do you have a license? We supply them."

"I do. Freedom of movement is important to me."

Mondu's face broke into a broad smile. The man was looking for one of the boss's special services—a passport, probably, but it could be national ID, or a false account, or any number of other things. It was a chance to do something fun. "We have many tools available."

The customer nodded. They understood each other. "My needs are specific. As you can see from my suit, cleanliness is important to me."

"Will you need privileges?"

"No. Just cleanliness."

"Understand. Take this," Mondu handed over a pencil and a paper form. Based on the boxes he checked, the man didn't just want a passport, he wanted an identity. He checked the whole sheaf—biometrics included.

"This should do me fine."

"Price is..."

"Not a problem." He produced a deck of cards from his pocket and set it on the table. With his left hand he cut them, then dealt the first card to Mondu, face up. "Put this through your assay—it should settle the bill."

A playing card? Mondu slid the card off the tabletop and threaded it into the assay scanner he'd used the day before to determine the molecular structure of the ring.

"Set it to x-band."

Mondu complied. Under the low level X-ray bombardment, the card showed platinum in the ink. A lot of platinum. The boss set the store's exchange rate at twelve hundred credits per ounce. Mondu looked back up at his customer. "You have how much?"

"Two decks." Mondu nodded and did some quick mental calculations. It would more than cover the fee.

"Two decks for a full ID jacket."

"How long?"

"Three hours."

"Done."

"Stand in front of the register, please." Mondu flipped open the camera port concealed in the cash register. "Eyes straight forward." The customer complied, and Mondu snapped the photo.

The customer donned his hat and tipped the brim to Mondu. "I'll see you this evening." Without another word, he turned and walked out.

Three hours was just enough time to work up a full ID jacket.

Mondu's fingers danced between the scattered devices on the boss's desk in the office. Taking the photo and laying it into the watermarked paper with the laser etcher, he carefully laid down a false name, encoded false issuing authority information into the threads laced through the paper for that purpose, looked up a copy of the notary's signature from three years ago and carefully forged it—this was the part that took the longest. It required an actual signature, not a printed duplicate, and it had to be autonomic. The difference between a deliberate signature and a thoughtless stroke of a pen from muscle memory showed up in the way ink bled into the paper where the pen hesitated. That wouldn't pass muster.

A lot of the fine details were like that—little touches here and there that had to be done by hand. It was the *imperfections* that authenticated the documentation—the right kinds of random defects in the right places. The ID card, the marriage license and death certificate for a fictitious wife, the passport, the digital thumb copies of all of them complete with crypt256m keys, and the biometrics jacket made the package complete. Once Mondu had it all in order he uploaded the keys to the SAA keyserver, from where they'd propagate across the different customs authority systems.

Biometrics were the easy part. DNA was easy enough to wrap or rewrite, fingerprints were easy enough to burn off or replace, irises were easily altered, even the bones of the facial structure or a person's gait could be tweaked enough that post-singularity intelligence couldn't recognize them. As such, biometrics cards were linked to the cryptkeys that didn't change, and travelers were required to renew every two years to update any changes that they'd made through cosmetic, medical, prosthetic, or cyberorganic procedures. When the customer returned, he could sample the fingerprints, the iris scan, the DNA, and the walk cycle.

Mondu gathered up the scattered instances of forgery, returned the gadgets to their proper places, and set everything up to give to the customer after he integrated the biometrics. He looked at the clock—1600. He had a good half an hour before the customer came back, enough time to inhale some pineapple and a breast of peacock.

"Hey! Boy!" The voice from the front room sounded like the owner of the gold ring. Mondu dropped the last of the bones on his plate and emerged from the back to find the weathered Asian man standing over the display case, looking with relief down at the property he'd evidently come to reclaim.

"Wanting back the ring?"

"Yes."

"Twenty two to get out the hock." Mondu reached into the display case and removed the ring from its pedestal. He set it spinning on the counter and reached for the proffered claim ticket and cash from the customer. "Thank you." He grasped the cash and felt the oily residue on it. Wet, he might have expected—everything was wet here—but not oily. He left the cash on the counter and lifted his hand to look at it. As he did, his hand seemed to melt before his face. He felt a strange euphoria as he watched the flesh run like wax and darkness closed across his vision like an iris.

Mondu felt nothing as his head hit the ground and his scalp split, trickling a generous rivulet of blood down through the floorboards to fertilize the forest.

Sound was the first thing to come back. The banshee wind of billions of crickets trolling for sex all around him. Buried in the noise, riding down below in the registers most humans normally spoke in, he heard the dull thudding of someone tenderizing a steak. After that, he heard voices. The voices didn't make sense for a while, but he knew they weren't the call of his ancestors welcoming him into paradise. They were angry. And they spoke English in accents you didn't often hear in Calabar, and never in the home he'd been born to.

"I've never heard of the man. Oof!" It was the voice of his customer—the man in the white Fedora who wanted the identity package—somewhere in the distance.

"No, I think we have our Mister Briggs." The rough, stilted voice of the ring's owner. What as going on? "The jungle will take him, I think."

"I'm not..." His voice was cut off by the sound of a body splashing in a puddle.

Mondu didn't consider keeping his place and playing dead. His customer was getting beaten just out the back door. He couldn't let it go on. Not in his presence. Not while he could do something about it.

The boss kept an old projectile pistol under the cash register, in case of robbery. While the sickening sounds continued, Mondu opened his eyes a slit and scanned around, making sure there was no one who could see him. The area behind the counter was clear. He inched his way along the ground—his head was still swimming, he didn't trust himself to stay below the glass so he couldn't be seen.

Under the cash register now, he reached up and snaked the gun out of its cubbyhole. The boss had given him some instructions when he was first hired. It was only a revolver, and a good thing, too. He'd seen tourists occasionally using automatics. The mechanism looked simple, but there were odd rituals they went through before shooting that, without training, made no sense to him.

Mondu pulled himself into a squat behind the cash register—the only blind available to him. He held the gun up against his chest in both hands, breathing as quietly as he could, trying to stuff the dizziness and the nausea down from his head and into his gut where it couldn't make him fall over. He mentally counted three, and stood up.

The front room was clear. As near as he could tell through his head swimming and swaying, the sounds were coming from behind him. Quietly as he could, he stumbled through the swinging door into the back of the shop. Past the boss's office, past his rooms, the soft thudding sounds of a man being beaten in the face kept him pushing forward.

The back door was half-open. Through it he saw three figures. Mondu took a deep breath, raised the gun and kicked the door open. Under the awning, the Asian man stood cruelly over the balding

American, while a taller, younger, and far more frightening Asian stood in the corner as backup. Mondu didn't have time to do more than survey the situation before the younger man whipped a taser off his belt and fired it at him. Paralyzing, itching numbness crawled over his skin and through his organs like a swarm of army ants, and he fell to the ground again, his senses quitting under the abuse.

Mondu awoke with water filling his lungs, spluttering and thrashing. He kicked like a giraffe, trying to keep himself afloat. Hands flailing, grasping for anything at all, he coughed until his lungs ached and his throat tore. The lake—or river, or deep bathtub for all he knew—was dark. The whole world was darkness and panic.

The water kept pushing in any time he tried to breathe. His body quivered with adrenaline, his muscles already exhausted after only a few seconds. He pushed against the water, trying to gulp air. There was no way to know even which way to swim, if he could manage to get control of himself long enough to remember how. He wouldn't last long.

With one last great burst of will, Mondu kicked with all his might and tried to get on top of the water so he could float. He splashed, crashed, and gasped above the surface before sinking back down feet first. Just as the water was about to close, his feet found the bottom.

He stood still for a minute, maybe two, hardly believing his luck. He'd found a rock or a...no. His foot tapped out carefully around him—the ground was solid as far as his feet could feel. He was standing in no more than a meter and a half of water. He'd been *drowning* in no more than a meter and a half of water.

Where was he?

Cautiously, Mondu slid his left foot forward as far as he could go without losing his balance. When it failed to find any resistance or dropoff, he put his weight on it and repeated the process with his other foot. Four long, slow, sliding strides brought him to a cinderblock wall extending over his head, and for farther than he could reach to either side. It only took him another minute to move around the circumference of his enclosure. He was in a well of some sort—round walls, too far apart to brace against, nothing to hold on to.

No escape.

The panic rose in his throat again. No escape. And no rest, either. The water was high enough that he couldn't sit down to sleep. There was no way to prop himself up.

He was dead.

Somewhere overhead he heard a thud, then the smash-tinkle of breaking glass. Someone yelled. Then silence.

He counted seconds by the sound of a drip. Overhead, the trees or the roof or whatever was over him leaked at a steady rate. A few minutes trickled by before he heard anything else.

"How many more?" The man from the rain. Screaming.

Mondu couldn't hear a response.

More minutes dropped by. He couldn't tell how many through the ache in his lungs and throat. The blood on his head was dry now, and it made his scalp itch. He wanted to sleep.

Yes...sleep. That was it. He could nap, just for a little while...

A crack snapped Mondu back to himself with the water at his chin again.

"You down there? Hello?" The passport customer.

"Hello?"

"Stand back."

Mondu pressed his back up against the wall. He heard two more hard cracks, then light flashed down into his hole. From two meters up, a board broke loose and fell towards him. Mondu covered his head as the sodden wood slammed into the water in front of him. Wan light streamed down through the hole, but to Mondu's eyes it was nearly blinding. A man's head poked into the opening.

"Are you the guy from the pawn shop?"

"Sid...yes!"

"Hold on a second." A terrible scraping pierced his eardrums as the heavy wooden cover was pushed aside, then the man shoved a cane down the pit to him. "Grab hold."

Mondu did. His hands in the crook of the cane, he hauled on it as hard as he could while his feet scrambled and pushed him up the wall. The man at the other end of the cane pulled him up until he could reach the lip of the pit, and then pulled at his arms and shirt while Mondu pushed himself up on the ground, swung his legs out and over the edge, and rolled out of the pit onto the ground.

He lay on the ground for a moment, catching his breath, and then pushed himself to his feet and looked back down the pit. "Vondu silah, what is that?"

"Looks like an old well, or...eh, it doesn't matter."

Mondu stepped back from the pit and regarded his savior. In the irregular light spilling through on them from a bare bulb just on the other side of the door, the man looked different. He wasn't the embodiment of deliberation and patience he'd seemed earlier today. His hat was battered, his white suit splattered and caked with blood. His own blood, viscous, flowed slowly out of a gash above his left ear. He dabbed at it unconsciously as he waited for Mondu to finish collecting his thoughts.

Who was this man? Did he even want to know? Looking over the mud and gore streaked across the once white suit, he decided he'd rather not. "Um...I...thank you."

"Don't mention it. Let's go. You still have that package for me?"

"Sid sid, it's ready."

"Then let's get moving." Without looking at Mondu again, he walked up the half-flight of decaying wooden steps and through the door. Mondu had little choice: he shrugged and followed after.

The door led to a landing, and the stairs doubled back on themselves. The top of the flight opened into a restaurant kitchen. Two steps in, the smell hit him. Acrid, metallic, and vaguely repugnant. Like rust and ammonia laid over a bedding of diarrhea. His stomach lurched.

"Excuse the mess, I've been doing some cooking. You still need some biometrics, right?" His companion grabbed a pair of poultry shears and ducked behind a counter.

"Sid...yes. Sorry, what is that smell?"

A crunching, squishing sound came from behind the counter. "Sorry about that. Like I said...urgh," the man grunted with exertion, "I've been busy. Messy business. What's your line? You haven't spent your whole life hanging out in the jungle."

"Special AI for custom apps."

"Like ship computers with personality?"

"No, no. Easy. Old. Take medical data—need special diagnostic AI with lateral mind, but don't want it making decisions." Mondu hung back uncomfortably. Something told him he should give his savior some privacy behind the counter.

"You did that?"

"One of them." The sickening sound came again.

"What the hell are you doing running a pawn shop at the ass end of nowhere?"

"In Calabar now, AI designs AI. No work. Looking for new thing."

"Well," he grunted again, and a dull, wet cracking sound echoed around the counter, "We all need a change sometimes."

Mondu's curiosity got the better of him, and he screwed up his courage and walked toward the counter. "Sid sid, and we..." he stopped as his lunch lurched up in his throat. The man in the once-white suit knelt next to someone in a leather vest. On that someone's back were three small sausages. Above the sausages, Mondu's customer held the body's hand.

Only his hand. The arm wasn't attached anymore. Neither were three of the...

Fingers.

Mondu turned around and spilled the remains of his last meal on the floor. He wiped his mouth on his soaking sleeve and tried to find his tongue in the burning. "What are...why are..."

"Biometrics. For the card." That sound again. Mondu heaved, but nothing was left to come up.

"Vondu!"

"Life is messy." Crunch. "Don't walk around this way if you can help it." The man—if he really was a man and not a demon—stood and grabbed a cup from the counter. He walked to the freezer as if it were the most natural thing in the world to eat a popsicle after dismembering another man's hand. He scooped the cup in the ice tray and returned to the floor. Mondu closed his eyes, trying to remember what life was like before it was filled with blood and electricity and dark pits full of water. "There," the jocularity in the voice unnerved him, "that should keep them nice and fresh until... oh fuck. Yakuza...I should have known. Well, that figures." He stood up and straightened his suit, as if an even lapel line would make him look like he didn't just walk out of a slaughterhouse.

"Yakuza?" Mondu had nothing else worth saying. He didn't even want to know the answer. He didn't want to know anything more. He just wanted to live through the day, or the night, or whatever it was alive and get lost in the morning. But he had to say something. He couldn't bear the silence. The dripping sounds kept on. He couldn't cope with not knowing whether those drips were water or blood. As much as the man from the rain frightened Mondu, he was the only way out. Talking was better than sitting in the kitchen like an animal wondering where the next predator would come from.

"Japanese Mafia."

Mondu shook his head, not understanding.

"They're hired muscle for organized crime. They used to have lots of power before the war, now the ones that are left are freelance hit men."

"Why are..."

"Some things, trust me kid, you don't want to know." The man stood up and brushed his hands. "All you really need to know is that the world is full people, and some of them are looking for me."

Mondu nodded. "I see."

"Don't worry about it. It's not your fight, and nobody's going to tie you to these two..."

"But how can you..."

"You learn. Hope you never have to. Come on, we'll go get that card and I'll get out of your hair. You're lucky enough to still have some." The man gave Mondu an incongruous wink and led him around the corner. "You may want to hold your nose and look away. It got messy through here."

Mondu tried to do as instructed, but when he plugged his nose he tasted the foul metallic tang, and he kept having to look up to avoid tripping over stools, and limbs, and cabinet doors. In front of them, hanging from his hair in the doorway, the Asian man who'd hocked the ring smiled ghoulishly at them with his neck. A dozen stab wounds peppered the front of his guaybera shirt, and long slits down his forearms opened the muscle arms to the bone. "Vondu..." He was getting tired of saying it, but prayer was all he could think of to do. He swooned a little, and his hip crashed against the counter as he caught himself.

"I said don't look! You'll have enough nightmares as it is. Through here."

He felt the stranger's strong hand grip his arm and pull him up, leading him through the rest of the kitchen, turning left at the meat gargoyle, and emerging out a back door into an alley.

Mondu knew this alley. It was behind *Touristas*, the seasonal restaurant at the top of the little hill, two blocks up from his own shop. The horror closed behind him with the door, and he greedily sucked in the thick, unbreathable air and all its earthy, living scents.

It was a different world out here.

"How..." he struggled to slow his breathing, calm his heart rate, pretend that he wasn't a hunted animal that this psychopath could snuff out and butcher at any moment, "How long have we..."

"About eight hours. They brought us up here about three hours ago and dumped you down there while they worked on me. I'd have come for you sooner, but I needed to make sure there weren't any others coming." The stranger patted him reassuringly on the back, as if they were brothers. Having walked through danger and blood together—literally—perhaps they were.

Mondu would have given anything for a computer terminal and a pair of headphones to shut out the jungle night's cacophony. The crickets sounded like thousands of dying men screaming and croaking their last breaths. In the thirty two degree heat of the night, he shook like he was covered in snow. He knew he should feel something—his body was breaking down—but his emotions were blank. What he had just seen sucked his soul out through his eyes, and he didn't know if it would ever find him again.

The rain started. Still standing behind the restaurant, the man from the rain took off his hat and spread his arms wide, looking up at the sky with pagan welcome. He scrubbed the blood off his hands, off his face, and took his jacket off, wringing out the silk and pushing all the blood out of the white, then hung it on a stray nail and did the same with the rest of his clothes. "Gotta love these stain proof silks." Finished with his cleansing, the man re-dressed and then turned back to Mondu and took him by the arm. "Come on. I'll walk you back."

Mondu stumbled forward, roughly, his legs not quite remembering how to walk. As long as he was still he was okay. When he started putting one foot in front of the other, the fear welled up in him, and he tried to run away and run back all at once. Tears of rage and terror pushed out of his eyes, and he looked for something—anything—to grab on to, but he didn't know whether to kill it or hold it.

"Keep going. It will pass. I promise." The smaller man's firm grip was the only thing that steadied him. Mondu let himself be marched out of the alley and onto the main street.

Descending the hill gave him something to do. Trying to keep his feet in the mud, trying not to take his companion down with him if he slid, keeping up some pretext of conversation as the rain washed them both clean—they kept his mind moving. They kept it from settling on the vulture's heap. It wasn't quite life, maybe, but at least it wasn't death.

Five minutes, maybe ten, brought them to the door of the hockshop. It could have been hours for all he could tell. The Amazonian night hung heavy everywhere, and the clouds and the canopy kept the stars concealed overhead. There was no way to mark time but the steady drip, drip, drip of water on the counter through the thatch.

Mondu detached himself from his escort and mechanically found the counter. Circle round, behind the counter, where the office was, on the desk, the envelope was still there. No one had bothered trying to break in. Nobody should have. It was the off-season. Mondu pulled out the card and fed it into the writer.

"Senor, come back."

The Fedora's white brim led the severe, haggard face around the corner. Mondu saw smile lines—at some point, it had been a happy face. Not anymore.

"Here." Mondu shoved the biometrics writer at him and looked away. He didn't want to think about what the rustling of ice from the man's coat pocket meant, or what he was feeding into the fingerprint scanners, or why he was putting them back in his pocket. He didn't want to imagine how it was that the man changed his iris—he had to have at some point, or he wouldn't need a new biometrics jacket. He didn't want to know anything more, ever, of this creature from the cafe.

"Thank you. This is the rest of the package?" Mondu looked up, and saw the man pointing to the manila envelope on the desk.

"Sid sid. It is yours. Take it."

His customer nodded and took the envelope. He pulled the contents out one by one, examining each in their turn, and pocketing them where appropriate. As much as would fit in his front trouser pockets, and the rest in his inside coat pocket—the places least likely to be picked.

Mondu didn't care anymore. He wanted to get his book and go to bed and pretend that the whole world was paved over by shining relays and intelligent protocols in giant shining glass fiber cables. He got up and led his customer back out to the front of the store, and stayed at the counter while he got situated. The stranger produced the store's revolver from a pocket and laid it down on the counter.

"Here. I didn't use any of the bullets." He followed the revolver with the promised payment—two decks of cards printed in platinum ink. Mondu would have to burn it down to bullion, but that was tomorrow's problem.

A small patch of dried blood, black in the yellow light, still lingered inside the top of his left ear as the man who came out of the rain donned his Fedora. The hat's white felt shone a dull orange as the man nodded to Mondu's book, still at the end of the counter where he'd left it when the Yakuza flattened him.

"You ought to find a way to put that into practice again."

Mondu nodded dully. "One day, there may again be a need."

The customer pulled his brim down and turned towards the door, stepping through from the yellow into the dark, pale blue. He called over his shoulder to Mondu, "The clouds have broken."

The man stood there, as if expecting Mondu to follow. Maybe the only way to be rid of him was to humor him.

Mondu strode across the entryway and stood by the shorter man. Looking up through the canopy in the clearing, he saw the galaxy sprawling edge-on above him. "A lot of space out there."

"Yup. A man with your expertise could find a lot of opportunity up there."

"No, I think not. Moving up...much money."

"There's a place up there, nobody knows about it yet. They're going to call it Nineveh. They'll need people like you to build it. If you can make it to the elevator, look for the MEO or the IBM pavilions."

"They will not want someone with a history like..."

"If you can do the job, that's what they'll care about." Clouds began creeping across the break in the canopy once more. Soon, there would be only the blank grey of the cloudy sky, and then more rain. Mondu wanted to go back inside before the clouds closed over him again. He didn't want to stand next to this man who he'd watched do...things he never thought he'd see. That man turned towards him and looked up to him. "Thank you for trying to help."

"I did nothing."

"You worried enough about a stranger to risk your life."

"It is the decent thing."

"The world's decency tank is empty most of the time." The stranger produced one more pack of cards from beneath his shirt. A money belt? Perhaps. He opened the box and dealt a hand of five, and handed them to Mondu. "Decent men should win sometimes."

The man had just handed him enough money to get somewhere —even to the elevator—if he really wanted to, because...Mondu couldn't begin to guess why. But it was clear now that the man wasn't going to kill him. He let out his breath, feeling the adrenaline subside. Not knowing how to respond to the gift, merely nodded at his companion and said: "You are a good man."

"Hmph." The corners of the stranger's mouth twitched up, and he shook his head as if trying not to laugh at a private joke. "I may be a lot of things. But that isn't one of them."

"You saved my life."

"It was...convenient." The man took his hat off, fiddled with the brim a moment, then nodded to himself and put it back on. "Now that you have it back, do something useful with it. Don't take too long. None of us lives forever."

"Forever. A long time." He wondered again who this strange, brutal creature was. As the man took his first step down whatever road lay in front of him, Mondu caught him around the arm. "Wait. What is your name?"

The man looked sidelong and raised an eyebrow, as if Mondu had just asked the most foolish question in the world. Then he smiled. "You gave it to me. Let's see..." The man dug down in his pocket, and flipped open his new passport. "Joss Kyle. Freelance trader. Pleased to meet you."

The newly minted Mr. Kyle returned the passport to his pocket, adjusted his hat, and walked into the night.

Mondu stood for a few more moments, watching the cloudbreak repair itself, and then returned to his counter. He went about his business of locking up the store, then picked up his book and retired to his room to dream of being in a modern world again.

The jungle was brutal. It was hot, and it was close, and he'd been here six months without getting to know anyone in the small community beyond a passing glance and an exchange of names. It was only ever supposed to be a way-station while he figured out what to do. If he could find a way *up there*, he might be able to find work in AI again. The space elevator the stranger mentioned was in Ecuador. And now, thanks to that stranger, Mondu had just enough money to hop a shuttle to the mountains.

The light from his hammock-side lamp burned steady and low, throwing deep shadows over everything. Through the walls, the sounds of the ever-living jungle played a riotous din, enough white noise to make any city-dweller happy. It settled into the back of his mind—not as good as the thermoregulator pumps in a cluster farm, but, for tonight, it would do.

Death of the Machines

By Emerian Rich

(Originally podcast: 11/06/08 on HorrorAddicts.net, Episode #011)

Edward felt trapped in a modern office world of horrid fakes. His days seemed a facade of purpose that only he could see through. What was the game they all loved to play? Why did they love it so? He detested their shallow laughs and deceiving looks.

"What are you going on about?" He wanted to scream at the top of his lungs.

The fakest bastard of them all, Mr. Ryan, was standing beside him in his unimaginative gray suit. He was bitching and complaining in his irritating loser way. Edward imagined tearing away Mr. Ryan's skin and finding not human bone, but metal spurting not blood on his starched white shirt, but oil. Mr. Ryan's oil had probably never been changed. It was sure to be clumped and stringy like paint left out too long. It would be black and murky like the secrets of lunacy he hid behind the plastic bag he called skin.

Edward sneered, turning from the idiotic figurehead, and surveyed the other replicas in the room. They were hanging on Mr. Ryan's every word as if gaining priceless information.

Fabricated laughs filled the room as Mr. Ryan made an unfunny joke.

Is it too much to ask that someone react humanly? Is it too much to ask that real emotion be shown? Edward wondered as he stood, not amused by the nonsense, next to the worthless piece of corporate synthetic junk in a mass-produced suit. Edward imagined the others being linked by USB cords to Mr. Ryan's backside, downloading megabytes of drivel into their neural networks. He knew that if the power source were cut from all of the droids, he would be the only being left.

If that glorious day did occur, he would run screaming through the garden of electronics. "Hello? Is anyone alive out there?" He would yell for other humans like himself. No response would come.

As he left the building, he would see a few small, crouched beings hobbling along, confused and desperate, searching for those cold metal eyes that had enslaved them for so many years. They would be searching for direction, but alas... not an order would be uttered. They would suddenly cry out to Edward, hoping that he would be their leader.

But there is no way he would ever stay! He would avoid the children of freedom and their moronic pleas.

"You are free my friends! Free to be what you want to be. Free from the mechanical masters." He would yell.

They wouldn't understand. No one had ever allowed them to live and survive without leadership. Natural instinct and human thought were stripped from each and every one of them the day they received their company badge. And no one had drawn up an emergency plan for a total loss of electronic guidance and so without a spreadsheet or company authority chart, they would crawl under their cubicle desks, assume the fetal position and die.

How could Edward know, as he stepped out of the conference room and journeyed back to his desk, that this very thing was about to occur.

It was 11:38am on Wednesday and he happened to look up from his eye-deteriorating machine, when Mr. Ryan's circuits went dead. At first he couldn't believe it. He wiped his eyes and shook his head, looking again at the immobile droid. As Edward leaned over to ask his co-worker if he saw it too, he realized his co-worker had the same dead look in his eyes. No more electro-light. No more plastic smile.

Edward stood, registering the time on the digital clock on the wall hadn't moved. 11:38am.

Though his sense of reason was telling him it was all too good to be true, Edward took the stairs to exit the building. Security guards, smokers, lunchers were all standing about in their normal position for the morning but none of them were moving.

A part of him knew this would happen. He had imagined it too many times before in meetings just like the one they'd had that morning, but now that he had his freedom, what would he do with it?

It was so quiet. The gargantuan building of glass and concrete loomed above him as some sort of digital cemetery angel. Unlike his daydream, there were no lost souls calling out to him.

"I must be the only human left," he said this aloud, perhaps only to hear his voice echo off the skyscraper walls around him. But no, there must be others like him. Glad to be free from the digital wizards of consumerism.

He walked. That was the first step.

Edward was amazed at what creatures of habit humans are as he finally journeyed on foot, in what seemed slow motion, to his dwelling. Passing the multi-story metal structures that appeared to be quiet ships in an ocean of nothingness, he felt as if the world had taken a deep breath in and it would never breathe out again.

Even though it was the time of day when horns should have been honking and tires screeching, the traffic sat still. The BMW next to him gave no gentle engine purr. Nor were there any signs of life from what must've been hundreds of people sitting in bumper to bumper traffic. It was amazing how quiet the city was without the hum of power. He clicked his tongue every once in awhile to keep from going insane from the silence.

Edward's daze thickened as the whole world seemed in a state of shock. He dared not stop the movement of his feet for fear he would become one of the many he passed on the sidewalk, mid chore.

I must pretend that everything is completely normal, he thought to himself. He unlatched the useless timepiece on his wrist and threw it into a large fountain filled with stagnant water. Like a pebble, the watch skipped before sinking into the putrid water.

This is all there is left. There are only the dead shells of electronic boxes and I. Edward's mind raced and his inner voice rambled as if he had some reason to record every moment of the day. *No one, scratch that, no thing is here with me. I am one lone being in a jungle of voltaic dinosaurs. What does it matter? There is no one to tell. Why would I want anyone to be, for they are empty, soulless machines with preprogrammed responses that will never be enough for me.*

He arrived at the place where he had been living for quite some time and it looked the same as it always did when he came home from work. He entered with a smile, because there was no computerized voice telling him the time or the date or what he had planned for the evening. He studied his worthless possessions.

Suddenly he was filled with inspiration and began to gather things he would take with him on his voyage thru the vast machine wasteland. He grabbed a few things that only a human would take: his favorite book, a picture of his parents, several changes of clothes and his fish, which he would release in the nearest waterway. A grin was ever-present on his face as he strolled about his home pulling the items together with a quiet urgency.

Edward hummed a song as he entered the closet. He reached up and pulled at a luggage bag on the top shelf. It gave him a bit of trouble so he yanked at it. Something seemed to be on top of the suitcase, stopping it from coming down. He peered up, grabbing the bag firmly with one hand and tugged it.

A large metal object began to fall towards his face and as if it was in slow motion, he tried to move but couldn't. His clothes iron slammed into his cheekbone, making a loud cracking noise and knocking him down.

When Edward woke, the gloomy room was stale. The sun had set and with no machines or power, he was in complete darkness. For a moment, he could not remember what state the world was in. He wondered if it was time to get up for work and turned his head to find the oversized digital numbers on his alarm clock... but the numbers weren't there and he began to remember that he was free. Yes, he was about to embark on an adventure, when he had been hit on the head. His hand went instantly to his face. Blood covered his right cheek and neck. He rose, flipping on the light switch. No light came.

The machines are gone. Stumbling over something on the floor, he pitched forward and knocked into his bedside table, hearing the crash of glass. Feeling the floor, he eventually found his industrial strength flashlight and switched it on.

His apartment looked strange with only the singular stream of illumination to light his way. He fumbled with the door handle and entered the bathroom to take a gander at his wound.

Staring into the mirror, he saw his face, the bloody thing, appeared to be cut through to the bone on his cheek. He took a cloth and wiped at the crimson stain, his eye watering even though he felt no pain.

Shock, Edward, that's what they call it. You're in shock. He continued to clean his wound with one hand while he searched the medicine cabinet for peroxide. The once tan washcloth was covered in deep stain. *The cut must be deep.* He panicked for a moment about infection. Were all the doctor's gone with the machines? What would he do if he needed real medical care?

Gripping the flashlight with one hand, he used the other to inspect the wound in the mirror. He ran the cloth over the gash, finding that under the blood was something hard and white. *Oh no, I've scrapped it clear to the bone!*

He angled the flashlight upright and got closer to the mirror, studying his cheekbone. Instead of a creamy white bone, something shiny and metallic flickered in the wavering flashlight beam.

What the... Edward set the flashlight on his shoulder, to steady the light and stared unbelieving into the glass before him.

His heartbeat increased, making him breathe heavily. He picked up his razor blade and scraped at the skin around the injury, exposing more of the silvery substance.

How could it be that my bone structure was replaced and I never knew it? What kind of trick is this? He stared into the mirror in disbelief, blinking erratically, attempting to refocus his eyes. His mechanical stare in the mirror was too unreal, too untrue. *This can't be!* An urgent thumping on his chest cavity told him his heart was beating irregularly.

The truth of it all was surfacing in his mind and he didn't want to give into it. He didn't want to realize that he was like one of them, that he was only *programmed* to have feelings of mortality. He wanted to scream, but his mouth was still as he took the blade and slashed his right arm. He stripped away the bag that he had once called skin. The force of the blade made his mortally programmed eyes close, though in reality, he knew he was not feeling pain.

Staring at the gash on his forearm, he willed there to be flesh. He willed there to be veins and puss and bone.

The circuitry in his wrist zapped and popped as the razor ran over it. His mechanical knees gave way and he fell to the floor.

"No!" Edward heard his computerized scream echo through the lifeless apartment. "I am what they all are. I am a machine. I have no natural purpose." His voice box electronically transmitted in a digitized voice. Tin eyelids slowly closed over his optical units and the microprocessor that assumed the position of a human heart began to fail.

"Let's get some light in here," a police officer with salt and pepper hair commanded as he entered a dark, musty apartment of a tenant who had not been heard from in over a week.

His partner, a young kid just out of the academy, flicked on his flashlight as they moved further into the living space.

"Shit!" The rookie covered his nose and mouth with his elbow. He held the flashlight with his alternate hand, flicking the light stream over the apartment to try to find the source of the odor.

"Jesus Christ!" the first cop exclaimed, smelling the ungodly scent. He pulled his gun and edged closer to the bedroom door where the smell seemed to be emanating from.

Seeing the feet of a man, the cop approached with caution. When he saw the decomposed flesh on the face, the cop pushed a button on the side of the radio on his shoulder. "We found him, but he won't be making any more rent payments."

Back at the station, the police officers that had found Edward's body spoke.

"Apparently, he was a top employee. Had won the Employee of the Month six times during the last year and his boss had promoted him the day he disappeared."

"Did he have any enemies?" the police officer asked.

"The coroner's report states the wounds were self inflicted."

Shaking his head and turning his chair to glance out of the window, the rookie sighed.

"What on earth would make a man like that do this?"

"These corporate types. They work themselves into the ground and then one day they just pop. Something about sitting eight hours a day looking at a computer. Those machines can really screw with your head."

Asleep at the Wheel

By Tee Morris

(Originally podcast at www.podnova.com/
channel/5102/episode/15/)

Tonight's traffic was, for a delightful change, light. Usually the infamous Beltway was nothing more than a perpetual backup of every make and model of car from the Virginia-Maryland-D.C. metro area, tags of all kinds either designating diplomats from foreign countries, nicknames, or quick little messages to other commuters who could make the long trip home a deciphering game. The rules of the "license plate game" were simple. First, successfully crack the plate's code. (For example, if a tag reads "CMORFIT," was it "Seymour Fitt" or "See more of it"?) Once the message is translated, figure out why the driver put that on their license plates. (See more of what?)

Tonight there was no such game. It was just a long drive home. Tom had been asking himself for the past month exactly why he was still working out with this acrobatic team. It was his *ex*-girlfriend's idea to work out with them, so why was he following this routine?

The past two years had been one big joke. Meghan had sold him on the idea of performing a dead art form from Renaissance Festival to Renaissance Festival. *All right,* he begrudgingly thought to himself, *maybe not dead but definitely in a deep coma.* Their workouts with the gymnasts were limited due to Meghan's "chronic motion sickness." That should have been his first warning. When had he stopped being honest with her? Tom thought back over the relationship. They started off great. The sex was amazing! When she left for the conservatory, the distance was manageable. It probably started when he actually met the staff of her "conservatory" and saw the footage of what the students had spent a good part of the year developing…

"One step above Children's Theatre," he muttered aloud.

Maybe it was the whole issue of seeing her there, but Tom could deal with it. The exercise routines kept him busy, fit, and out of Meghan's way when she did show up to "work out" with the team. He was no acrobat, but he did learn how to do a killer cartwheel and enjoyed the results of these aerobic workouts, far superior to any gym or weight room. It was nice to be in better shape now than in high school or college. Now he had graduated to another routine—cardio-kickboxing—courtesy of the gymnast's next-door neighbor. It was a "user-friendly" approach to martial arts and a satisfying workout, especially when turned loose on a punching bag.

He turned the music up a hint louder. The down side to all this physical conditioning was the long drive. The routine began with finding a seat (hopefully) on the metro by eight, catching a return metro train by half past four, out to the gym for martial arts and acrobatics, then home sometime after ten. Eat a late dinner (usually his own "Burrito Supreme" creation), try and wind down, fall asleep by midnight, and begin this cycle again at the sound of his clock-radio alarm. Following one of his workdays in Virginia, the last thing Tom relished was a trip deep into Maryland, but the return trip home guaranteed downtime. During the drive, he silently assessed how much his consulting firm wanted him involved in the day-to-day operations and how this commitment would affect his acting career currently in a "rebuilding" phase after Meghan's influence.

Suddenly, Tom remembered his checkbook was in desperate need of balancing.

His mind was much like his lifestyle, working in several directions simultaneously and he liked it that way. He took after his dad in this multi-tasking approach to life. Tom loved being an actor, but he also took great satisfaction in teaching computer applications. Now he could feel a martial arts bug gnawing at him. Then there was his personal website. His first design. It was still a hobby, but he could easily see it becoming a nice little side business. *Yeah, that's me,* Tom thought to himself. *Jack of All Trades, Master of None.*

He blinked his eyes a couple of times, turning up the music. Or was it talk radio? It was a surreal feeling. Tom could not ascertain what he was listening to. It could have been classic rock. It could have been a late night shock jock. The sounds of the radio, the wind, and the hum of the Ford all coagulated into a dreamlike static.

How loud was the radio?

How far was the window down?

He *was* aware of being in his own lane.

His last conscious thought was that he had just passed the Georgia Avenue exit. *Not much longer. I'm halfway home…*

The plexiglass slid away as he felt a wave of consciousness come over him. The taste in his mouth was horrific and his biggest annoyance with the whole hyper-sleep process. He could deal with the muscle stiffness, waking up with five to ten minutes of disorientation (but he actually got it down to three with a couple of yoga exercises he pulled from a CentralNet site), and removing the intravenous feeds of chemicals and nutrients attached to his body. Tom let out a loud yelp as his feet touched the cold floor of the *Walter Raleigh. Okay,* he thought hazily, *maybe the taste in the mouth is a close second to the cold floor.* Close by the sleep chamber was the mouthwash he swirled around in his mouth and forced down like cheap gin. It was considered hazardous to swallow the company's mouthwash, but it was the closest thing to alcohol on the ship.

Tom instinctively slipped his feet into the 'bear-foot slippers,' a late twentieth century novelty that never wandered far from his chamber. He constantly got ribbed from other pilots about these ridiculous slippers. They were obnoxiously huge and faux-fuzzy with farcical claws protruding from the front. Tom could care less what they had to say about his slippers. They were his and they were warm. He had found them on a CentralNet "Antiques & Heirlooms" site where collectors were placing bids on them, probably for some collector who would have taken these mint-condition slippers and put them in a glass case for display. It cost him a good chunk of his savings from his last few hauls, but with the chill of the ship's metal floor the cost was justified.

Worth every credit, Tom thought pleasantly as he wiggled his toes inside the slippers.

The cockpit appeared exactly as he last left it before going into hyper-sleep. The comm-set was attached to the headrest of his pilot's chair and the checklist panel was in its pocket next to the armrest. The computer displays indicated the artificial gravity had been active for the past hour. *Ah, I see. You activated the artificial gravity but didn't bother to warm up the floor. Thanks, Cujo. I'll remember that.*

"What time is it, Cujo?" Tom yawned.

"Ship's chronometer reads that it is 0321 hours," the ship responded. The computer's voice was a disturbingly calm female voice, void of emotion. No mistaking that it came from a computer. "Thirty-seven years, two months, two days, and seventeen hours since leaving Jupiter's orbit. Nine years, one month, six days, and eleven hours since passing through the Alpha Centauri checkpoint."

"I just wanted the time, Cujo. I just wanted the time."

Tom stared at the display for a moment, knowing full well that the computer could not see the frustration in his face. He laughed in spite of himself. At least he always got the last word with this computer every time he addressed the interface. In the fleet of colony ships, every central computer was called "Watchdog" as it protected the ship from space debris, changed course to avoid any ship-to-ship collisions, or activated its defense grid when threatened. Tom's sense of humor and love of classic literature could not stop him from calling the ship's computer "Cujo." While his fellow students bought "Cliffe Disks" that poorly summarized and analyzed the Academy's required reading, Tom actually read this author's works in school. This one book, *Cujo*, was his favorite. Reprogramming "Watchdog" to respond to this new name was just a start. Tom went so far as to change the alert signal to bark as a wild, rabid dog in case of virus infestation or operating system errors.

Tom glanced at the navi-grid to the right of him, a dotted line deviating from a solid line that stretched across a star map. Currently, according to stellar charts as drafted by Earth Central, they were traveling through the IR24 system, about ten years clear of the Alpha Centauri colonies. *Those checkpoint hotshots probably did their fly-by's so close they knocked an antennae out of whack,* Tom thought bitterly, *and it's taken this long for Cujo to pick it up.*

To reach a colony's destination, computers and company navigators plotted extremely precise courses, the computers for accuracy and the company navigators to pinch pennies where they could. Be it an asteroid or a star, if it had any kind of gravity, the company men would make it part of the slingshot formula. Any deviation from that course and Watchdog would correct. If it failed, essential crew would be awakened from hyper-sleep.

Tom was the pilot and therefore the essential personnel.

"So is this the problem, Cujo? Course deviation?"

"Yes, sir."

"I see." Tom cracked his knuckles and flipped a couple of switches on the controller stick in the right armrest. "Starboard thrusters at twenty percent."

There was a flash from the right side of the ship. Tom watched the field of stars slowly move. The computer was supposedly a "state-of-the-art" product of Artificial Intelligence, but Tom was essential in performing a function any "shake-and-bake" of five could perform. The genetic "shake-and-bake" prodigies programmed for flight are considered "too valuable" to risk on deep space exploration, and now "homegrowns" are back in demand. Humans created "the old fashioned way" were needed to do the dirty work. He sighed and ran his fingers through close-cropped hair now turning gray at the temples. *I'm not even thirty,* Tom thought grumpily, *and my hair is turning gray.* One of the lovely side effects to repeated hyper-sleep. He could not help but wonder when he became so jaded on the job.

When space flight become so…isolated. That was probably what made him so grumpy. Not the hyper-sleep, but an overwhelming sense of loneliness. He could not remember ever feeling this lonely.

He should have felt this after his first haul.

Tom enrolled in the Mars Academy Pilot's Program. It was a better alternative than spending the rest of his life on a planet of rust or returning to a dying planet. He was six when the *Unity* Incident of 2103 occurred. The station's orbit began its decay, and projections indicated it would splash harmlessly in the Pacific Ocean. The computers, however, were pulling information from the station's original schematics, not from its upgrades between 2014 and its decommission. When it impacted the Earth, the nuclear reactor upgrades on board exploded with such force that it was similar to the "Asteroid Calamity" scientists had been continuously droning about for centuries. Hawaii, Japan, and half of Australia were buried while the San Andreas Fault in North America gave way. The debris kicked up in the air reeked havoc with the environment. Orbital way stations and resorts on the Moon and Mars quickly became science experiments as to the potential of life on other worlds. Colonization programs were accelerated.

So for Tom, there were very few options.

The Academy emphasized from Day One the majority of a pilot's life is spent in hyper-sleep. Outside of other pilots, family, friends, and intimate relationships were impossible. Tom recalled his first assignment. It would take him on a fifty-year orbit. He said goodbye to his mother and father for what would be the last time. The pay was fantastic. He felt no regret. No loneliness. It was something he had to do to survive.

So is it finally catching up with me? Am I finally suffering from Hyper-Sleep Isolation Disorder? His mind wandered back to a time far gone when it was a different kind of ocean pilots like him navigated. He read all about it on CentralNet. The oceans were not a void of black but a vast uncharted region of the deepest blue, sometimes calm and inviting and other times turbulent and rebellious. There were no sleep chambers or slipspace propulsion drives. Only the wind carried ships from port to port. It was a far simpler time.

A far simpler time, Tom thought languidly as he stared across the stars stretching out to infinity before the *Walter Raleigh.*

Some people called him a "romantic" and fellow pilots took great delight in reminding him of problems in ancient history, right up to the twentieth century. No, the first millennium was a far-from-perfect age. Still, there was something far superior to that ancient method of travel. What a time that was. No artificial air. The warmth of true sunlight. Tom could hear the sounds of the ocean lapping against the sides of the vessel. The sunlight baking his skin to a golden brown. He could feel the wind on his face, cool, refreshing, full of the scent of life. Turning up the volume of the radio, enjoying the sound of classic rock. He could feel his grip tighten light on the steering wheel…

Tom paused. *Steering wheel,* Tom asked himself. *Where the hell did that come from?*

"Cujo, perform a diagnostic on my sleep chamber." Tom returned the comm-set to its headrest and slowly made his way back to the cylindrical bed, "Was I programmed for REM sleep?"

"No, sir. Sleep chamber is operating within normal parameters." The computer's voice continued as Tom took a seat on the bed of his sleep chamber. "Article 24, Section 3 of your contract states that you are not to be subjected to Rapid Eye Movement. Your chamber is regulated to keep you in a state above REM, its benefits synthetically replaced during your hyper-sleep."

This was a constant clause in his contracts: REM sleep was prevented by the ship's medi-computer. If Tom did happen to slip into this state, his dreams were monitored and recorded by Watchdog. The company kept careful documentation of his dreams to assure he was not slipping into deep space dementia. Cujo would not have hesitated to mention a faulty sleep chamber or if his supply of the synthetic adrenaline, Stimuline, failed to keep him out of REM as it was supposed to do, was low or empty.

"Report the last dream I had since departing the *Galileo* Way Station."

"No dreams have been documented on this journey."

"When was my last attempt at REM?"

"Last dosage of Stimuline administered in 2353, thirty-one years, six days, 3 hours, and 24 minutes from this present awakening. I would comment the yoga exercises downloaded from CentralNet have proven quite beneficial in regulating your sleep."

No, Tom thought anxiously, *I was dreaming. I wasn't here. It was vivid. It was real. I remember turning up the radio and hearing the Classical music station. The song was "Love in an Elevator" by Aerosmith...whoever they are. I was driving a car...*

Tom only knew of cars from his history disks and CentralNet. The author of Watchdog's namesake wrote about a car once...

"Captain Martin," the ship's computer chimed, interrupting his thoughts. "I cannot return you to hyper-sleep unless you fully recline."

"Cujo... access Mainframe." Dreams were still believed to be the first symptom of deep space dementia, but there were other studies and theories. He wasn't cracking. This dream was so clear, like a memory. "Tell me about lucid dreaming."

"Mainframe accessed. *Lucid Dreaming*: the term was coined by Frederik van Eeden in 1896 when he used the word 'lucid' in the sense of mental clarity..."

Tom sighed heavily, "I don't want the details, Cujo, just the general idea. Simply put, what is lucid dreaming? How does it occur?"

The computer's voice hesitated as if editing its search results, then continued with its findings. "Lucid dreaming is a dream within a dream. Dreamers will dream within their dreams and become aware of a second dream when noticing impossible or unlikely happenings, such as encountering deceased loved ones, walking through walls, or obtaining flight without mechanical assistance. Lucid dreaming is achieving awareness in a dream that one is dreaming."

Would that explain how real it all was? I could feel the grip on the steering wheel. I saw the exit signs. Georgia Avenue—that was the last one I passed. Could I have confused the medi-computer in dreaming within a milder dream? Or could I have slipped into a deeper REM the computer couldn't recognize?

"The quality of lucidity in a dream varies from subject to subject," the computer continued. "Lucidity at a high level is an awareness of everything experienced is a dream. There is no threat. The dream subject is fully aware of being asleep in bed and will awaken shortly."

"Is it the same as dream control?" Tom asked. He had never heard this tone in his voice before. It reminded him of his mother trying to convince him not to become a colony ship pilot. It was imploring, desperate.

"No, sir, but it is possible to control dream parameters without being aware of the initial dream. Lucidity in a dream increases the extent of the dream subject's influence of both the initial dream and the second dream. Dream subjects can resume the second dream with full knowledge of existing in a dream and maintain the ability to redesign their dream parameters."

"Is it possible to be in a state of lucid dreaming and accept the dream reality as present reality, thereby obtaining a higher level of lucidity within a dream?"

Tom thought about what he just said. *Maybe I am losing it…*

"Insufficient data to comply to query."

He hated it when a computer said that. Was that supposed to be a more intelligent way of saying *I don't know*? It made sense to him. Achieving a state of consciousness within a dream. If it were possible then maybe his idea would work.

"Thank you, Cujo, that will be all."

A far simpler time.

Tom knelt by the sleep chamber and pried open the control panel. The multi-colored wires extended back to the motherboard. *I can do this. I can. This will work!* His hands shook lightly as he checked each wire, tracing where it led. The green-white wire controlled the medi-computer. This was what prevented him from dreaming. With a quick jerk and a shower of tiny sparks, the medi-computer was taken offline for his sleep chamber.

"Captain Martin, I detect an error in—"

"Thank you, Cujo, that will be all."

"Captain Martin, I am programmed to inform you of—"

"Thank you, Cujo," Tom snapped. "That. Will. Be. ALL!"

Tom searched for the red wire, the last and most crucial in the array. This was the connection to all environmental controls such as oxygen, temperature, and other critical systems. It was this wire that was the only flaw in his plan. Disconnecting this would keep him asleep. Disconnecting this could kill him.

If he could return to his dream, why would he want to wake up? He could see his parents waving goodbye to him. He could see out of his transport's window a dying Earth. As it was on Mars many decades ago, there were few options for him. It was a far simpler time waiting for him. A better time.

A far simpler time…

Tom climbed back into the sleep chamber and reinserted the intravenous feed to make certain nothing appeared to be wrong to the others when or if they awakened. The cover slipped over him as he began his breathing exercises.

I am asleep at the wheel… I am asleep at the wheel…

He closed his eyes and breathed deeply, each muscle in his body easing into a more relaxed state.

I am asleep at the wheel…

Holy—

The median wall was close enough to catch serial numbers off each individual segment. It was close. Far too close. He didn't know how fast he was going but it was too fast.

Across four lanes…

Across two lanes…

I'm losing control of the car. Please God…

The wheel began to steady.

I'm awake! I'm awake!

The car was back in its original lane. Tom was wide awake. The most wide awake he had ever been in his life.

He glanced in the rear view mirror. The closest car was a half-mile to a mile away. There was no one in front of him. *Talk about riding with the angels.* He looked up and saw the exit for Rockville. The window was opened a crack, and the winter air rushing in hit the newly formed sweat on the back of his neck, sending chills down his back. The music deafening. A talk radio show host was playing Aerosmith. *Is that what woke me?* He turned down the volume, but there was still the bass track reverberating in his ears.

Tom then realized the "bass track" was his own heartbeat reverberating in his temples.

He was now aware of every detail, signaling turns well in advance. His speedometer never challenged the limit. Tom refused to relax, even when he turned right to go into his apartment complex.

He sat in the car for a moment, the only light coming from the street lamps in the parking lot. He hated this car. It was such a lemon he was convinced a mechanic could make lemonade from it during an oil change. A piece of crap. If he were to describe it in a single word: unreliable.

Tonight, he wanted to give its bug-encrusted grill a big sloppy kiss.

Get out, Tom told himself. He got out, his legs unsteady. *You're okay and you're home.* He was still taking deep breaths. *Not until I walk through the door.* The keys were shaking but they found their way into the lock of Apartment 301. When the door shut behind him, he let out a heavy sigh.

He was home. He was okay.

Tom remembered passing Georgia Avenue. Then he saw the median wall. *Did I really nod off?* He couldn't recall what had happened in the long stretch between Georgia Avenue and Rockville Pike.

He set his gym bag by the couch, thanking whatever it had been—God, a guardian angel, or just plain Fate—that woke him.

He walked over to the mail awaiting him by the answering machine; and in an instant, it all came back. The damage control on his acting career, the upcoming bills, dealing with this computer training firm, and balancing his checkbook. The fear now yielded to the reality of what was. The bills were arriving.

Life goes on, Tom sighed *Thank God.*

Tom's eyes happened to land on his tiny library in the entertainment center just underneath the television. It was a modest collection of books in his entertainment center, a varied collection of different science fiction authors. Bradbury. Roddenberry. Bauchman. He thought with a wry grin, *Wouldn't it be nice just to get away for a while?* Far off worlds where computers took care of mundane responsibilities like bills, cooking, and programming the VCR. One hour car trips were a mere blink of an eye and other worlds were only a short space cruise from Earth. He smiled at what fantastic place he wanted to visit from his flights of fancy.

If only I could see that time, thought Tom, *a far simpler time…*

Hero

By Scott Sigler

(Originally podcast: 07/30/08 at
www.scottsigler.com)

He looked, but he saw nothing.

Nothing that posed a threat.

He looked again—there had to be something. It couldn't be this easy.

Alex Devryasek stood at the edge of broken lift tube, staring into the fading blackness that led to the basement. He looked around the filthy, reeking, grime-streaked lobby, eyes hunting for the trap, the trick, the thing that would try and stop him now that he was so close.

But still he saw nothing.

A dry, cracking tape strip held a yellowing piece of paper to the lift tube's frame: "Out of order." This had to be a set-up, some kind of defense. How could Timmerman live in a place like this? War heroes didn't live like this. Emperor-slayers didn't live like this.

The stairs—that's where the guards would be, hunting for danger, utilizing the high ground, waiting to fire straight down.

Alex felt the glow of fear in his chest. His nose itched. It always itched when he got scared. He considered the fear for a moment, considered his weakness, then scratched his nose and pushed the fear away. He headed for the stairs.

Tension wormed through his lithe body, threatening to cramp and knot his well-toned muscles. He ran through a quick breathing exercise, calming himself, bringing his body, mind and spirit under one unified control. The mantra of the Rillek Assassins ran ceaselessly through his head.

There is no defense against a perfect weapon.

The perfect weapon is cunning, calculating and ruthless.
I am all of these things.
There is no defense against me.

The words would die with him, for he was the last. Five centuries of tradition would fade from existence, probably as soon as he killed Timmerman. But that didn't matter, not as long as Timmerman died this day. Poetic justice is all the more eloquent with your enemy's brains cooked a crispy-brown.

Alex reached up to his gray plastic headband and flipped down the eyepiece, which hung in front of his left eye like a red monocle. The headband looked like the typical equipment for a street reporter, a hands-free recorder that captured everything the reporter saw and heard. This headband, however, held a full array of sensor equipment designed to ferret out cameras, motion-sensors, auto-guns, trip beams or any other security device. Alex stared through the ruby-red eyepiece, scanning the door to the stairwell.

Nothing.

He nervously scanned the lobby for the third time, as if somehow he'd missed something the first two times, or perhaps threats had suddenly and miraculously appeared where seconds ago there had been none.

Where was the security?

Alex opened the door and stepped into the quiet stairwell. One of the light banks hung dead and gray, the other flashed with an erratic pulsing, filling the stairwell with a dim irregular strobe effect. Thick layers of garbage, both rotting and fresh, almost blocked the steps. He scanned every corner, every shadow, even the garbage itself. Nothing. His nose demanded another scratch. Eyes wide and alert, pulse rocketing through his body, he started up the steps for the fifth floor.

At the third floor, the lights evened out, but trash still abounded, as did the ubiquitous anti-League graffiti. He reached the fifth floor—Timmerman's floor. He stood very still, listening, seeking any sound that might filter through the landing door.

Nothing.

Alex's skin prickled, a wave of needle-pokes rolling up and down his spine. Where were the damn guards? This was Timmerman's floor, of that Alex was certain, but if Timmerman lived here, where the hell was his protection? The sweeper picked up nothing—not even a single security device.

He focused his thoughts, knowing full well he might open the door to face a half-dozen armed League guards. The fear blossomed up again, a little bigger this time, a little more cancerous. But again he pushed it away. Or at least he tried. One way or another, this was the end of the line, either for himself or for Timmerman, and he'd bridge any obstacle to complete the mission. The pinching fear made him want to draw his weapon, but he resisted. He had a plan. His reporter disguise would probably get him close enough to take out the guards before they could sound an alarm. The odds were against him, probably, but that was nothing new. He flipped up the eyepiece, took a controlled breath, then let it out slow and easy. A lifetime of training had led to this moment; the mission was his destiny.

Alex calmly opened the landing door and stepped into the hallway.

Nothing.

Nothing but a dirty carpet and bits of trash littering the hall. Grime streaked the walls, as did spots of bad graffiti. The place was a dump. He'd thought the conditions downstairs some sort of ruse, thought that the fifth floor—Timmerman's floor—would be a palatial apartment. What else would you expect for the man who'd almost single-handedly brought down a galactic empire?

This time Alex needed two fingers to scratch his nose. The Rillek Empire had fallen to the League of Planets. Timmerman had brought the empire down. Timmerman the Legend. Timmerman the Brave. Timmerman the Savage. Timmerman the Unkillable.

Timmerman, the fucking *hero*.

That's what they called him in the history books. Alex knew the truth, knew that Timmerman was a criminal of the highest caliber, but it's the winners who write history.

Leon Timmerman, a sergeant in the Imperial Marines who threw his lot in with the Uprising. The man who fought his way onto an Imperial dreadnought in order to rescue Lieutenant Pamela Timmerman, his young bride, who'd been taken prisoner along with all the officers of the rebel cruiser *Listaine*. Leon Timmerman, who'd killed the Emperor himself in a quest to rescue his wife.

Well, Timmerman's heroic days were over. Alex was there to make sure of that. It was far, far too late to save the Emperor, the Empire, or any vestige of the old ways. But it wasn't too late for retribution.

Alex walked down the hall, feet crunching on discarded candy wrappers, sheets of used-up net-reader, and an occasional empty tube of bender.

What was this place? How could Timmerman live in a drug-house, a slum? The answer must lay inside Apartment 5-C.

It had taken years to find Timmerman, a decade-long search across two-dozen worlds and a hundred orbital settlements. The funny thing was no one seemed to know where Timmerman lived. He was the icon of the Uprising, yet he never showed his face and no one had seen him in at least a decade. At great risk, Alex finally developed a mole in the League Office for Veteran's Affairs. The mole obtained the address for Timmerman's benefit checks. The address was an apartment registered to Timmerman's daughter Celeste, of all things, under her married name of Brinswager. The benefit records showed she'd moved a dozen times in the past ten years.

Alex flipped down the eyepiece and checked his sweeper again—still nothing. The eyepiece went back into the headband housing. He felt anxious, out of his element. He'd expected a dozen elite guards, the type of protection you'd see for a king or the Prime Minister, expected he'd have to blast his way into the hall using the modified Transteel G-6 Enforcer tucked neatly into the holster at the small of his back. His nose never itched when he had the G-6 in his hand. But nothing. Not a damn thing. Not even a frigging camera.

If the League scum were fool enough to let an assassin this close, then they deserved to have their timeless, un-killable hero blasted into soggy pieces. Trick or no trick, it was time.

Alex straightened his tie and rang the buzzer for apartment 5-C. Inside the apartment, a baby started crying. He heard the droning voices of a holovision, then footsteps. The door opened.

He'd studied the surveillance pictures enough to know every detail of Celeste Timmerman's face, even though the pictures had been taken some fifteen years ago. She was in her early forties but looked a hard fifty. Celeste held a crying baby in the crook of her right arm, held the door open with her left. Heavy bags lined her eyes and her brown hair looked dry and unkempt. A blotch of wet baby vomit rested on her shoulder. The faint smell of shit drifted out of the apartment. She looked exhausted, as if responsibility were the only crutch that kept her standing.

The baby bawling in her arm, she stared at Alex. "Can I help you?" Impatience and frustration tinged her voice.

"Yes ma'am," Alex said. "I'm from League Showcase Magazine, I called earlier."

Recognition and anger flashed in her eyes.

"You again? Look, I told you, he's not seeing any visitors."

She tried to shut the door, but Alex slid his foot forward to keep it open.

"Please, Mrs. Brinswager, I've waited a long time to talk to him." He towered over her, even though she had the thick build and height reminiscent of her hulking father.

Her voice went cold and staccato. "I don't care how long you've waited, he's not seeing anyone. And don't call me Mrs. Brinswager… that bender-sniffing bastard is out of my life for good."

"Fine. Miss Timmerman, then? Please, I only need a few minutes. What's a story on war heroes without Leon Timmerman?"

"Jesus, mister—that was *fifty-seven* years ago. The galaxy has moved on, ya know? He's an old man. I'm sure he's not what you're hoping for."

"Please, Ms. Timmerman, I'll only be a few minutes."

She took a small step back, considering. Alex knew he was close, almost in the apartment, and his senses hunted for the trap, the secret defense that must be waiting for just the right moment to take him out. But he didn't see anything. Celeste Timmerman held a baby, not a weapon; there was nothing dangerous in sight.

He threw out his best smile, white teeth blazing from behind his tanned skin. "Please, Ma'am. I promise I'll keep it short."

Her brow furrowed for a moment, then the baby erupted into fresh screeches. Its little face wrinkled into a mask of misery. She sighed a tired, frustrated sigh, then switched the child to her other arm, letting the door swing open. "Alright, mister, but I'm telling you I'll be surprised if he can even hear you. Keep it short."

"Don't worry," Alex said as he strode into the apartment. "This won't take long at all."

He casually flipped down the eyepiece, yet still it gave no hint of a monitoring device. He surveyed the small apartment: a kitchen, perhaps two bedrooms, a living room where the holovision droned a football game. The Ionath Krakens vs. the Quyth Survivors. Alex smiled at the irony—he'd bet his entire savings on the Krakens, the risk seeming insignificant when he figured that he'd never live to know the game's outcome. The living room was dark, lit only by the holovision's blue glow. The flickering images framed the silhouette of a huge man.

Timmerman the Hero.

Alex walked towards the living room, feeling the danger now, feeling the adrenaline rocket through his system with a kick stronger than the purest bender ever distilled. His nose screamed to be itched. How many Rillek assassins had Timmerman killed? How many elite Imperial Guards? Timmerman had been called "the galaxy's deadliest man." But that was a long time ago, Alex reminded himself. Timmerman was old, Alex was young, and in a few moments all this concern would be purely academic.

Alex entered the living room. Celeste followed, jostling the crying baby in her arm, trying to comfort its misery. Alex monitored her position without looking, always keeping a fix on her, ready to kill her in a blur of movement, ready to kill the baby, too, if need be. Whatever it took to get at Timmerman. If there was no security, well, that made his duty even easier.

He was close, so close—the last mission of the last assassin of an empire five-decades dead, an empire that Alex had never known. He was thirty-two, and all he knew of the old days was the League's revisionist propaganda and the tales of his father, also a Rillek Assassin, heard through the partition of a war-prison visiting room.

All of that, and now he was here with Timmerman. The big, bald man sat in a beat up grav recliner, the kind of chair used for fat people or invalids. Beyond him, the holovision showed the Krakens were up 17-13. Alex took that as a good omen.

Even as Alex came around the chair, he knew he'd found his prey. There could be only one man with those broad shoulders, that inch-thick scar running from between his shoulder blades to the top of his head, and that iguana tattoo on his throat, tail wrapping all the way around the neck. But the tattoo looked faded, blurred. And the shoulders looked somehow wrong, perhaps not as broad as they should be... or perhaps they just sagged.

Training told him to pull the G-6 and put a hole in the back of Timmerman's head. But the old man wasn't going anywhere, and Alex wanted to see his face, wanted to see the expression as death came to claim the criminal.

Alex came around the front of the chair and stared at his target, ready to kill instantly in a dozen different ways—and despite decades of single-minded focus and training, his breath escaped him in a sigh of astonishment.

Leon Timmerman sat in the grav recliner, staring more into space than at the dancing holovision images. Wrinkles lined his face, etched as clearly and deeply as his trademark scar. He wore blue pajama bottoms with no top. A terrycloth bib hung round his neck, resting on a chest that was once huge but now sagged like an old woman's tits covered with gray gossamer hair. A thin string of drool ran from the corner of his mouth to the bib, which was wet in a dozen spots. Rough, patchy, gray beard covered his face, clear in the holovision's flickering light.

The smell of shit was stronger here, and a scent of piss also filtered through the air. Leon Timmerman was slumped in his chair... no, not just slumped, but *limp*. Alex noticed a strap around Timmerman's broad chest—a strap to keep him from falling forward. Timmerman stared blankly, probably as unconscious of the football game as he was of the spit hanging from his toothless jaw.

He was *old*.

Not just old, fucking *ancient*. Could this be the same man? Could this be the man who'd brought down an Empire? The man who'd killed so many men that even League historians had lost count? The man they sang songs about? Made movies about?

With one smooth motion Celeste expertly shifted the baby to her free arm, reached out and wiped away the spittle. Her expression wasn't pity or satisfaction, but rather a beleaguered sadness—she appeared long-since resigned to the drooling *Behemoth* strapped into the chair.

"Not what you expected, eh, mister?" With her free hand she lifted Timmerman's bib and dabbed at his mouth.

"I... uh... no, he's not what I expected."

"I told you, but you wouldn't listen."

"What happened to him?"

"Same thing that'll happen to me, to you, to everyone. He's just plain *old*. His 87th birthday is coming up in a week."

It made perfect sense, of course—Timmerman's reign of terror ran its course almost sixty years earlier. Alex had expected an old man, sure, but nothing like this, nothing like this drooling moron. Here was Timmerman the Unkillable, Timmerman the Savage.

Timmerman the fucking *hero*.

"How long has he been like this?"

"Oh, he started going downhill when my mother died. Let's see... that was about twenty years ago."

"Twenty years? Pamela Timmerman has been dead for twenty years?"

"Yeah, twenty years... that's about right."

Unexpected thoughts ricochet through Alex's head. Pamela Timmerman dead. For two decades, no less. Sure, the Uprising had been in full swing when she'd been captured, but the Emperor had the situation under control—right up until the moment Leon Timmerman cut off his head. All because of that whore Pamela Timmerman. The very cause of the Empire's demise, and she'd been dead for twenty years.

Leon and Pamela's story had been told a dozen different ways in a dozen different media, and in all that time it had never crossed Alex's mind that the pair would get old and die. There was something so immortal about the Timmermans' story, their timeless love and all that shit. But she'd been dead for twenty years, back when he was just a little kid who hated the League for putting his father in prison.

He stared at Leon Timmerman, seemingly a caricature of the once-imposing man. As he watched, Timmerman's head lolled forward; another thin string of drool swung from his lower lip. Celeste dabbed at it with the bib, a reaction so automatic she probably didn't even register it.

The small of Alex's back tingled, right under the spot where the G-6 Enforcer rested. Not yet. Not just yet. He wanted Timmerman to see it coming, wanted him to know the Rillek Empire won out in the end.

Alex realized that his nose no longer itched.

"Why is he here, Ms. Timmerman? Why is he here and not in some veteran's hospital?"

"They won't take care of him anymore," Celeste said. She bobbed the baby up and down with one hand, the other hand gently caressing Timmerman's bald head. The baby's cries steadily faded away. "Can you believe that shit? They say they need the space for vets of the Sklorno conflict. It's hard to argue with them, really—you ever see the wounded from that war? It's horrible, what with those little bugs crawling around inside them and all. But still, you'd think they could take care of Leon Timmerman. It's crazy that the people who make the decisions now weren't even born when daddy rescued mom, when he killed the Emperor."

"He gets benefits, right?" Alex realized he'd never thought to inquire about the amount of the benefit checks, only their destination. He'd just assumed Timmerman had all the money a hero could want.

"They're still paying, but money at 2620 values doesn't go that far in 2667 thanks to inflation, now does it?"

"No," Alex said, his voice coming from some faraway place. "No, I guess it wouldn't."

"My ex-husband spent most of the benefit checks on booze and bender. Fucking bastard. Maybe things will be a little better now that he's gone. It's funny… Leon Timmerman is in all the history books, a real hero to the cause and all that shit, and they can't even take care of him. No one wants to remember him like this, they all want the man that cut off Emperor Shimoto's head. Like I said, mister, all that shit went down fifty-seven years ago. Things move on, you know?"

Alex shook his head. It astonished him, even angered him, but he felt a pang of pity for Timmerman. Timmerman was a criminal, but he was also an incredible soldier, a man who'd beaten odds so great it was still hard for people to understand. The Rillek Empire would have never allowed this to happen to a warrior, to a hero. But the League was a far cry from the Empire. In a way, this was a just reward.

But still, Timmerman was alive. The Emperor was dead. Alex's father died after spending four decades rotting away in a League penal colony. Rotting away as a war criminal. A *war criminal*, for God's sake, when he'd served his Emperor faithfully. And during his father's sentence, the real criminal was treated like a hero. Drooling waste or not, this was the man that brought down the greatest Empire in the history of mankind. He had to die.

"Mister Timmerman," Alex said, voice automatically slipping into a tone most people use for small children. "Mister Timmerman? Can you hear me?"

Timmerman's blank eyes never strayed from the football game.

Alex raised his voice. "Sergeant Timmerman? Can I ask you a couple of questions?"

Still no response. Celeste said nothing, just stood there jostling the baby, whose cries were now only tiny sobs.

Enough of this shit. What did it matter if he saw it coming or not? He had to die anyway. Alex reached behind his back and pulled out the G-6 Enforcer. Celeste inhaled sharply. She covered the baby with both arms, trying to shield the toddler, but kept her wide eyes riveted on Alex.

Celeste stared at the weapon, than at the stranger she'd let into her apartment. "Mister, what the hell are you doing?"

"He's a criminal, Celeste," Alex said, using her name for the first time. "Old or not, he's a criminal, and he's got to pay."

"Put that gun away!" She felt her pulse racing, pounding through her body in a rapid beat. Was this guy nuts? Was this some publicity stunt? "Put it away—he doesn't like guns."

"That's too bad," Alex said. "He's not going to like it when I blow his brains all over this shitty living room, either."

Celeste tried not to move, tried not to stare as she saw her father blink once, twice, then slowly swivel his eyes to stare at the gun. *Oh God, not again, not again…*

"Mister, listen," she said in a quiet voice. "He's a veteran, for God's sake. Put that gun away now before he has a flashback."

"The sad thing, Celeste, is that I have to kill you too. You and the child. The evil of the Timmerman line stops here, stops now."

Terror spiked through Celeste's soul. This wasn't a media stunt, this nutcase was for real. He was here to kill them all. Maybe she could talk her way out of it, talk some sense into the guy. She stole a glance at her father and her fear cranked up another notch—Leon stared at the gun now, his eyes no longer vacant, no longer empty. She forced herself to look away, look past the gun and look into the eyes of the would-be killer.

"Mister, please, listen," she said. She tried to sound reasonable, but she just sounded scared. "Listen, I don't know who you are, but my father isn't a criminal."

"Oh really?" Barely controlled rage coated the stranger's words. "What if I told you I'm a Rillek Assassin? What if I told you your father is responsible for my father spending four decades in a penal colony? What if I told you my father was in prison for two decades before they let my mother have a child, and then only by artificial insemination? What if I told you I never *once* touched my father? Can you see my point now?"

She started to answer, started to try once again to get him to put the gun away, but Leon Timmerman ended all discussion. His giant hand reached out. She heard a slap of skin as the hand closed on the assassin's wrist.

The gun fired once, the blue beam passing to Celeste's left by a few inches. It blew a huge, smoking hole in the wall. The smell of scorched plastic filled the room.

The assassin turned. The brief look of disbelief on his face evaporated—he tried to pull free, but couldn't break her father's iron grip. Instantly the assassin brought his free hand around, punching Timmerman twice. The old man's crooked nose erupted in a gush of blood, the second punch split the skin above his right eye, yet his head barely budged.

She saw her father smile.

Celeste heard a sharp snap—the assassin let out a small scream as his arm twisted at an unnatural angle, broken just behind the wrist. The gun fell to the floor. The assassin's face screwed into a mask of pain, then of fury; in a blur of blinding speed he brought his free hand towards her father's throat—but Leon seemed to be waiting for just such a move. He pulled hard on the broken wrist. The assassin tumbled into her father's lap with another grunt of pain. Leon's free hand shot forward, fingers extended like claws, thumb heading for the assassin's eye.

"Daddy no!"

But it was too late. His thumb sank into the assassin's eye with a soft, squelchy pop. His huge fingers wrapped around the man's skull, palming it as a child might hold a toy ball -- then a brief twist, a crunching sound, and the assassin went limp. A snarl of primitive fury still covered her father's old, wrinkled, weathered face.

Celeste took a step forward and kicked the gun under the chair, out of sight. It was as if a light went off in the old man's head; the savage expression faded away, the blankness returned—he fell limp, held up only by his strap. Once again he stared blankly at the holovision, a new thread of spit falling from his lips to land on the dead man in his lap.

Celeste felt weak. She sat on the floor, the baby—now silent, of all things—cradled in her arm. She felt the tears come and did nothing to stop them. A roar rose up from the holovision. She absently stared at the replay screen. A Survivor's defensive back had intercepted a Krakens pass and ran it back for a touchdown. The Survivors kicked the extra point, taking the lead 20-17.

"Damn you, daddy," Celeste said quietly. He'd saved her life, the baby's life, but those lives would have never been in danger if not for him.

Another flashback, another body.

"Damn you, daddy... now we've got to move again. I love you, daddy, I love you so much, but why can't you just die?"

But she knew the answer to that. She wondered if he would *ever* die. He was, after all, Timmerman the Undying, Timmerman the Unkillable.

Timmerman...the Hero.

Soapbox 1.1 Beta

By E. A. Zefram

So, you want me to help you, Matthew. I am so honored, truly I am. And it's a wise choice."

"Thank you Mr. Griffiths, it's much appreciated. Would you please take a seat," said the younger man in a white lab coat as he pulled a neon green chair towards the round, technology-covered table. Very little of its white surface peeked through the piles of laptops, monitors, wireless thingamajigs, papers, pens, cables, CD-ROMs, computer language books, a Blackberry and an assortment of empty paper coffee cups sporting various pseudo-inspirational slogans.

"Quite the operation you have here, Matthew," Mr. Griffiths remarked, adjusting his grey suit jacket, making himself as comfortable as possible in the rubbery plastic chair. "Lots of technical stuff I see," he eyed the table, the surrounding bookshelves stuffed full of papers, hard drives laid to rest, spindles of CDs and his gaze stopped at a large whiteboard covered in strange figures. The man's forehead wrinkled up slightly into a worried expression. Matthew ignored it, "yes, we're in our very own high tech cave and it keeps getting smaller."

"Smaller?"

"By all the accumulating crap we refuse to throw out!" Joked another man who had been unseen behind a large monitor.

"Oh, sorry Mr. Griffiths, this is my associate, Roger." Matthew gestured over to Roger, whose too-wide grin looked menacing in the monitor screen light.

"Hello Roger." Mr. Griffiths shifted around in his chair, eyeing the room for any further potential hidden programmers. The suited man smiled but his forehead's collection of worried wrinkles remained in place. He turned back to the man in the lab coat,

"Matthew, is anyone else going to be involved?"

"Nope, just you, me and occasional help from Roger here." Roger kept baring all his teeth, looking quite pleased with himself.

The older man composed himself, sat up and cleared his throat, "Of course. I suppose we wouldn't need much help, we have *us* after all," he pointed to the room in a circle. "Me, and scientists like you two."

Matthew smiled, "Yes, that's true. Though, we wouldn't be doing this if there wasn't so much that is unknown."

"Yes, yes, of course, of course. Ahem, well, yes, we will definitely bring that unknown into the truth of the light now won't we, yes?"

"Yes, Mr. Griffiths," Matthew hid his smile behind a new DVD disk. "OK, we're about ready."

"Ready?"

"Yes, to record your first podcast," the young researcher slipped the disk into the drive and typed something into the keyboard.

"We'll need a web site," Mr. Griffiths offered.

"Yes, that's underway."

"But, you'll need my help with that too," the older man offered, hands clasped in front of him.

"We'll be ok," Matthew kept his eyes on the monitor.

"But, my content? You'll need my input. It must reflect my podcasts—everything people see must be one cohesive complete whole, yes? I thought that—"

Roger interrupted, "Mr. Griffiths, we have everything under control, everything's set to go."

"Actually..." Matthew leaned back, tapping the top of his pen on his upper lip. A few moments passed and only sound in the screen-illuminated room was their breathing and the whirs and hums of all the computers and servers thinking away—as if it was all intended to add to the image Matthew presented of a keen intelligence concentrating on the world's great problems.

"...we *could* use your input Mr. Griffiths. Yes, we'll definitely want to have your web site reflect your thoughts and ideas."

"And what I think as well..."

"Yes, that too," Matthew was nearly successful at hiding his smirk. Out of sight of the older man, Roger rolled his eyes as if in pain. Matthew turned to Roger but continued, "Yeah, we'll want it to be a whole package. Words, vision, the whole experience. I *like* it." Roger looked panicked. Matthew typed him a quick "Don't worry!" through Messenger and turned to Mr. Griffiths.

"Ok, if you'd please put on your headset. Yeah, that one … no…no, the other way, that's it. Okay then … we're good to go. Whenever you're ready."

"Ready?" Mr. Griffiths was still holding the headphones on his head.

"When you're ready I'll hit record."

"I want to hit record."

"Oh, um, alright," Matthew turned his laptop around and pointed to the screen, "click the red button here and then start talking."

"I know that of course," scoffed Mr. Griffiths. After a few long moments he clicked the record button and then sat.

"Um … Mr. Griffiths? We're recording now."

"Yes, I'm collecting all my thoughts. You can edit the final product, no?"

"Sure we can, of course, yes, please continue when you're ready," Matthew sat back, visibly annoyed at not being able to use his laptop during the recording.

The older man cleared his throat, loosened his tie, cleared his throat again, wiggled slightly in the cheap neon orange chair and then he finally spoke.

"Hello! Hello everyone! Hello all! Now, what will we talk about today? Let's just talk. And as this is my first podcast on the computer let's begin with introductions. I am Mr. Professor Griffiths and I will tell you all that I know about the world and what I know that is true on it, around it, and of course, inside it all."

Matthew and Roger glanced at each other, blank-faced in shock. Neither could smile—yet.

"First, let's get some misconceptions out of the way—like,

math and monkeys. We don't have mathematics to explain where monkeys are born do we? But we accept that we need to learn math in school. Then, as a child we see a monkey in the zoo. You don't put the two together intuitively now do you? Of course not, never. So why do that when you're an adult. No. Let's try tying in another interesting concept. The concept of bananas. For they can explode, did you know that? It's true. You need math though, to decide how many bananas you need to make an explosion. Monkeys don't use math so they don't need to worry about the bananas. Though, not all monkeys eat bananas. Try adding that one up in your head! Ha ha ha..." finally he stopped for a breath. "More about jungles in a moment. Let's think about darts. We know math helps with that. And we all want to be smart forever. My family already knows that. Monkeys know that. They stay away from large quantities of bananas. Or bugs. But it depends where in the forest the bugs are. But, I digress..."

After 25 minutes Matthew used Roger's laptop to send a message to Mr. Griffiths. "We've got 5 minutes left, you will want tie things up soon." And then added, "Please, thanks." Mr. Griffiths shot Roger a sharp look of displeasure. Both researchers ignored it.

"And so, I must conclude, if you carry one of those all-in-one screwdriver sets with you in your car you can start assembling your brand new entertainment unit even before you've entered your house. This will facilitate keeping on schedule for the barbeque you will have later that day when your in-laws arrive."

He took a deep breath in and looked around at the monitor and keyboard, "Um, how do I stop recording."

"You click stop."

"Where?"

Matthew swiveled his laptop around and stopped the recording. "Excellent Mr. Griffiths, excellent. This will sound great. I'll edit out the silence at the beginning and it'll be ready to be podcast."

"Oh! Wonderful! Thank you! I want to do more! How about tomorrow?!"

Roger's eyes widened at Matthew.

"Actually Mr. Griffiths it would have to be in a week's time. There's other research I'm doing at the moment—very busy. How about next Tuesday?"

"Oh yes! Yes, wonderful. Yes. Looking forward to it! I have much more wisdom to dispense!" And before Matthew could tell him what time, the older man almost danced out the door and into the hallway.

"Again?!" Roger started laughing out loud.

"Roger, this is *perfect*. This is exactly what I was looking for. Before he agreed to help with our project I thought we would fail before it even got started." Matthew was smiling now. "I think it'll be a huge success. The only question is how huge. And stop smirking so much while the guy is recording—it makes me want to burst out laughing."

Roger put on a mock innocent look.

"No seriously! I want this experiment to go as well as it can. How far will it go, who knows? But if we put too many limits on Mr. Griffiths, we'll never find out." He closed his laptop, slipped it into its padded bag and added, "Okay, time for lunch. I'm starving!"

Roger nodded picking up his backpack, "and he's *not* a professor."

The other laughed. "Oh I know, let him enjoy it. Then let's see if he becomes a demigod over the next few weeks." They left the glowing, humming workspace to continue calculating, uploading and thinking for itself.

"How was it? How did it go?!"

"Calm down Mr. Griffiths, it went great! Two thousand listeners! Great for a first podcast." Matthew was setting up his laptop getting ready for recording.

"Where's your assistant?"

"Exams."

"Oh....OH! I need to help you!"

"Um, what with?"

"The web site! Oh, I wrote out pages of ideas and some drawings

—you need to photocopy these so you can use them."

"Er, 'scan them' you mean. Um, okay, let's have a look then," Matthew carefully took Mr. Griffiths' diagrams and lists and spread them out in front of him. "Where….what… okay, um, now… what's this part?" He pointed to a large box with a squiggle going through it diagonally.

"That's the flow of the web site's entire thought," he leaned back, hands clasped on his belly, and looked very proud of himself.

"Right. Okay, is this here the navigation?"

"Pardon?"

"Are these lists of words what your links will be?"

"Oh yes, yes, I modeled them after many web sites I saw last night. Just make everything work the way I have there and it should be good. See? There," he pointed to the collection of circles. "See those? Those are my thoughts, they will be all over the site. Maybe have some pop up everywhere too. Bits of wit and wisdom."

"Okay." Matthew gathered up all the papers onto Roger's chair, removed his lab coat and handed Mr. Griffiths a headset. "Time to record. Oh, and last week's theme was very mathematics-natural-sciences, so maybe this week something more philosophy-astronomy? Shake things up a bit?"

"Oh! I love talking about those things! Yes, yes… definitely," and he adjusted the headset. "You may click record this time, Matthew." And he grinned in anticipation.

Matthew nodded, and Mr. Griffiths leaned forward. "Greetings to all my new, wonderful fans who have heard what I have talked about last time which was of most interest to everyone I have no doubt indeed and today I will be talking further in the same vein and, ha ha ha, *artery*, ha ha ha, pardon me, but the topic will be different but I'm still, ha ha, *pumped*, get it? To tell you all about today's topics! Topics which always remain at the *heart*—ha—heart of what I always care about."

Matthew barley managed to hide his shudder from the man across from him.

"Today, *the sky*! That big huge place above us. Sometimes it's light, sometimes it's dark. Sometimes it's in between. Why do we let this happen? No one knows. But I know. Sadness. Yes, that feeling you get, you know, when you're not happy. This can change. Like the sky changes color. Don't let your philosophy about your inner dark or light make you not see the light—the light to your inner wisdom to know when it's time for happiness again. If you're a smart enough man, of course. No matter—no matter what time of the day—or year!—it may be. And that includes when you can see a planet in the sky—you know, they look like stars, but not really, but we all know what I mean don't we? Well, not everyone does."

After 20 minutes Matthew handed a scribbled note to Mr. Griffiths in the attempt to keep him on topic.

Please remember today is about philosophy and/or astronomy. Please tie this new advice about growing your own herbs into the overall theme soon—please! Thx

"And so, *use*! Yes, use the sun! The big star in our very own solar system to your very own uses—for it is yours to use. We don't want the sun to feel irrelevant now do we? And neither do we. No."

After the podcast recording was complete, Mr. Griffiths bounded over to Matthews side of the room nearly knocking an iPod and a graphic tablet off the table in his rush. "Sorry! I'm just so excited! Now, the web site…"

"We'll work on it and show you what we have next time—we can't make it in a day—especially with the features you are wanting."

"Like a place to talk, make comments. I want to know what my new fans have to say!"

"Sure, no, that's a great idea, thanks. See you next week, and, if you like, you're free to prepare what you wish to say entirely ahead of time if you want. You don't have to improvise. There's no reason you can't have notes in front of you."

Mr. Griffiths' eyes widened, "Of course! Brilliant! I'll start writing as soon as I get home! Thank you!" He slapped Matthew hard on the shoulder and left the room. When he was alone Matthew grabbed his shoulder in pain, stared at the pile of paper on Roger's chair and sighed. "This is going to be a coffee-charged, all-pizza weekend. Great."

"He'll hate it."

Matthew sighed. "Roger, he'll love it! It's got everything he wants—and so what if the entire site's navigation is on one giant, big-ass, dropdown menu, who cares. What matters is the site actually functions! Well, sort of. This alone could get us an award out there."

"Okay, *I* hate it," Roger sat in front of the neon blue, dark brown, lime green and grey web site with its random thought bubbles popping up, dispensing short nuggets of wisdom. *'Your life is your story. You don't know how many chapters there are so always use a bookmark.' 'Things look better when your eyes are open all the way. Squinting suggests you're not sure. Or you need sunglasses.' 'Men and women see things differently—be smart and know the difference.'*

"For the record, I hate it," Roger kept clicking to make the annoying bubbles go away. "Can we have a stop button? Please?"

"For what?"

"The thought bubbles of condescension, that's what! And what's with this moronic menu? And the sitemap page is an essay about how to buy the right map for driving out of town—probably to his mother's house!"

Matthew laughed. "It's all part of the whole project. Short of putting on a parade and an air show our 'celebrated professor' has to get his way."

Mr. Griffiths arrived early for his recording session. "I am here to cast my pod! All ready to go! Oh, hi Roger!"

"Hi," he mumbled.

"Your web site is ready, Mr. Griffiths, please come see," and Matthew scooted his chair in, allowing the older man to see his site for the first time.

"What—is that?"

"Your site, Mr. Griffiths sir," Roger gave up closing thought bubbles. "Something wrong?"

"No, no, some of it I like, very nice bubble pops there, very nice, yes. But, why, why can't I see the entire list of topics?"

Matthew started before Roger could answer, "Uhhh, Mr. Griffiths, that's a technical problem we're dealing with at the moment. Um, a server problem has caused a site, um web menu cascade failure for all web sites using the brown and lime green design scheme… thing." Matthew winced.

"Oh, that would be it then. That's too bad. Maybe it can be fixed soon."

Roger grinned, adding, "Yes, a patch is being developed as we speak… um, a fix so that all web sites with brown and lime can show stuff below the bottom of monitor screens…thing." Matthew shot Roger an angry look. Roger just grinned more.

"Well, I trust you'll do what you can. Thank you boys, you've done well."

'Boys?' Roger mouthed to Matthew as Mr. Griffiths turned away. Roger rolled his eyes.

After two months of podcasts about topics from plastic paper clips to philosophical digressions into the true meaning of alarm clocks, it was time for the researchers to share their latest findings.

"It's better than we could have expected. Unique in fact. Here, look at these stats," Matthew handed a printout to Mr. Griffiths.

"Oh my!" he took off his coat, fanning himself. "These numbers!"

"Yep, nearly a million listeners. And many more downloading later. You're a hit Mr. er, Professor Griffiths!"

The older man sat there, beaming, clutching the results in his hands. "T-shirts!"

"What?"

"T-shirts! Everyone wants t-shirts on the web—we could make money! I could pay for the initial production of course," and he reached for his wallet.

"Um, yes, Mr. Griffiths we can do that but let's have a design first shall we?" Matthew's knuckles were white, clenching the armrests of his chair, while Roger simply glared at Matthew in horror.

"I can design one," Mr. Griffiths piped up.

"You?" Roger and Matthew said in unison.

"Yes, I do that, too. I could have made the web site as well but I don't want to take away from your fun. And that poor server problem is still obscuring my list on my site. Those server people should get that all patched up."

"Yeah, they're working on it. Um, can we design the t-shirt? Our gift to you," Matthew was smiling in earnest, "Roger is skilled at vector drawing tools, he'll come up with something fantastic for you."

"Well, ok, vector huh? Well, so long as there're no birds in my design. My podcasts aren't normally about birds."

Roger and Matthew exchanged looks. "No birds, Mr. Griffiths. Oh, before we forget, some comments that have been collected on your site, I'm sure you'll feel more connected than ever."

Mr. Griffiths gazed over them, eyes wide like he was reading what he would receive for Christmas.

> simdarlo4EVA: so helpful are Professor Griffiths thoughts on life and the universe that I find myself repeating his words throughout the day—days feel more balanced now. There is a clarity I didn't know before.

> MrFairweather: Such insight. Such delight. Thank you for sharing Professor! I am truly thankful to my wife for getting me my iPod last year.

> BarTerminal666: Mr professor FTW! I use yuor stories to help my homework. Thx 4 helping. The story about teh sun made lots of cence and I can c where they relate to the universe. I will bcome scietist like u.

"So…so heartwarming…I…yes, I am overwhelmed. I wouldn't know where to start with a t-shirt for these fine people…I…"

"We'll, take care of it, and Mr. Griffiths, our aim over the next few weeks is to double our numbers. We're linking everywhere—everyone's talking about you. On MySpace, Facebook, Twitter, you name it!"

"Twitter?"

"The place where you tweet 140 characters—short tweets like a little bird—to other users."

"Oh, but I said I didn't want a bird used in my t-shirt design."

Matthew looked at Roger's blank face and turned slowly back to Mr. Griffiths. "Don't worry. No birds."

"OK, good…can we record now?"

"Why of course!" Matthew handed over the headset impatiently. Roger hadn't moved pretty much for the last five minutes, his face still frozen.

Thirty minutes later, Mr. Griffiths was finishing his weekly podcast, "and so, if all humans, everywhere, regardless of where they are, were to enjoy the simplicity of having clean underwear daily, every day, then what I have revealed to you will prove that we would no longer have any more war. Peace would be as simple as getting a new pair of underpants out of one's dresser drawers. Now, this won't apply to women of course because they wear more than underpants and frankly, brassieres are NOT my department as I am a man. War must be resolved with wisdom and there's no place for the nonsense of lacy undergarments in all that. Go in peace all my faithful listeners—hold onto your high thoughts—especially to the sounds of the timber wolf howling around the Asian tundra. Good bye for now."

The room was quiet except for the usual hums, whirrs and clicks.

"Oh Matthew."

"Yes?"

Mr. Griffiths rose holding a pile of papers, "I have more web additions for you. Pages to help promote my ideas, my philosophies,

I want them to be clear. Especially a new section on child-rearing, gender roles and discipline."

Roger stood up suddenly, "Matthew, I really have to get to a meeting—totally forgot about it, sorry, um, bye." And he bolted right by Mr. Griffiths and out the door.

"Uh, no problem, Mr. Griffiths, we'll have a look at them soon, thanks." Matthew half smiled.

"So, good then. Thank you. I'll see you next week then. Goodbye," and the 'celebrated' podcaster left the room.

Matthew gingerly leafed through the web changes for a few moments until he finally rested his forehead into the palms of his hands. "Oh no."

The t-shirt was carefully placed on the table without a fold to best display its unique design. Roger had spent the better part of the morning setting up the site changes Mr. Griffiths had requested and he'd already placed the headset at the table in front of the neon chair. Matthew entered the room, followed by an exuberant Mr. Griffiths who rushed directly to the t-shirt.

"Incredible! Beautiful! My compliments to the artist!" Roger grinned triumphantly while Matthew stood frozen with his mouth gaping open. "No, I don't know what it means but I'm sure it's perfect. And no birds either. Superb."

Matthew stepped forward, looking from the shirt, to Roger and back again. "Yes, Roger, please explain the design to Professor Griffiths."

Roger held up the lime-colored shirt with its bold brown logo.

"It's ancient Latin for the complete oneness of everything," he began with a cheeky grin.

"Latin?! Oh I know all about Latin—the numbers especially!"

Mr. Griffiths pointed carefully at the edges of the print.

"Oh, well, then you'll know they only wrote in upper case letters back in the days of ancient Rome." Matthew gave Roger a look of pained suffering. Roger continued grinning. "And only the oracles who lived along the mountain sides knew the secret Latin language of the lower case letters. You see, it's a clue—and the 3 lowercase characters—especially in an ellipse—to convey everything. The continuousness of everything."

"Oh... oh my... thank you. You know, I've always wanted to visit Rome. All those huge buildings and such," Mr. Griffiths continued staring at the logo completely oblivious that Matthews face was starting to turn crimson.

"The site?"

"Oh yes," Roger just kept on grinning. "Incredible additions, thank you. So many areas for visitors to explore your ideas in greater detail, thank you."

Matthew stepped foreword, "Roger, before the recording can I talk to you?" He stepped dizzily into his chair.

"Sure. Oh, Professor Griffiths..."

"Yes?" He was already seated, just about to place the headset over his ears.

"We believe visitors to your site now exceeds one hundred million."

Matthew let out a choked cough and Mr. Griffiths shot up out of his chair. "Oh! Oh! ...um...Oh!"

"Okay, okay, calm down... we're not surprised by the figures! Your listeners are not only devoted but bring new visitors—I'm thrilled to see the results."

Matthew stared into space.

"It's miraculous!"

"No miracle Mr. Griffiths," Matthew interrupted. "It's technology. Now let's record." Roger sat down slowly, his smile disappeared.

"Hello hello, to my millions of fans—my devout listeners—the gracious few that became a gracious many! I have a delightful gift for all of you! In gratitude for your continued support we have a free t-shirt for you that –"

"Stop! *Free*?!" Both researchers were staring at Mr. Griffiths.

"Oh right, um, let me rephrase all that—you can edit later right?"

"Yes, we'll edit later. Continue. Please," Matthew's face was still red.

"We have a special offer, yes, offer for you! A custom designed piece of art—on a t-shirt you can wear anywhere—no matter where you are! The design reveals the total everythingness of nothing in a continuous manner..."

Roger chuckled quietly.

"And we can have it on our—*my* web site where you can buy the shirt. I don't know how much it is but I'm sure my web page will tell you. Please check it, thank you. Alright! Now! For all your multitudes out there I ask, how can flying buttresses help you? How?"

Matthew and Roger shook their heads in confusion.

Mr. Griffiths smiled ear to ear, "Support! We all need the flying buttresses of life all around us—and they take many forms. The vaults of our doubts hold up the ceiling that we think will fall down upon us when we don't remember our buttresses. Think of buttresses for a moment and the columns of hope will lift you out of the pit of confusion that you are probably in right now. My goal is to motivate you to identify the flying buttresses in your own life. Right now. They may be your car. Your neighbor. The raccoon that goes through your garbage at night. You will already know what the dark corner has to reveal with that bright crayon left out in the sun too long."

After the half hour was over, Mr. Griffiths shook both of the researchers' hands and marched triumphantly out of the room, "till next week! Remember your buttresses!"

Matthew for a moment had forgotten to stop recording. "*How many visitors? Why don't you tell me stats and* –"

"Look. If I'm supposed to create Purgatory's official web site, create some bizarre t-shirt inspired by that man's ponderings, then I think I can use a bit of creativity with the site visitor numbers.

You did want to see how far a person would run with the idea that they're famous on the web."

Matthew sat, his face now pale.

"Look, I'm sorry, Matt, I got carried away with the t-shirt and the numbers but jeez, this guy isn't just podcasting he is a *pod*. What's scary is the possibility that some people could actually follow what he says. He's not the only nutter out there."

"I sometimes feel sorry for him," Matthew started preparing the recorded file. "He just doesn't know anything. And he doesn't know that he doesn't know anything. It must scare him."

"No it doesn't. He's not scared at all. His delusions are firmly held up by his flying buttresses - don't you forget that," Roger making a sweeping gesture with his hand. Matthew laughed.

"Okay. So what happens next week. What if he starts preaching that everyone should shatter the delusions of postmodern architecture in favor of some medieval ideal?"

"Then maybe for once we'll laugh out loud," Roger grinned packing away his laptop and the new t-shirt.

"Or we can let Master Griffiths work on his own site," laughed Matthew.

"He's not touching my buttresses!" and he left the room with a grin.

"Over a billion ... how did ... how did that happen?"

"The buttresses. Your speech about life and architectural elements must really have struck a chord in everyone," Roger spoke gently and directly to Mr. Griffiths. Matthew rolled his eyes.

"I'm so... oh... I'm so overwhelmed. All those people. Are you sure we can't continue with our podcasts after today? All those people will be lost without hearing what I have to say. Things to brighten their day, bring meaning, clarity. To bring reason to the things that make sense without which the only clarity will be confusing reason and what not."

Matthew handed Mr. Griffiths his headset. "We're ready to record.

Your audience is one sixth of the entire human population—not to make you nervous or anything, but, you may want to have a theme that ties together all your other podcasts. We're sorry we can't continue... at least not for a while."

Mr. Griffiths looked down into space for a moment and then in a determined move put the headset on in one motion and sat up straight and proud. "Alright, let's begin."

"Recording," Roger leaned back.

"Dear followers, my brilliant audience. I am humble before you and must bring sad news—yes, news that is darker than when it's in the middle of the night. Our podcasts must end for now. Do not be lost! I repeat! Do not feel abandoned. I will give you the elements you need to survive in my absence. So, be calm and get a piece of paper handy. And a pen. Or a pencil. Whichever you like best. Or have handy. And I will tell you all you need to know. First, you will need a package of about twenty or so medium-sized birthday balloons. It doesn't matter what color. I know this must sound odd but... but, the meaning of everything you seek is within grasp and I, I will share it with you—it will amaze you, thrill you, bring all the understanding you've ever had into one single moment of peace and then—"

A young man with a goatee stormed in the room. "Matthew! Roger!! Guess what?!"

Matthew hit 'stop' and grinned at the newcomer. "What is it, Clem? Can it wait? We're in the middle of recording."

"Oh, oh, I'm sorry," he glanced at the man in the bright plastic chair. "I was just asked to DJ on Friday, Saturday and Sunday evenings; and if it goes well, then...more! Okay, I'm really excited and, yeah, it's really cool!"

"Mr. Griffiths," Matthew held out his hand, "meet the newest on-air personality at our university radio station!"

"Er, hello..." Mr. Griffiths stood up slowly.

"My DJ name will be Darth Melody!"

"Clem that's terrible, don't use that."

"Aww, c'mon Roger, what's wrong, too nerdy?"

"Nerdy is insufficient of a word," Roger grinned. "Why not just call yourself 'DJ of the Sith' or something?"

"Or Caption Quasar!"

"Um, Mr. Darth...um,.." Mr. Griffiths was cautiously holding up his hand.

"Yes?"

"Can I be on your show? After today I can no longer podcast to my over a billion listeners."

Clem glanced over to the others, both with very worried looks on their faces.

"Um, what do you talk about?"

"Everything. I help people with everything. From the practical to the all-encompassing."

"Cool! I'll think about it. How would I get hold of you?"

"My web site of course," he looked over to Matthew and Roger who were shaking their hands telling Clem to stop.

"Sure, 'K, I'll do that. Anyway, Roger, I'll need your technical help here..." Clem stepped around Matthew and glanced at Roger's screen. He burst out laughing. "Oh, dude, is this the link you gave me yesterday?"

"Yeah," Roger grinned. Matthew was covering his mouth.

"Dude! It's bloody hilarious! It's like the House of Winchester—but as a web site! Nothing goes anywhere. You go around in circles. Things just sit there—looking pretty—nothing. Oh man, we were all laughing in the lab this morning. Those popups are *beyond* stupid!"

"Thanks. Thanks so much," Roger kept smiling. Mr. Griffiths was smiling but Matthew remained motionless.

"Sounds like a funny web site," Mr. Griffith's was craning his neck to see what Clem found so amusing. "What is it?"

Clem turned to the older man still laughing. "Oh, some experiment site full of philosophy crap. It's a scream! It's a mess—like you're never supposed to find out the fricken meaning of life ever—too funny!"

Mr. Griffiths stopped smiling and wrinkled his forehead looking confused. Matthew could barely meet his eyes.

"Well, I'll annoy ya later, 'K Roger?"

"Sure, text me or something."

"Oh and tell me when the bloody disaster of a web site goes live will you? I can't wait to show it to my Mac head cousin back home!" He slammed the door shut behind him and the room seemed quieter than it ever had before.

Mr. Griffiths spoke first. "What does it mean by 'go live'?"

Matthew and Roger quietly looked at each other. Roger spoke up, "it means it... it gets launched onto the internet."

"Oh, I see, but my web site is already alive on the web, right?"

Roger relaxed his shoulders, "Oh yeah, yeah, *your* site is online for the public, yes. This experiment one is just a demo." He gave Matthew a quick glance and watched Mr. Griffiths start smiling again.

The recording of the last podcast continued uninterrupted. When finished, Mr. Griffiths looked up from clasped hands to see the other two staring at him in silence. "I'm going to miss this." He rubbed his chin for a moment. "Matthew, why are the podcasts ending?"

"Run out of funding and I have to prepare for my Masters defense," Matthew said quietly.

"Oh, but, what about all of my listeners?"

Matthew stood up slowly. "Um, they'll be fine. Matter of fact, they all get a free t-shirt, just like you'd wished. I think everyone who heard your podcasts will be forever changed." The older man stood, grinned and shook Matthew's hands.

"True...true. I appreciate you making this possible. I'll miss these recording sessions." He walked hesitantly to the door.

"Oh, Mr. Griffiths!" Roger reached into his bag. "You should have this too." He handed him the t-shirt with the encircled 'wtf' on the front.

"Thank you! Oh, you are both just fantastic, thank you. Remember, if you ever need any helpful advice or someone to communicate to the masses, you know who to contact." And Mr.

Griffiths walked out of the room for the last time.

Matthew just stared at the door in disbelief, "he can't wear that!"

"It won't fit him, don't worry," Roger was packing up his laptop and bag.

"What did I do?"

"What?" Roger was pulling on his jacket.

"To Mr. Griffiths… I mean, he really thought he was speaking to millions—billions—of listeners. All hanging on his every word. Ok, I'm still wondering what the deal is with the math monkeys and all that but –"

"Matt, look. Seriously, what did you do? Nothing more than give him the electronic equivalent of a soapbox. He was the one who stood on top of it and spewed his nonsense—did it matter that not a single soul outside this room heard? Not to *him*. He thinks he knows everything. He's happy. Why ruin it for him? And you *did* get your answer to how far a person could take this. Now you just have to defend the thesis."

As Roger was reaching for the door handle Matthew plunked himself back down, "Roger…"

"Yep?"

"How different is it for us? What if we're just in someone else's experiment to see how far we'll take our own ambitions. When we're done our degrees, how many people will be listening? Am I just standing on my own soapbox?" Matthew was minimizing and maximizing application windows at random.

"Um… no."

"How can you be sure? It's still just us… behind a wall of words, numbers, results and code… who's on the other side?"

"Matt… people are listening. You've been staring at that screen too long. I intend to thoroughly bug Darth Disco about his terrible DJ names—all weekend in fact. We'll have a great time. Are you in?"

"Yeah," Matthew mumbled.

"You sure?"

"Yeah, I'm sure!"

"Completely? Wrapping together the total meaning of everything? Encompassing the immense magnitude of the awesome — " Roger was spreading his arms.

"Stop it! I'll go!" Matthew laughed and Roger left.

After burning the entire collection of podcasts on to a DVD, he dragged the 'podcast-experiment1a' folder icon into the Recycle Bin.

"Goodbye soapbox," said Matthew and he shut his laptop.

Uncle Julius

By Timothy G.M. Reynolds

We buried my Uncle Julius today. He was 72, and, *yes*, he was dead when we set him in the ground. It's only noon, but I've had a couple drinks already and right now, while I'm stringing his dog tags onto my keychain and waiting for them to get the wake buffet set out in the dining room of the farmhouse I grew up in, I'm trying to decide what a fitting tribute would be for Julius.

Maybe I should get out my long-ignored, dust-covered brushes and finally paint the portrait of him that Mom wants, based on a couple of the published photos taken of him when he was the eye of his own personal media hurricane (my favourite is the one from the Topeka Capital Journal where he's facing down Jack Happer's prize bull and smiling). Also under consideration is finally finishing composing the song about him that I started back in college when he was on some Wichita morning show trying to roll an egg across the host's desk with just the power of his mind. I finally digitalized the old video tape we have of the show so maybe it's about time I finish the song.

Then again, although the painting and the song both need to be done at *some* point, based on the massive influx of emails that's bombarded me in the last twenty-four hours, I think I'm going to have to at least address his hundreds of thousands of fans he found through my odd little podcast, RS: RELATIVELY SPEAKING. I'm kind of loath to use the podcast because I'm pretty sure it was a podcast that killed him. On the other hand, maybe the podosphere is the perfect place to take this, since it made at least *some* of his dreams come true.

Although possessing strange planet-wide popularity now, RS started out a few years ago with really, *really* limited appeal, since

I was just getting my feet wet in the new medium to see if it was a good fit with the material I wanted to get out on the 'net. I'd always wanted to host my own radio show so once a week I put together a podcast involving my strange relatives, usually starting each half-hour 'cast with a short interview with Mom's lawyer-cousin, Leon. Leon and I chatted mostly about the legal ups and downs of incorporation and contracts within the farming community and I'll be completely honest and straightforward and tell you flat-out that no one could ever describe those early podcasts as either riveting or captivating. That all changed, though, the week after I upgraded my portable digital audio gear and started recording and podcasting a couple of the Wichita County Fair performances by my infamous singing aunts, The Warbling Wichita Wrens.

Infamy is far too easy to achieve in this day and age with YouTube and all the other upload-your-shame-on-video websites, but my aunts more than earned theirs. For as long as I can remember, Fair Time meant that my aunts were often either half in the bag drunk from judging the entries in the home-made cider competition or high on the medicinal weed Aunt Elise smoked for her glaucoma. Some days it was both. The worse the glaucoma got, the higher they got, and the performances were always gems, in a 'did she really just sing what I think she just sang?' kind of way. They don't sing anymore, but the archives of those early podcasts are still as popular as ever.

The Warbling Wichita Wrens were definitely a hit, but my subscriber list didn't grow into triple digits until Uncle Julius, the family's token Vietnam vet, caught wind of the attention his sisters-in-law were getting and suggested I interview him about some of his conspiracy theories. From Marilyn Monroe's murder by Abbot and Costello to Elvis' reincarnation as a humming llama in Decatur, Illinois, he was privy to them all and more than happy to disseminate them to the world at large.

Then one day he shocked the shit out of me with his completely unexpected 'on air' description of the time he spent with a French-

Canadian psychic while they were POWs in 'Nam. How could I do anything but let the 'tape' roll and then dedicate an entire podcast to the stunning tale? In a matter of hours my subscribership set sail into the sea of high five-digits, with fans writing in from McMurdo Station in Antarctica to Nassau to Beijing. Julius was an almost instant hit and the Warbling Wichita Wrens were forgotten, which is probably a good thing because one died and two are in rehab.

As much fun as Julius and I were having, though, the ride wasn't expected to last because, like everything else he *ever* got involved in, I assumed my uncle would quickly get bored and find something shining to draw his attention away. And did my prediction come true? Not a fricking chance! My uncle who had lived much of his life under the thumb of family and friends' mediation, regulation and social 'filters', was drawn inexorably to the one form of media totally lacking in mediation, regulation and filters, social or otherwise. Much to my dismay, I discovered that there was no way in hell that Uncle Julius was walking away when he finally had an audience who wanted to hear *everything* he said, no matter how outrageous it originally sounded when he'd lobbed the idea onto the table like a conversational grenade during a family dinner.

He got so caught up in the whole podcast process that after only three truly scintillating episodes of Telekinetic Tales from the Hanoi Hilton he brought in his own intro music to 'spice up' my humble little narrow-cast. Starting that day, "TT from the HH" always opened with a portion of the Jimi Hendrix solo in Gypsy Sun and Rainbow's 1969 Woodstock rendition of 'The Star Spangled Banner'.

Then, holy crap of craps, once he found out that he could actually subscribe to the podcast and download the whole thing to an MP3 player so he could listen to it all again and again, he nagged and nagged my mother until she finally drove him into town to get an iPod! He would have asked *me* to drive him, but Mom was the custodian of his finances so he pretty much had to have her along to pay for it anyway so why not have her do the driving, too.

Uncle Julius was actually the first member of his geriatric

generation in town to get an iPod, and after only an hour of his showing it off to the Thursday Morning Folgers & Glenfiddich crowd down at Legion #1, the local Circuit City was inundated with walker-supported, curse-muttering, half-informed senior citizen veterans joining the 21st century with 'one of them there I-music-pod-people thingies'. When Circuit City ran out of stock, the Crestline minibus from the Eleanor Roosevelt Retirement Palace was quickly commandeered for an impromptu road trip to Wal-Mart's Electronics Department. There was even a little side-trip to the in-store McDonald's, wedged between the Portrait Studio and the Crafts Department, because nothing says "I'm on the cutting edge of technology" like fumbling with a too-damned-small-to-read instruction manual over regular Freedom Fries and a deep-fried Filet-o-Fish sandwich that sticks to your dentures.

All was goofy but pretty quiet on the podcast front for awhile when all of a sudden, one cloudy afternoon, Uncle Julius made the seemingly harmless offer to actually channel some of his psychic energy through the podcast, to share his 'gift' as it were with the masses. Oh, it didn't matter that I explained fairly patiently to him that the show wasn't *live*, that it was all pre-recorded and then uploaded—he wanted what he wanted, and why on Earth would his favourite nephew deny him that bit of joy? So I didn't. I suppose part of the reason I went along with the idea was that Julius had laid claim to special powers for almost as long as I'd known him, and I figured at worst, it would make an interesting episode for his growing fanhood but at best, he would actually succeed and we'd *both* become famous.

My memory is a bit spotty when it comes to any of my childhood before the age of five, but since I was one of those kids always hitting my head on things when trying a stupid stunt while my big brother, Lucas, egged me on, I'm hardly surprised. That said, my first memory of Uncle Julius' 'strange and wonderful gift' was when he used it to stop me from running away from home on my brother's bike. It was my fifth summer and I was one pissed-off little brat.

I went tearing past him down the old lane out back of the barn with my school bag stuffed with my G.I. Joe, my entire Hot Wheels collection, fresh underwear and a half-crushed bag of Hostess Salt & Vinegar Potato Chips bouncing on my back. The fact that I wasn't stopping to pick up the Hot Wheels as they tumbled out of the incompletely-closed bag and onto the dusty lane told my uncle something was *seriously* wrong—my Hot Wheels were my life! He shouted four or five times for me to hold up and he even made an attempt to chase me on foot, but I was peddling like all four of our school bullies were on my tail and stopping meant being beaten to death.

The stupid thing is that I was only running away because Mom wouldn't let me eat a third post-school, pre-chore chocolate chip cookie, having already consumed my standard-issue allotment of two. Like I said, I was a brat.

The way my brother—the ever-reliable prosecution's witness against me—tells the story, Uncle Julius stopped shouting, dropped to one knee, put his hands to his temples and fixed his Stare of Power at the fleeing bike. Lucas said that our uncle simply willed the bike to stop and it did, 'dead' in its tracks. I, on the other hand, flew more than a little awkwardly over the handlebars and landed on my unhelmeted head. Come to think of it, that was probably the first of the many such minor head traumas to come.

When my senses finally cleared, I swore up and down that my tumble was caused by the front tire slamming into a fist-sized rock lying in wait in the lane, but since the rock was nowhere to be seen, Lucas insisted it was Julius. All these years later I've come to suspect that I probably hit the damned rock hard enough to knock it over into the weeds, but good old Uncle Julius claimed it was his psychic powers that had stopped me and who was I to argue? I was only a cookie-deprived five-year-old fugitive escaping from the drudgery of helping Mom hang the wash out to dry.

That's my first memory of the strange and wonderful world of Uncle Julius and his 'powers'. Unable to work due to the pain and limited movement of a shrapnel-punctured left shoulder from his second tour in 'Nam, my uncle had all the time in the world to dedicate to strengthening his mental powers. From that day on, Julius spent one-hundred-and-forty-four minutes each day working to refine his gift. He said that one-hundred-and-forty-four was a number of power. He'd read it somewhere—probably in the back of one of the comic books he loved to pore over while sitting in the barber's chair every third Tuesday—and he accepted the fact without question. So it was one-hundred-and-forty-four minutes each day, day in and day out without fail for the rest of his life. I have no idea why he couldn't apply that kind of dedication to the simple things in life, like learning to play the guitar we bought him for Christmas in '88 or changing his dirty socks before the rank smell chased the dog and every other living thing off the front porch after dinner. It had to be one-hundred-and-forty-four minutes each day.

This 'working to refine his power' took a number of forms over time. In the first two years all he really did was a daily drill of sitting in front of the old, over-heating, static-spouting, G.E. radio he kept out in the barn. He would stare and stare and concentrate on adjusting the volume with only the powers of his mind. This was back in the days before cable television took away humanity's imagination and, from what I remember of that damned radio, when it did actually occasionally pick up a broadcast, the volume was known to vary all on its lonesome, with or without Uncle Julius' mental intervention.

Then the G.E. blew a tube and nearly burned down the barn. Mom was a whole lot less than impressed and said her brother-in-law was putting crazy ideas in her young sons' heads so it had to stop. Julius took that as the challenge it was not meant to be and since he was satisfied that he had some measure of control over his powers he graduated himself to tougher tasks.

One Saturday in my seventh summer he finally made the leap in faith to try influencing a living creature. Bicycles and radios were one thing, but God's creatures would *really* test his power, he whispered when I slipped up beside him out in the yard. Uncle Julius was up at sunrise that day and had spent the first two hours staring at the swallows swooping and diving from their nests in the barn to the fallow field and back. When I noticed his focus I asked, in all childhood innocence, if stopping a flying bird would make it drop like a stone to the ground where it could be hurt, or worse. Well, that ended the experiment with the swallows pretty damned quick. Julius wasn't a cruel man, sometimes he just needed someone to point out the flaw in his single-minded methodology.

He thanked me for the insight and assured me that, if they could, the birds would thank me, too. Then he took my kid-dirty, seven-year-old hand in his soft, dry, oversized paw and led me around to the side of the house where Mom had her vegetable garden.

"Lad, there's a rabbit hereabouts who's bin eatin' your mother's carrots'n tomatas. She wants me to set up a snare to kill him but I think I have a better way, and it starts with becomin' invisible."

By "invisible", Julius meant the very mundane method of using a blind, like Dad did when he went duck hunting every fall; but this kid was still excited to be included in such seriously adult goings on so off we went to find the materials necessary to our becoming invisible. We eventually built our blind out of some of Mom's lesser bed sheets and planted ourselves in the wicker chairs carried over from the porch so we could watch through the spaces between the sheets in comfort. I really didn't expect to see the rabbit because I'd seen him out there earlier, getting his fill while Uncle Julius was staring at the swallows. Mom said I was to throw rocks at the rabbit if I ever saw it, but *it* wasn't growing carrots and *it* didn't make me eat carrots. Matter of fact, it ate the carrots I hated so so much and that, in my books, made Little Bunny Foo Foo my friend, and I don't throw rocks at friends.

Now, Uncle Julius may have had some strange ideas over the years, but except for last week's freight train 'incident', he had the most incredible luck of anyone I've ever met. If a flipped coin landed heads five out of ten times for me, for Julius it would be heads eight out of ten. At the time, like him, I believed it was his powers, but when Foo Foo the rabbit hopped out of the bushes only five minutes into our vigil, even my uncle said, "Well, ain't that lucky."

Then he leaned in, hands raised, palms forward, one eye closed and stared kind of lopsided at the bunny; and this seven-year-old blood kin who hoped some of the power could rub off, leaned forward, raised my hands, closed one eye and lopsidedly stared, too.

In my experience, rabbits, when not being chased, are cautious little critters. Even at seven I knew that. To this day I've never seen one hop more than a couple feet without stopping to listen and sniff, and that little carrot-eater we watched way back then didn't disappoint me. He took two hops and froze. After a second or so he moved again only to stop again after two more hops. It was typical cottontail behaviour, but the barefooted seven-year-old in dungarees and his thirtyish uncle in his dusty cammo combat pants, drab olive t-shirt and floppy U.S. Army-issue jungle hat swore that every stop that rabbit made was caused by nothing less than the powers held in our brains. I started that simple little vigil just wanting to keep my off-beat uncle company on a sunny Saturday, but I finished it a firm believer in the extraordinary powers of certain human minds.

I became a true convert that day and, as is typical in rural communities, word spread faster than a ticked-off bumble bee. Pretty soon some of the more superstitious farmers came by to ask the psychic if he could heal or predict. Well, if he couldn't before, Julius certainly found that he could now. Never as popular a man as my hard-working father, his brother, Julius now had visitors on a regular basis, and he loved it. They came to him for bunions, breaks, sprains, gout and one daring old gent brought his piles, but Julius was wise enough to refer him to the herbalist down the road.

Let me point out something before I go on: Julius Flack may have been shell-shocked and gullible enough to believe himself a psychic, but he *was* a thinking man. As my mother never failed to point out, Julius always had an answer for everything.

"Why don't you make it rain an' save the crops, Julius?" a neighbour asked.

"If'n I make it rain now, Bill, we'll have a colder winter due to the variation in pressure caused by the unexpected cloud cover and the new level of humidity during this new moon."

"Why cain't you heal my leg faster, Mr. Flack?"

"If'n it heals too quickly, Mitchell, the break will take calcites from the rest of the bone and weaken it, an' then your limp'll be worse than before."

"Julius, if you kin make a hoppity rabbit stand still, why not make my chickens lay twice as many eggs?"

"Chickens only got so many eggs in them, Mr. Wilkins, an' if you force them to give them to you all at once it'll kill them an' then all you'll have is one good roast, a handful of feathers, a bunch of eggs and an empty spot in your coop."

Even my brother sought his sage advice. "Uncle Julius, kin you use yer powers t' make the girls at school like me?"

"Lucas, lad, I'm a psychic, not a miracle worker."

He didn't always make sense, but he *did* have a sense of humour. If he got a dilly of a question, though, he simply countered with "That's more a question for the good Lord in church on Sunday" and that shut up the lot of them. They were willing to believe a psychic healer walked among them but they were also good Episcopalians and some questions threatened to lead them onto sacrilegious ground where the devil sows his wicked ideas.

It may not sound like it, but every once in a while Uncle Julius had a flash of common sense and it was usually when was at his healing. While he was concentrating his power on a back injury he would knead the muscle with his hands. He said it was to help the transfer of power but I know now that a good circulation-aiding muscle rub has been known to do wonders for an injury.

Another time, I sprained my left ankle while playing with Dad's snowshoes and Julius applied his power while my foot was propped up in a snow bank. Whether I now credit the snow's cold or my uncle's powers, the swelling did go down with uncanny speed.

Did Julius notice any of the coincidences? He never said, one way or another. And Dad? Well, Julius *was* his little brother, and it never hurt business having a healer in the family—someone who drove from two counties away to see that same healer could quite often be convinced to take home a bushel of fresh corn or apples, for a small price.

Then, as I said, one day my somewhat mixed up, but harmless 'telepathetic' uncle (as Lucas used to call him at school to keep from being pummelled when the others mocked Julius behind his back) offered to share his healing power with the subscribers of my podcast and took his game to a whole new level. Before we knew it, what seemed like half the world was coming along for the ride. I guess people will believe just about anything if it'll make them feel special and less alone in a continually more disconnected and lonely world, so them wanting to develop their psychic abilities through a pre-recorded podcast shouldn't have surprised me as much as it did.

In two blinks of an eye Uncle Julius went from being a self-proclaimed psychic war vet trying to predict the upcoming seasons better than The Farmers' Almanac, to being the talk of the internet, the prince of the podosphere and the lord of every general store front porch and Wal-Mart checkout-line in the great state of Kansas and well beyond. And then he went and got himself hit by a train.

Being hit by a train has that effect on a person's reputation, psychic or not, and before I set about putting together a podcast tribute for a man almost triple the age of the average pod-monkey, I'd better tell you about the end.

Two weeks ago Julius returned from one of his forays into the city, walking on a cloud of sheer enthusiastic joy. It was the 8th, a fact I remember because it was Lucas' son's eighteenth birthday and we were all getting ready for the party. Mom, ever the practical one, asked her brother-in-law if he'd found a job. He was seventy-two but she never gave up hope.

"A job? Nope. A calling? Yes ma'am."

And that's all he said until dinner, when the whole family was gathered around the table while young Lucas Jr. blew out candles and talked about his first year of college. I, myself, was flashing back to my childhood, making a mountain and lake of my mashed potatoes and gravy and most everyone else was eating as much of Mom's incredible home-cooked feast as they could. Mom still cooks as though for growing sons, even though we're now well into our forties, and these family events were a welcomed chance to purge the fast food crap that was clogging up our intestines and top up on free-range, organic, Mom's Good Cookin'. As a matter of fact, Lucas Sr. did happen to grow up to be a giant of a man a full head taller than my own five-nine, and I swear it was because of Mom's cooking. Since he'd happily taken over the farm when Dad retired in '99, I guess it was a good thing he was the size of a reliable Clydesdale. But back to my uncle.

Julius told the story all at once, in an uncharacteristic blurt. "I stopped a streetcar today. It came to a complete stop. They tried to say it was a power surge on the 3rd Street line, but they just can't admit the truth. It was me."

Mom stayed quiet, Dad looked up and made some weak, non-committal agreement, my sister-in-law Lisa just nodded, her pretty little mouth full of fresh bisquit, and my brother paid no attention whatsoever, intent as he was on his roast beast. Only Lucas Jr. and I showed any real enthusiasm, and it was me that didn't get the brain into gear before releasing the park brake on my mouth, again.

"A streetcar, Uncle Julius? That's better than a rabbit or a bike by far. Next thing you know you'll be stopping a freight train." Shit. I'd said it. I couldn't take it back even if I'd known what idea I'd just put into the head of my well-meaning fool of an uncle. 20/20 hindsight isn't much of a gift, people.

"A freight train..." He just locked his gaze on the centrepiece candle for a moment and his smile grew from a single seed to a whole crop in a handful of blinks. This time no one but me noticed, most of them having found that hot sweet potatoes are infinitely more interesting than yet another story from Julius. Needless to say, my own family weren't subscribers of my podcast.

For a week things went on as usual with a new podcast recorded and uploaded, with folks still dropping by to visit with Uncle Julius, ask for his help and maybe even buy some corn or a handful or two of carrots from Mom's smaller-than-it-used-to-be vegetable garden.

It took a day or two, but once the trickle of fan responses to the podcast started, it became a flash flood too fast for me to do a damned thing. If it wasn't bad enough that I gave the freight train idea to Julius in the first place, I'm sure I compounded the whole thing when I didn't stop him from expounding on the podcast about the whole streetcar incident and what was next for the telekinetic power of Julius Flack. The fans were ecstatic and supportive and everything Julius' own family had never been of any of his wacky ideas. But as well-meaning as they were, they didn't know my uncle like I did and I'm pretty sure none of them imagined that he would take it so far that he might get hurt. Then again, there were probably more than a few who hoped we'd videotape the event and post the results on the web, however gruesome they might be. Maybe if there had been some reg or rule forbidding old men from trying to send psychic powers to his legion of podcast subscribers, then maybe I wouldn't be planning a memorial 'cast. Maybe Julius would have become bored and tried road-kill taxidermy or rock tumbling or macramé. But there wasn't and he didn't.

Two nights later, on Tuesday, the moon was full ripe and the night felt thick with energy. It just might be that's what inspired Julius to follow through with his plan, because he sat on the porch until 2 a.m., leaning forward, arms up, palms forward and one eye closed, staring at the moon's disk as if he could soak up all its mystical powers to augment his own.

Maybe my uncle really did stop that rickety old streetcar, and maybe, after more practice, a small, empty freight train could have been within his reach, but at 11:55 Wednesday morning, the fully-laden three-engine Wichita-bound Kansas Central ran over the kindest soul to ever come back mixed up from a war that never should have been. They said his end was quick, but I wonder if he even saw it coming, what with his hands up in front of him and his one good eye closed as he focused his power on the not-so-simple task at hand.

The Eyes Have It

BY J.D. WILLIAMS

H e prepared for casting. Tonight was going to be special. Never bothering to write anything down, he ticked off the things to get done in his head. Update the elaborate plan to his viewers, give the clue for the next cast, choose an identity.

Excitement made him dart back and forth across his one-room apartment. He stepped from his mattress on the floor, around the stacks of electronics boxes and to the black drapes nailed to the ceiling that formed a small square in the corner and served as his broadcast area. He was sure many of his viewers could guess he didn't live any better than them—yet—but he didn't see any point in taking away the mystery.

So, who would he be this time?

He had been hacking computer databases and establishing several identities. The most developed were Harold Boggins, M.G. Mayer and Emmitt Pfingston. For his new plan, he needed something that sounded serious, with an automatic touch of legitimacy. M.G. Mayer was the choice. *Special homicide consultant M.G. Mayer.* He laughed.

He jumped into the only chair he had, raised his legs onto the table and grabbed the large, white plastic touchboard. Picking up the slender stylus, he wrote across the touchboard. Images of numbers appeared wherever the stylus touched. These were the random numbers his computer had generated that would be programmed for the code of his *next* cast.

Too bad that idiot Burris had to go and get himself killed.

Detective Ellen Jackson looked out of the moving police van and wondered if she was watching anyone using Remote Eyes. Remote

Eyes — "REs" for short — seemed like just an expensive fad last year. Now the pundits opined they would revolutionize the country. Businesses and some government departments were quick to jump on the bandwagon. Millions of others were signing up for the government program to have the nano-devices installed in front of their retinas (and similar listening devices in the aural canals). REs functioned similar to a computer monitor, displaying images and data seemingly right before the user. Two years ago, the so-called experts pondered who would want machines surgically embedded in their eyes. Now everyone was asking, "Who wouldn't?"

The police van passed a mechanic leaning over the battery compartment of a dead, two-seat car. If he had possessed REs, instructions could have been beamed into them so that diagrams of what he was supposed to do appeared laid over what he worked on.

Two city workers looked over a malfunctioning traffic sign. Maybe they had REs. They could be seeing directions for what to do.

Three people walked down the street, shoulder to shoulder. They were talking, but not looking at each other. A business meeting conducted on the go, courtesy of REs?

Jackson heard a faint beep in her ears, the distinct tone announcing an RE signal coming in. She tapped the controls of her RE on the flexible band around her left wrist. She got the code wrong on the first attempt. *I'll get the hang of this yet.* Silvio's face appeared before her, just to the left of her field of focus. No matter how she turned her head, Silvio's face stayed in the same orientation.

"We've heard from the consultant," Silvio said. "He'll meet you at the crime scene in three hours."

"Thanks," she replied. The signal ended, and a brief flash of the carrier company's logo appeared before her. She was curious as to why a consultant would be assigned to one of her murder investigations, but since it didn't violate any of her Three Axioms, she wasn't going to let it bother her.

Jackson's Three Axioms were the golden rules she tried to live by. The first was "Hide in plain sight." It was far easier to overlook the obvious than to fail to assemble enough clues to solve a puzzle. The second was "Rules usually serve a purpose." As a child, she had been a stickler for conformity, in spite of the derision of her peers. Now, more than ever, she saw how just the right amount of rules kept society civilized, or at least away from anarchy. She had acquired discretion, not disregard, so her peers now respected her. And her third axiom was "When in doubt, trust instinct." Nine times out of ten, her subconscious would tell her when her conscious mind was missing something.

Jackson and the other two officers stepped out of the van. They had arrived in front of a brown brick building, built almost a century ago in the 1930s. Her REs gave her directions to the crime scene three floors up, where a dead body had been found by the landlord last night. Medical already determined the time of death as two days ago. A uniformed officer stood outside the door to the victim's apartment. By luck of the draw, the investigation was another case in her busy workload.

She walked around the two-room apartment. Bed, kitchenette, sofa and bookshelves were in the first room. What should have been the bedroom was instead stocked with computer devices, a desk, two tables and other electronics. Like the city, it was cluttered, needed a good cleaning and had too many poorly lit corners.

She spent the rest of the morning gathering the information she required. While her two companions used the latest high-tech gadgetry—DNA scanners, 3D imagers and cameras that could photograph fingerprints invisible to the naked eye—Jackson did things the old-fashioned way: by looking closely and touching carefully. She found everything she needed except for one thing. She confirmed the ID of the dead young man as Burris, found leads on acquaintances, and gathered enough data from his computer to put together what kind of life he led. All that was needed was a clue to the murderer.

"Let me guess," came a voice from behind her. "You're thinking, 'What a waste. All that potential gone.'"

Jackson turned to the young man entering through the open

apartment door. He wore a brown leather jacket and well-creased dark blue slacks. His wavy, blond hair was too thick to comb well. He shouldn't have been older than his early twenties. The officer stationed at the doorway watched the man with a keen eye. Jackson nodded to the officer that the visitor was okay, and the officer returned his gaze to the corridor outside.

The blond man activated a palm-sized tablet with his thumbprint and handed it to Jackson. His assignment information flowed up the display. She caught the pertinent bits. M.G. Mayer, consultant, assigned to homicide, photo identification, authorization to access his RE codes. She had already seen it all this morning during briefing. And no reference to the higher-up who had assigned Mayer to her investigation. *Typical.*

Jackson gave the tablet back. "I'm only thinking about finding the murderer."

Mayer nodded. "We're all working for our fifty. And that's why I'm here, to lend you my area of expertise."

Jackson was fifty-two years old, which put her barely halfway through her fifty years of work until retirement. She was glad she made detective twelve years ago. She felt too old for patrols and foot chases now, and there were days when she thought she was too old to fully trust the complicated new technologies that kept coming along to supposedly make her job easier. "I have a dozen open cases I'm juggling. Why you, and why this case?"

"Remote Eyes," Mayer replied.

"How can Remote Eyes relate to a murder?"

Mayer shrugged. "That's what I'm here to find out. Someone in your department thought those techno gizmos might factor into this in a big way, and I know Remote Eyes backwards and forwards. So they gave me a retainer, and here I am."

Jackson knew the ad campaign. "'See the country through the eyes of others.'"

Mayer nodded his head slowly. "We're probably talking about illegal upgrades here. The hacking that's created a growing subculture of casters and watchers."

Jackson had been briefed months ago when the RE corporations realized their brand-new "impenetrable" security had been broken. "Voyeuristically watch other people's lives through their eyes, whether they know it or not."

"Look, I'm just toeing the line. Some fancy suit calls and asks me to look into this as soon as I can, so I come over here and look into this as soon as I can."

"You seem young to be an expert the department would call in. How'd you become so good so young at something so new?"

"Talent, refined skill, and duplicating what others do until I learn their techniques through simple repetition. I'm after the same thing you are, Detective Jackson — who killed Burris. Did you confirm his name?"

Jackson nodded.

Mayer went to the victim's computer table. "I'm going to focus on what the victim was killed over. Is it alright for me to touch anything?"

Jackson waved him on. "Be my guest. We've scanned for prints, videoed the place, and copied Burris's computer's memory." If this murder was all just a robbery gone lethal, then this Mayer was wasting his time. Nothing suggested otherwise so far to Jackson. She watched him lean close and carefully lift components. "Looking for anything in particular?"

"Yeah. Modding RE implants takes more than just ingenuity. You need the illegal tech to interface a computer with the RE control card. Did you or your people turn up anything like that?"

Jackson tapped the RE controls on her wrist. The filenames of everything they had imaged and logged this morning floated before her. A few more taps on her RE card and she accessed Mayer's RE ID codes from his police file and forwarded the filenames to him. "Here are scans of what we've gathered so far. You're free to look it over."

Mayer tapped his RE controls a few times and said, "Nope, nothing there."

"You're sure about that so fast?"

He turned to her. "How long did it take you to ascertain the body was dead? I know my job, detective." He resumed poking through the collection of electronics on Burris's computer desk table.

Asshole. "I'll leave two uniforms here to assist you. Keep us posted if you find anything." As Mayer left, she told the officer at the door to keep a close eye on Mayer and make sure he didn't take anything without it being logged. She glanced one more time into the apartment before leaving and saw Mayer staring at her.

Mayer dragged his chair into the corner, pulled the black drapes together and attached a metal clip to keep them closed. He tapped at his RE controls as he sat down. Hooked to the wall was a mirror at eye level as he sat. He stared into his reflection as he spoke. Anyone remoting into his cast would see his reflection as if he were talking directly to them. The single light overhead sent shimmers along the edges of the sunglasses he wore as his head bobbed.

"Well, Faithful, did you all catch that? M.G. Mayer successfully made his debut with the homicide department today. How'd it feel being a part of my charade? Did your pulse race, did your breath go dry? I think I did a fairly good job, if I say so myself.

"I'm sorry I couldn't let you, my Faithful, in on my earlier excursions into the police department, but hey, trade secrets are at stake, right? I can't reveal *everything* about how I pull these escapades off, can I? But I can promise you this: M.G. Mayer will be making a visit to police HQ, and soon. Keep going to Ebon to check for my next code display."

He rubbed his stubbly chin, thinking about what else he needed to add to this broadcast. "Oh yeah, and to the fuckwaste who blanked Burris: You should know I was hacked into Burris's REs at the time you killed him. I saw your face. If I see you anywhere near me, I'm reporting you to the cops. And I will be with a lot of cops. So fuck off, and fuck off as far away as you can.

"Goodbye for now, my Faithful. More to come soon. Keep

checking in at Ebon."

He switched off his Remote Eyes and leaned back. He made a mental note to broadcast a new set of randomly generated codes for his next cast to Ebon, the black market Remote Eyes site where unknown devoted fans of REs took turns spending all day staring at walls of large touchboards with scribbled broadcast codes. If he ever found out who those wonderful folks were, he would thank them for their service. But like him, their success depended on anonymity.

As for Burris's killer, he knew the odds were astronomical that the fix-crazed druggie would be one of his viewers, but Mayer was still angry that someone had randomly ruined his negotiations. The druggie had yelled about cash before killing Burris. As desperate as he looked, he probably had died from withdrawal or an overdose by now. The idiot never imagined there was data worth a thousand times the cash Burris had on hand right there in that apartment, waiting to be plucked, if only someone knew the right place where to look. And M.G. Mayer was going to be that someone who looked in the right place.

The next day, Jackson talked to potential witnesses of another murder before she went in to her precinct headquarters. Once there, she slid into her squeaky swivel chair and verified her notes had transferred from her field computer to the system's main drive. But the Burris murder occupied her thoughts. In particular, she couldn't get M.G. Mayer out of her mind. He didn't violate any of her Three Axioms, but she didn't care. She was curious.

Jackson tapped at her RE controls and called Personnel. "Hey, Ed. I had a civilian consultant at my murder scene yesterday. Do those things go through Personnel?"

"Nah. The Liaison's office handles those things these days. You got yourself a clumsy know-it-all walking all over evidence?"

"Know-it-all, yes. Clumsy, no. Thanks, Ed."

"Hey, we can always use some good help to ease the load. We shouldn't have to work for our 50 on our own."

"I hear ya."

"Talk to you later, Detective Jackson."

She leaned back in her narrow chair, only to have her hip squeezed by her taser in its holster. Stupid, narrow chair. Her hips weren't that wide. Why'd Supply give her such a tight chair? Without looking, she pulled her taser out and put it in her jacket pocket as she called the Liaison's office to ask how she could find out who assigned Mayer to the Burris murder. The man who answered was polite, but that was all.

"I'm sorry, Detective Jackson. Mrs. Krauss handles those procedures."

"How does she select applicants, and how does she choose cases?"

"Detective, it varies by case. Mrs. Krauss is out of town for the rest of the week. If you really need to talk to her, I can get a message to her. I'm sorry. I wish I could be of more help. I'm just toeing the line like the rest of us."

"Thank you." She leaned back, ready to move on to reviewing the information for another case when a thought struck her.

What had Krauss's assistant said? "Toeing the line?" Mayer had used that phrase. And the guy in Personnel had mentioned working for his 50. It was like a mantra for civil servants but less so for private sector workers — and especially consultants, who had the opportunity to make enough to retire much sooner.

Something didn't feel right. She didn't know what, but she fell back on Axiom Three: *When in doubt, trust your instinct.* Mayer had also said he became good at what he did by repeating what others did. What did he mean by that? If he was knowledgeable about Remote Eyes and hacking, did that mean he himself was a hacker? Had he become good at pretending to be a police consultant by illegally tapping into police RE casts? If so, why? The answer would tie into Burris's murder, and that meant the solution to all this might be at the apartment.

Jackson grabbed her badge and strode out the door. She didn't bother to log out or tell anyone where she was going. She felt for her taser and twisted to look at her empty holster. *Oh yeah, jacket pocket. Stupid tight chair.* She was in such a hurry, the taser would be fine in her pocket. Before she got into a car, she turned off her REs. If what she suspected was true, then Mayer could be hacking into her Remote Eyes or anyone else's at the precinct.

Did she know? How could she know? Mayer was so nervous, he had to go to the bathroom and pee again.

He had watched through Jackson's REs as she left the precinct headquarters, but she had shut off her devices. He didn't know where she was going. It had to be the apartment, but he saw its door had been sealed earlier with an electronic bar. The brute force necessary to remove it would send a signal to the police, and they would be at Burris's apartment in minutes, too soon for Mayer to locate what he needed. And breaking in might tip Jackson off that this whole thing was about more than a hacker killed randomly by a druggie.

Mayer looked through his digital notes through his Remote Eyes for the codes for Tech Specialist Suarez. Mayer slipped on his sunglasses and activated Suarez's codes.

Mayer saw a full cup of coffee. How clichéd. A hand—Suarez's hand—grabbed the cup. Suarez walked down a corridor and turned right. Inside the dark room was a wall covered with monitors. A few were off. Several displayed what were clearly cameras mounted on cars or shoulders of officers on duty. The rest showed the distinctive binocular view of active Remote Eyes. The Holy Grail of hacking—cracking the most sophisticated codes ever devised in order to convert RE broadcasts into a digital format that could be recorded. Breaching the simpler codes of RE users had been far easier, even though the RE development corporations thought *those* codes were unattainable. Broadcast codes were even more so.

Mayer had spent months, after acquiring a series of hacked RE codes, to get Suarez's codes. From there, all he had to do was observe Suarez do his job with his REs on. Eventually, Mayer obtained more police RE codes merely by waiting until Suarez happened to look at them. Police chief, personnel director, liaison head—even Detective Jackson. The RE corporations had done everything they could to create their super-codes, but all the precautions in the world were useless if somebody looked at the actual numbers when their REs were on and hacked.

Suarez tapped at a keyboard, then switched on a microphone. "Dispatch? Detective Jackson has left without an itinerary and her REs are off. Did she say anything to you?"

"No," a woman answered. "I saw her leave. Thought she was off duty."

"Nah. She's day shift. She's scheduled to be on duty till five."

"Can you keep an eye on her codes, see if they come back online?"

"Will do," Suarez replied as the link to his Remote Eyes was terminated.

Mayer grabbed a handgun and raced out of his apartment.

Jackson stared at the police bar across the door to Burris's apartment. She swore as she had to activate her REs, if only momentarily, to get the code. She stared at a shadowy corner of the floor the entire time she had them on, because the nature of Remote Eyes was, whenever they were on, you were casting what you saw. For once, the code was in the active file, so she didn't have to link with anyone else. But she had kept her devices on for more than a minute.

Once inside, she looked around the apartment again. Rule One, "Hide in plain sight." Had she missed something? At least the afternoon sunlight kept things well lit, and the apartment was a corner unit that faced west and north.

She focused on the trivial. Small, stuffed animals on bookshelves. A framed commemoration of one of the last music CDs pressed in the 2010s hanging on the wall behind Burris's desk, with a scantily clad young vixen posing on the disk's printed label. Mardi Gras beads hanging from a light fixture. Were those for future use?

Dammit, the disk!

Maybe it wasn't a pre-pressed music CD after all. It could just as easily be an old-style recordable disk with a printout affixed to it. Jackson raced to the framed CD and lifted it off its hook on the wall. She carefully disassembled the back of the frame and slid out the cardboard holding the disk. Switching on Burris's computer, she sat down and put the disk in. One folder appeared, but it was encrypted. She had no clue what the password could possibly be, but whatever bonehead made the disk left the name of the folder for anyone to see: *RE Tower Schematics.*

She didn't need to know what the files actually showed. If they were indeed the schematics to Remote Eyes transmission towers, that was illegal in itself. The devices implanted in human eyes had only enough power to send out a short-range signal. It was up to the towers, positioned virtually everywhere, to boost signals to and from individual users. Hackers had long been breaking into the software within the devices, expanding the functionality of broadcast and reception. But hacking into the towers was something else. Why would they want to do that? Terrorism? Techno-blackmail? No, that would be antithetical to hackers. They wanted to *add* to Remote Eyes, not bring it offline.

The signals.

RE towers relayed thousands of encrypted signals. If hackers could decrypt those signals, they could acquire the RE access codes to users in the vicinity. Want politicians' RE codes? Hack into the towers closest to City Hall. Want military codes? Look for any restaurant where off-duty soldiers might be casting. Want police codes? Get to the tower nearest a precinct. Heck, hack into a tower near the facilities of one of the corporations that develops and maintains RE devices, and a hacker might acquire an RE engineer's codes. It was one thing to break the encryption of random signals. But if you wanted someone *specific...*

A floorboard creaked. Jackson's body stiffened. She slowly stood up, careful not to allow the desk chair to make a squeak of its own. She stepped into the front room, and Mayer stood there, staring at her.

"Detective Jackson." There wasn't a hint of surprise to his voice at all. "Hands out to the side, fingers apart. Please, do not activate your Remote Eyes. Leave them off."

"Mr. Mayer." She was alert. This was no coincidence. Mayer's nonchalance was in indirect proportion to his potential threat. What would he do if she reached to activate her Remote Eyes? She would find out what she could before making a desperate move. He may have been the one to kill Burris. Then it hit her. M.G. Mayer. Metro-Goldwyn-Mayer, the long-ago movie studio? "Or whatever your *real* name is." That made him look a bit surprised. She decided to put him off balance more. "Tell me about RE transmission towers."

"Ah, void it all, you found it. Hidden in plain sight, right? Where was it?"

So he shared one of her golden rules. She would admire that after she had him cuffed. But first, she wanted to try to get more out of him. Why was he after the disk, and what did he know about Burris's murder?

Mayer moved his hands and arms slowly as he talked. Was he trying not to spook her, or was he getting ready to make a move at her? "Ah, Ellen, Ellen... I can call you Ellen, can't I? Do you know what the hardest part is about hacking into Remote Eyes? It isn't how to get paid in a world where cash is only used one percent of the time. It isn't about acquiring the incredibly advanced and highly illegal equipment. The hardest part is finding the time to do the hacking and then enjoy the fruits of your labor. No matter how much I charge —and I can charge a lot, Ellen, 'cause I'm really good—no matter how much I charge, I can't buy myself more time."

"So you're going to hack into tower signals to acquire specific RE signals for yourself?"

"Hell, no. I'm going to figure out how to do that even more efficiently than I do now, and then charge people even more to give them the means to do it for themselves. I figure, if I can't buy more time, I'm just going to make myself even richer than I already am."

He couldn't have been that rich already, she thought, or else he wouldn't be taking such risks. Or maybe he was an extreme risk taker, in which case he could be that rich already. None of that mattered right now. "Did you kill Burris?"

"No, but I know who did. Burris and I were casting to each other when he got voided. Some butthole druggie, but I already know Burris didn't give anything to him. The druggie was a stealer and a quick seller, not a hacker. The schematics would've been up for sale almost immediately, if the idiot had even realized what Burris had somewhere in his possession."

Jackson put the pieces together in her head. "So... you put yourself into the investigation, hoping to find what you wanted. A police bar across the door made the apartment almost impenetrable, but it wouldn't be there forever. You wanted an edge."

Mayer spun around, dancing around her cluelessness. "Oh, come on, detective! Don't you get it? I was already hacking into numerous police REs. Even yours."

"That's how you picked up the procedures and faked your way into the consulting position. The person who would've assigned you is out of the office this week. You made that work to your advantage."

"See? That's why I'm so good. I don't just hack Remote Eyes. I hack all computers! But hacking into REs is becoming more and more sophisticated. The government and the mega-corporations behind Remote Eyes are sinking more and more money into improving the encryption. It's a wild chase that is leaving the slower hackers behind."

He was telling her too much. Never a good sign.

"You look skeptical, detective."

No, asshole. Seriously worried. "Go on."

"Most people aren't satisfied with their own lives. That 'grass is always greener' feeling leads many to believe anyone else is more interesting than they are, which in turn leads to a rise in tech such as chirping and now remoting. Remember chirping? People would cheep the most mundane aspects of their lives, and others read those cheeps.

"I guess I've always been old," Jackson said. "I could never get into that."

"Well, the real advance was casting your life. Don't just read snippets about others' better lives, live it through their eyes. Remote Eyes casting."

"Remote Eyes were supposed to artificially augment people's knowledge and skills. Instead, it may have dumbed this nation down further than anything else ever has."

"Don't be a luddite, Ellen."

"I'm not. The tech has tremendous positive potential. Hackers dying for their illegal secrets is not part of that. Just so I'm clear, the hacking was your entire angle?"

He chuckled. "No. I've been promised a bundle by a Hollywood production company to find the means of converting RE signals into recordable data that can be projected for anyone to see. Hollywood is struggling desperately to replace the revenue it's losing from movies as more and more young people turn to remoting as their entertainment. 'The eyes have it'—that's going to be the slogan I suggest for the new product. Imagine it: Every time we turn on our Remote Eyes, we're casting everything we see. What if we could pay to receive pre-recorded RE casts by category and topic, recorded live but viewable whenever we want it? And not just the random crap that's mostly too boring to pay for, but the rare, really juicy stuff that people stay up all night trying to find the codes for."

"That's an illegal concept. Part of the construction of Remote Eyes guarantees recording can't be done except by the proper authorities, such as police, and then only police REs, no one else's. Part of the legal mumbo-jumbo to ensure privacy rights, from what I recall."

"But big businesses can't survive without big profits, right, detective?"

Jackson nodded. She may have learned everything she needed to know. Now, how to take him in?

"It's really too bad you were in such a rush to get out of headquarters. You shouldn't have left your taser behind."

"If you've told me all this, it must be because you think I won't be able to make use of it. But you don't strike me as a killer."

"That's where you're partly wrong. True, I've never killed anyone. But I've watched dozens of killings over RE to know how it's done."

"You're that cold hearted?"

He shrugged. "Remote Eyes is my passion. Everything else, well, is just life's nuisances. I think we need to wrap things up here."

"Agreed." She had learned more than enough from him.

He reached behind himself with a slowness born of overconfidence and pulled out a gun from the back of his belt. Jackson whipped out her taser and pressed the trigger. His body convulsed and crumpled to the floor. One stray shot blasted harmlessly from his gun into the wall to the left. A twisted look of agony scrunched his face and replaced the briefest look of surprise. Was he surprised she still had her taser, or was he surprised at how much it hurt?

She made a mental note to ask him later during interrogation.

ElectroFunkSeppuku

By Jennifer Rahn

M issed it that time."

Tez was muttering to himself as his fingers ran over the design board, the grey light coming from it washing over his bearded face and dark dreads with an unnatural glow. He didn't seem to lose his place though, and kept on sketching out the *plan*, flipping the digital pages faster than Emil could read them over his shoulder.

"Go back. Hold on! Wait."

"Feck out. I'm busy. You can set up when I'm done."

Emil lifted his keyboard as if he were going to hit Tez with it, then just rested the device on his head, folding his skinny arms over it.

Davey wasn't really interested in what they were doing or why and he was growing bored as nobody was paying attention to him. He was just in it to perform, but he would nod and pretend to be listening whenever Tez went on his rants.

The download lines were clean and secure now, ready for tonight's fiasco, so he hooked up his jPod and helped himself to a few 'casts from the off-site nodes before Tez irritably unhooked his cable and waved him away. Shoving his hands into the pockets of his sequined jeans, Davey pushed his narrow hips away from the desk he'd been leaning against, thinking he might as well go get ready while the two of them were fighting with the new *plan*. As he made his way through the securehouse, trying not to knock over any of Tez's gear or trip over the inexplicable mess of cables lining the floor, Len charged past him with a load of circuit boards and wires, deliberately knocking against his shoulder, hard enough to make him spin around. Davey heard him say something about a 'pouf', followed by what should be done with him, and wondered yet again why someone like Len would bother being a part of the group if he felt that way. He huffed and turned back the way he'd been heading, hoping he'd come off looking swag, like he was trying to be. Len was building up to spinning something, he could feel it, but it wasn't going to throw him off his game. Not tonight, and not when all of this was over and he went pro. *As if.*

Flicking on the lights around the makeup table, he sat in front of the mirror. He'd already varnished his nails black, gelled his blond hair up in spikes and frosted the tips violet, so all there really was to do was paint. Foundation went on to cover up what he couldn't shave off, followed by contour powder and blush. He lined his eyes with electric blue, put on pink mascara and drew a slash of sparkly pink across his entire face to further enhance his eyes. He could feel himself warming up. The colour was making him feel good. Pursing his lips, he painted them a matching hue.

"Davey! You're on in five," Tez snapped.

"Yeh?" Davey got up from the table, carefully pulled his tee off over his head and wrapped a pink and black boa around his neck. "Emil is ready?"

"He's gonna be. C'mere. Let me show you this."

Leaning over the design board, he listened obediently as Tez tried to explain.

"Word went out over *horroraddicts.net* last night. Emerian gave you several good plugs to her audience. We're going to upload your 'cast to these fifteen nodes here. We're already getting pings from about thirty-seven billion IP addys waiting for your next gig. When we open it up to the wolves, we're expecting about 87% of SolCorp's bandwith to be chewed up, they'll have to switch over to the contingency channel and when that happens, their firewall will have to reroute as well, causing a 0.2 nanosecond breach. We'll send in the hack then. Should knock out security at the Third Node wall for maybe another 0.5 nanoseconds. Shanna will get through and deliver payload."

Tez grinned at him triumphantly, sending warm shivers up Davey's spine. He smiled back cautiously, knowing that although he loved it when Tez was manic like that, it wasn't meant for him. He turned away before he got himself worked up about it. The reality of it was, that Tez was into Shanna and they all lived behind the Wall, and that's where they'd die, probably sooner than later, since every podcast they sent out brought them one step closer to getting caught. They were growing exponentially in popularity, which was essential to increasing the number of downloads to hit the bandwidth threshold Tez needed to find the cracks in the Wall, and although Davey lived for these nights, it was ultimately going to kill them. He knew he was being used, but someone like him didn't get famous without someone like Tez.

"OK, let's record. I need you to hit this note exactly when Emil plays this chord. See the amount of data needed to code for that? It'll create the pulses we need to break up the bandwidth tracer enough so that we'll have time to run before the trackers show up." Tez had grabbed his arm and was propelling him toward the stage waving the pages of music in front of them. He resisted just a bit, increasing the pressure on his arm and enjoying the infinitesimally prolonged contact. "Get up there. Do your thing."

Davey let his head fall back as he zoned into Emil's magic swelling out of the speakers, feeling the thrum of the vibrations supercharge the blood in his veins, letting the flow of energy in the sound catch him up in a vortex of ecstasy as he slowly raised his arms, and turned to the camera. He began by speaking to it, in that strange baritone that always emerged from his narrow chest whenever he was *on*, beginning the story that was emerging from the papers Tez was holding up behind the cameras. He flipped his hair from his eyes and ignored his friend. He didn't need any help to do this. His mind and soul were being lifted into a stream of superconsciousness that connected him to all in existence, that fed him all he would ever need to accomplish anything. Anything at all. The patterns and structure of the music shaped his movements as he merged with it, finally unleashing his voice in song. This was lyrical disdain, and he let it show on his face with a heavy lidded stare and curl of his lip while he sang, completely oblivious to anything but the music and the audience he knew would be adoring his every strut and twitch on the other side of the cameras. All thoughts of Tez's instructions, Len's threats and the enclosing Wall were obliterated by the passion shining out of his skin. He was light, divine knowledge and secret release. When he was done, the ending silence still searing with his final hollered note, he let one hand rise to push his hair up from his forehead, then turned his head to show off his profile and earring. He held the pose until the lights and mist were shut off and he heard Tez's slow, heavy applause.

"Fantastic, Davey. Nailed it. Every last note."

"Wicked," said Emil indulging in one of his characteristic full-body spasms. "I'm starting upload."

"Wait, you feck!" Tez brutally smacked him away from the control panel. "We have to add the effects first. This is visual, not just about your sounds. The downloads will drop next week if we don't get it swag!"

"I know, I know!" Emil wrapped his arms around his head again. "It was just so awesome. I just want to get it out there."

"Yeah, and completely forget the plan, which is why we do this anyway."

"Yer bowf poufs," muttered Len as he slunk away to load the stealth crates.

"Davey, clean up and get out of here before we start upload. Don't forget the nail varnish and earrings. You too, Emil. You guys can't run fast."

Davey felt the energy draining out of his body as he slouched off the stage and went into the portable washroom to wash out his hair and scrub his face.

"Hey. Here's your stuff." Emil was reaching into the small room, holding out a hanger with street clothes on it. His eyes were invisible behind the reflection on his lenses.

"Thanks. Hey, I just noticed your tee matches your hair."

"Yeh. Planned it that way. You were awesome tonight, Davey. I'm gonna risk a download later to see it after Tez is done."

"That's shaky, man. Why don't you just get it from Tez after?"

"Can't wait. And downloading with a trace is half the rush. See ya. Get to work safe, hey?"

He punched Davey's shoulder as he left.

After toweling his hair to one side and using paint thinner to clean his nails, Davey leaned against the sink and stared at himself in the mirror. There was nothing left of the glam, just a tired, too thin, too pale sack of bones reflected back at him—so unremarkable the trackers would probably walk right past him on the street. He was now, officially, unplugged from everything. Wanting to feel at least a bit of the warmth his stage persona lent him, he took a gauzy pink scarf and wrapped it around his neck before slipping on the heavy black sweater, jeans and jacket left by Emil.

The sky outside was overwhelmed with stars that Davey could watch move if he had the time to stand still for a few moments. A few times he had gone to the spin poles just to see everything twist above him. The citioid behind the Wall wasn't that big, so the spin was noticeable, and it was almost always dark on this half, unless a big enough freighter was passing by with a reflective surface. Looking up, he thought of the Others on the Outside who would be downloading his gig tonight, maybe feeling like they were connecting with him, experiencing an awakening from the energy of his performance—at least that was how he imagined it. The Outsiders were safe from SolCorp, who could politely complain about the nodes overloading, but still needed the colonial trade and information flux, which stopped them from completely shutting down the nodes. And, their corporate nerds had so far been unsuccessful in figuring out the word puzzles Emerian used in her podcasts to tip off Davey's fans of which nodes to download from, and when.

His work shift was excruciating. The anemic light in his cubicle at the water recycling plant seemed to leach the colour and life out of his skin until his hands seemed to be the same shade as the paper on which he scratched out the quality assurance test results. Batch, after batch, after batch, watching the tank in front of him fill with greyish liquid, spill into the analysis columns, resolve, then spit out numbers at him, for sixteen hours. His nose always plugged up after half a day in his cubicle and he began to slouch into a small mass at the bottom. Every time he sniffed or cleared his throat, the sound that bounced back at him seemed unnaturally plastic and loud. He was supposed to be grateful for this life. Grateful that when the unwanted frozen embryos from SolCorp HumaniDesign were ordered discarded, some lobbyist had looked out for his welfare and forced SolCorp to hatch him and put him here instead of the biowaste incinerator. Despite SolCorp's official 'compassionate support' of the citioid's residents, they still wanted the hatchlings gone, and would get rid of one or two every chance they got.

Davey flipped his hair out of his face for the nine hundredth time, again resisting the urge to reach under his collar and touch the pink scarf, just for a second, and relive last night.

"Jones! You're outta here."

He startled into alertness as the shift manager lifted the seals on the cubicles and he was released along with the other 92 of his coworkers at the plant. "C'mon. Get out. Why you sittin' there staring at the water? Thinking of drowning?" Sheft chuckled like he thought he was funny or something.

Yeh, thinking of drowning a shift manager, Davey thought.

"Back in sixteen hours, ladies and gents. Make the most of it, because in two shifts your sorry arses are again mine!" More laughing from Sheft. More dark thoughts from Davey.

When he got back to his home cell, he found Emil spasming in the hall outside his door.

"Omigod, Davey! Omigod!"

"Shut up, Emil. Get inside." Davey hit the button on his fob that unlocked his door and shoved his friend through it. They weren't supposed to be seen together—ever. There wasn't much room in his cell to stand, and Emil was too agitated to go sit, which left Davey standing very close to a thrashing man he cared about who smelled wonderfully like the securehouse and music. He took a deep breath to control his impulses and crawled awkwardly over the chair next to the door so he could sit on the bed.

"What's eating your brains, man? You're gonna get us lynched."

"Can't help it. Can't help it, Davey. Shanna got picked up last night, before she got through. Tez fecked her over and sent a second code through that she didn't know about. Thought he could get a two for one."

"Shit. What happened? Why'd he send in two hacks?"

"Dumbass couldn't wait. Thought he was smarter'n he is and the nerds wouldn't catch it."

"Did she give us up?"

"No. I don't think so, but she still had payload. She went down for smuggling. Davey, they executed her this morning."

Davey's head spun and if he had eaten anything, he would have thrown up.

"What was payload?" he finally asked.

"Tokes," said Emil.

"She died for *that*? Why the hell was Tez smuggling tokes?"

"Don't you get it, Davey? Tez just wants to break the Wall. Shanna was all impressed with him because she thought he was some sort of revolutionary and she wanted to be involved. He set her up with lameass missions so she'd stick around and it was an excuse for him to program bits of code and test it against the Wall. Now he's gone nuts. He wants to break SolCorp."

"*What?* He can't! He's gonna get us killed."

The citioid spun a bit more and Davey grabbed his head with both hands in an attempt to keep it still.

"I'm done, Emil. I can't do this anymore." The moment he said it, he knew it wasn't true. There was hell on either side of the coin, but the side without the gigs was worse.

"Aww, Davey. Don't say that, man. What else we got? It's the same reason Shanna did what she did. You just wanna sit at the waterplant and nothing else? You're a feckin' *star*, man. It's just getting a bit hot, that's all. And Tez, if he breaks the Wall, maybe we can get *out*."

"You think we can get out?"

"Well." Spasms. "Well. No, but dying's getting out too—like if they catch us. And dying quick doing the 'cast is better than dying slow without it. It's still better'n slowly fading out in the gutter."

"'cast without Tez, then."

"Shit, man. You think we can do that? We don't have all that stuff. And even if we did he'd find a way to shut us down."

Davey closed his eyes for a bit and wished that Emil would sit next to him on the bed, maybe put an arm around him and warm him up. Tell him things would be right. But when he opened his eyes, Emil was leaning up against the wall, one hand hanging on to the elbow of his other arm, one knee up and the foot tapping ceaselessly against the wall, staring at him through those super reflective lenses. He only did that when he was getting pissed.

"Okay."

Emil said nothing. Didn't even spasm, just tapped his foot. Really pissed. He was expecting more.

"*Okay*. But I'm worried you know. Angry Tez might not be as safe as Crazy Tez."

"Doesn't matter. He always makes us leave before he does anything risky anyway. We got nothing to lose." Foot still tapping. Still mad.

"Yeh. I guess."

"Don't you give a shit about Shanna?"

No. "Well, yeah, I just, didn't know her really. You know? And I'm kinda stunned. Hasn't all sunk in yet."

"Yeh, whatever." Emil let himself out and left Davey sitting there, colder than ever. Was he wrong to not care about Shanna? She'd never really talked to him. She'd never been like Len or anything, and yeah, she'd died, but was that so bad? Maybe she'd wanted to get off the citioid bad enough so she'd slipped—on purpose. Wasn't so hard to imagine that. Living here like fungus that had been irradiated to make sure it didn't overpopulate, then forced into slavery to make sure it was self-sustainable. What was the point? They could let everyone off the citioid. Was that so crazy? But it seemed the society that had discarded them once had no real interest in assimilating them again. Let Emil get all worked up if he wanted to, if it gave him something to feel alive about. Maybe Davey should go be Tez's toke mule. *As if.* He'd never be allowed, being the star 'pouf'.

He sighed, stretching out on his bed, and plugged into his jPod, flipping to the 'cast he'd swiped from *horroraddicts.net* before his last gig. It was a pretty crazy tale. Some guy named Davy, go figure that, was a crewman aboard a water ship that had sailed around the oceans of Terra Prime a thousand years ago. They'd sailed into a dense fog and then some dark witch they'd picked up from one of the islands they'd visited started speaking to them in their language, which she hadn't known before, and cursed them for kidnapping her. A ghost ship came up out of nowhere and all these undead skeletons charged on board and killed everyone, all except Davy, who was just bitten several times and then woke up later. He was super cursed because he'd been the one who'd kidnapped the witch in the first place. Seeing everyone else dead just made him miserable and guilty, and all he wanted to do was go join his mates in the afterlife, so he tried to drown himself, but he couldn't die, so he turned into an ocean vampire, and then became the evil lord of the ocean who kept kidnapping and drowning any sailor who came from the same land as the ship who had taken the witch.

Davey smiled to himself as the ending music cued and he let himself fall asleep. The author of the 'cast had described Davy as being cursed, but *damn*, he got the freedom to roam the entire ocean. Didn't sound so bad, being that free. Dead to the world so no one would come looking for you, or could make you spend 16 hours a day watching toilet-flush water get purified, and you could just swim on and on, forever. It was a nice dream.

Morning came, and looked exactly like last night. Davey got out of bed and decided what he had worn to sleep was still good enough, so he just left his cell and went to Mexie's for his once-a-day meal of beans and bread that was considered in the best interest of all the citizens of the citioid. The canteen was basically converted from an underground parkade of the concrete palace that was the central admin building, which had been rezoned once the citioid planners realised no one would ever be driving a car. If Tez wanted him, there'd be a note somewhere in the food, depending on what kind of mood Mexie was in. The old 'chef' wasn't one of Davey's fans, but still seemed willing to do what Tez wanted. Maybe he hated the Wall also. Davey didn't expect a note today, considering what had happened to Shanna, so he ate slowly, trying to push back the looming sadness at the thought that all he'd get to do was go to work.

The note was there. Davey felt it mush up against his teeth, and carefully pulled it out of his mouth without tearing the sodden paper. Wiping off the beans, he read the coordinates for the next 'cast and felt his spirits lift a little bit. He shoveled down the rest of the food, threw out the container, wiped his hands on his jeans and ran to catch the subway. He went to three extra stops he didn't need, hoping that would actually help obscure the route he was taking to the securehouse.

The entryway to the coordinates on the note was a covered alleyway with no lights. Usually Tez would make sure all the doors were clear and secure, so Davey didn't worry about the darkness and hurried through it in a shuffling jog. His whole body was already warming up with the anticipation of the lights, colour and music, Tez's wide smile afterwards, his slow applause...

Davey got tripped and felt someone grab the back of his collar to slam his face against the wall.

"Where you goin', poufboy?"

"Feck, Len!" Davey tried to push himself up, but Len didn't let go. "What're you doing? Tez called us!"

"Yeh, yeh. You like that, don't you? Being a pouf. Think yer goin' somewheres with that now? Now you got Shanna out of the way? Think Tez is gonna like you? I seen how you looks at him, like yer hoping he's a pouf too. I think Tez likes yer looks at him, but he's just jerkin' you around. He likes messin' wif yer head, and that's all how he's ever gonna mess wif you."

"Why do you care? Why are you even in this? You hate me so much, why even come?"

"Maybe I like messin' wif poufs."

Len pulled him up like he was nothing more than a rag doll and slugged him hard. Davey felt something snap in his middle and fell to his knees, spewing his meager breakfast over the concrete ground. Len kicked his backside so hard he flew forward and smashed his face against a garbage tank lining the alley. A few of his teeth broke and swam around in the blood filling his mouth.

A door banged open somewhere behind him.

"Len! Where the feck is Davey? We're running late!"

"You wan' the goddamn pouf, you can get him by the rest of the garbage."

Davey managed to roll over and spit before he swallowed his teeth, and saw Tez looking at him, horrified. He couldn't stand being looked at like that, so he began to sob mindlessly and pick his teeth fragments out of the mess on the ground. Everyone seemed to be hating him because he didn't care about Shanna. Probably Tez, too.

"I'm sorry," he mumbled to Tez. "Sorry about Shanna." The words came out garbled and slurred.

"Aw, shit, Davey." Tez knelt beside him and put a hand along one side of his face, turning his head gently to inspect the damage. "Come on inside. We gotta get ice on this." Davey's head spun as Tez hauled him up and dragged him into the securehouse. Emil's head snapped around when they came inside, and whatever he had been thinking about last night, whatever had been scrawled all over his face just now, fell right off his expression as he ran towards Davey and spasmed before obeying Tez's commands to get cloths and ice.

Davey couldn't see much past all the towels packed against his face by Emil, but he could hear Len and Tez fighting well enough.

"You think you're such a feckin' hot coder? Huh? Think you're gonna come in here and mess up my plans? I can't feckin' 'cast with him like that, you feck!"

"Yeh? You think I feckin' care what you do wif that pouf? Think you can pull off this shite wifout me? Go ahead and try. You an' yer big *plans*. All gonna bring down the Wall. Ain't seen shite for it, Tez. Big man Tez. I'm sick to feck listenin' to yer crap about the Wall. All it got any of us is dead. You wanna be dead, big man? Come on and hit me then."

"Get the *feck* out of my securehouse! Go code your shit somewhere else! Think you can beat me? Bring it! Let's see what you got. You ain't got shit, 'cept in your goddamn head!"

"Yeh? Bring it? Already brought it, to yer pouf here. I'm gone. Have a nice feckin' life."

Len's heavy boot steps faded after the metal door clanged shut behind him. There was a long, empty pause, when all Davey could sense were Emil's hands trembling as he held the towels against the ice.

"Emil!" shouted Tez. "You're gonna have to help me with this now. We gotta check all the code. We gotta scan for any hacks Len put in here. Probably planned to bring us all down. Come on. We gotta find it quick and then move."

"Can you hold this yourself?" Emil asked Davey, lifting his scraped hands to the towels. "Here, you can listen to Emerian for a while." He put a set of headphones over Davey's head and set the channel to the live streaming podcast. Too upset to really listen, Davey tried not to cry, since it would make his face swell up more and it was already going to be hard enough to get cleaned up for work. Sheft was really gonna ride his ass for showing up like this, and then he probably wouldn't be able to breathe at all in his cubicle. He pulled the towels away from his face to see how much blood there was, and felt a little relieved that the ice seemed to be helping. The hole where his teeth used to be seemed alarmingly large, so he kept his tongue away from it. Maybe he could apply for some dental help later. For now, there wasn't much to do but lean back and relax. There was no way they were going to get a 'cast off now. He wondered how he could paint around the damage until he could maybe get some fake teeth put in. Or maybe he could go without. Could he make that look work? Have to see what the rest of his face looked like first.

The 'cast coming through the headphones was resolving into a gutteral chant with no background music. *Emerian's getting into some real freaky stuff,* he thought, before slowly realizing that this wasn't even the right channel. The white noise hiss behind the recording was completely different. He sat up and dropped the towels so that he could press the foam earcaps closer to his head. Now all he heard was a hiss with something that sounded like whispering embedded in it, too subtle to make out what was being said, then the 'cast exploded into electronic screaming. Davey yelled in surprise and ripped off the headset, staring at it angrily. The electronic noise could still be heard coming through the earcaps, changing in pitch and frequency every few seconds.

He looked up to see Tez and Emil staring at him, then Tez came over and pulled the headset away, putting it on himself.

"It's code," he said after a few minutes. He stood up and punched a few keys on the console, checking the channel. "The 'cast has been hijacked. Someone's transmitting code over it."

"What's it for?" asked Emil.

"Don't know, but it's high level. I would've said military, but all the usual signatures have been changed."

"You can tell that by listening?" Emil demanded.

"Well, yeh." Tez flicked a glance at him. "You can if you hear it enough. You guys get out of here now. I'll clean up. I gotta find out where this is coming from."

"Be careful, man."

"Yeah, I will. Go on, get out of here."

The next note from Tez took six weeks to show up. Davey's face had mostly healed, and the stumps of his teeth had been painted over with sealant. The health commission promised him he could apply to get a proper fix sometime next year. Overall, it wasn't too bad, especially with the idea he planned to borrow from Emerian's podcast. His broken face would work marvelously with the persona of Davey Jones, Vampire and Oceanic Master, who of course would still be very glam. He smiled to himself as he plucked Tez's note from the folds of his napkin. Mexie was being a lot nicer after seeing what Len had done to him.

He approached the securehouse a lot more cautiously that he usually would have, still wary that Len might somehow have gotten wind of it and was lying in wait. As he opened the door and slipped inside, Emil scared the crap out of him by pushing in directly behind.

"Hey. Was hiding there, waiting for you to show up, just in case, you know."

Davey took a deep breath and let it out. "Yeah, thanks."

"How you doin'?"

"I'm alright. How are you?"

"Never better." Emil grinned and his lenses flashed in the dim light. "Been needing to play like crazy. Been a long time!"

Tez hadn't set up his usual rig. The soundboards weren't up, and the console hadn't been assembled. Instead he was leaning over some naked girl who was all hooked up to wires that snaked into a row of computers.

"Guys, look at this," he said. "I'm calling her 'Shanna.'"

"What the hell," breathed Emil as he stumbled forward. "Is she dead?"

"No. She came from the code. The one that Davey found on that weird channel, that day when..." Tez broke off, suddenly looking down.

"I don't get it," said Davey.

Tez took a deep breath and started talking again. "I had to run it through, like, five different decoders until I got it all. That channel was carrying about seven layers of overlapping info. Some of it was machine code, some of it genetic. Took me a hell of a long time to figure it all out. Once I got it sorted, I had to scam new equipment to plot out the genetic stuff and grow out the clone. I had to go back to that channel a few times, and man, it was hard to find because it kept jumping around the net, and each time I got more and more pieces to put her all together. Now here she is. All I need is an activation code. At least that's what keeps getting referred to whenever I try to wake her up. I've been searching for it, but it's taking forever. It's become next to impossible to find that channel again and it's driving me nuts. Guys, I need your help to find it."

"Uh. OK." Emil was looking perplexed. "Might be stupid to ask, but what does this have to do with the Wall, or sending out our next 'cast?"

"Guys, she *is* the plan. Nobody knows about her, so there's no trace. She can go right through and not come back. That's way more than just deliver payload, because no one will know she's missing. And she's a feckin' *computer*. We'll have our own private node on the Outside. One completely free from SolCorp."

"Wow. 'K. I get it." Emil's agitation was showing through his foot tapping. "What do you need us to do?"

"Right now, just help me find that channel."

"Um. OK." Emil had a hitch in his voice and his head was twisting around, the way it did when he was trying to keep something in. "So we're not recording tonight?"

"Well, not tonight," said Tez. "But we're gonna. We still have to get Shanna through."

"And after that?"

"We'll be free, man! Then it'll all be about the 'cast. Nothing but."

"'K."

"Emil, look—"

"Ya, OK, I know, Tez. You understand that this is everything to me, and we're not splitting up after, and it's not gonna come down crashing around us, because we're not gonna get caught and executed. I get it. But I don't believe it, and I never have. I'm OK with that. I knew the score starting in. I just... I'll see you guys in a bit, OK?"

Tez sat for a long time after Emil left, with his head bowed and hands dangling over his knees. He finally looked up at Davey with red-rimmed eyes and asked, "Are you still in?"

"Yeah," said Davey. "I mean, I know all that stuff too, but I don't care. If it lasts or doesn't, I'm in. Wondered for a while, but I'm in."

Tez reached over and put a hand along the side of Davey's neck, sending a warm flush down his spine. "It's the last piece, Davey. This is going to work. It has to. I don't know where this code came from, but it has to be from the Outside. Someone's trying to help us. If we can just get out, I'm sure they'll be there, waiting. Why else would they bother sending this to us?"

"Do you think it was sent to us? Not just sent out to everybody?"

"Nah, I tried tracing it. I couldn't find the source, but I could track where it went once it was on this side. I'm telling you, Davey, that podcast was meant for us. The wavelengths, the frequency, it was only showing up on our gear. No one else is even seeing this. Their hardware isn't calibrated for it."

"Cool."

Tez was staring at him intently, leaning close, his hand incredibly warm. Davey swallowed hard, filled with hope that absolutely anything could happen. He'd always felt it before, whenever he sang for the 'cast, that he was connecting with something larger, something Outside and meant to be, but now it was like it was coming full circle. Someone who had heard him, was finally reaching back. Something big was about to happen.

"Help me find the channel, Davey."

"Yeah. Of course."

The moment ended. Tez took his hand away, stood up, went over to a computer and tossed Davey the headset attached to it. "I usually find it by scanning the regular podcast channels. Once you start hearing the code hissing through, you adjust the reception here."

Tez opened a window on the monitor showing a graphic equalizer. "Get the frequency window set so that you're capturing just the code signal and not the background noise. Then hit 'record'. OK?"

Davey nodded and sat down next to the computer and began scanning the channels. His work shift at the waterplant came and went, and he didn't care. The personnel monitors had probably already raided his home cell, since there was no way Sheft wouldn't have reported his absence, and were now putting out an APB on him. He could probably get away with it once, if he said he was depressed about his face, but they'd watch him pretty close after that. If Tez could really get them out, none of that would matter. It didn't matter now. He was so caught up in the joy he was feeling that when he found the signal he almost scanned right past it into the next channel.

"Tez! I found it!"

"Good man! Hit record!" Tez came over and clicked the button himself, then rubbed Davey's chest and back at the same time, making him giggle. "Awesome! Look at it! That's definitely it!"

"How can you tell?"

"Because it fits, man! See this end sequence? It lines up exactly with the last bit I downloaded. Still gotta decode it, though. Get in some of the blank spots. I still have to write in some of it myself." All of his attention was on the monitor now, but Davey still felt good. Cramped and curious, he got up to stretch and went to examine the decoded woman on the worktable. Was she really meant to get them out? She did kinda look like Shanna, dark hair, narrow face, delicate features. He touched the pseudoskin of her face, surprised that it felt cold and rubbery. He wondered if they should warm her up first, before loading in the activation code—if that's what this last bit really was.

Tez was muttering to himself as he madly struck his fingers against the keyboard. Davey wrapped himself in his sweater more securely and yawned. He wanted to help, but if there was anything he could do, Tez would let him know. Otherwise he'd just be getting in the way.

After pacing for what seemed like an hour, Davey noticed that Tez was just sitting there, staring at the screen. He shoved his hands into his pockets and sauntered over. "Are you done?" he asked.

"Yeh," said Tez.

"Are you going to try it?"

"Sure." It took Tez another few seconds, but he finally hit a few more keys to transfer the code to the worktable, then made his way over to the pseudowoman and connected another wire to her head. "Here goes nothing." He punched the upload button.

A humming noise came from the body, then her neck muscles contracted. Her eyes fluttered open and she smiled.

"Can she see us?" Davey asked.

"I don't know."

The woman sat up and slid her legs off the table. She stood up and walked towards the wall, the wires and tubes pulling and popping out of her unnoticed as she went. She stopped just in front of the wall, then turned and walked to each edge of the room, as if mapping it out. Her head turned and her body twisted around to follow it as she gazed at the ceiling, then the floor, still smiling. Finally, she walked up to Tez and stopped in front of him.

"See?" she said. "I *can* beat you."

"What?" Tez frowned into the woman's face.

She suddenly jammed her hand through Tez's neck, her fingers entering under his jaw, and exiting at the base of his skull. "Thought you could outcode me. You and yer feckin' pouf. Goddamn asshole. Shoulda shown me more *respect*. Walked right into this one. Knew you would, because yer too feckin' *arrogant* to think that this could be anything other than part of yer big *plan*. Too caught up in yerself to *think*, to even *imagine*, that ol' Len could *possibly* code better'n you!"

Davey felt his bowels start to loosen as he scuttled backwards. The woman freed herself from Tez's neck, turned her head towards him, and then he just got his feet under himself and *ran*. He could hear her coming after him, and when he risked a look over his shoulder, he could see her running more smoothly and agilely than he ever could. She would catch him in a matter of seconds.

Where can I go, he thought desperately. *Gotta go where she can't follow. So sick of this running and hiding for yet another reason. I just want to be free!*

He ran to the edge of the block and found himself looking down to the next level of the citioid. If he could just jump across, he could end up on the roofs of the next terrace, but it was a good six feet across.

The pseudowoman's fingers dug into his shoulder, and Davey instinctively twisted away, losing his sweater in the process. He tumbled over the edge and fell, his hands scrabbling at the air, seeing the woman jump over the edge after him. She wasn't going to let this go, even when he was surely about to end up dead. Wouldn't even give him a few minutes to himself to die.

His back hit the icy cold surface of the water reservoir, and he sank into it, the shock of the cold water closing in over him, the impact of his landing, forcing the air out of his lungs. Surprised that he hadn't hit pavement, wondering if there was still chance he could get out of this, he tried to kick his way to the surface but couldn't see where he was. The water was being pumped into the large metal tubes that carried it to the secondary stage of purification, swirling around Davey and forcing him down into the next tank. It was so cold. He couldn't breathe. His mind was becoming empty.

A white spot of light was growing before him. Was he seeing it, or was it just forming in his mind? He could still feel the rush of water around him, tossing him where it would, forcing his body to move with it. *Davey Jones*, he thought, *you're about to die.*

Numb. Cold. Pain, gradually resolving into warmth. Chest cramp easing. Strange airless euphoria, taking over. This feels... like when I sing...

As Davey's brain starved to death, he imagined he could hear angels singing to him. A song of comfort, of promises, of a home that Len and SolCorp and godamn mushy beans and toilet-flush water couldn't follow him to. No, he didn't imagine it. They were really there, on the Outside, waiting for him. Caring about him.

Wanting him as badly as he wanted them. The Outside just wasn't what he'd thought it would be.

An old ship from Terra Prime rose towards him, out of the depths of the light, the submerged sails tattered and drifting with the flow of the water as it came to collect him. He could see the undead crew celebrating his arrival, waving scimitars and roaring their delight into the ocean. That was alright. It was his ship. He was going to leave, to sail free in the water, anywhere he wanted to go. Where would this ship take him, he wondered? Could Emerian really have known that there was a locker at the bottom of the ocean with his name on it? Huh. Maybe Emil would give as much of a shit about him dying as he did when Shanna died. Maybe not. Didn't matter. He'd still let Emil and Tez come on board his ship.

The singing of the crew was reaching him and he joined his voice to it, letting himself become immersed in the shared passion of the music. His mind was again opening up to the superconsciousness, and this time it wouldn't leave him behind when his song was done.

From Anna to Yousef

As reported by Alexander T. Crisp

Syndicated PodioFeed (Arts/Opinion/Editorial)
Alexander T. Crisp, Canadian Image Press. May 29th, 2009.
On October 30th, 2008, Zeke Boggs, 28, a Londonderry massage therapist, received sixty-two emails regarding the poor quality of his most recent weekly podcast, Zen of Zeke.

Boggs investigated and determined that an unintelligible audio track had been overlaid during or after the upload. After deleting the corrupted file and re-uploading, the podcast was reported as stable.

Twelve days later, on November 11th, at 1900hrs GMT, podcaster Allyson St. James, 31, of Dubai, received 497 emails complaining about the 'mixed up' audio of her erotica podcast. St. James looked into the problem, confirmed the poor quality, and also re-uploaded, just as Boggs had. According to *PodioAudio Tracking and Review*, the audio problem occurred another one-hundred-and-forty-two times in the podosphere over the next forty-eight hours.

A development was made from occurrence eighty-one, on the philosophically-inclined podcast of Toronto sound engineer, Seth Waisglass, 26. Waisglass posted a note on the 'wall' of his Facebook group asking if anyone else had experienced the same thing. The response was almost instantaneous: twenty-three of his four-hundred-and-ninety-four Facebook 'friends' confirmed similar corruptions. Waisglass compared the embedded tracks from 34 different instances and found 96% similarity of the tones. After successfully separating out one the audio tracks he discovered it was a recording of a woman speaking.

Waisglass recognized the language on the embedded track as Russian and enlisted the help of his maternal grandmother, Ruth Wahlmstein of Rochester, NY, formerly of Ekaterinburg, Russia, to translate the clip into English. What follows is the translated transcript of the message which somehow found its way onto one-hundred-and-forty-four apparently random podcasts between October 30th, 2008 and March 13th, 2009.

"Dearest Yousef, my rebel brother, it's me, Anna.

Surprised to hear from me? I know, I know. It's been a long while but I'm here at the cabin, curled up in Opa's wicker rocker, and thought that this would be a good time for you to get a letter from your little sister.

I've been up here for a couple days now, waiting for an old friend of mine. He didn't say exactly when he'd arrive but I have a feeling he'll be here soon. As it happens, I have time to kill and this place reminds me so much of you, therefore I'm writing.

From my vantage point, wrapped in the old quilt in the rocker, I can see the stuffed fish on the wall. Remember it? Not much bigger than my hand, now, but back then it was your pride and joy. You must have taken half the morning to reel it in. Even at eight years old you had that determination to succeed. Next to it on the mantle is that cracker-dry sparrow's nest I found under the cedar hedge. Mother called me a 'little Cossack' that day when I spent more time examining the dead fledgling than caring for the living one. I didn't know then what she meant by that comment (I was only five) but I'd heard the tone many times before, and was to hear it for many years after.

There's a question I've always wanted to ask you, Yousef, and this is a good time, I think. Do you believe Mother ever forgave me for living while Marina died? I don't. I've always believed she hated me more every day. She almost died giving birth to Marina and me, did she ever tell you that? If we both had died early in the pregnancy she maybe could have tried again for healthy babies, but the midwife saved me and that destroyed Mother's chances for more babies.

She was ashamed of herself, I think. She believed that God had judged her and cursed her with one dead baby, one crippled baby and no more hope. It didn't take long for me to start wishing I'd died with Marina.

I'm getting morbid, again, sorry. You had enough of that when we were growing up. No point in wondering about Mother—she's as dead as your fish, now.

Oh, the rain is starting up again. It rained all last night and it lulled me to sleep. I love a rainy night. Everything so dark and damp with nature's rhythm tapped out on the shingle roof and on the hearth when the wind is soft and the drops make it down the chimney. I left the kettle on the hook this morning and now the rain is playing a copper drum song. If I close my eyes and concentrate I hear the marches they used to play for us in school. I missed many things, having a twisted leg, but not marching like a good little communist didn't break my heart.

So, how have you been, Yousef? Your own children growing tall and strong? Did Karl ever get through that book I sent him last birthday? I was afraid he might find a collection of folk tales too old fashioned.

I only have the one oil lamp burning, now, so that I might see the lightning while still writing this. There's a current in the air tonight, the light hairs on my arms are standing up and the wolf skin rug under my foot is charged with power. My friend is coming. I'm using the stove for heat tonight because there are always fewer stray embers that way. The scent of the burning cedar is an opiate to me, lifting me to planes of existence my leg has kept me from reaching.

Do you ever talk to your dead wife, Olga? I talk to Marina, sometimes. I did it a lot when I was young and recently have started again. She doesn't answer me, of course, but sometimes it helps just to talk to her. I wonder if she forgives me.

Oh my, that lightning flash lit up the whole world, I think. The shadows all came to life and started to dance. When my friend arrives we'll dance, I think. He doesn't mind my leg. We've been close a long time, he and I, and now that the time is nigh (I read that in a book, once: "The time is nigh, and I must fly" and have always wanted to use it. Doesn't sound like something I'd say, does it?) Where was I? Oh yes, now that the time is... here, I'm looking forward to the dance.

I heard from Konrad last week, or maybe it was the week before. He thinks I should get out of research and back into teaching. He just doesn't seem to listen when I say that doing research is much more interesting than sitting in a classroom guiding narrow minds down old roads. He says that I spend more time with dead historians than living friends. Sometimes he's so touchy sensitive—he should be an artist, not a government clerk.

The rain is heavier now. The drum beat is more of a loud thrumming, and I had to stir out of my warm chair to move the kettle—I was afraid the little thing was going to be beaten into slag by the rain and hail coming down the chimney. The old cast iron pot can catch it all now. The lightning is more frequent now and the thunder is shaking the place like the echoes of the footsteps of a colossus or two trampling Oma's long dead cabbage patch. Maybe they're doing the dance, too, and are waiting for me to go out and partner up. I'll wait, thank you.

Have you ever danced in the wan moon light, Yousef? I don't think there'll be moonlight getting through the cloud to fall on the cabin tonight, though. I hope he's happy with just the light from one oily lamp, but, then, I don't suppose it matters much to him.

It's been almost too long since he last came around. I think Papa's funeral was the last time. He's been busy, of course, but when you get used to someone looking over your shoulder for most of your life, well, you miss him when he's off doing what he does.

Ah, the old cuckoo clock Papa smuggled up from Bern is sounding eleven o'clock. I suppose it would be too Chekhovian of me to expect him to arrive at the stroke of twelve. His schedule is his own secret and while in my heart I know he'll be here tonight, he never actually promised me. When it's time it's time, he once said. That answer will just have to keep me happy and, to tell you the truth of it, it does. Not knowing exactly when adds an edge to life, believe it or not. Mmm... there is a current in the air that has nothing to do with the storm pounding the cabin.

Yousef, I wish you could be here with me to see that I am happy, and not crazy at all. You're not ready to dance, though. You have too many things left to do. I just thought... oh, my. I think the clock has stopped. Has it ever done that before? Probably once or twice, I'm sure.

The air is so charged, now. I can almost see sparks. The rain has stopped, too. Oh! Yousef! I see moonlight! Pale and beautiful and casting more dancing shadows! Wait. One shadow is separating from the others! He's here and it's my turn to dance. God bless, Yousef! I'll"

None of the support staff at the dozens of affected servers were able to offer an explanation. There are no apparent trails to follow, no e-files to open, no digital viruses or worms to quarantine—only the audio.

Yousef, if you read this article, please contact Alexander T. Crisp: ATCrisp@CDNImage.net.

𝔄uthor 𝔅ios

TALENTED PEOPLE

JARED AXELROD: Jared Axelrod is an author, an illustrator, a graphic designer, a podcaster and quite a few other things that he's lost track of but will no doubt remember when the situation calls for it.

He is the writer and producer of two science-fiction podcasts, *"The Voice Of Free Planet X"* and the serial *"Aliens You Will Meet."* For more information about those podcasts, as well as Axelrod himself, *www.JaredAxelrod.com* is place to look.

MIKE BENNETT: Mike started podcasting in 2006, with his first novel 'One Among the Sleepless', and then his short story collection, 'Hall of Mirrors', and from which 'Salvation' is taken. He is currently podcasting his second novel, the vampire thriller *Underwood and Flinch*.

He was born in London, England and currently lives and works in Dublin, Ireland. *www.MikeBennettPodcast.com*

MARIE BILODEAU: Marie Bilodeau's first love is to share stories in current available formats, including (but not limited to) print, podcasts and while standing on tables in bars.

'A Pint to Prophecy' is part of her *Shades of Ragnarök* cycle. She often adapts myths as a nod to her BA in Religion and Culture.

Novels include her fantasy trilogy, *Heirs of a Broken Land* (Absolute XPress) and her space fantasy, *Destiny's Blood* (*Dragon Moon Press*). More info at *www.MarieBilodeau.com*.

ALEX T. CRISP: Born in London, Alex Crisp has a diploma in Journalism and Short Story Writing from ICS (International Correspondence Schools), as well as two unused bachelors degrees in the less useful fields of History and Education. He likes pina coladas and getting caught in the rain. He's not much into health food but he is into champagne. He apologizes to Rupert Holmes. Alex T. Crisp is a pen name. *www.AlexTCrisp.com*

JUSTIN MACUMBER: Justin Macumber once had a job. A real job, I mean. Now he no longer has that job, so he's trying to give this writing thing a try. The jury is still out on whether or not it'll take off, but for the time being he's keeping a glass-half-full attitude about it. Good for him. Help him out by going to *www.JustinMacumber.com* and reading his work there. It would mean a lot. And hey, you can buy stocking stuffers for the kids!

JACK MANGAN: If you've heard of Jack Mangan, then you're probably familiar with the Deadpan podcast and its community. Or maybe you know of his novel, "Spherical Tomi", a former #1 title at Podiobooks.com. Jack's writing, music, and voice have also appeared in many prestigious print and online venues, including *Interzone, Tales of the Talisman, SFReader, Variant Frequencies,* and *Internet Review of Science Fiction.*

If you haven't heard of him, then that's ok too. More info: *www.JackMangan.com*

TEE MORRIS: Tee Morris has been writing adventures in far-off lands and far-off worlds since the fifth grade. His first published work, *MOREVI: The Chronicles of Rafe & Askana,* a Historical-Fantasy epic written with Lisa Lee began in the most unlikely of places—a chat room on the Internet. He lives in Virginia and continues to freelance as a professional public speaker, New Media authority, and all-around daydreamer. *www.TeeMorris.com*

JENNIFER RAHN: Jennifer Rahn lives in Calgary and wanted to attend Hogwarts, but had to settle for a PhD (Medical Sciences) from the University of Alberta. Her novel, *The Longevity Thesis,* was podcast as a weekly series on Mevio.com. ElectroFunkSeppuku had been stewing ever since Jen experienced 80s hair, rollerskating rinks and glam rock in junior high. It finally flared to life when she was writing for *Podthology: The Pod Complex,* and she's mighty happy about that. *www.LongevityThesis.ca*

TIM REYNOLDS: Originally from Toronto, Tim has been in Alberta since 1991, following his passions of writing, photography, music and stand-up comedy. This is his second editing project for Dragon Moon Publishing, the first being Darwin's Paradox by Nina Munteanu. Visit *www.tgmreynolds.com* for more information on both his non-fiction (Stand Up & Succeed and The Cynglish Beat) and upcoming fiction projects. His blog & podcast can be found at *www.TheTaoOfTim.com.*

EMERIAN RICH: Emerian Rich is the author of *Night's Knights* Vampire Podnovel, which came out in print in late 2009. She is the host of the podcast *HorrorAddicts.net,* writes for *dashPunk.com,* and is the author of the romance podcast Sweet Dreams. She lives in the San Francisco Bay Area with her husband and son. To find out more about Emerian or her work, go to *www.emzbox.com.*

PHIL ROSSI: Writer, musician, and embracer of new media, Phil's passion for story-telling is matched only by the pleasure he derives from keeping his fans awake at night. *Crescent,* Rossi's debut novel (originally podcast in 2007), has lured tens of thousands of listeners and readers into a dark, twisted world of nightmares and things that go bump in the night. Phil lives outside of Washington, DC in Virginia with his wife, daughter, and menagerie of rescued animals. *www.PhilRossi.com*

J. DANIEL SAWYER: A longtime producer, activist, filmmaker, and photographer, Dan began podcasting in 2004, hosting *The Polyschizmatic Reprobates Hour.* His fiction includes the anthology series *Sculpting God: Bedtime Stories for Adults,* the science-fiction spy thriller *Predestination* (both Parsec Award-nominated), and the mystery-dramedy mashup *Down From Ten*—all of which are fully scored and soundscaped, and feature full voice casts. He is also a regular participant at Zach Moore's philosophy roundtable *Apologia*. Find him at *www.jdsawyer.net*.

SCOTT SIGLER: New York Times best-selling novelist Scott Sigler is the author of *Infected, Contagious* and *Ancestor*, hardcover thrillers from Crown Publishing.

Before he was published, Scott built a large online following by giving away his self-recorded audiobooks as free, serialized podcasts. His loyal fans, who named themselves "Junkies," have downloaded over seven million individual episodes of his stories.

Michigan native, Scott lives in San Francisco with his wife and dog. Visit Scott at *www.scottsigler.com*.

JD WILLIAMS: JD Williams lives, writes and makes typos in Central Ohio (USA). His novel *TimeStream* was released by Lyrical Press in January, 2010. When not writing…well, apparently JD does a lot of writing. Podcasting has intrigued JD enough for him to ponder its future, where he expects its influence to evolve as computers and communication evolve. For more about JD and his writing, please visit *www.jdwilliamsauthor.com*.

E.A. ZEFRAM: With a BFA degree in her pocket and a twisted sense of humor up her sleeve, E.A. Zefram has been painting, cartooning and writing short stories for over two decades. Her first published story, Ascension, appeared in the printed *Aced* Magazine Summer 2005 issue. Working as a web designer for nearly 10 years made discovering podcasts inevitable. A native of Alberta, Zefram now lives in beautiful San Francisco. *www.eazefram.com*

To learn more about podcasting, check out *Podcasting for Dummies* by Tee Morris & Evo Terra, published by Wiley Publishing, Inc.